## PRAISE FOR *THE S̲____*

"*The Secret Stealers* is a flawlessly crafted and engrossing story of the unexpected ways in which war changes who we are. Once again, Healey gifts readers with her trademark characters: everyday women who prove themselves to be extraordinary—women so relatable, so endearing, and so brave that they jump off the page and into our hearts."

—Lynda Cohen Loigman, *USA Today* bestselling author of *The Two-Family House* and *The Wartime Sisters*

"Set against the fascinating and well-researched history of the OSS, Jane Healey has crafted a remarkable story of perseverance, friendship, and the adventurous spirit and bravery of women who were instrumental to the Allies' efforts during WWII. This novel captured my heart while speeding up my pulse with its triumphs and tragedies; suspense and struggle; and ultimately, redemption, revelation, and reflection. Fans of Kate Quinn and Martha Hall Kelly will love this book."

—Susie Orman Schnall, author of *We Came Here to Shine* and *The Subway Girls*

"*The Secret Stealers* is World War II historical fiction about women spies that offers the rare balance of nail-biting action with strong, fully-developed characters who embrace friendship, empowerment, and romance. Jane Healey's crew of intrepid women are equally at home navigating the intrigue of the OSS in Washington, DC, and the dangers of war-torn France. This one's not to be missed!"

—Elise Hooper, author of *Fast Girls*

# The
# SECRET
# STEALERS

## ALSO BY JANE HEALEY

*The Beantown Girls*
*The Saturday Evening Girls Club*

# The
# SECRET
# STEALERS

A NOVEL

## JANE HEALEY

LAKE UNION
PUBLISHING

Published by Lake Union Publishing, Seattle

www.apub.com

Amazon, the Amazon logo, and Lake Union Publishing are trademarks of Amazon.com, Inc., or its affiliates.

ISBN-13: 9781542023559
ISBN-10: 1542023556

Cover design by Faceout Studio, Jeff Miller

Printed in the United States of America

*For my parents, Tom and Beth Healey*

*What is the use of living, if it be not to strive for noble causes and to make this muddled world a better place for those who live in it after we are gone?*

—Winston Churchill, former prime minister of the United Kingdom

*It's okay to stumble, as long as you fall forward.*

—Major General William J. Donovan, founder of the US Office of Strategic Services

# Chapter One

**June 26, 1942**
**Washington, DC**

My watch said it was fifteen minutes before eight in the morning, but I could already feel the oppressive DC humidity rising as I stood under a tree and gazed across the street at the three-story brick building with enormous white columns. I looked down at the sweaty piece of notebook paper in my hand, where I had scribbled the address, checking for the fourth time to make sure I was at the right place:

> *The East Building, 2430 E St. NW, across the street from the State Department. A brick building with columns. Enter through Gate Two. Ask for Alice Montgomery at the main reception desk.*

A large chain-link fence with barbed wire lined the perimeter of a complex that comprised four buildings. I couldn't see any signage or markers, nothing whatsoever to indicate what went on inside.

For the hundredth time I questioned my decision to do this, to come and interview for a government job I didn't actually need in an organization I knew very little about.

"Excuse me. Can I help you?" I turned to see a young woman observing me from a few feet away. She was a couple of inches taller than me, five foot five, with pale blonde hair, and wore a light-blue-and-white-striped summer dress with cap sleeves and a navy-blue straw hat that flattered her heart-shaped face. I looked down at my dull, plum-colored shirtwaist dress and wished I had gone shopping for something new to wear today. I hadn't set foot in a department store for months, since well before the funeral.

"It's just that you look like you might be lost." She gave me a small smile.

"Well, I think I'm in the right place, but I'm a little early for my eight o'clock interview." I pointed at the building. "That is 2430 E Street Northwest, yes? I didn't see any sign."

"There's no sign, but you're correct," she said. "I work there. Do you want to walk in with me? I can point you in the direction of reception when we get inside; it can be a little confusing."

"Oh, thank you. I would appreciate that," I said, relieved. "I'm Anna. Anna Cavanaugh." I held out my hand.

"Irene Nolan, happy to help," she answered as we crossed the street.

"What kind of work do you do here?" I asked, eager to hear from someone who actually worked in the building. Irene paused before answering.

"Oh, mostly research, organizing, you know . . ." She waved her hand. I glanced at her sideways as she quickly changed the subject. "So, let me guess. Wellesley grad? Or maybe Smith?"

"Radcliffe, actually," I said. "I graduated four years ago and did a postgraduate year in Paris."

"Ah, well done," she said with a nod. "I adore Paris. Did you enjoy living there?"

"I did," I said. "It was one of the best years of my life. Such a beautiful city. The culture and food, the people—I fell in love with all of it. I might not have come back if not for the war."

"I'll bet. I'm a Vassar girl, class of '38, like you. Do you know who you're meeting with today?"

"I'm supposed to ask for Alice Montgomery when I arrive, but I'm also meeting with William Donovan."

Irene nodded and gave me a wide smile, clearly impressed.

"Wow, Wild Bill, the legend himself, is meeting with you? Is that right?" she said. "Now, that's interesting. He's so busy these days, he rarely has time to interview anyone."

"He's a friend of my father's," I said. "I'm sure that's the only reason he's meeting with me in person."

"How do they know each other?" she asked. "He's been pulling recruits from everywhere he can to try to build this place up fast—business connections, social circles, family and friends."

"They grew up together in Buffalo, New York," I said, not really thinking of myself as a "recruit" and wondering what she even meant by that.

"Ah, no wonder he's meeting you in person," she said. "That's much more than a casual acquaintance."

I nodded. We arrived at Gate Two and walked up the incline toward the building. Irene wasn't done with her questions.

"Is your husband in the service?" she asked, glancing down at my wedding band. I felt my stomach drop as she kept talking. "Mine is. Military intelligence, which means we can discuss absolutely nothing at the dinner table, except for baseball, which he obsesses over and I barely tolerate. He's a Yankees fan."

She looked over at me for a response.

When I got dressed that morning, I had agonized over whether or not to wear my wedding ring, as I had every morning since January 22, when I had first learned the news. I didn't want to make her feel uncomfortable. There was no casual way to say it, so I chose not to say it at all.

"He was shipped out to Hawaii after Pearl Harbor," I said. "He's a Harvard Medical School graduate, and a group of them went there to help with the injured, implementing some promising new medical procedures."

It wasn't a lie exactly, just an omission of the entire truth.

"Oh, wow," she said. "Does he know you're interviewing here?"

"No," I said, feeling my cheeks burn. I had never been a good liar.

"I'm sure he'll be so proud when he finds out," she said.

I just gave her a small smile as we walked up the granite steps toward the main entrance. Men in uniform and smartly dressed women were hurrying by us, ready to start their day. I still had not seen one single sign declaring what government department actually resided in this building. It was so odd, but then, given the rumors in the newspapers about Donovan and this department, not entirely surprising.

A dark-haired young man tipped his hat and opened the door for us, and we entered the high-ceilinged main hall. It looked like any modern-day office building and had a musty sweet-and-sour smell, a combination of something like floor polish and ink. Still, there was no placard listing any departments, and no numbers on the few doors I could glimpse from where we were standing.

"Reception is down that hallway to the right. Check in with the secretary," Irene said, pointing. She reached out and shook my hand. "It was so very nice to meet you, Anna. If they offer you a job here, just know it's a fascinating place to work, like nowhere else. Truly. And there are more than a few young women like us. Smart women. The hours are long, but it could be the type of job to keep you busy while your husband is away."

"Thank you," I said. If I never saw her again, I wouldn't have to feel guilty about not telling her the truth. "And thank you very much for your help this morning. I appreciate it."

"Good luck," she said. "I hope to see you soon." She turned and joined the throng of employees hurrying to their various destinations as I headed in the opposite direction.

"Alice Montgomery is no longer working here," the secretary at the reception desk told me in a clipped tone when she glanced up, peering over the top of her tortoiseshell cat-eye glasses at me after I announced my arrival.

"Oh, okay, that's who I was told . . . ," I started.

"Maggie Griggs, who is in charge of recruiting and hiring women, will be coming to get you, but you're going to have to wait at least thirty minutes," the secretary added. "Maggie is very busy and wasn't anticipating having to meet with you herself. Have a seat. Today's papers are on the table."

I sat down in one of the black leather chairs and picked up the *Washington Post* from the glass coffee table. There was an article about Major General Eisenhower's arrival in England and another about the recent Battle of Midway in the Pacific, but I was too distracted to read beyond the headlines.

≈

The last time I'd seen William Donovan was the evening of Connor's funeral. When I thought back to that terrible period, the first thing I remembered was how my body had ached with bone-weary exhaustion. I had never realized before how physically draining grief could be. I also remembered feeling numb, shocked about the turn my life had just taken. It had all been so surreal, like playing a part in a play, or living someone else's life.

At the post-funeral reception at my parents' house in Cambridge in late January, I prayed for the moment when all the guests would leave and I could go upstairs and collapse onto the twin bed in my childhood room. I had been sitting in the corner of the dining room with Mary, my best friend from the Winsor School, the all-girls private high school we had attended. She stayed beside me most of the evening, slightly protective as I greeted the endless array of friends, relatives, and strangers that felt obligated to personally offer me their condolences.

After a group of Connor's friends from Harvard Med School hugged me good-bye, I asked my younger sister, Colleen, to get me another cup of coffee from the kitchen. When she returned, she handed Mary and me glasses of red wine.

"I think we could all use this more than coffee—especially you, Anna," Colleen said with a wry smile, sympathy in her eyes as she kissed my forehead before heading back to the kitchen to check on things.

"I may fall asleep in this chair if I drink the whole glass," I said to Mary.

"Nobody would blame you," Mary said, putting one arm around me and resting the hand holding her glass of wine on her enormous pregnant belly, her black dress stretched to its limit. For a second I placed my head on her shoulder, smelling the apple scent of her shampoo in her chestnut-brown hair, always pulled up in a bun. Mary and her husband, Joe, lived only a few blocks from me in DC, and I'd never been happier about that—because I'd never needed a friend nearby more than I did now.

"Mary, you and Joe have stayed long enough. You don't have to sit here with me all day; my parents and sisters can . . ."

"He's fine," Mary said. "He's out back with Colleen's fiancé, smoking and having a couple of beers." She took a sip of wine and gazed across the crowded room, a quizzical look on her face. "Who's that man that just came in, the one your parents are talking to? Where do I know him from?"

I strained my neck to see my mother and father in conversation with William Donovan, Congressional Medal of Honor winner and the most decorated military officer of the last war. My father and Donovan had been friends since they were in grammar school.

"That's Major General William Donovan, the legend himself," I whispered, shocked to see him standing in our dining room. "I wasn't expecting him to come."

He had only met Connor once, at our wedding reception eight months earlier.

With his arrival, I felt the atmosphere of the funeral reception change. There was a palpable excitement, a charged electricity not usually felt in such a somber setting. The stocky, silver-haired Donovan had the kind of magnetism that changed the energy in the air around him. He embraced my petite mother in a hug that nearly lifted her off the ground. And when he put her down, she laughed with tears in her eyes, clearly touched that he had come to pay his respects.

Hollywood had made a film about his unit in the war called *The Fighting 69th*, which had elevated his profile to an almost movie-star level of fame. After making a fortune as a lawyer on Wall Street, he was now working for President Roosevelt as an advisor. My family members and friends still in attendance were trying not to stare or whisper, but they were failing miserably across the board.

I watched as he gave my youngest sister, Bridget, a hug, and then my father and Donovan made their way through the crowded dining room to me. My father looked as exhausted as I felt, with dark circles under his large blue eyes that matched my own, and I swore his salt-and-pepper hair was saltier than it had been a week ago.

"General Donovan," I said, getting up to give him a warm embrace. "Thank you so much for coming."

"Ah, dear Anna," Donovan said in his quiet voice. He held on to both my hands after our embrace. "I am so very sorry for your loss. Connor was a fine man, with such a brilliant mind."

"Yes, he was brilliant," I said, feeling myself blush. Every single person who had offered their condolences had mentioned Connor's brilliance.

My father went to fetch Donovan a drink as I introduced him to Mary, and we talked a little more about Connor and the service. He looked at me with the empathy of someone who knew loss far too well. His twenty-two-year-old daughter, Patricia, had died two years prior in a horrible car accident on the way home from American University.

"Anna, might I have a quick word with you on the front porch, where it's more private?"

"Of course," I said, frowning a little, wondering what he might have to say to me. I picked up my glass of wine and nodded to Mary, who gave me a look of curiosity as she headed out to the backyard to find her husband.

The cold winter air felt refreshing after the stuffiness of my parents' crowded house, and I took a deep, grateful breath. It smelled of snow and a hint of cigarette smoke wafting from the guests in the backyard.

"I will keep this brief because I'm sure you're very tired," Donovan said. "I know firsthand what grief can do to a person."

"I know you do," I said, giving him a sympathetic smile in solidarity.

"I also understand that your world has been turned upside down, and you don't know what you're going to do in the next hour or day, much less months from now," he said, pulling out his wallet. "But I wanted to give you my card. If you ever need anything in DC, I can be reached at this number day or night."

"Thank you," I said when he handed it to me. "That's very kind of you."

"The other reason I want you to have it is because, if you decide to remain in DC, and if you're interested in a job outside of teaching, I could use somebody like you in the government organization I'm building."

I looked up from the card, completely surprised by his words. The truth was, I had been interested in a job outside of teaching for a long time. But life, specifically married life, had gotten in the way of those plans. "Someone like me?"

"Top of your class at Radcliffe, fluent in French and German, *and* you've studied abroad in Paris—yes, someone like you," he said, smiling, his cheeks turning ruddy from the night air. "Why wouldn't I?"

*Why wouldn't he?*

"Thank you," I said, nodding. "I don't know what I'm doing next, to be honest . . . You're right, I'm still . . ." I struggled to find the words.

"I understand," Donovan said, putting a hand on my shoulder. "But if you ever decide you're interested in learning more, call this number. Please consider it."

~

"Hello, Anna Cavanaugh? Excuse me, Miss Cavanaugh?"

I dropped the unread *Post* and jumped up from the chair, embarrassed to have been caught preoccupied with my thoughts.

"Yes, hello," I said, reaching out my hand. "I'm Anna."

"Maggie Griggs," the woman said, shaking my hand as she sized me up. "Nice to meet you. Come, let's go to my office to talk before you meet with Donovan."

Maggie Griggs was a handsome woman I guessed to be in her late forties. Her chestnut hair was streaked with gray, and she had an angular face. She wore a red-and-black plaid skirt and a white blouse under a short-sleeved black cardigan. We walked down the hall, and she greeted various people we passed.

"How old are you again, Anna?" Maggie asked.

"I just turned twenty-five," I said.

"That's right." She gave me a sideways glance and nodded. "You could pass for seventeen."

"I get that a lot," I said, trying not to sigh. "It makes teaching high school students a little difficult . . ."

I was petite, with thick, jet-black curly hair, large round eyes, and dimples in both cheeks—a combination that made me look very young for my age.

"I can imagine that it might," she said. "Donovan says he's looking for girls that are 'a cross between a Smith grad, a Powers model, and a Katie Gibbs secretary.' You've certainly got the looks and the education."

"Um, thank you," I said, not sure how to take the compliment.

We reached her office, and she opened the unmarked door for me. The room was small and spotless with a desk and two file cabinets. We sat down, and my eyes landed on a rather thick, cream-colored folder with my last name on the tab in the middle of her desk.

"Mrs. Griggs, forgive me, but the only things I know about this organization come from the vague references to it in the papers. I know it's now called the Office of Strategic Services—could you please explain what goes on in this place?"

"Ah yes, you've read about Donovan as FDR's 'international man of mystery' and all that nonsense in the *Post*?" Maggie said, laughing. "The press loves Donovan. And I can't say he minds the attention. As for the recently named Office of Strategic Services, the OSS, it's the brainchild of General Donovan and President Roosevelt. It was formed about a year ago and dubbed the Office of the Coordinator of Information, or COI, with Donovan reporting directly to Roosevelt. It was actually just renamed the OSS this month—same mission, but now it's an agency under the Joint Chiefs of Staff."

"Okay," I said, frowning since that still told me nothing.

She pulled a letter from the top of my file and put it in front of me.

"But, before we get into any more details, Miss Cavanaugh, I need you to sign this confidentiality agreement. You will be legally bound to keep this and any conversations you have today secret, regardless of whether or not you end up working here."

I nodded and gave the letter a quick read, knowing there was no way I wasn't going to sign it. I had to know what in the world was going on in this mysterious building with no signs or numbers on the doors. I had to know what kind of job they had in mind for me. I wanted a reason to stay here in DC this summer, instead of going to the Cape, where I would have to endure the constant, pitying looks of friends and family and also deal with my mother's overbearing ways. I was supposed to be getting on a train in three days, but this place might offer me an alternative plan.

Maggie Griggs paused as if for dramatic effect, pulling a pack of Marlboro Slims out of her top drawer. She offered me one before she lit her own. I declined.

"The mission of the OSS is multifaceted," she said. "But its main objectives are analyzing all data related to national security and coordinating espionage activities behind enemy lines for the armed forces."

"So, research and . . . espionage? Spying. *Spies*," I said, not quite believing what I was hearing. I didn't know what I had expected her to tell me about the OSS, but that was not it. "You're sending spies behind enemy lines?"

"Yes, spies, to gather intelligence and engage in guerrilla war tactics, among other things," she said. I'm sure she could tell my interest was piqued. "However, we do much more than that. We have a large division here devoted to research and analysis of strategic information, such as the geographical studies of various war zones, and another that focuses on how to create and spread disinformation and propaganda. There are multiple groups within the organization working on ways to subvert the enemy.

"As the person in charge of recruiting women—*lots* of women—I've got my work cut out for me," she said, leaning to crack the window behind her, as the little office was getting smoky. "I've been cautiously taking out ads in magazines and newspapers, but of course they have to be vague. Since I can't describe exactly what the job is, it makes it difficult to compete against the recent, more glamorous recruitment campaigns of the Women's Army Corps. Meanwhile, every damn morning

Donovan gives me more positions that need to be filled. Yesterday it was a 'combination seamstress and secretary for the North Africa office.' That one's not going to be easy."

"So, you're even sending women overseas," I said.

"We've started to, yes," she said.

"How many will you be sending?"

"Oh, in the hundreds at least," Maggie said. "To Africa, England, Switzerland—wherever we need them."

"France? To Paris?"

"No, none to France," Maggie said. She paused for a second. "Well . . . let's just say not yet."

"Wow. I had no idea," I said. I felt like I had stumbled into a secret club, which in some ways I supposed I had.

"Yes, this is a chaotic and frenzied place to work," Maggie said. "We haven't hired nearly enough people to staff these operations, but everything we're doing here makes me thrilled to be a part of it, and most people here feel that way—passionate about the mission."

"I can understand why," I said, more curious than ever as to what type of work she had in mind for me.

"After the breathtaking intelligence failures that led to Pearl Harbor, Roosevelt tasked Donovan with building this organization from scratch very quickly. There's been little time for tight security checks. So, many of the people he has hired are people he could trust due to personal connections or referrals. This has included close friends, business clients, club members, professors from elite colleges, linguists, and established writers."

"And sons and daughters of friends?" I asked.

"Yes indeed, many of those as well, including President Roosevelt's son."

"Are there any female spies?"

"A very select few," she said. I couldn't quite decipher the look on her face. "But let's talk about why you're here and what role we have in mind for you. The timing of your phone call last week was seren-dipitous, Miss Cavanaugh. Alice Montgomery's role was as General Donovan's secretary and right-hand woman. Her last day was supposed to be in two weeks, but her father's health has taken a turn for the worse, so she had to head to South Carolina yesterday. We would like you to consider being her replacement."

My mouth dropped open, and I was about to start asking questions, but she kept talking.

"The job requires, first and foremost, ultimate secrecy," she continued. "You may not keep a diary of any sort. You are not to discuss anything about what goes on here with anyone in the outside world, not even family. Like many others here, you know him personally, but you'll have to be prepared because, as a boss? Donovan is hard driving. The man never stops. There will be long hours, evenings, and sometimes weekends."

"Um . . . okay . . . ," I said, trying to process what she was saying to me.

"But I will tell you, he thinks you'd be perfect for the job—given your obvious intelligence, as evidenced by your grades at Radcliffe and your language abilities," she said, thumbing through the pages in the folder. "You spent a successful postgraduate year at the elite École Libre des Sciences Politiques in Paris before coming home to teach high school French in Boston and then here at the Sidwell Friends School in DC after getting married to your fiancé last May. I'm very sorry about the loss of your husband, my dear."

"Oh, um, thank you," I said. I felt my cheeks burning. Her knowledge of Connor's death and my background had thrown me. "My French is very strong overall. My German is good. I can read and understand it very well, but my speaking ability in German is not as strong."

"Thank you for being honest, dear, but to have those two languages? Well, it's still quite an asset," she said as she continued to look through my folder. "Your recommendations from Radcliffe were stellar, of course. Particularly Professor Moore, who said you were . . ."

Maggie riffled through papers, and I felt my face grow even hotter as she read. "'Highly intelligent and hardworking. A near photographic memory like few I've encountered. And my only student who sounds like a native Parisian when she speaks.'"

"Wait . . . you have letters from my professors?" I said, raising my eyebrows. "But I only called here last week . . ."

"We have references from your professors, as well as from some of your colleagues from both the Winsor School in Boston and the Sidwell Friends School. Donovan had you properly vetted months ago," she said, showing me the letters.

I blinked at them, slightly stunned at the revelations about the OSS, and the fact that they'd already vetted me.

"Did Donovan have me vetted after he talked to me at Connor's funeral?"

"Oh, long before that, dear," Maggie said. "Since the day he started working for Roosevelt, he's been building up his list of possible recruits."

"And I was vetted a while back, but this position became available yesterday?"

"Yes, he wasn't sure what role you would fill initially," Maggie said, watching my reaction. "But, as it turns out, we have an immediate need for a secretary for him, and . . . he'd like you to consider it."

So many thoughts were running through my head. Donovan had vetted me before the funeral, meaning he wasn't offering me a job out of pity because I was a widow. That mattered. He wanted me here based on my intelligence and abilities, not because he was doing me a favor.

I had a train ticket to Cape Cod in my purse. According to my mother's meticulous plans, I should be "relaxing and healing" this summer on the Cape and moving back to my family home in Cambridge after that. My parents would try to convince me I wasn't ready for something like this, that I still needed time to get over my grief.

But just the thought of spending the entire summer on the Cape made me feel suffocated. I pictured my mother dragging me to play bridge at the club or pushing me to go out with summer friends I barely knew anymore. My sister Colleen had already told me how she planned on setting me up on dates that I definitely wasn't ready to go on. This job, this opportunity, was the perfect solution. I would tell my parents that I had to stay in DC because this was an opportunity to serve my country that I absolutely had to take. And it could be a chance at the kind of work I had once dreamed of doing.

"So, what do you think? There is a great deal more to tell you about the role and this organization. But I need to know, are you seriously interested?"

"Well . . . I . . . are you offering me the position?" I asked, thinking there was no possible way this could be happening so quickly.

A loud knock on her office door made me jump.

"Come in," Maggie said, raising her voice. William Donovan walked in, his silver hair in a fresh military cut. Maggie and I both stood up.

"Dear Anna," he said, and I gave him an embrace. "I know we were supposed to meet later this morning, but I've been summoned to the White House, so I won't be able to after all. Maggie has given you some of the details?"

"She has, yes," I said. "And thank you."

"Anna was just asking if we were offering her the position." Maggie looked at him, arms crossed as if to say, *You tell me.*

"Of course we are," Donovan said. "You'd be perfect. And I'm sure Maggie's told you, we don't have any time to interview a hundred girls, especially when I know you'd be the best of the lot anyway. What do you think? Do you want to work for me? To be a member of the OSS?"

"I . . . when would I start?" I asked.

"Monday," Donovan said.

"This Monday?" I said, taking a deep breath. There wouldn't even be a short family vacation. There would be no going back home for a long time. But I didn't want to spend the entire summer on the Cape being treated like some hothouse flower. I knew that for sure now.

"Of course. There's a war going on, my dear." He looked me in the eye, his face very serious now. "Now, Anna, if you're not ready for something like this yet, if you need more time, I understand. Maybe in the future, something else—"

"I'll take it," I said, interrupting him. "I don't need more time; it's such a great opportunity."

His face lit up, and he clapped his hands together.

"That's my girl! You won't regret it, Anna. I promise you that. Maggie, you'll get her all the paperwork and get her squared away so she can start Monday?"

"That I will, sir," Maggie said, lighting another cigarette.

"Thank you," Donovan said. He patted me on the shoulder. "Do you want me to call your father, tell him about it?"

"Thank you, but I'll take care of my parents," I said, not looking forward to my conversation with them.

"Well, if you need me to talk to Dick and Deidre for you, let me know. I'm happy to make the call and explain to them why I need you here more than they need you on the Cape," Donovan said with a wink as he turned to leave.

"Thank you, sir," I said.

"Now I've got to get to Roosevelt before he has my head," he said. "I will see you both on Monday."

He was going to meet with the president. I had accepted a job working for the president of the United States' right-hand man. I felt a mix of elation and fear, and a kind of giddy anticipation about the future that had eluded me since long before Connor died. Maggie's talk of sending girls overseas was one of the things that excited me the most. If I proved myself working for Donovan, maybe that could be in my future as well.

"Congratulations," Maggie said to me, holding out her hand.

"Did I . . . I just accepted the job, didn't I?" I said, shaking her hand, a little incredulous, though I couldn't stop smiling.

"You did," she said, grinning back at me. "Donovan has that effect on people."

"So he does," I said, nodding, still not quite believing what had just happened.

"Welcome to the OSS, Anna Cavanaugh."

*Chapter Two*

I felt like celebrating after my interview, so I headed straight to the Woodward & Lothrop department store downtown and went shopping for clothes for the first time in almost a year. I bought a blue-and-green plaid skirt, a short-sleeved white button-down shirt, and two dresses. One was pale blue and the other was red with white polka dots. I even treated myself to coffee and a Wellesley fudge cupcake in the tearoom on the seventh floor to celebrate this unexpected new chapter in my life.

I arrived back at my apartment in Georgetown's East Village late that afternoon, laden with shopping bags. It was the first floor of a Federal-style, pale-yellow clapboard row house that had been built before the Civil War. I grabbed the mail out of my mailbox with one hand, and the moment I saw the envelope with red-and-white trim and an airmail stamp, I put down all my bags in order to open it. There was another envelope inside it, and I immediately recognized the handwriting on it.

*28 mars 1942*

*Chère Anna,*
*How are you, ma très chère amie? I think of you and your family in these difficult times after Connor's death. I wish I could be there for you in person.*

*My sister, Yvonne, promised she would try to get this letter to you. She is still in Dinard with the rest of my family, but I am back in Paris, as I am no longer allowed to stay in Dinard for reasons too difficult to explain here. I recently started working as a German translator for some French industrialists. Their offices are on the Rue Saint-Augustin.*

*Like many French soldiers, Henri was captured and held as a prisoner of war in Germany for some time. My father and uncle were able to get him out, thank God, and he is working with Georges LaRue. Do you remember him? He was a professor of mathematics at Sciences Po, but only a few years older than us.*

*Wish you were here, but then again, I don't because you would not recognize this place. What is happening here fills me with fury that is hard to suppress, as I walk the streets of a Paris that is no longer our Paris. Sadness hangs over this city like a sickness. The Nazi flags are everywhere, and I often shiver when I walk by them. There is so much German signage, and of course, there are so very many soldiers and tanks. The constant, guttural voices over loudspeakers and their boots clicking on the cobblestones—these ever-present sounds have become the anthem of this occupation. I dream of our city returning to its former beauty and peace, and of reuniting with our friends and having an aperitif on the banks of the Seine.*

*Are you moving back home this summer as planned? I am sure it will be good for you to be close to family again.*

*So much more I want to tell you, so much I want to ask, but it's most important that this letter reaches you, so at the very least you have my current address and know that I am alive and safe, as is Henri and the rest of my family.*

   *Please write and tell me how you are, my dear friend.*
*I miss you. So does Henri.*
   *Je t'embrasse fort,*
   *Josette*

I had so many questions. Josette and her family had fled Paris for Dinard when the German occupation of the city began in 1940. So why was she no longer allowed to stay there now? And what were her reasons for being back in Paris? It was odd, but it was also clear she wanted to make sure that the letter got past censors, so she did not share more details. I reread the letter, trying to read between the lines for clues as to what was really going on with her. I was worried. Nothing felt right about any of this news.

Josette Rousseau had been my best friend during my year in Paris. We lived in the same dormitory at "Sciences Po," as the university was called. A native Parisian, she also spoke German like me, and thanks to her, my French was now flawless. Her tight-knit circle of friends had welcomed me as one of their own. The group of us would spend our weekends lingering for hours on café patios, smoking and drinking cheap red wine, or having picnics on the banks of the Seine, trying to ignore the drumbeat of war on France's doorstep. I had fallen in love with Paris and often thought about how different my life would be now if I had found a way to stay, though the reality of the war would have most likely prevented a permanent relocation.

The last words, *So does Henri*, warmed my heart and made it ache, filling me with guilt at the same time. Josette's cousin Henri was tall and handsome, with a shock of dark hair and a Roman nose, as well as a charming personality and a zest for life. He was a brilliant math major with a love of photography and American jazz. My time with him in Paris had given me clarity about everything that was wrong with my relationship with Connor. And yet I had still come home and married him.

I put the letter in my dress pocket, picked up my bags, and pushed through the door. Milo and Mabel, my two calico cats, immediately greeted me with loud meows of hunger. After feeding them, I poured myself a glass of lemonade from the red ceramic pitcher in the fridge, put an Artie Shaw record on the player, and sank into the velvet sofa in the living room, holding the cool glass up against my forehead as I closed my eyes.

The memories of my marriage still haunted me whenever I first arrived back at our apartment alone, knowing nobody else would be joining me. Although it had never really felt like *our* apartment, if I was being honest with myself.

I thought back to December 30, the day Connor had left for Hawaii. He had been standing in the middle of this very living room with his bags packed at the door. He had been wearing his new black-framed glasses, his brown hair freshly cut per army standards, as he waited for the military truck that would take him to the airport. It was an awful memory that was branded onto my brain, and recalling it was like summoning a ghost. I felt like if I opened my eyes, I could relive it all again. I could even smell his Old Spice aftershave, which I had adored when we first met but had come to loathe in time. The tension between us on that fateful day had been so thick I had felt like I could swipe at it, like a heavy, damp fog in the air between us.

Now, I heard four quick knocks at the door in a familiar staccato pattern, and both cats scurried under the sofa.

"You cowards, it's just Mary," I said to them as I opened the front door to see my dear friend looking frazzled, her hair up in a messy bun. She wore a yellow sundress and balanced a large brown paper bag on her hip.

"You have to stop bringing me food," I said, giving her a hug hello. "I am perfectly capable of cooking supper for myself, you know."

"Oh really? What did you have for supper?" she asked, walking past me to put the bag down on my kitchen table.

"Um . . . I had a chocolate cupcake at Woodies this afternoon. Does that count?"

"Definitely not. Anna, you are too skinny. You need to eat," Mary said, taking out a wax-paper-covered dish and six bottles of Narragansett beer.

"Where's the baby?"

"Joe's with him," she said with a sigh. "I came over because I need a break. Joey Jr.'s been fussing all day. He's teething. I made franks and beans with brown bread tonight. Nothing fancy, but I know you like it. Also, I need a beer, so I brought us some." She handed me a bottle and took one for herself.

"Well, thank you as always," I said. "I feel like you mother me almost as much as you mother Joey Jr. But I'll eat later. It's beautiful outside. Let's sit in the garden and have a beer."

My favorite part of my row house apartment was that it had a tiny secret garden in the back. It was private, surrounded by brick walls on all sides, and contained a pretty vine-covered trellis, some ancient trees that provided shade, and all kinds of mature perennial flowers—bursts of purple, yellow, and pink among all the green. Mary and I sat down at the small wrought-iron table and chairs and sipped our beers.

"You're going to miss this garden when you head to the Cape Monday," Mary said.

I took another sip of my beer, bit my lip, and just looked at her.

"What?" Mary said, elbows on the table. "Oh no. What's that look?"

"My summer plans have changed," I said. "That interview with William Donovan's organization? That was today. Believe it or not, they offered me a job. And . . . I accepted."

"What?" Mary said. "Holy cow, Anna! You got a new job? In DC? With the glamorous William Donovan?"

"I did," I said, smiling at the shock on her face. "I'm going to be his assistant."

"I cannot believe it," Mary said. "I thought you were just going out of curiosity. I never thought you were serious. Have you told your parents?"

"No, not yet," I said, "and I have no idea what I'm going to do about the lease." I was supposed to come back at the end of the summer to pack up my apartment, but that wouldn't be happening now. "When I had my interview this morning, I saw all these young people working there, and everyone was filled with purpose and energy, and I just . . . I *had* to take the job. I had to do it."

"This is nuts, but it's also terrific," Mary said. She jumped out of her seat and gave me a hug. There were tears in her eyes. "I was going to miss you so much. I need my best friend here, especially on nights like this when motherhood has worn me out."

"So, you don't think I'm crazy?" I asked.

"Maybe a little," she said, sitting back down. "You're not exactly an impulsive person. Do you know what you're getting yourself into?"

"If I'm being totally honest? No."

"Then what the heck made you say yes?"

"It seems like such an incredible opportunity," I said. "They're even sending women overseas—to Europe, Africa. And Donovan's this remarkably charismatic leader. He's one of Roosevelt's top advisors now. He was on his way to the White House this morning when he offered me the position."

"Fascinating." Mary nodded. "Do you know there's a comic strip in the *Washington Star*, *The Exciting Adventures of Wild Bill Donovan*?"

"I did. Did you know the *Post* has nicknamed him Hush-Hush Donovan?" I asked. "That part is strange for me. Not that we've ever been close, but he's a family friend. So, to see him as this famous figure now? It's just not how I know him."

"You have to tell me all about it. What are these exciting adventures? What's his 'top secret' organization do exactly? Why so hush-hush? I want to know everything."

"That's the one lousy part," I said. "I can't tell you anything about it. It's classified war work." I made a motion like I was zipping my lips.

"Come *on*," she said, her eyes wide. "You're joking."

"I swear, they made me sign papers. I have to keep my mouth shut about everything that goes on there."

"No wonder you took the job," she said. "Just to find out what goes on there will be worth it, I bet. Although it's going to kill me that you can't tell me anything."

"I'm sorry . . . And I hope you're right, about it being worth it," I said.

I paused for a few seconds as a breeze passed through the garden. I could hear two mourning doves calling to each other. I wondered for a brief moment what Connor would have said about it all. He had been so traditional, with such an oversize ego. He would not have approved.

"I appreciate what my parents are trying to do," I continued, "but it's like they've reverted to treating me like a child instead of a young widow."

Mary just gave me a sad nod.

"So, the thought of going home, getting another teaching job in Boston? Deep down, I've been dreading it. And you've heard me complain all year: I've come to realize I don't even *like* teaching languages. I don't have the patience for it. Today was the first time in forever that I felt truly happy and excited about something. The first time since before Connor died."

"Sounds like the right decision, then," Mary said quietly.

"And you know what else?" I said. "They had me vetted months ago, before Connor was killed. They discussed *my* intelligence and language abilities, and they had recommendations from my Radcliffe professors and the faculty at Sidwell Friends and the Winsor School."

"Seriously?" Mary said, eyebrows raised. "That's impressive."

"It was, and it was so refreshing. And it's an opportunity to really contribute to the war effort and to use my brain in a whole different way than teaching. For a while now, I've been living in a world where only Connor's intelligence mattered, his accomplishments, his . . . everything."

"Don't I know that," she said. "How are you feeling lately, by the way, about all of that?"

"The same roller coaster of emotions. Grief and guilt, regret and sadness," I said.

"For the thousandth time, please, I'm begging you, stop being so hard on yourself," Mary said, passing me a second beer.

"I'm trying," I said. "I play back everything my life has been in the past couple of years. I should have listened to my gut instead of everyone else in my life. If I had, we would have broken off the engagement. Maybe I would have stayed in Paris and gotten a job at the embassy, doing the kind of work overseas I always thought I'd end up doing. And maybe he wouldn't have even ended up on the wrong road in Hawaii and his jeep wouldn't have—"

"Now you absolutely know that's crazy talk," Mary said, interrupting me. She sat up and reached out and grabbed my hand. "Not the part about Paris, the part about him in Hawaii."

"I know," I said, "but he was going to help with Pearl Harbor victims, he wasn't going off to fight in the war. To die in a jeep accident in the rain? It sounds so naive now, but I was honest with him about our marriage, about my unhappiness, because it never occurred to me he wouldn't come back. I thought he had a long life ahead of him . . . I just knew it wasn't going to be with me."

"That's it, Anna," Mary said, giving me a sad smile. "That's why you shouldn't feel guilty at all about your honesty. You did what you thought was right."

I found myself blinking back tears and squeezed her hand. We sat there in the peace of the garden for a few minutes, just listening to the birds and enjoying the breeze.

"I finally heard from Josette today," I said.

"Oh, how is she? Is she safe?"

I pulled the letter out of my pocket and handed it to her.

"Why would she have to leave Dinard?" Mary asked, frowning at the letter.

"That's the exact question I had," I said.

"She says Henri misses you too," Mary said, giving me a knowing look.

"That," I said, pointing at the letter, "was more than a lifetime ago."

"Do you really think that matters?" she said. "I'm going to bring out some of the food I brought. You should eat."

My time in Paris felt like a dream now, the details beautiful and blurry like an impressionist painting. On my final day there, after months of conversations and laughter, flirtatious glances and subtle brushing of hands, Henri and I had spent the day together. He took me on a tour of his favorite places to take pictures: the Passy Bridge, with the Eiffel Tower in the background; the steps of the Sacré-Coeur in Montmartre; and under the trees in the Tuileries Gardens. I posed for him, trying to be serious but often laughing as he snapped away on his small silver-and-black 35mm camera. With the hours before my departure ticking away, and a fiancé I didn't love waiting at home, I found myself unable to deny my romantic feelings for Henri any longer. And from the way he held my hand as we walked, sometimes putting his arm around my shoulder, or kissing the top of my head, it was clear he couldn't deny his feelings for me either.

After my going-away party that night, and after too many glasses of red wine, Henri Rousseau and I had stood on the rooftop of the student apartment building where we both lived.

"Please stay in Paris," he said to me as he held my hand and pulled me into his arms.

"If only I could," I said, looking into his dark eyes, their sadness mirroring my own. My heart ached because that day I realized that what I felt for Henri—the dizzying, magnetic pull of what could only be described as love—was everything I didn't feel for Connor.

That night, with his warm breath on my cheek, I remember thinking how I'd never wanted anything like I wanted to kiss him at that moment, on a Parisian rooftop under the stars, a spot so romantic it was almost cliché. His lips tasted like red wine and cigarettes. He pulled me in tighter, our kisses becoming more intense and passionate, and then he broke away and grabbed my hand.

"Come with me . . . please?" he said, pulling me to the staircase, to his studio apartment two floors down. The fact that I didn't even hesitate spoke to how broken my relationship with my fiancé was. When we reached the door of his apartment, he picked me up and carried me over the threshold. Laughing and kissing, we tumbled into his bed as we undressed each other. I stayed until dawn, kissing him good-bye while he slept and leaving a note on his nightstand before departing for home. While the guilt of making the decision to stay with him that night and then going home and marrying someone else still haunted me, that night remained the most romantic one of my life.

"Have you ever thought of writing Henri a letter?" Mary asked, interrupting my thoughts as she came out and put a plate of food in front of me.

"What?" I said, shaking my head and blushing despite myself. "No. Yes. Okay, maybe I've thought about it once or twice. But I doubt I'll ever see him again."

"Okay," Mary said, giving me a pointed look.

"It was a mistake, Mary," I said, turning even pinker, putting my head in my hands. "I was engaged. I should never have let it happen."

Mary was the only one in America I had ever told about that night and my feelings for Henri.

"I truly hope someday soon you forgive yourself for being human," she said. "I know what Connor was like, what your relationship was like."

"I know you do," I said. "I guess that's the other part of this that I still can't forgive myself for . . . I'd always considered myself a really intelligent, moral person, and yet I had an affair and then went ahead and married Connor. Even though I knew I shouldn't, even though I fell for someone else, spent the *night* with someone else. What was I thinking?"

"There was so much pressure on you two to get engaged," she said. "So much pressure on *all of us* to get married. Remember the *Boston Herald* articles keeping track? 'Thirteen Radcliffe Seniors to Marry Harvard Men.' It was obnoxious. Never mind your mother pushing marriage after your first date with Connor."

"True," I said, looking up at the darkening sky. My mother thought I had landed the catch of the century with Connor Cavanaugh, the golden boy of Harvard Med. We had agreed a long engagement made sense due to the demands of his burgeoning medical career. I should have interpreted that as the bad sign it was. But once the wedding date was set, it felt like a runaway train nobody would let me jump off of, one that, for some reason, I had lacked the courage to stop myself.

"Thank you," I said. "I don't know what I'd do without you."

"And I don't know what I'd do without you and this garden to escape to this summer. I'm thrilled you're not going anywhere. They aren't going to send *you* overseas anytime soon, right?"

"No," I said, "but, to be honest, that might be what has me the most excited about this job. I'd do anything to get a post overseas at some point."

"That doesn't surprise me," she said, her voice quiet. "I think part of your heart is still in Paris—maybe more than that."

"You're not wrong," I said.

"So, when do you start?"

"Monday, when I'm supposed to be on a train to the Cape," I said, and Mary laughed.

"Oh boy," she said. "So, you're not going to the Cape *at all*? Dick and Deidre Shannon are not going to be pleased. When are you going to tell them?"

"I was thinking Sunday night?" I cringed at the thought of the call. Mary nearly spit out her beer from laughing.

"Good luck with that," she said, tapping her beer bottle with mine.

"Thanks," I said, lifting my bottle in a toast, praying my parents would take the news well.

# *Chapter Three*

**June 28, 1942**

My parents did not take the news well.

"I'm confused. Why did he offer *you* a job?" my mother asked when I called them Sunday night. "Do they need French teachers in the government now? Because that's the only work experience you have. Why would Bill Donovan want you to work for him?"

I rolled my eyes at this comment. Even with the war, Mother still had a hard time believing women belonged in the workplace in any capacity.

"Mother, there are many teachers leaving their positions to support the war effort. Judith Carr, one of my coworkers, is leaving to join the Women's Army Corps. I know of others . . ."

"Yes, but you already have plans for the summer, with your family. Colleen and Bridget will be so disappointed you're not coming," she said, sounding peeved. "If you want to serve the war effort, couldn't you just come to the Cape and volunteer a few hours a week for the USO? Do you really have to take this job? You don't need the money. And you've been through so much, dear. You insisted on going back to DC and teaching for the rest of the year. I just think some rest this summer would do you good, after . . . after everything."

"I know you do, but I just can't imagine sitting on a beach all summer with a war going on," I said. "I think I'll be better off being busy and productive. I really do."

I heard my youngest sister's voice in the background.

"Oh . . . here, maybe Bridget can talk some sense into you," she said.

"Can you get me a job with you?" Bridget said, her voice soft. "I could move in for the summer, maybe I could even do my senior year down there somewhere . . ."

"Bridget, can Mother hear you?" I said.

"No, I stepped into the closet with the door shut on the phone cord," she said. "I can't bear summer on the Cape without you. I am going to be bored to tears."

I felt a pang of guilt. Of my two sisters, I had always had more in common with Bridget. Recently engaged Colleen wanted nothing more than to be a housewife and a mother, despite a mind for numbers and a Wellesley degree. And seeing how happy Mary was as a mother and wife, I understood that decision more than I ever had before. However, Bridget, now a senior at Radcliffe, was also incredibly bright but with an independent streak that rankled my mother to no end. She had very different aspirations than Colleen.

"Bridge, you know that's not possible," I said. "And you know you've got to finish up at Radcliffe."

"Please, Anna," she said with a groan. "It's going to be all country club cocktail hours and tennis lessons. And Colleen trying to fix me up with Boring Brad's friends."

Boring Brad was the nickname Bridget had given Colleen's fiancé. Unfortunately, it suited him well.

"Shush," I said. "Poor Brad is *not* that boring. And I'm so sorry, Bridge, but coming to live with me is not a possibility. I—"

I heard the click of a door and then my father's voice as he took the phone, despite Bridget's protests.

"Anna," my father said, clearing his voice into my ear. "I appreciate you wanting to serve your country. But we just want to make sure that this is the right time for you to make a change like this. After . . ."

"After Connor was killed in Hawaii?" I said. He had a hard time saying it out loud.

"Yes," my father said in quiet voice. "It's barely been six months, after all. Are you sure you're ready for this?"

*No, I'm not sure at all, and I'm slightly terrified, but I still need to do this.*

"I am sure, Father," I said out loud, hoping that would make it true. "I'm excited, and if you have concerns, you can take them up with Donovan. Please understand, he made me an offer I really couldn't refuse. I need something like this right now. Desperately."

"I know when you've got your mind made up," he said with a sigh. And then he dropped his voice to a whisper, slightly muffled. I knew he must be holding his hand around the receiver, trying to keep my mother from hearing. "I'm proud of you. Donovan chose you for a reason—you're smart and capable of more than you know. I . . . I'm not the least bit surprised that he offered you this position. But promise me you'll quit if it gets to be too much?"

I felt the pride in his voice. And the concern. And I knew, no matter what happened, the OSS would have to fire me if they wanted to get rid of me. But still, I told him what he wanted to hear.

"I promise."

∾

*Dear Josette,*
*I will write more very soon, but I'm sending this quick postcard to your sister to pass on to you, just to let you know I'm staying in DC for the summer, so my address*

*remains the same. I have a new job working for the government.*

*I was so happy and relieved to receive your letter. I miss you, my friend, and think of you and Henri and your family often. Please try to stay in touch so I know that you are safe in Paris. Please take care and tell Henri hello . . . and that I miss him too.*

*Je t'embrasse fort,*

*Anna*

I dropped Josette's postcard in a mailbox a block away from OSS headquarters. I had hardly slept all night due to nerves and excitement about my first day. At five thirty, I gave up trying to go back to sleep and got up to feed the cats.

Though it was unmarked, Maggie had shown me where Donovan's office was on Friday and told me it was room 109. Just outside 109 was a sitting area with a coffee table and chairs; a desk and matching chair were positioned right next to this setup. This was where I would be spending a large part of my days.

I put my purse down in the chair and ran my fingers across the cool, dark wood desk, not quite believing where I was and why.

"Well, aren't you the early bird?" Maggie said. She was holding a cup of coffee and walking down the hall toward my desk. "You even beat the boss; he and I are usually the only ones here before eight."

"I don't think I slept a wink last night," I said.

"I understand," Maggie said. She took a sip of her coffee, and I looked at her cup with longing.

"Do you want a cup?"

"Am I that obvious? I would love one," I said, smiling with gratitude.

"Let's head down to the cafeteria."

"Sounds good."

We reached the other end of the first floor, and Maggie pointed to a large classroom-sized room with several desks. All the walls were lined with file cabinets.

"So, there are six departments in the OSS—but two you'll be interacting with the most: this one, Research and Analysis, or R&A, as we call it," she said. "The other is Secret Intelligence, SI, which is on the floor above us.

"Some of your responsibilities will be pretty typical: keeping Donovan's calendar, typing up notes for him, pulling research for him, and answering his phone, of course. Some . . . will be not so typical. And the work pace might overwhelm you at first, but you'll get used to it. My advice to every girl that starts here? Work hard and find a way to get the job done. And most importantly, don't talk to anyone about anything that goes on here, ever."

"Got it." I nodded. I didn't know if it was nerves or the fact that we were walking so fast, but I was starting to sweat and felt a little sick to my stomach.

We went down the stairs to the basement level of the building. The smell of coffee and baking bread was strong, and I spotted double doors to the cafeteria. A woman was walking toward us, coffee in hand. She was so tall that her light-brown curly hair nearly brushed the top of the low-ceilinged hallway.

"Oh, here's someone you should meet. Julia McWilliams, this is Anna Cavanaugh. Julia is in SI and serves as one of the liaisons to Donovan's office. Anna is Donovan's new assistant."

"Oh, thank goodness you're here," Julia said, shaking my hand and giving me a warm smile. She had a long face and kind eyes and had to be over six feet tall. "Someone needs to help us rein him in. We've all started calling him Seabiscuit, because he's constantly racing around this place." She made a galloping motion with her hand.

"I'll do my best to help with that," I said, laughing.

"Maggie, why don't Irene and I take Anna to lunch today?" Julia said. "Irene also works in SI, and you'll be dealing with her a lot, too."

"Oh, I met an Irene. Is her last name Nolan?"

"That's her," Maggie said. "And that's a great idea, Julia. Thank you."

I thanked her, we said our good-byes, and got in line for coffee.

"She is *so* tall," I said.

"Yes," Maggie said. "They wouldn't even let her in the Women's Army Corps because of her height. Julia is one of my favorite people here; you'll love her."

"Another new girl, Maggie? What are you, getting them straight out of high school now?"

I turned to scowl at the tall, blond-haired young man in an officer's uniform standing behind us in line. I guessed him to be around my age, and he was handsome enough to be arrogant about it.

"I'm four years out of Radcliffe, believe it or not," I said, not able to hide my sarcasm as I paid for my coffee and one for Donovan, per Maggie's suggestion.

"Radcliffe? Well, pardon me." He winked at me. *Ugh.*

"Yes, Anna is taking over as Donovan's assistant," Maggie said. "Anna, this is Reggie DuPont."

"Nice to meet you. And boy, I hope you last longer than the others," Reggie said. "What is this, the third? Or is it the fourth assistant in three months?"

"Is that true?" I looked at Maggie, a little nervous.

"Shush, Reggie, don't scare her, for God's sake," she said, glaring at him. "Don't listen to him, Anna."

I gulped my coffee and hoped she was telling me the truth.

"Maggie, I wanted to tell you, the new girl, Evelyn Roberts, in my department? She's just great," Reggie said. "Really smart gal."

"Well, she does have a PhD from Columbia, is a world-renowned expert in Asian studies, and speaks fluent Japanese, so I can't say I'm surprised," Maggie said matter-of-factly, and I had to bite my lip to keep from laughing.

"Um . . . uh, yeah, that's true," Reggie said, stuttering a little. "Thank you for finding her; she's a big asset. Nice to meet you, Anna."

We said our good-byes as we walked away.

"He's barely out of Yale. Evelyn Roberts is a brilliant doctor with years of experience, and yet *she* reports to *him*," Maggie said, shaking her head. "All thanks to family connections—and before you ask, yes, he's from *that* DuPont family. There are more privileged Ivy League boys working here than I care to think about. OSS is very much a man's world, Anna, although I'm guessing you've already figured that out."

"I gathered that based on his attitude," I said.

"Yes," Maggie said, rolling her eyes. "Let's hurry back, I'm sure the boss is here by now."

~

When I got back to room 109, Donovan was in his office on his black telephone. I had learned on Friday that the white telephone on his desk was a direct line to the White House, and the black one was for all other incoming calls. He gave me a wave and a smile as I placed a cup of coffee—cream, one sugar—on his enormous mahogany desk. Papers were scattered all over it. Some were marked *Top Secret*, and all of them were marked *109*. It was a high-ceilinged corner office; the walls were covered with maps stuck with thumbtacks, and tall windows provided a view of the Potomac River. He put his hand over the phone as I started walking out.

"Welcome, Anna," he said in a loud whisper. "I'll meet with you after this call. Please type up these notes for me in the meantime." I grabbed the enormous stack of papers from him and nodded.

About an hour later, he yelled my name, and I grabbed a notebook and went back into his office.

"How are you?" he said, holding his coffee and leaning back in his chair. A low bookshelf behind him featured several framed pictures of his family, including a portrait of his late daughter, Patricia, that made my heart ache for him.

"I'm good. Excited to be here. My mother was not thrilled, but my father understood my decision."

"And your father, old Dick, took it well in the end, did he?" he asked.

"I appealed to his patriotism. How could he say no?" I said, smiling. "Especially when *you're* the one asking? There was no way."

"Lucky for me," Donovan said with a smile. "Did you get fingerprinted? Get all the paperwork done?"

"Yes, Maggie took me to do all of that on Friday. Thank you," I said.

"Now, we're all learning as we go here, Anna, even the economists and PhDs on staff," he said. "You're whip smart, so I'm sure you'll get the feel for your role and for this place right away."

"I'm sure I will," I said. My cheeks turned red at this statement. I wanted so badly to live up to his expectations. He motioned for me to have a seat across from him.

"I need the most help managing my calendar and my phone calls. With my meetings, nobody gets extra time with me except President Roosevelt himself. Got that?" He handed me his calendar book.

"Yes, of course," I said, taking it from him. I looked through his schedule for the week; most days were filled until at least seven in the evening.

"And some of these politicians show up here and think they can chew the fat with me for hours, and I don't have time for that either. I leave those conversations to Edgar Huntington, my chief of staff. He's also in charge of making sure they keep giving us money to keep the lights on—another thing I don't have time for. You'll meet him later."

"Okay, sounds good," I said.

"You know what? Let's take a tour of the place, and I'll explain more about the job as we go."

We started walking, and as he talked I took notes about various departments I needed to understand and the people I needed to meet, the reports I needed to file, and the record keeping required. Donovan was more than twice my age but seemed to have the energy and enthusiasm of a teenager. As I hurried to keep pace with him, it didn't take me long to understand why they called him Seabiscuit.

We stopped by Special Operations, known as SO, which helped organize guerrilla warfare against the enemy on land, and the Maritime Unit, or MU, which helped do the same at sea. Though it was all fascinating, I started to get a headache from so much information coming at me at once.

What struck me as we walked the halls was how much the men and women of the OSS adored Donovan. From the seasoned economists and analysts to the typing pool, people's faces lit up as soon as they spotted him coming their way. He stopped to talk to anyone who wanted a word with him, though it was clear they all knew to keep it brief. He introduced me to everyone by name, knew their roles, and often knew them well enough to ask after their families. He was a football fan, so more than once, someone brought up the Giants. I had also learned he was, like me, a fan of Broadway musicals.

We arrived back in the basement of the building, on the opposite end from the cafeteria, but I could smell the aroma of stale coffee mingled with the savory smells of whatever they were preparing for lunch.

"This is the last stop on our tour, Anna. It's our secret communications center," Donovan said, excitement in his eyes. "This is off-limits to most of the people who work at the OSS, but not to you."

Donovan explained that the women and men working at the center worked in six-hour shifts, twenty-four hours a day, sending and receiving coded messages from OSS detachments as far away as the China coast.

"My code number is 109, like my office," he said in a quiet voice, as he rapped on the last door in the hall. "You'll need to know that."

"Good morning, girls!" he bellowed as he opened the door into a loud, smoky room where about a dozen women were sitting with headsets on, clacking coded messages into machines, notebooks and pens at their side.

We were greeted with good mornings and hellos and smiles, although a couple of the girls eyed me skeptically.

"This is my new assistant, Anna Cavanaugh," he said.

"Hello. I look forward to meeting you all personally," I said, giving an awkward wave.

"I know you're busy. I just wanted to give Anna the tour. Thank you, girls. I don't know what I'd do without you all," Donovan said, pointing his finger throughout the room. A couple of the women blushed.

"General, hello." Irene Nolan was coming down the stairs as we were about to head up.

"Irene, you're just the gal I wanted to see," Donovan said. "This is Anna. Anna, Irene is going to be your first line for SI and secret comms."

"Yes, we met last week. I knew you'd take the job," Irene said, reaching out to shake my hand. "Welcome. Sir, I actually came to find you. Huntington is looking everywhere for you; he says he needs to discuss the Cynthia project. It's urgent."

In a heartbeat, Donovan's face transformed from jovial to deadly serious.

"Thank you, Irene. I'll head to his office now," he said. "I thought it would be good for Anna to really get an understanding of what your group does. Can you spend some time with her this morning, show her what information gets sent up the chain to me, all of that?"

"Of course. Then Julia McWilliams and I are taking her to lunch," Irene said.

"Perfect," Donovan said. "I need to check my calendar; I know I have at least a couple of off-site meetings this afternoon."

"Yes sir," I said. "According to your calendar, your driver is picking you up after lunch for those two meetings. You have a two o'clock at the White House and then a four-thirty at the Ritz-Carlton. You then have a seven o'clock back here with Edgar Huntington, although maybe that won't be necessary since you'll see him now?"

"Right," he said, surprise on his face. "I'll have to see what he wants in order to know if I need to keep the seven o'clock. Thank you, Anna. I appreciate that."

We said our good-byes, watching him bound up the stairs.

"Is he always like this?" I said, eyebrows raised.

"Oh, he never stops. I'm not sure he even sleeps," Irene said with a laugh. "Speaking of, how are you holding up on your first day?"

"I'm not exactly sure what I got myself into," I said. "It's a little overwhelming."

"It is, but you'll be settled here in no time."

"I hope so," I said. "And now I fully understand why you were so vague about your job when I asked you on Friday."

"Yes, but now I can tell you *everything*. Come on," she said, grabbing my arm to head upstairs. "I'll start by showing you one of the least glamorous but most fascinating parts of my job."

"Sounds good."

"But just a warning," Irene said, looking me up and down and cringing. "You may regret wearing that pretty blue dress."

# Chapter Four

"I wish I had an apron I could give you or something. I apologize if you get that new dress really dirty," Irene said as she used a key to unlock yet another unnumbered door, this one on the top floor of the building in a dimly lit corridor off the main hallway.

"I'm not worried about getting it dirty," I said. "But how do you know it's new?"

"Because I saw it at Woodies last Saturday," she said. "I've got a bit of a shopping 'problem,' according to my husband. It looks darling on you—brings out your blue eyes."

I thanked her as she opened the door to reveal a hot, stuffy office with no desks, just an oak conference table piled with duffel bags covered in dust and grime.

"Wow, more than I expected today, actually," Irene said. She motioned me to one of the chairs at the table, then grabbed a duffel bag and handed it to me, taking another for herself before sitting down to open it.

"Basically, in SI, we're like air traffic controllers for classified reports from OSS field agents across Europe, Asia, Africa, and the Middle East. These duffel bags are delivered by secure courier, and in them are pouches that could contain anything from intelligence on German troop movements to requests for ammunition from OSS agents behind enemy lines. Almost all of this information is top secret."

She started pulling out large canvas pouches from the bag that were even grimier than the duffel bag itself. Inside the pouch were a few handwritten reports, among other papers.

"Our job today is to sort through these classified documents, all raw intelligence, and figure out where to send it. Some of the more basic intelligence we simply pass on to the indexing department. More critical information will be sent elsewhere, such as to one of the desks assigned to a geographic region—Spain, North Africa, Italy—to analyze it. You get the idea. We'll go through it all together at first, until you get the hang of it."

"Sounds good," I said. "I'm completely intrigued."

"I know," Irene said, pleased that someone understood her fascination. "It's so interesting, but you just have to remember that it's also critical we do this quickly and thoroughly. Delays or breaches could blow the cover of these field agents—which would be disastrous."

"Understood, of course," I said. It was a somber reminder of the stakes involved. I looked at the bags from that perspective, trying to imagine the people stationed all over the world who had risked their lives to deliver this information to the US in order to help the war effort.

We dumped out the first two duffel bags and went through pouch after pouch of communications from men and women in the field who were identified only by code names. Some of the communications were just dirty, torn bits of paper with notes on them. On this particular day, there was a great deal of raw intelligence for the North African desk.

Irene also explained to me that anything designated *109* meant I had to jog down the stairs and deliver it straight to Donovan's desk. I did the same for documents marked *Eyes Only* for specific OSS officers. After two hours of sorting in that stuffy room and running up and down stairs multiple times, I was sweaty and dusty, and, as Irene had predicted, my new dress was no longer looking pristine.

At one o'clock, there was a knock on the office door.

"Hello, ladies! I have cold Cokes and mediocre cafeteria egg-salad sandwiches for you," Julia said, as she walked in holding a brown bag, the soda bottles under her arms. Once again, I was struck by her height and the warmth of her smile.

"Bless you, Julia," Irene said. "Let's take a quick break. Anna, I'm so sorry we won't be able to take you out to lunch today. I didn't realize we'd have so many bags to go through."

"When I saw these come in earlier, I had a feeling we'd have to change plans," Julia said as we cleared a spot on the table to eat. "So I thought I'd bring lunch to you."

"Thank you both," I said. "I just appreciate having you here to show me the ropes. It's all so interesting, but a little daunting."

"Yes, it's both," Julia said, eyeing her sandwich with skepticism. "And you should probably know—we rarely have time to go out for lunch."

"True," Irene said with a sigh. "We usually eat at our desks, we're so busy. But that makes the days fly by."

"Now, Anna, tell me all about yourself," Julia said. "Where you're from, school, family, any juicy scandals in your past—all that good stuff."

I laughed and gave her a brief overview of growing up in Boston and spending summers on the Cape, about going to Radcliffe and studying in Paris. When I got to the part about teaching French in Boston and then here in DC, I was filled with increasing dread. There was no getting around telling them about Connor.

"Now what about your husband?" Irene asked, taking a sip of her Coke. "What's his name? Have you been able to get in touch with him in Hawaii, to tell him about your new job?"

She asked the question just as I was searching for words to explain. I lost my appetite for lunch, twisting my wedding band around my finger.

"I didn't realize your husband is away. Is he stationed at Pearl Harbor?" Julia asked, leaning forward. "Was he there during the attack?"

"I have a confession to make," I said, putting my sandwich down and looking at Irene, praying she wouldn't judge me too harshly. "My husband . . . he . . . well, he died in Hawaii six months ago. I'm a . . . widow. It still feels odd to say that out loud."

Julia gasped and put her hand over her mouth.

"He died in a freak car accident. He was a medical student and had been working with the military there after Pearl Harbor. I'm sorry, Irene. On Friday, I just didn't know what to say . . . I—"

"Anna, please, don't apologize," Irene said, interrupting me, sadness in her eyes. "Please. I completely understand. And I'm so sorry."

"Me too," Julia said, her voice quiet.

There was a moment of awkward silence.

"I have a fabulous idea," Julia said. "Why don't the three of us go out to dinner on Friday night to celebrate your first week? We can go to the Del Rio. It's about a mile from here, and they have this divine shrimp and oysters in curry sauce."

"I'd love that," I said. "Are you sure?"

"Absolutely," Irene said. "Michael's never home for dinner anyway. He's always working late, even on Friday nights." I detected a bitterness in her voice that I understood all too well.

"And I live at the Brighton Hotel by myself—just me and a hot plate. I live for going out to dinner," Julia said as she started cleaning up the table.

"Okay, let's do it, then. Thank you," I said.

"It's a date. Whenever we finish work on Friday night, we can walk over," Julia said, pleased with our plan.

"Perfect. Now we'd better dive back into these sacks, or we'll be here till midnight," Irene said, grabbing another duffel bag to unload.

∽

We didn't finish sorting through all the intelligence until after seven o'clock that evening. I headed back to my desk outside Donovan's office feeling disheveled, covered in a layer of dust. But it had been a fascinating and sobering afternoon, reading reports and being privy to the covert operations of OSS field agents all over the world. The reports detailed supply requests in North Africa, propaganda efforts in Asia, resistance groups being organized and armed in occupied France. I had a front-row seat to history and tragedy. I'd spent the afternoon viewing the on-the-ground details of a war that was raging with no end in sight, and there were no guarantees of what would happen in the future. The propaganda efforts might have no effect; the troops in North Africa might not get the supplies in time to help their efforts. And even if they were successful, lives would still be lost. The only thing inevitable in war was sacrifice. It wasn't lost on me that some of these American agents around the globe wouldn't make it home.

When I got back to my desk, the door to Donovan's office was open, and I could hear him talking to other people. I knew one of them had to be Edgar Huntington, his chief of staff. I glanced at his calendar to see that the name Phillip Stanhope had been penciled in for this meeting as well.

I was exhausted and in desperate need of a hot bath, but I was determined to keep the same hours as my new boss. I sat at my desk to review Donovan's calendar book and go through the messages and folders that had piled up in my absence. Being so close to his office, I couldn't help overhearing the discussion on the other side of the door.

"As you know, it's a black bag job, but the president and the joint chiefs gave it the okay last month," Donovan said. "The question is, When are we going to be ready? I'm feeling pressure from the president to get it done as soon as we can."

"Cynthia wants us to meet regularly with her and her contact at the Wardman Park Hotel. We'll go over logistics and pick a night to execute the plan. We're thinking before the end of August." A voice with an upper-class British accent said this, which I knew belonged to Phillip Stanhope when he added, "Huntington, have we had any luck getting in touch with the convict?"

"*Ex*-convict. And we have," Huntington said. "The Georgia Cracker is quite the character. He's considered to be one of the best safecrackers on the East Coast. Many tattoos, not many teeth."

I heard Donovan and Stanhope chuckle.

"Sounds perfect," Donovan said. "Look, we can't delay any longer than August. We desperately need to get our hands on that intelligence for North Africa, and unfortunately this is our only viable option. I know it's high risk, but that's why we're the ones to do it. Now, who's going to be the runner that night?"

"Young chap on my team named Archie Thayer," Stanhope said.

"Ah yes, Jonathan Thayer's son," Huntington said. "He's a friend of Roosevelt's from Harvard."

"Are you sure he's up to the task?" Donovan asked.

"He better be, or he'll be out of a job, won't he?" Stanhope said and then paused for a moment before adding, "He's up to it. Just out of Yale, very bright bloke with a bit of an ego, thinks he was born for this kind of work, and he's desperate for a shot at it. He's done good intelligence analysis for me since I've been here. Plus, he's on the small side and very quick—a cross-country champ. I thought those attributes might come in handy, in case running like hell is actually required."

*Safecrackers and Yale grads running like hell. What in the world?* I typed up notes as they talked more about meeting at the hotel and assembling a small OSS team for the "high-risk" mission with the mysterious Cynthia. I wanted to know more about her—what her background was and how she ended up becoming a part of this world.

"Ah, brilliant, you must be the general's new girl." I nearly jumped as Phillip Stanhope walked out of Donovan's office.

"I prefer assistant," I said, trying not to bristle at being called "Donovan's girl" or "the general's girl" for probably the twentieth time that day. I stood up and held out my hand to Phillip Stanhope, who was a couple inches taller than Julia McWilliams. "Anna Cavanaugh."

"Delighted to meet you, Anna. I'm Phillip Stanhope." He gave me a wide smile and took my hand and, for one awkward second, gestured like he was going to lean down to kiss it, but then, apparently remembering where we were, he shook it instead. He was not dressed in uniform like many of the men at the OSS, but in a very dapper pale-gray suit tailored to fit him perfectly. I guessed he was in his late twenties, with his boyish good looks, dirty-blond hair, and green eyes, as well as a mischievous smile that probably broke more than a few girls' hearts at Cambridge or whatever posh British university he had attended.

"Nice to meet you too, Mr. Stanhope," I said.

"Oh please, call me Phillip. No need to be all formal," he said, leaning against my desk, confident, I gathered, that I wouldn't mind him doing so. "First day?"

"Yes."

"Settling in quite well, are you?"

"I am. It was long, but all in all a very good first day, thank you."

"Lovely. But I'm surprised you're still here. It's almost eight o'clock," Phillip said. "A pretty girl like you must have some dashing husband waiting for you at home." He looked at my wedding ring and gave me a wink.

"Anna," Donovan said, walking out of the office with Huntington. "Thank you for staying so late on your first day. I'll radio my driver, Louis, right now, so he can give you a ride home. You've met Stanhope, I see. This is Edgar Huntington, my chief of staff. You'll be seeing a lot of both of them."

"Nice to meet you, Anna. I'm thrilled that you're here to help me corral the general. I've heard great things about you," Huntington said, shaking my hand with both of his. Edgar Huntington was a man in his late forties, stout, with a long face and deep-set eyes that reminded me of a basset hound. I liked him immediately. "I've met your father on the Cape, on the golf course on a couple of occasions. Please tell Dickie hello from me."

"I will do that, sir," I said.

"And I was very sorry to hear about the loss of your husband, Connor," he added, a look of sincere sympathy in his hound dog eyes. "I'm a Harvard man too. I saw the article in the *Crimson* in February. Quite a brilliant young man. I'm so sorry."

Phillip Stanhope put his hand over his face and let out a small groan.

"Thank you, sir," I said, touched at his kind words.

"Well, I'm a bloody tosser," Phillip said. "I'm so sorry, Anna."

"What? What did you say to her?" Donovan said, frowning and looking like he was going to smack him.

"I don't know what 'bloody tosser' even means, but please don't worry about it. You couldn't have known," I said, feeling my cheeks grow warm.

"It means I'm an idiot," he said. "Please forgive me."

"Of course. Don't give it another thought," I said, desperate for this awkward conversation to end. "The wedding ring throws people off. It's my own fault."

I realized it was time to put the ring away, or this scenario was going to keep repeating itself. And, if I was truly being honest with myself, I wasn't wearing it due to love or loyalty to a man or our marriage. I was wearing it out of guilt. Guilt for a young man who lost his life too soon while I survived. Guilt over a failed marriage. The irony was that if Connor had come home as I had assumed he would, the ring on my finger would have been off as soon as his plane landed.

"The car will be out front in five minutes, Anna," Donovan said, clearly also wanting the awkwardness to end. "I let Louis know he'll be driving you home first and coming back to get me. I've still got another half hour or so of work to do."

We said our good-byes. Phillip and Edgar started to walk down the hall, but then Phillip turned and trotted back to me.

"Since we're going to be seeing a lot of each other . . . can we just . . . may we start over tomorrow?" Phillip asked. "I apologize for the dreadful introduction. We British really can be quite charming."

"We can start over," I said with a smile. "Good night, Phillip Stanhope."

"Good night, Anna Cavanaugh."

I gathered my things to go find my ride home. The office clock said 8:25. I had officially survived my first day at the OSS.

# Chapter Five

**July 24, 1942**

Irene, Julia, and I did not end up going out to dinner my first week, or for several weeks after. We worked such long days we were usually too exhausted to make the effort. Donovan was in the office at six every morning and rarely left before seven in the evening, so I did the same. From the moment I got in every morning, senior personnel were hurrying in and out of briefings with him.

I soon realized the OSS was composed largely of young professionals like me, men and women who were either just out of college or had been lured away from new careers to serve the country in wartime in this unique way, selected for reasons and objectives that were incredibly varied. There were cryptographers and cartographers, propagandists and typists and translators, and then there were some people in positions so top secret I had no idea what they did.

And even more intriguing than the work that went on within OSS headquarters was everything happening around the world. Classified cables and memos crossed my desk, detailing the endeavors of OSS men, and a few women, working overseas. Many of them were risking their lives living undercover in occupied areas. The OSS field agents were gathering military intelligence, arranging safety nets for downed Allied fliers, and organizing guerrilla groups, among many other responsibilities. I had no concept of what it took to be qualified for those kinds of roles, but I was terribly jealous of the women who got the chance to do it, and as with Cynthia, I wondered how they were ever granted the opportunity in the first place.

On my fourth Friday morning, I was going through Donovan's calendar when I heard a knock and the now familiar voice of Julia.

"Good morning, Anna. I brought some more eyes-only reports from North Africa for the general, and a jelly donut for you from my favorite neighborhood bakery."

"Why, thank you," I said, taking from her the reports and a white paper bag that smelled like powdered sugar. I smiled. "You just made my morning."

"I'm about to make your morning even more, because Irene and I were talking, and we decided, even if we all fall asleep on our plates, we are taking you out to the Del Rio tonight for dinner," Julia said. "You've been working your tail off trying to keep up with Seabiscuit in there, and you deserve a night out."

"Okay, sounds like a plan," I said with a laugh. "Thank you."

"We'll swing by at the end of the day to pick you up," Julia said.

Just then, there was another knock, and Maggie Griggs was at the door of the outer office, wearing one of her signature plaid skirts, this one green and navy blue.

"Good morning," I said.

"Good morning, Anna," she said. "The general's eight o'clock interview is here." She had an expression I couldn't quite decipher, and it seemed she was trying to silently communicate something with her eyes.

"Ah yes," I said, glancing down at the calendar. "I remember the name because it's John Wayne. So funny. Just like the act—"

"Like the actor? No, miss, I am the actor," John Wayne said in a low, slow voice I would recognize anywhere. He was standing in my office next to Maggie now, giving me that understated smile that had launched his movie career. I jumped up and glanced over at Julia, who appeared beyond delighted that this was happening.

"Oh, um, I'm sorry, I . . . Forgive me, Mr. Wayne," I said, holding out my hand, more than a little bit starstruck. He was a huge bear of a man, a long, lumbering six foot four. "I'm Anna."

"Nice to meet you," he said. That smile again.

"And I'm Julia McWilliams," Julia said, shaking his hand and pumping it up and down so hard I thought I might have to intervene. "What a thrill this is. I am just an enormous fan. And I'm from Southern California like you."

"You don't say," he said, smiling wider now. "Whereabouts?"

"Pasadena," Julia said.

"Not far from Glendale," John said.

"Um, Anna, could you go in and let the general know Mr. Wayne is here?" Maggie asked. "You know he's got quite a full day."

"Oh yes, yes, of course," I said, as John and Julia kept talking. I tried to stop staring at him, not quite believing he was standing in the middle of my office. I noticed the traffic in the hallway had increased. Women from far-flung departments just happened to be strolling by our corner of the first floor.

"Mr. Wayne, you can have a seat." I motioned to the chairs across from my desk as Maggie and Julia said their good-byes, Maggie literally dragging Julia off by the arm.

I knocked, stepped through Donovan's door, and shut it behind me. He was lost in thought, looking at his wall of maps.

"Sir, Mr. John Wayne is here to see you?" I said. "As in, the movie star John Wayne."

"What?" Donovan said, frowning. Then he rolled his eyes, coming back to reality. "Oh yes, right. You can send him in. Sorry, Anna, I've got a lot on my mind, and I don't really have the time to talk to Hollywood types this morning."

"May I ask what he's doing here?"

"He's got some connections at the White House, so we let him fill out an application," Donovan said, looking up at me, eyebrows raised. He glanced down at the papers in front of him. "On his application here, he says the reason he thinks he'd be a good spy is because *he's an actor and is . . . a very good horseback rider.*"

"You can't be serious," I said, trying not to laugh.

"I wish I was joking," Donovan said with a tight smile. "I appreciate his willingness to serve, but he's not really fit for undercover work, is he? I get calls from Hollywood all the time wanting to help—actors, directors, producers. And some of them work out—we've got a couple directors in the OSS field photo unit. But it's not like I can stick John Wayne undercover in a village in Italy and just hope nobody there has ever gone to an American movie."

He smiled wider and chuckled. "Oh, and I heard Julia talking to you about dinner tonight. You gals should go, even if I'm still here. Things are only going to get crazier in the coming weeks, so have a little fun while you can."

"Thank you, sir," I said.

"You haven't missed a beat, by the way. The OSS is lucky to have you."

"Thank you very much," I said, thrilled he felt that way. "I'm happy to be here."

"Now, let's get this interview done. Send him in," Donovan said with a sigh. And I went to fetch the Hollywood movie star who was sitting across from my desk drinking coffee.

~

"Wait, did he actually put *a very good horseback rider* on his application? You're lying," Irene said, laughing, sitting back in the enormous red leather cushioned banquette. She was holding a cigarette in her left hand, looking much more relaxed than I'd ever seen her at the office.

"Irene, I swear to you, I saw it myself," I said, raising my hand as if taking an oath.

"I was really hoping Donovan would hire him for something. What a thrill it would have been to see him around the building every day," Julia said.

It was eight o'clock in the evening, and the three of us had finally made our dinner plan a reality. We were sipping rum and Cokes, sitting around a corner table against the back wall of the Del Rio restaurant. The place smelled like cigarette smoke and broiled chicken, and it was packed with young Washingtonians celebrating the end of the work-week. A few I recognized as fellow OSS employees. The Ink Spots' song "I Don't Want to Set the World on Fire," one of my favorites, was play-ing on the restaurant's jukebox. I took a deep breath, looked around, and smiled. It felt good to be out socially. It had been a long time.

"Julia, I didn't realize you were from Southern California until you told John Wayne," I said. "What made you come all the way out here?"

"Same reason I think a lot of people are here," Julia said, sipping her rum and Coke. "With the war going on, this is the place to be, the center of things. And I love the East Coast. I went to Smith, and then lived in New York for a time after graduation. I had moved back to California for a job in advertising. I had just turned down a proposal from my boyfriend before I moved here. It was the perfect time for a fresh start."

Irene gasped. "Now that is a scandal you've never discussed. Tell us more."

"No, I assure you, nothing scandalous, I'm afraid," Julia said. "His name was Harrison Chandler. He was lovely, and he loved me . . . but I didn't feel the same." She shrugged.

"Wait . . . Harrison Chandler." I paused, trying to remember how I knew the name. "Is his father Harry Chandler? Publisher of the *L.A. Times*?"

"Precisely." Julia nodded, impressed that I knew the name.

"Julia, what did your parents say?" Irene said, shocked. "The Chandlers must be one of the richest families in California."

"I'm pretty sure they're one of the richest families in the *country*," I said. "My mother would have dragged me down the aisle."

"Mine practically did," Julia said, giving us a wry smile. "And she also kept reminding me that I may never receive another offer of marriage, given my height and my other failings. But accepting Harrison's proposal wouldn't have been fair to me or to him. I'm craving some more adventure before I settle down. *If* I ever settle down."

"Do you want to go overseas?" I asked. It was the question I'd been wanting to discuss with them since the day I had started.

"Of course," Julia said. "Just like every other gal here. I want to go to the farthest-flung place I can go. I tried to put in for that North Africa assistant-slash-seamstress position a couple of weeks ago, but I can't sew worth a damn, so Maggie just laughed at me."

"What about you, Irene?" I said.

"Absolutely. Like Julia said, almost every girl here wants to get a post overseas. I want to go desperately," she said. "I'd love to go to work in the new London office. They're hiring a ton for that one, but so far, Maggie and the general won't consider me."

"Why in the world not?" I said. Irene was one of the more impressive women I'd met at the OSS, meticulous, hardworking, and no-nonsense.

"Because I'm married," Irene said. She exhaled cigarette smoke, her mouth in a knot. "Maggie said the general doesn't want to be responsible for the breakup of any marriages. He says it's always a risk when you send women overseas."

"Have you talked to your husband about it?" I asked.

"I have," she said, looking down at the table, flicking her ashes in the tin ashtray. "He's fine with it. Thinks it would be good for us . . . I mean for me."

Julia and I exchanged a brief glance. Clearly there was more to that story, but neither of us wanted to pry.

"Well, maybe they'll change their minds," Julia said. "So, Anna, I'm guessing you're also interested?"

"Yes," I said. "I'd love the chance to go anywhere, really. London would be a good start. The Continent definitely—anywhere closer to Paris and my friends there."

"Yes, tell us more about these Parisian friends and what it was like living there," Julia said. "I bet it was fantastic."

This led to a discussion of my time studying abroad at Sciences Po. I told them all about Josette and Henri and our other friends from university, leaving out my feelings for Henri. I also told them about my last letter from Josette and her being back in occupied Paris for reasons she couldn't say and how I wondered if there would be another letter anytime soon.

"You're right, it was fantastic. Paris was the best year of my life," I said with a sigh. "It was the first place I've ever been that felt as much like home as my family home in Cambridge."

"Wait. The year you were married wasn't the best year of your life?" Irene asked.

"Irene," Julia said, swatting her arm. "Anna, you don't have to answer that. It's entirely too personal."

"I'm so sorry. Julia's right," Irene said, waving her hand as if to swat the question away. "I have a habit of asking too many questions."

"No, it's okay. It's a fair question," I said, taking a long sip of my rum and Coke as I considered how to explain. "And since you're my first friends at OSS, I want to be honest with you. Paris *was* the best year of my life. My year—well, eight months—being married was . . . definitely not. Connor had already been living down here for a year when we got married, so our relationship had been long distance for a while. When I moved down here after we got married and took the teaching job at Sidwell, my long-term plans were to go to graduate school here and, after that, work for the government, maybe even work overseas at some point, in an embassy or consulate like I'd always wanted to. When we were engaged, Connor seemed supportive of my ambitions; he had even encouraged me to study abroad in France. But when I returned from Paris and took my first teaching job in Boston, Connor's star was rising in the medical world, and his studies and his career had become all-consuming. And by the time we were married, he was constantly frustrated that I wanted to be anything more in life than his doting wife. It was pretty clear that we were not the perfect match everyone always told us we were."

"I understand," Irene said in a quiet voice.

"So . . . ," I said, eager to change the subject and curious too, "have either of you ever considered applying to go into the occupied territories or to be trained as an agent?"

Julia burst out laughing. "Yes, I think I would be absolutely perfect in the field. I mean, look at me. I wouldn't be conspicuous in the slightest. Especially in a village of petite French peasants, nobody would ever suspect I was an American *spy*." And in a convincing French accent, she added, "*Mesdames et messieurs*, please pay no attention to the new woman in the village who is taller than anyone who has ever lived here in the last hundred years."

Irene and I couldn't help but crack up.

"No. An overseas post? Definitely. But a field agent? I don't think so," Irene said. "I don't think I have the temperament."

I was about to ask what kind of temperament she thought was required for the job, when our waitress came over with the Blue Point oysters, canapés of caviar, and imported boneless sardines Julia had insisted we order for appetizers, as well as another round of rum and Cokes.

"Oh, we didn't order these drinks," I said. The waitress put them on the table anyway. She had her dark hair done up in victory rolls and exaggerated black cat-eye liner around her eyes.

"No you didn't, honey. That good-looking English fella at the bar sent them over for you," she said, nodding her head in that direction.

Phillip Stanhope was standing at the bar with a slight, red-haired young man who looked no older than seventeen.

"Stanhope," I said. It was the young man from Donovan's office I had met at the end of my first day. Since then, he had breezed in and out of Donovan's office on several occasions, but we had both been too busy to do more than exchange a few pleasantries.

"Stan-who?" Julia said. "Is he that tall glass of water over there?"

"Phillip Stanhope," Irene said. "I haven't met him yet personally, but I know he works for the British equivalent of the OSS, although he seems to be working for us more than them."

"Ah yes," Julia said. "I thought he looked familiar. He is quite good-looking."

"Yes, and I believe he's well aware of that fact," I said.

"Um, he's coming this way," Irene said. "Who's that with him? His *son*?"

"God no," I said, laughing. "But . . . I think I know who that is."

"Ladies," Phillip said, coming over to our table with the other man. "Congratulations on making it out of the office at a decent hour this evening."

"Thank you for the drinks," I said, introducing him to Julia and Irene. "And let me guess, you must be Thayer."

Just my height, slim with ginger hair and freckles, Archie Thayer fit the description of the Yale grad who could "run like hell" if required. This was the man I had overheard Donovan, Stanhope, and Huntington discussing on my first day.

"How do you know that?" Thayer said, looking surprised and almost annoyed as he shook hands with us. "I'm Archie Thayer. I just started at OSS a couple of months ago."

Phillip gave me a look, clearly not pleased with my guess.

"Maggie Griggs mentioned you were one of the new fellas starting," I said, making up an excuse as to why I knew his name. "A little before I did."

"Well, sit down and share some of our snacks," Julia said, moving over to make room. "You must try the sardines."

Archie was already taking a seat and helping himself to the canapés.

"Let me guess: You pretty ladies are in the typing pool?" Archie said, seated next to Julia.

"That's exactly right. Amazing. Clearly, you're born for this type of intelligence work," Irene said, so straight-faced that Julia had to hold her fist in front of her mouth to suppress a laugh.

"Anna, might I have a word in private?" Phillip asked.

"Oh. Yes," I said. "Be right back, ladies."

Irene and Julia both gave me looks like this might be something more than a chat. I rolled my eyes at them. Phillip Stanhope was handsome, but I'd become numb to the idea of getting involved with anyone romantically. It was easier and safer to dream about Henri, about what might have been with him, than to let my guard down with anyone real.

"I'm sorry," I said when we reached the bar. "I know what you're going to say. I shouldn't have guessed his name. That's why I lied about Maggie telling me."

"No, you shouldn't have," Stanhope said, eyebrows raised. He offered me a Chesterfield, but I passed. "He doesn't show it, but the chap is a nervous wreck. Don't need to make him even jumpier now, do we?"

"I won't do it again, I promise," I said. But then, frowning, I added, "If he's a nervous wreck, are you sure he's up to the task? And what is the task, anyway?"

Stanhope examined my face for a moment before answering.

"I suppose I can discuss this with you, since you work for the man himself, making you privy to most of what goes on at the highest levels," he said.

"At this moment, I only know what I overheard from that meeting when we first met. I haven't learned any more than that from the general."

"Well, you know it's a black bag job approved by Roosevelt himself."

"Yes," I said. "So 'black bag' means a break-in somewhere? To obtain information?"

"Right you are," he said with a nod. "We are desperate to gain this particular bit of intelligence for the war efforts in North Africa. By we, I mean my country *and* yours." Stanhope blew out a puff of smoke, his frustration evident.

"His is a small job in the grand scheme of the whole thing, but I'm not sure if the lad's up to it, to be honest. I brought him out tonight to give him a talk. He's got an ego, and despite his pedigree—Yale and all that—he's not as bright as he thinks he is, more of a bon vivant than a spy. His father is rich and powerful and has Roosevelt's ear, so I think he was foisted on General Donovan. I have to tell you, though, by hiring the Archie Thayers of the world, Donovan's giving this place a bit of a reputation as more of a country club than a serious organization."

"I've heard the nicknames—OSS stands for 'Oh So Snobby.' And trust me, I know Archie's type," I said, thinking of the men like him I'd met since my first day: freshly minted Ivy League grads given high-level roles they had not yet proven they were worthy of having.

I looked over at Archie, who was inhaling the appetizers, much to Julia's horror. He was bouncing his leg up and down under the table, and he had just called the waitress over to order another martini.

"Did your talk work?" I asked.

"It better have," Stanhope said, watching him. "We're getting close to the date, and we cannot afford to have him muck it up, can we?"

"I wish you could tell me some of the details. I'd love to be involved."

"Ah, not with this particular mission, you wouldn't. I promise you. Nearly impossible odds—this one is a beast. I just hope it's not a spectacular failure, or Archie and I will be out on the street. Or in jail."

"I doubt that will happen," I said. "Can I ask—who do you work for, anyway? The OSS or your country's version of it?"

"You might say I'm here on loan from the Special Operations Executive, otherwise known as SOE," Phillip said, which I knew was the OSS's counterpart in the UK. "I was with MI6, my country's foreign intelligence service, before we started up the SOE specifically for the war efforts. You Americans are so new at this whole espionage game. We've been doing it for four centuries. You've been doing it for about four months, haven't you? You hardly know what you're doing, so we're giving you a hand."

"Ah, how good of you."

"Pleasure, really," he said, winking at my sarcasm. "There are much worse places to be in the world right now. I can tell you that."

"That is very true," I said in a quiet voice. I thought of Josette and Henri in occupied Paris and wondered for the thousandth time if they were safe.

He paused for a moment and looked in my eyes, serious now. He had a small horizontal scar on his forehead, partly concealed by his hair. I couldn't deny that he was very handsome, and there was something charming about a British accent.

"I wanted to say again that I'm very sorry about the loss of your husband. And I apologize for being so daft a few weeks back."

"Thank you," I said with a pang of guilt, as he had misread who I had been thinking about.

"I'm not going to presume I know what you've been through, but so you know . . . I've experienced loss in this war too. My older brother was an officer with the British army at Dunkirk. He's missing, presumed . . . presumed dead. My poor mother is the only one holding out hope at this point."

He spoke slowly when he said this, as if the words hurt on his lips. I knew that sharing grief brought it to the surface in a way that could be hard to bear.

"Oh, I'm so very sorry for your loss," I said. "Your family's loss— how horrible."

"Yes, it's . . . well, it comes in waves, the grief, doesn't it?"

"Yes," I said. We were both quiet for a moment.

"I . . . took the ring off. You weren't the only one who asked, so please don't feel too badly."

"Do you mind my asking what happened? To him?"

I had gotten used to talking about it when people asked, but it always managed to summon all my conflicted feelings about Connor—the guilt and the many regrets.

"He was training to be a doctor—Harvard Medical School," I said. "They had been researching some very promising blood plasma treatments for soldiers in the field when Pearl Harbor happened. So, he was sent down there, and . . . it was a freak car accident shortly after he arrived. Bad weather. A jeep on a dirt road."

"Horrible," he said, shaking his head. "And how have you been holding up?"

"I'm all right," I said, giving him a small smile. "Thank you for asking." For a moment, I wanted to tell him that our marriage had been in trouble, and then I felt guilty for wanting to tell a perfect stranger something so personal.

"I was planning to move back home to Boston when I met with Donovan. Taking this job? It was one of the best decisions I've made in a long time."

"Well, you're certainly fitting in well, aren't you?" He nodded to Julia and Irene.

"Yes, and we better go back to the table before Julia punches Archie for eating the last oyster," I said.

He laughed. Before we rejoined the group, I decided I needed to say one more thing. Because of the general's relationship with my family, I knew he would be resistant to me going abroad or getting involved in anything he deemed too dangerous. I'd need some allies to help me convince him otherwise. I was hoping Maggie Griggs could be one. Maybe Phillip Stanhope could be another.

"Look, I barely know what you and Archie are involved in, but I envy you," I said. "I know I haven't been here long, but I'm capable of doing so much more than I'm doing. I want to be *in* the room like you are, not sitting outside it. I mean, if a kid like Archie Thayer can be part of an SI mission, certainly I deserve a shot. Would you . . . would you keep that in mind? In case any opportunities arise?"

"Ah yes, yet another young American eager to do her part in the field, are you? Well, Cavanaugh, not sure I can help you there," Stanhope said, but, seeing the look of disappointment on my face, he continued, "but I promise I'll keep that in mind in case I can."

# Chapter Six

**August 10, 1942**

*27 mai 1942*

*Chère Anna,*
*It is getting more and more difficult to get letters out into the world from here, but my sister in Dinard promised to mail this to you. I hope that you receive it, even if it takes many weeks.*

*Paris is dark, and it is dangerous. We had the coldest winter here that I can remember, and there is never enough coal or food. And Anna, now everyone knows someone who has been arrested.*

*Do you remember our friend from university, Simone Monteux? She has vanished. I went to her home today, and her entire family was gone. I begged the concierge of their building for details about what happened to them, but she would not tell me anything.*

*And Monsieur Drucker, the owner of our very favorite fromagerie in the Marais? He and his family have also disappeared. Their store is boarded up, and when I knocked on the front door of the building to ask what happened, someone looked at me from behind the curtain but would not answer.*

*Life is difficult here for everyone, but it is even more difficult for families like Simone's and Monsieur's, because they are Jewish. The lives of Jews, even Jews that are native French, are restricted more every day, and it fills me with an indescribable anger. Please say a prayer that our friends made it out of this city to somewhere safer, because the rumors are dreadful. It is said Jews are being sent to prison camps in occupied Poland.*

*I still work for the French industrialists as a translator, so I often have to also work with a group of German officers. Some are kinder than others. I want to ask them where Simone and Monsieur Drucker and their families are. I have so much more I'd like to say to them, but I bite my tongue and do the work. It's all I can do for now.*

*I miss you, my dear friend. Do you remember the night a group of us joined the tango dancers on the banks of the Seine? Georges and Henri were there, and out of the group, the only one who could dance the tango well was you? I was looking through some pictures Henri took of that evening. He took more pictures of you than of anyone else, which is no surprise. That night is one of the memories that keeps me going in these dark times. I dream of all of us reunited again, listening to the music and figuring out the steps together.*

*If you write, please address the letter to my sister.*
*Je t'embrasse,*
*Josette*

I sat at my desk outside the general's office and read the letter for a fourth time. It was August 10, but Josette had written it to me in May.

The letter had arrived only the day before, and I had brought it to work with me because I couldn't stop thinking about it. I had so many questions. Josette's words filled me with dread. I wondered if she had finally received my postcard, or if it was even worth trying to get another letter to her through her sister because mail delivery to occupied France was likely to be more unreliable than ever.

Why hadn't she said anything about Georges and Henri, beyond a memory of all of us on a night out dancing? It was an explicit omission. Wherever Georges and Henri were now, she wanted to make it clear to the mail censors that she knew nothing about their whereabouts. I prayed that meant she knew where they were . . . and that they were safe.

Henri had often snapped pictures when he thought nobody was looking. The thought of him taking so many pictures of me without my even realizing it warmed me inside. A validation. What we had felt for each other had been real.

I kept reading the letter because I felt like I was missing something . . . like there was . . .

"Anna. Oh good, you're still out here. I know it's late, but can you come in for a second?" General Donovan said, leaning out of his office. I nearly jumped at the sound of his voice and shoved the letter back in the drawer.

"Are you okay?" He looked at me, eyebrows raised.

"Yes, sir. Sorry, lost in thought for a moment," I said. "I received a letter from my friend in Paris. She sent it by way of her sister in Dinard. Times are very tough there."

"So I have heard," he said. "I know that . . ." He stopped himself mid-sentence, catching himself from saying something he couldn't share. "Well, never mind, I just need to dictate a few notes to you before you leave."

"Of course."

I grabbed my notebook and pen and joined him in his office. He was sitting behind his desk, which was forever scattered with papers marked *Eyes Only* and *Top Secret*. Many of the reports had to do with North Africa as of late. Much of the most recent intelligence included maps and diagrams of port locations and facilities, and some had to do with where warships belonging to France's collaborationist Vichy government were stationed in the Mediterranean.

There had been a frenetic energy emanating from him in the past few days. He was keyed up, getting prepared for something big. And I knew that, whatever it was, it had to do with the Allies' upcoming plans in North Africa and the connected, critical intelligence operation Phillip Stanhope and his sidekick Archie were involved in.

"Have a seat, Anna," he said, continuing to read a report.

I sat down.

"I appreciate you working late, but please don't feel like you have to every night," he said, looking up at me with a smile.

"To be honest, sir, I don't mind at all. There's not much waiting at home for me these days except my cats and the dinners my best friend leaves for me."

"Ah yes," he said, giving me a small, sympathetic smile. "You don't feel it's too much for you? Too much too soon, like your father—"

"No, not too soon at all. I prefer being busy," I interrupted him, blurting out the words I'd been thinking since I started at the OSS. "In fact, I'd love to take on more. I haven't even utilized my language skills. I know from Maggie that you're sending more women into the field as agents. I . . . I'd like to be considered for those kinds of posts."

Donovan leaned back in his chair, looked up at the ceiling, and sighed.

"I knew you'd bring this up at some point. You're a wonderful assistant. Maggie thinks you've already proven yourself way overqualified for this position," Donovan said. "But . . ."

My arms broke out in goose pimples. The fact that he'd even thought about me being a field agent was more than I had hoped for.

"But I have a couple of concerns. For one, you are Dick Shannon's daughter," he said. "And I don't take the decision to put my old friend's daughter in harm's way lightly."

I glanced at the picture of his late daughter, Patricia, behind him on the bookshelf and simply nodded.

"I understand that, but I can handle my father," I said, knowing my parents would think the idea of overseas work was ridiculous. "What are your other concerns?"

"Being a field agent is incredibly dangerous," he continued. "We're highly selective about the women and men we choose for this work for a reason. It's not a life for everyone. It's not a life for *most*. You live for the work and not much else."

"Yes, but right now? I think it might be the kind of life I need," I said.

"Why do you say that? And don't tell me, 'To serve my country.' I know that already. Why would you want to do something as dangerous as this? Why *now*?"

I shook my head and paused, trying to articulate this yearning I had had since, well, since I came home from Paris. "Before I got married, I always thought I'd do something more, and that I'd definitely travel the world somehow. I had dreams of maybe working for the foreign service, at an American consulate or embassy, maybe in Paris or Berlin. At the very least, I thought I'd use my language skills for something other than teaching French to snobby high school students."

The general laughed but then turned serious. "I'll tell you what—"

Just then, Scotty Halloran, the portly nighttime security guard, burst into Donovan's office.

"There's a gunman loose in the building. He's looking for you, General," Scotty said in a breathless voice.

His chubby face was beet red and shiny, and I glimpsed circular sweat stains on his uniform dress shirt.

"Police are on their way, but Anna, you and the general need to hide out someplace safe. Get him outta here."

"What in the hell?" Donovan said, not believing his ears. "Scotty—"

"Now! You need to hide. Get away from this office," Scotty said. "I've got to make sure there's no other employees still here."

Scotty darted down the hall as the general jumped out of his chair, swearing a blue streak.

"Jesus Christ Almighty," he said. "I was just telling Roosevelt this building needs tighter security."

"Follow me, General. I know exactly where we should go," I said, trying to ignore the feeling of my heart beating out of my chest and praying my idea would work.

We hurried down the dimly lit hallway, not speaking and walking gingerly on the tile floor so as not to make too much noise. All the offices were empty, as everyone in our corner of the building had gone home for the night.

We reached the ladies' room at the end of the hall, and I swung the door open and motioned for him to go inside.

"What?" the general whispered, looking at me like I had lost my mind.

"There are no women in the building right now but me," I said in a whisper back, knowing he was mortified at the idea of being caught in the ladies' room, armed intruder or not. "Go to the last stall. I'll be in the one two down from you. Stand on the toilet seat."

He hesitated for a moment, his pride getting in the way.

"General, please. *Now*," I said.

He sighed and quietly but quickly walked down to the last salmon-pink stall, and I opened the door to mine, crouching on top of the toilet seat.

I heard the sound of police sirens right outside. Five minutes passed, and I had to wipe the trickle of sweat dripping into my eyes. Where were the police? Then I heard a booming male voice coming from the hallway.

"General Donovan! Show yourself," the voice said. "Wanna talk to you about hiring too many commie bastards." The gunman was getting closer, as was the sound of office doors being kicked in. I swallowed down a cough. Another kick, and this time the ladies' room door swung open. I had to bite down on my fist to keep from screaming.

A pause. I froze in place and only took a breath after the door swung closed again.

"Police, drop your weapon!" a voice hollered, and I heard a stampede of feet outside the door.

A gunshot rang out, and I jumped. I bit down on my fist again and tried to make myself even smaller on top of the seat.

There was a cacophony of sirens outside and the sound of more police storming up the stairs. The shock of what had just happened paralyzed me for a moment. Mere seconds before, a man who wanted to shoot the general had been standing a few feet from me, just a flimsy bathroom stall door between us.

"All clear. Intruder is down. I repeat, intruder is down," a policeman in the hallway said over a bullhorn.

"General! Anna! Coast is clear. Where are you?" I heard poor Scotty's frantic voice.

"We're here, Scotty," I called out, finally pulling my half-numb legs out from under me and putting my feet on the floor.

I stepped out of the stall at the same time General Donovan stepped out of his, and we looked in each other's eyes and silently acknowledged the danger.

He was a decorated veteran and had been in combat, but being so close to guns was a first for me. I tried to hide my shaking hands and hoped he couldn't see that I was sweating through my shirt now, just like Scotty.

We walked out of the bathroom.

Cops greeted us. One of them shook Donovan's hand, and another one asked if he could get me a glass of water. Someone threw a gray cotton blanket around my shoulders, and I didn't refuse. I could still hear the sound of the shot ringing in my ears.

"Oh, thank God." Scotty came running over as the general and I made our way back to Donovan's office. "You all right, Anna? General, you holding up okay? Can I get you anything?"

"We're okay, Scotty, thank you. Good job tonight, my friend," the general said, shaking Scotty's hand.

General Donovan looked completely unruffled by the incident. Just another day at the office.

"Anna, come get your things. I'll call Louis to give you a ride home in a few." He steered me back into 109, hand on my shoulder.

"Have a seat for a minute," he said, taking two shot glasses out of his desk drawer and grabbing a bottle of Tullamore D.E.W. Irish whiskey from the bookshelf.

He handed me a glass. We toasted and both downed our shots. I winced as the strong alcohol burned my throat, then put the glass down on his desk, my hand still unsteady.

"You okay?" he said.

"I . . . yes," I said. I took a deep breath. "I mean, I will be. I'll be fine."

He studied me, looking down at my hands.

"You did well," he said. "Better than most people would in that situation."

"Thank you," I said, then I frowned at him. "Are you surprised?"

"A little . . . but not completely," he said with a chuckle. "And now you have to make me a promise."

He held the bottle of whiskey over my shot glass, but I declined another drink.

"You cannot tell anyone where we hid tonight. Not a soul," he said. His face was so serious I couldn't help but break into a huge smile. After what happened, he was mortified about hiding on a toilet in the ladies' room and afraid that news would get out.

"Of course. I would never," I said. I couldn't help but start giggling, which made him break into a wide grin.

"I'm serious, you know," he said, pointing at me. "Don't get me wrong, it was a brilliant hiding place, but I do have a reputation to uphold."

"Your secret is safe with me, General," I said.

"Good." He paused for a few seconds. "What I was going to say, before we were interrupted earlier this evening, is that I will *think* about your desire to be a field agent. In the meantime, let's give you a little more responsibility here. This black bag intelligence-gathering operation for North Africa—I'm sure you've heard at least parts of the discussions I've been having about it?"

"Yes," I said, literally sitting on the edge of my seat. With my head spinning a little from the alcohol and adrenaline, I shared my thoughts more freely than I would have otherwise. "From what I've seen in the documents coming into the office and overheard from your meetings, it has to do with gathering intelligence regarding the Vichy France Navy movements in the Mediterranean, specifically around North Africa. You need more information on their navy; that is the missing link."

"Very good. Well done, you," he said, leaning back in his chair, his expression somewhere between impressed and amused. "And why do you think we need this information?"

"Why? Well, my best guess is the most obvious one—it's obvious to the world at this point that the Vichy French government is collaborating with the Nazis. And the Allies have future plans in North Africa."

Though most of northern France was now German-occupied territory, there remained a so-called "Free Zone" in the south, governed by a French government headquartered in the city of Vichy.

I tucked one of my curls behind my ear, my hand still shaking. The general noticed and poured a little more whiskey in my shot glass, which I didn't refuse.

"Now, based on what you've learned, where do you think we're going to get this intelligence?"

"That's what I can't figure out," I said, standing up, studying the maps on the wall. "It feels like this operation is not only soon, but it has to be close by. You're breaking in somewhere in DC, aren't you?"

"Yes," Donovan said, definitely impressed now. "Which leaves only one place."

I thought for a moment and then hit my forehead, annoyed that I hadn't figured it out sooner.

"The embassy," I said. "The Vichy French embassy, of course. Where else could it be? Am I right?"

"You are right."

"But wait, the operation that Stanhope and Archie are involved in—they're not . . . the OSS isn't *actually* going to break into their embassy. Are we?"

"We are," he said. "We've recently confirmed that the Vichy French embassy is sharing information about the US and its allies with the Germans. In April, Pierre Laval took over as prime minister of the Vichy French government, and now we know they're nothing more than a Nazi puppet state."

"I'm surprised there's still an embassy here at all," I said.

"I doubt it will be here long, which is why we have to act soon. We're going to steal their navy ciphers so we can read their cables. It's critical that we know their plans for their battleships. If they're planning to hand those over to the Germans, we need to stop them."

"How and when are you going to do this?" I said, stunned at the boldness of the plan. No wonder Stanhope thought it was a "beast" of a job, as he called it.

"When? The night of August 20 . . . *How* is a complex question, obviously. But I'll tell you what, Anna. If you stay late tomorrow night, I have a meeting with the team involved. We'll fill you in on more of the details, make you understand what field agents like Stanhope and Cynthia truly have to contend with. You can take notes for me, be my second set of ears. That is, if you're up for it?"

"Thank you so much. Of course I can stay," I said, stumbling over my words, trying to contain my excitement. "I am ready, sir, I promise you."

"You should go home and get some sleep. I'll call Louis."

I agreed and went to grab my purse in my desk.

"And Anna?" he said as I was leaving his office.

"Yes?"

"The more you learn, the more you may decide it's not the life for you after all."

"I doubt that, sir."

"I was afraid you'd say that," Donovan said, downing the last of his whiskey.

# Chapter Seven

**August 11, 1942**

I was wide-awake at 5:00 a.m. the next morning. All night my mind had raced between Josette's letter, the armed intruder, and the impending meeting regarding the embassy break-in. I got up, fed the cats, and was back in the office by 6:30. The general was at meetings off-site until at least eleven, so I worked and enjoyed my cup of coffee in the quiet of the early morning as other office lights were flicked on and people started to arrive.

"Ah, it's the hero of the hour," Maggie Griggs said as she walked up to my desk, clapping her hands.

"Oh no. What are you talking about?" I asked.

"I just heard about what happened last night," Maggie said, handing me a stack of mail she was holding under her elbow. "Well done hiding the general in the first-floor ladies' bathroom."

"No, no, no," I said, covering my face with my hands. "He's going to be beside himself. How could you know that already? I swore to him I wouldn't tell anyone."

"Did he honestly think he could keep it a secret?" Maggie said, eyes wide and incredulous behind her glasses. "There's already a team from the Pentagon here this morning evaluating the building's security. They told me the whole story. Everyone's going to know what happened by lunchtime."

She paused, looking me up and down, no doubt noticing the dark circles under my eyes.

"How are you doing, by the way?"

"I'm all right; didn't sleep that well."

"Nobody could blame you for that," Maggie said. "I'm proud of you."

"Really?" I said, thinking it was an odd thing to say. "I honestly didn't do much."

"You didn't panic. You didn't cry hysterically. You're back at work today," Maggie said. "You proved yourself tougher than most women. Or men, for that matter."

"Thank you," I said, feeling my cheeks grow warm. "Maggie, do you have a minute to talk, confidentially?"

"For you? Of course," Maggie said, grabbing a chair and pulling it over to my desk. Since I had started working at the OSS, I had learned two things about Maggie Griggs: one, that she was the person you went to if you needed to talk; and two, that she knew as much as Donovan about the inner workings and secrets of the organization.

I filled her in on my conversation with Donovan, thanking her for the kind words about my being overqualified and telling her about the invitation to the meeting that night.

"He's bringing you into the fold on this latest intelligence mission? That's unexpected, to be honest," Maggie said.

"Is it?"

"Yes," she said. "It's highly classified and critical. I only have a vague idea about what's planned. And I have to be frank, Anna. I could see him relenting and letting you take an overseas position, but a field agent? Those roles . . . All I can say is they carefully recruit and curate the people in those positions. For now, I would just focus on the meeting tonight. See what happens."

"You're right," I said. "I get too impatient."

"I'd never guess," she said with sarcasm as she gave me a wink. "Good luck. Speaking of field agents, one of the fellas you're meeting with is quite a character."

"Oh, you're talking about the Georgia Cracker, aren't you?"

"Yes," Maggie said. "That's the only name I know for him. It was his nickname in prison. He's known to be one of the best safecrackers in the country. We've got more than a few ex-cons working for the OSS now."

"Are you serious?"

"I am. I've seen the employee files myself. It makes sense when you think about it—why train Dartmouth grads to crack safes when you can hire professionals who've been doing it their whole lives?"

"Um, because you shouldn't hire convicted criminals to work for a secretive government intelligence agency?"

Maggie just laughed and shook her head. "You'll like the Cracker. He's one of a kind."

~

"Irene and I came up with a name for your heroic mission last night," Julia said, looking at Irene, barely able to contain her laughter. We were sitting at a table in the corner of the cafeteria picking at the sad-looking turkey sandwiches we had all chosen for lunch. We tried to have lunch together in the cafeteria at least once or twice a week, and we had met for drinks at the Del Rio once more. I had leaned so much on Mary since moving to DC, and I had even more so these past several months since Connor's death. It was nice to have some new friends, to give her more time with her own family.

"I'm so afraid to ask," I said, covering my mouth with my hand. Maggie had been right. By lunchtime, at least a dozen people had asked me how I was doing or for more details about the events of the night before. I dreaded seeing Donovan's reaction to the entire OSS knowing the ladies' room had been our hideout.

"Operation . . . Johnny on the *Pot*," Irene said, and she and Julia started laughing, unable to contain themselves. I scowled at both of them for thinking they were so clever, but then I couldn't help it. I started laughing too, even though their "Operation Johnny on the Pot" joke was ridiculous.

"In all seriousness, though, are you okay?" Julia said. "I would have run from the building screaming in terror."

"I'm fine. Don't get me wrong, it was terrifying, but it was over in minutes," I said. "Sleep was nearly impossible last night, though."

I told them about my racing thoughts at 5:00 a.m., which led to my sharing Josette's latest letter with them.

"Georges is a friend from university, a former professor," I said after they both read it. "I didn't tell you this before, but Henri might have been more than a friend."

"Might have been, or was?" Irene asked.

"Was . . . for a brief moment in time," I said. "I was engaged. I'm not proud of . . . of letting something happen. But as I've mentioned, my relationship with my fiancé only looked good from the outside."

"I just knew there was something there," Julia said, looking pleased with herself. "Something about the sparkle in your eye when you talked about France."

"It was so long ago," I said, feeling myself blush. "I just hope he's safe. Last time she mentioned both of them being there with her; this time she didn't, which is odd."

"These are dark times for the French," Julia said. "Reading about all those poor people being taken away gives me the chills."

"That was another reason I couldn't sleep last night. Where are they taking them?" I asked.

"Based on reports coming in, things are getting much grimmer all over occupied France," Irene said, still looking over the letter, as if she was trying to see beyond the writing. "If they're not in the military, men over the age of twenty are being drafted to work for the Vichy government—basically forced labor—and many are sent to Germany. My guess is your friends went underground, into hiding, so they wouldn't be forced to go. Many young men are doing that, joining up with various resistance groups."

"How do you know?" I asked, guessing she was right about their going underground.

"I just read a report from SI this week before I handed it over to the French intelligence desk," Irene said. "And before you say we're not supposed to discuss these things, as Julia and I have said on more than one occasion, this all stays between us and goes no further." She swooped her arms as if the three of us were in a protected bubble.

"Exactly," Julia said with a nod. "Nothing goes beyond this corner lunch table."

"After all, if we can't talk to each other about this stuff, who can we talk to?" Irene said. "I certainly can't talk to my husband."

"I appreciate your honesty, and thank you for including me," I said, happy to have earned their trust.

"And now I have some news," Julia said, putting down her sandwich and picking up her Coke bottle as if to toast. "I have applied for an overseas position in the OSS in . . . drum roll please . . ." She paused for dramatic effect, tapping her fingers on the table to make the sound effect.

"Julia, please, out with it," Irene said, swatting her arm, laughing.

"Ceylon," Julia said.

"Wow." I clinked my bottle with hers. "Exciting. When do you hear?"

"Very exciting," Irene said, then, frowning, added, "but I think I need to look at a map. Where exactly? See-what?"

"Ceylon," Julia said. "It's a British territory in South Asia, in the Indian Ocean."

"The other side of the world," I said.

"That is why I applied, my dear," she said smiling. "If I get selected, it'll be an exotic adventure. Maggie said I should hear in a few weeks. And I think both of you should apply with me. They're looking for more girls. Think of how much fun we could have."

"I think living in Ceylon is a little too exotic for my taste," Irene said, "but I am meeting with Maggie this week to see if I can finally convince her to let me apply for one of the London openings. Michael is going to be traveling a great deal for his work in the next six months. He'll be so busy he's not going to have time to miss me . . . not that he would anyway."

Julia and I just looked at her.

"Look, by now you've probably both figured out that things are less than rosy in my marriage," Irene said, chewing on her thumbnail. "I don't know what we're going to do. I'm Catholic. My parents will disown me if I even mention the word *divorce*. We married too young."

"I'm Catholic too, so I understand. Have you talked about it?" I asked. "About separating or getting a divorce?"

"No, I haven't gotten the nerve up," she said. "He's a more devout Catholic than I am. But devout or not, I don't think either of us can live like this for the next fifty years. I'm at the point where I dread when we actually have time alone together. We have nothing to say. It doesn't help that he's working in Japanese intelligence for the army and I'm here. But it's not our work that's pulling us apart . . . it's just us."

Her story sounded so similar to mine in some ways. I reached over and squeezed her hand. "I empathize more than you know," I said.

"Oh, Irene, I'm so sorry. I didn't realize things were that unhappy at home," Julia said.

"Yes, well, I think some time away will help me see things clearly," Irene said with a tight smile. "And what do you think, Anna? Will you apply with me?"

"Well, wait, what about applying for a post in Ceylon with me?" Julia said, pointing at me. "Think of all the handsome officers in tropical dress uniforms, the warm weather, the delicious new foods to try."

"They're both tempting offers," I said, flattered by the invitations. "But jeesh, I just got here, and now you two are planning on leaving me already? I like having friends at work."

"And that's why you need to go with one of us," said Irene.

I wasn't ready to discuss my recent conversations with Donovan and Maggie yet, partly because I thought they might think I was crazy and partly because I felt like doing so might jinx any chance I had.

"I'll think about it. Let's do dinner again soon to talk about it more—maybe next weekend?"

"Sounds perfect," Julia said. "I'm about to throw my hot plate out the window of the hotel."

We made a date for dinner, tossed our half-eaten lunches away, and headed back to our desks.

# Chapter Eight

The black bag meeting was scheduled for seven that evening. Phillip Stanhope strolled in ten minutes early, followed by Huntington at seven on the dot. Donovan called me in to join them just as Archie Thayer was arriving. His face was flushed redder than his hair, and his brow was damp with sweat.

"Sorry I'm a few minutes late," Archie said, taking the chair across from the general that I usually sat in when we had meetings.

"GC still hasn't shown up yet, but we might as well get started," the general said.

"What is she doing here?" Archie said, pointing at me as I dragged my desk chair into the general's office. Huntington and Phillip both jumped up to help.

"Excuse me?" I said, my face growing hot.

"Anna is my assistant, and I've asked her to be in this meeting because she's helping me with the logistics of this operation," Donovan said in a growl.

Phillip Stanhope glanced over at me, raised his eyebrows, and gave me the slightest nod, as if to say, *Well done.*

"Okay. That's fine, I guess," Archie said with a shrug.

"Son, it's not up to you to decide whether it's fine or not," Huntington added.

"Sorry," Archie said, raising his hands in defense. Then he turned to me, looked me up and down until his eyes settled on my chest, and said, "Hey, Anna, sweetheart? Can you at least get us all some coffee? I know I could use a cup."

He pulled out a packet of Pall Malls and lit one.

"Thayer, what in the hell is the matter with you? You're acting like a bloody arse," Phillip said, leaning out of his chair and getting in Archie's face. He looked like he was going to punch him. Instead Phillip paused and took a long breath in.

"Wait . . . you've been drinking," Phillip said.

"Well, yeah, what of it?" Archie said, getting defensive now. "Who has a meeting this late in the day anyway? I just went to the bar with a couple of fellas from propaganda and had a few. You're from London, you 'chaps' do it all the time over there." He made quotation marks when he said the word *chaps*.

Phillip stood up and put his hands on his head, looking like he was about to explode. He looked at Archie, furious.

"Get out of my office," Donovan said.

"What?" Archie said, entitled and naive enough to be shocked.

"Get the hell out of my office, or I'll call Scotty from security to drag your scrawny ass out of here," Donovan bellowed.

"Get out, Archie," Phillip said. "You're fired. I'm not sure how I ever thought you could handle this job in the first place."

"It was just a couple drinks," Archie said, looking around the room at all of us. "You can't be serious. Huntington, you hired me."

"And it looks like it was a colossal mistake," Huntington said. "Good-bye, Archie."

"You can't do this," Archie said, his chin up in defiance. "Do you know who my father is?" He directed this question at Donovan, who stood up now, an eerie calm in his demeanor.

"Do you know who *I* am?" Donovan said, his voice quiet but menacing. His eyes glinted with an anger I'd never seen him reveal before.

"Now, you have ten seconds to leave this office before I pick you up and throw you out the damn window. I'm starting to count now . . . Ten . . . Nine . . ."

Archie Thayer finally got the picture, because he jumped out of his chair and backed out of the room, only to bump right into a skinny middle-aged man in dirty blue jeans, a well-worn green-and-red plaid shirt, and ancient black work boots with broken laces.

"Whoa, fella, you're in a hurry," the Georgia Cracker said to him as Archie whirled around and sprinted out of the office. The Cracker turned and looked at all of us, completely amused, and started laughing, revealing a jumble of teeth—he *was* missing a few. His upper-right front tooth was crowned in shiny gold. He was entirely bald, and there were tattoos peeking out from the collar and sleeves of his shirt.

"You all look like you're ready to lock that boy up and throw away the key," the Cracker said, his Southern drawl distinct. "What in the hell just happened?"

Huntington gave the Cracker a brief summary.

"Oh, and I don't believe we've met, miss. I go by the Georgia Cracker, but you can call me GC." He walked over and shook my hand, giving me a sincere, crooked grin.

"Nice to meet you," I said. "I'm Anna Cavanaugh, the general's new assistant. I've heard a lot about you."

"His behavior was abhorrent, Anna," Phillip said.

"It's fine," I said. "I can handle men like Archie Thayer any day."

"Like hell it's fine," Donovan said. "And now who will replace him?"

"I'll never allow myself to be pressured into hiring someone again," Huntington said, looking exhausted.

"I should have fired him myself sooner," Phillip said. "Bloody hell."

"Your apologies are appreciated but don't help the situation, gentlemen," Donovan said, unable to hide his frustration as he sat back in his chair and stared out the window. "Right now, I don't have the time to discuss how the incompetent Archie Thayer ended up here. We're meeting with Cynthia and Brousse next Thursday at the Wardman Park Hotel and executing the plan that night. We cannot change the date; we're running out of time as it is. Can we please review and then figure out how to patch up the hole we just punched in the plan? Huntington, provide some of the background for Anna's benefit."

Huntington spread out pictures of the Vichy France embassy and surrounding neighborhood, along with floor plans of the building itself. The embassy at 2129 Wyoming Avenue NW was a white Victorian with a sloping roof, bay windows, and a wraparound porch. An office-building-style second story had been added onto the back of it, so now it was an odd Frankenstein combination of architectural styles.

Huntington explained that the spy called Cynthia had been posing as a pro–Vichy France writer and was currently embroiled in a torrid affair with the embassy's press attaché, Charles Brousse. It was through Brousse that the OSS had learned that the Vichy France government was now sharing Allied secrets with the Nazis. At this point, he was completely besotted with Cynthia, and so not only was he providing intelligence to her, he had also agreed to help her with the ambitious plan to steal the naval codes.

Recently, Cynthia and Charles had befriended the night guard at the embassy and convinced him to allow them to use the embassy some evenings for an occasional lovers' tryst, because Brousse's American wife was getting suspicious. Brousse and his wife lived downstairs from Cynthia in the Wardman Park Hotel.

Phillip Stanhope was watching my incredulous reaction.

"You following so far, Anna?" he said, amused.

"Yes, but is this a story about spies or is it a romance novel?" I asked, eyebrows raised.

"All of Cynthia's operations sound like romance novels, for better or worse," Huntington said, rolling his eyes. "That said, it's hard to argue with her success."

He explained that the plan would take place on the evening of Thursday, August 20. The lovebirds would have a glass of champagne with the security guard, a man named Chevalier. They'd slip Nembutal, a sleep-inducing barbiturate, into the guard's glass and would put some in the guard dog's water bowl, enough to put both the guard and his dog to sleep for the evening. Then they would let GC in through the window located in the reception area outside the naval attaché's office. Thankfully this was in the back of the building, not visible from the street. GC would proceed to pick the lock on the naval attaché's office door, go inside, and crack the safe that contained the ciphers.

"Anyone bother to check if the windows have alarms on 'em?" GC asked.

"Yes, and they don't, fortunately for us," Huntington said.

"And what kind of dog are we talkin'?" GC asked, eyes narrowing as he lit another cigarette. "Don't remember you mentionin' the dog before. Don't like 'em."

"It's an Alsatian, otherwise known as a German shepherd, but no one wants to call them that these days. His name is Alphonse," Huntington said. "You don't need to worry about him; he'll be out cold when you arrive."

GC just grunted, unconvinced.

"So, GC here opens the safe, and then what happens?" I asked. Donovan was pacing back and forth in front of his wall of maps, his eyes mostly on North Africa, listening to Huntington, his brow furrowed.

"Then, whoever replaces Archie as the runner will be waiting in the alley under the ladder for a signal from the team that they have the books. When the three Bible-sized cipher books are in their possession, that person will jump in a waiting car on the street behind the embassy, driven by one of our people. They'll take the books to an OSS team waiting at the Wardman. The team of specialists will be standing at the ready in suite 215B there. They will photograph every single page; we estimate it will take about three hours.

"Then the driver and Archie's replacement will get the original books back to Cynthia and Charles and GC before dawn. They will put everything back in order and be out of the embassy before the five a.m. cleaning crew arrives for work. It will be like they were never there."

We were all quiet for a moment, absorbing the details of the plan. Phillip gave me a look that said, *I told you so*. He was right. The whole thing sounded impossible to pull off. The inside of the embassy was designated as foreign soil. If the OSS was caught red-handed with the Vichy naval codes in the French embassy, the international political and military consequences would be massive.

"Now the big question is, Who is our new runner?" Huntington said.

"Well, GC, you could do both jobs, couldn't you?" Phillip asked.

Donovan winced at this suggestion.

"Nah," GC said, waving his hand. "General and I talked about this a while back. I got a bum leg from a hunting accident and a rap sheet a mile long. And look at me. I'm not exactly innocent looking, walking through that fancy neighborhood in the middle of the night. Better we stick with the original plan. Before midnight an OSS driver, a fella I've worked with on other jobs, is going to use one of them government vans we've used before and drop me and my ladder off in the alley next to the embassy, right under that window I'll be climbing through." He pointed to the window in one of the pictures.

"That makes sense then," Phillip said with a nod. "In that case, I've got a couple fellas on my team who would be up for it. I promise you they'll be better than Thayer. And I've decided I'll be the driver; I don't want to be pacing the floor at the Wardman all night."

"I like that guy Madison for the job, the one from Princeton," Donovan said. "And Huntington, I'm sure you've got a couple men in mind."

"I don't care who you get to do it, but that mutt better be sleeping like the dead when I get there," GC said.

I looked around at the four of them, as they came up with a list of names of young men at the OSS who might fit the role. A female spy was the central player in this nearly impossible plan, and yet none of them had the imagination to envision another woman being involved in it. If I didn't have the courage to offer to do it myself, they wouldn't think to even ask me. And this thought aggravated me enough to speak up.

"Gentleman," I said, clearing my throat. "I'm sitting right here in front of all of you, and it doesn't even occur to any of you to consider me for this job?"

"Are you serious?" Phillip said. "You?"

"Why not?" I said, feeling my cheeks flush.

"Well, you haven't received any training in the field, for one thing," Huntington said.

"From what you told me, it's pretty straightforward," I said. "I don't think I need training to carry books from the embassy to a car. Plus, look at me—if anyone spots me, I can pass for a college student who stayed too late at her boyfriend's apartment. Personally, I think I'm far less suspicious than Archie Thayer."

"I think she'd be perfect, not that you're askin' my opinion," GC said, picking at his gold tooth with the corner of an envelope he had taken off the general's desk. "She looks like she's seventeen, for God's sake."

"Thank you," I said, giving him a grateful smile. "I've already memorized the floor plans; you are welcome to quiz me on them. And I'm fluent in French. Given that it's the French embassy, that might come in handy? And remember, sir, I did keep my cool last night . . ." I looked at the general when I said this last part.

"Operation Johnny on the Pot?" GC said, slapping his thigh and letting out a laugh. "That was you? Well done."

"Ah, bloody brilliant. I didn't know you were the accomplice," Phillip said, trying very hard not to laugh. The general did not look pleased.

"I swear to you, I've never called it that, sir," I said, making the sign of the cross. "And I wasn't the one who told the entire OSS."

"Never mind that," General Donovan said, his voice tight as he looked at me. "I brought you into this as my right hand . . . I wanted you on the team back at the hotel, copying the codebooks, helping to oversee that part of things."

"Yes, but with Archie out, circumstances have changed," I said. "You need someone, and like you said, you're running out of time. I know I can do this."

*Can I do this?* My stomach was churning from nerves, but I knew this was a chance to prove myself. And I wasn't sure when there would be another opportunity like it. Huntington looked at the general, and the general looked up at the ceiling and let out a deep breath.

"Okay, Anna," he said, and I almost leaped out of my chair to hug him, but I kept my cool.

"I'm giving you this shot because I trust you, and you've made a good argument for yourself. In the next few days, Huntington, Stanhope, and GC here will make sure you know everything you need to know beyond what we've discussed tonight."

"Are we sure this is a good idea?" Stanhope said, and I shot him a dirty look.

"'Course it is," GC said, also giving Stanhope the same type of look. I gave him a nod of thanks.

"Yes," Donovan said, "I'm sure."

"I support it," Huntington said, looking at me like a proud uncle. "I think you're up for the challenge."

"Thank you. I won't let you down," I said, silently praying I wouldn't. I looked over at Phillip in defiance, annoyed at him. He wouldn't look me in the eye.

"Good," the general said. "Now let's call it a night before I change my mind."

# Chapter Nine

**August 20, 1942**

On Thursday evening, August 20, at nine o'clock, Phillip Stanhope and I took a generic-looking navy-blue Ford sedan over to the Wardman Park Hotel for the prep meeting before the Vichy embassy break-in later that night. I had worked twelve-hour days all week. In addition to my usual responsibilities, I had met with Huntington, Stanhope, and even the Georgia Cracker in the evenings, reviewing every single detail of the plan. We had reviewed floor layouts and the timeline, as well as contingency plans if things went wrong. Earlier that week, I had taken a couple of trips over to the embassy on my own, walking around the neighborhood so I could get a sense of the building, including where the window of the naval attaché's office was located. It was twelve feet up, not too high, but high enough to require a ladder.

Irene and Julia knew I was involved in something particularly sensitive, and though I desperately wanted to talk about it with them, to share my excitement and my nervousness, I knew this one was too classified even for our classified corner cafeteria table conversations, and they knew not to ask.

Phillip and I rode in silence. I rolled down my window and looked at the darkened buildings we passed, trying to quell my nerves and praying he couldn't tell how anxious I was. I had been distant with him since he had questioned my ability to be part of this operation, and I hoped I would prove him wrong.

"You certainly look the part of the all-American co-ed, don't you?" he said, nodding at my outfit. He rolled down his window and lit a cigarette. I was wearing a straight red skirt with a short-sleeved black-and-red cotton cardigan and a white button-down with a Peter Pan collar underneath. I had even dug out my scuffed black-and-white saddle shoes and paired them with white bobby socks. My hair was pulled in a high ponytail with a red ribbon, and I had my Radcliffe College canvas bag on my shoulder, to transport the codebooks.

"Yes, as we discussed," I said, not looking at him as I brushed invisible lint off my skirt.

"Anna, listen. I know you're mad I questioned you for this job when you suggested it to the general."

"I am," I said. "Especially since I had already told you at the Del Rio how much I wanted to take on more. And then I finally get the chance, and you almost prevent it from happening."

"Well, it's not because I don't think you're capable."

"It's not? Because that's what was implied."

"I don't know you well, but from what I've seen, you are probably more than capable," he said. I scoffed at this, and he continued. "Truly. But I told you at the Del Rio what a beast of a job this is . . . And as a friend, at least . . . I didn't want your first job in the field to be this fraught with potential problems. If this plan ends up in shambles, you know they're going to blame the new girl, don't you?"

"Oh," I said. "That wasn't how I took it."

"Clearly," he said.

"Thank you. Though, honestly? You're not helping my nerves by saying I'll be the one to blame if the whole thing goes south."

I heard a quiet sigh and saw him toss his cigarette butt out the window.

We were quiet as we pulled up to the Wardman. The valet opened the door for me to get out, and Phillip grabbed my arm. I caught a whiff of his now familiar cologne, a woody bergamot scent that mingled with the smell of the Pall Mall he'd just finished smoking.

"Look, you're in it now, and there's no turning back, so please understand that I am on your side," he said, his face serious. "We'll get it done. And I will do everything in my power to make sure all goes smoothly tonight."

"So will I," I said, giving him a grateful smile.

"You and I . . . we are friends, aren't we?" he asked. His eyes crinkled up when he smiled in a way I found annoyingly endearing.

"Yes. We are."

He let go of my arm and handed the keys to the valet, and we headed inside the hotel.

The Wardman Park was a grand eight-story redbrick hotel set among several leafy acres.

I nodded and gave a small smile to the front desk clerks, and the two of us walked through the lobby to the bank of elevators in the middle of the building. I was keyed up for what was in store and was walking far too fast as a result. I hit the call button outside the etched bronzed elevator door and was startled when it dinged a second later.

"You need to relax, Cavanaugh," Phillip said when the elevator doors closed and we were inside. "You're jumpy, I can tell." He hit the button for the second floor.

"Am I?" I said, fidgeting with my ponytail, trying to tuck one of my curls back into it.

"Yes. Can't say I blame you," he said. "First time out and all that, but just try not to show it, won't you?"

"I will try," I said, not sure if I could.

The second-floor hall was painted in muted beige and cream tones. It was empty and quiet as we made our way to the door of suite 215B. Phillip knocked, and I took a deep breath and exhaled just as Huntington opened the door.

"Welcome to central command," Huntington said, smiling and spreading his arm wide as we walked in. Instead of the usual suit and tie, he was wearing his US Army colonel summer uniform. Something about seeing him in it underlined the seriousness of the occasion for me and only fueled my uneasiness.

The contrast between the quiet, empty hallway and the organized chaos inside the suite could not have been more striking. The small space was jammed with equipment. Lights, cameras, tripods, and cables covered almost every surface. Over a half dozen technicians and operators were busily milling about, adjusting the equipment and conferring with one another.

"Everything is a go," Huntington said. "Cynthia, Brousse, and GC are in the bedroom waiting to review the final details of the plan."

Phillip knocked on the door of the bedroom, and a woman's voice said to come inside.

"Ah, it's about damn time," GC said, giving us a huge grin. He was sitting at a small table in front of the bedroom's French doors, which opened to a small balcony. The gauzy ivory curtains were billowing in the night breeze.

The super agent known as Cynthia, the enigma I had been eager to meet since I had first heard her name, was sitting to the left of GC. Her beauty was jaw-dropping. She wore a tight silk dress that matched her emerald-green eyes, and her long blonde hair was in a chignon that highlighted her long neck and creamy skin.

Charles Brousse was sitting to the right of GC, smoking a cigarette, an empty martini glass in front of him. He looked to be in his midforties, his dark hair cut very short so as not to overwhelm his receding hairline. His tweed suit was tailored perfectly to fit his frame.

Cynthia nodded a silent greeting at Phillip, then her eyes turned to me. She looked me up and down, squinting as if she couldn't believe what she was seeing. She shot out of her chair as Brousse was lighting her cigarette.

"*C'est la relève? Cette petite écolière? Ils ne peuvent pas être sérieux. C'est une catastrophe.*" Cynthia was speaking French to Brousse, a seething anger in her voice. And then she hollered, "*Où est* Huntington?"

*This is the replacement? This little schoolgirl? They can't be serious. This is a disaster. Where is Huntington?*

My face turned hot. She had no idea I could understand her. And the veteran spy didn't think I was up for the job. With a few words in French, she had homed in on my quiet, underlying insecurities about this role. It was mortifying. Part of me felt the urge to run from the hotel and take the next taxi home.

But I wanted this opportunity so much I could taste it. Deep down I was still filled with nagging self-doubt, but there was no way in hell I could let this woman know that.

I kept my face calm and expressionless and began to speak in quiet, flawless French just as Huntington was opening the door.

"Pleasure to meet you, Cynthia, and you as well, Monsieur Brousse. My name is Anna," I said. "Though I am dressed like a 'little schoolgirl' for the mission tonight, I am twenty-five years old. I graduated at the top of my class at Radcliffe a few years ago. I have been well briefed on this job, and I believe that I am meant for this kind of work and that things will go just fine tonight."

I paused for a few seconds. I knew I had done well because Cynthia's red lips were wide open in surprise. Charles Brousse was looking at her expression, trying to conceal a smile behind his hand.

"Oh," I added, still speaking French, "I'm fluent in German as well as French. So, if you want to talk about me without my understanding, may I suggest Portuguese? Now, can we review the plans for the night?"

My face still flushed, I walked over and sat down at the empty seat at the table, putting my canvas bag down next to me, praying nobody saw my hand shaking or the sweat marks on my cardigan. GC gave me a wink when I sat down, as if to say, *Well done.*

"Are we okay in here, Cynthia?" Huntington asked, giving her a pointed look. "I have other things to attend to right now."

Cynthia was now pacing the bedroom, smoking. She sighed, gave him a quick nod, and waved him away.

"Your French is very good—no detectable accent," Cynthia said to me in English as she joined me at the table. She didn't apologize for her outburst, but there was a tone of grudging respect in her voice, which was better than nothing.

"Thank you," I said.

She leaned back in her chair. Brousse still looked amused.

"Did you study abroad?" she asked.

"Yes, I studied at Sciences Po in Paris for a year."

"Ah. You speak beautifully. I would have mistaken you for native French," Brousse said in thickly accented English.

"Thank you very much," I said to him.

Cynthia just nodded and continued to size me up.

"Anna has been well briefed on the plan," Phillip said, pulling the desk chair over to the table.

"Let's review."

Phillip explained that Cynthia and Charles would drive to the embassy at eleven, and GC would be dropped off in the alley, with his ladder, thirty minutes later. The couple would enter the embassy with a couple of bottles of champagne and offer a glass to Chevalier, the guard, saying they were celebrating an anniversary. Once the guard and his dog, Alphonse, were asleep from the drug, they would go upstairs and let GC in the window outside of the naval attaché's office. He would proceed to pick the lock on the office door and then crack the safe inside containing the codebooks.

"Anna and I will drive over to the embassy by midnight, parking on the side street, Thornton Place NW. She'll walk over at half past midnight and wait at GC's ladder under the window. When you have the books ready, you'll signal Anna with your flashlight. She'll climb up, grab the books from you, and I'll take her back to the Wardman for the team to copy them. We'll get them back to you to return to the safe by four a.m. at the very latest."

"You better," Cynthia said, giving me a look as if to say this was all on me if things didn't go well. I just gave a slight nod, stared back at her, and tried not to blink.

"We will," Phillip said. "And GC, after you close the safe and wipe it down for prints, you'll come with us, along with the ladder."

"Sounds good," GC said, rubbing his hands together. "Now can I get one of them martinis, extra olives?"

"I suppose I can make you one," Cynthia said, giving him a sly smile. "But just one—don't want you too tipsy for the job."

"Sweetheart, if anything, it will make me *better* at my job," GC said, laughing. "Anna, you should have one too. May loosen you up a little."

Cynthia rolled her eyes at this comment.

"No, thank you," I said. "I'm fine."

I felt nauseous and wondered how anyone could drink martinis on a night like this. Desperate for a distraction, I went back into the living room and observed the technicians at work. I introduced myself and had one of them talk me through the steps of what they would have to do to copy the pages of the codebooks later that night. I wanted to be able to help in some way and not just stand idly by when they were making the copies.

Eleven o'clock came quickly, and Cynthia and Brousse said a few words to Huntington and slipped out of the suite without fanfare, bottles of champagne in hand and with two vials of Nembutal—one for Chevalier and one for his dog—tucked into Cynthia's black leather envelope bag. With a quick wink and a nod, GC left shortly after they did. At a quarter to midnight, Phillip and I were about to depart when Huntington called me over.

"Just follow the plan. Do not deviate from it, and you'll be fine. It's a straightforward job," he said to me, kindness in his hound dog eyes.

"Thank you, sir," I said, swallowing hard.

The embassy was minutes away from the Wardman. We drove by it before parking on Thornton Place. I spotted Brousse's black Pontiac parked on the street first. And then I noticed a second car parked a couple hundred feet away from his. There were two men in suits sitting in it. It was hard to make out their faces, but it was evident they were there to observe the embassy.

"Phillip . . ."

"Yes, I saw them," he said in a quiet, tense voice. "Look a little dodgy, don't they?"

"Who are they?" My arms were breaking out in goose bumps.

"Could be a number of different groups, couldn't it? Nazi spies, because the embassy has been leaking secrets and they want to find out who it is . . . Or it could be the FBI, because of course they have no idea what the OSS is up to . . . I don't know."

"What do we do?"

"We go ahead with the plan. You go to the side of the house and wait. Cynthia and Brousse will let you know if they can't get the code-books out to you tonight."

"Okay," I said, gathering my bag and looking in the mirror, tightening the bow on my ponytail and smoothing out my skirt. "I'm ready."

"Good luck," Phillip said. He looked into my eyes, and for a few brief seconds he put his hand on mine. "I'll be waiting for you."

I looked away first, still feeling the warmth of his hand on mine as I got out of the car. I didn't want to feel anything for Phillip Stanhope, or for any man for that matter. I had too much I wanted to do.

"And Anna?"

"Yes?" I said, looking back in at him.

"For God's sake, make sure you aren't seen. You don't want to cock up your first job in the field."

"I won't be seen," I said, rolling my eyes and shutting the door.

I strolled down Thornton in the opposite direction of Wyoming Avenue. The air was humid and still on the tree-lined street of embassies and residences. Given the late hour, most of the homes were completely dark, leaving only a couple of dim streetlamps to light my way. I was trying hard to control my breathing and act the part of the co-ed coming home late from her boyfriend's apartment, though it had occurred to me before this that no decent boyfriend would send me home alone after midnight.

I rounded the corner, glancing around to see if any other cars with strange men were visible before I ducked down the alley behind the embassy. Taking quiet steps, I spotted the wooden ladder under the window of the naval attaché's office and jumped when I felt someone come up from behind me and grab my arm. Before I could scream, the Georgia Cracker put one hand on my mouth, holding his other hand to his lips, pleading with me to stay silent.

"What are you doing here?" I whispered, still shaking. "Why aren't you up there?"

"I've been waiting," he said, frustration in his voice. "They was supposed to let me inside since before those two goons showed up. But they didn't slip the guard the sleep drug. The dog neither."

"How do you know that for sure?"

"Take a careful look through the bushes," he said, pointing to the hedges behind us. I peeked through, and there was Chevalier, a short, middle-aged Frenchman in a guard uniform, with his trusted dog Alphonse, the largest German shepherd I'd ever seen. He was standing in the street, leaning over to talk to the two men in the parked car I'd spotted earlier.

I let out a barely perceptible groan and rubbed my face. Nothing had gone right yet.

"So now what?" GC looked at me.

"I think we wait a little longer, stay out of sight, and see if Cynthia signals us to do anything."

GC nodded and sighed. "I was afraid you'd say that."

At that moment, I heard the sound of an engine and peeked through the bushes to see the car with the two men drive away. Chevalier and his dog headed back inside the embassy. Fifteen minutes later, Cynthia signaled us with her flashlight to let GC know it was safe to come up.

"I'll stay here. Tell her to signal when she's ready to hand me the books," I said. GC nodded and scurried up the ladder without making a sound, no doubt a skill he'd acquired as a professional thief.

I sat in the shadows on the narrow walkways bordering the house, my arms wrapped around my knees as I watched the window, waiting for the flashlight—three short pulses—to signal when it was time for me to climb up. Instead of a martini, I had downed a cup of stale coffee one of the technicians had given me. I now wished I had drunk the whole bitter pot.

It was one of those nights in the city that offered no relief from the August heat and humidity. My skirt was sticking to my legs, and I wished I had left my cardigan in the car.

I stood up at the sound of rustling in the hedges. An enormous raccoon emerged, his eyes glowing when he looked up and caught sight of me, quickly lumbering off in the opposite direction.

At two o'clock, I knew we were running out of time, and I tried to silently will Cynthia to signal me. If we didn't get the documents to the Wardman in the next half hour, we would never be able to copy them and bring them back before dawn.

Finally, at sixteen past, she signaled. I climbed up the ladder, my palms sweaty and my saddle shoes slipping on the wooden rungs. At least I was wide-awake again, thanks to nervous fear, my heart beating out of my chest.

Cynthia, to my surprise, was wearing only a lacy pink satin slip and a string of pearls when she opened the window, her face grim as she smoked her cigarette.

"If GC can't get it open in ten minutes, we're out of time," Cynthia said as I climbed inside what appeared to be a small reception area with a large burgundy sofa, dark wood coffee table, and desk in the corner for a receptionist. Charles Brousse, fully dressed, was also there looking stressed, pacing the room, a glass of champagne in hand.

"GC's inside there, the inner office, he picked the lock on the door without a problem." She pointed to a door on the opposite side of the space, a former bedroom but currently the Vichy naval attaché's office. "But, he said the safe is a different model than the one on the embassy invoice we used to identify it; that's why it's taking longer."

"Darling, someone's coming!" Charles Brousse said in a loud whisper. "It's Chevalier on his rounds. I can hear him singing."

"Goddammit," Cynthia said. "Charles, get undressed—now!"

"What?" he said, looking at her like she was insane.

She whipped off her slip and, entirely naked except for her heels and pearls, shoved me toward the door behind which GC was working. I couldn't hide my shock at her bare breasts, which were at eye level. "Hide under the desk in there with GC. Hurry now. Go!"

I hurried into the office and headed straight for the desk. GC, having heard everything, was already underneath it. We just nodded to each other, and I tried to curl myself into a ball so small I might disappear.

We heard a knock on the outer door and the sound of it opening, followed by Alphonse's ferocious barking.

"Ooh la la!" Cynthia said in a loud voice. The dog went quiet, and I pictured Chevalier and Alphonse both shocked by her large milky-white breasts in the glare of a flashlight.

"I beg your pardon, a thousand times, madame. I thought . . . didn't rightly know . . . my apologies . . . ," the flustered, accented voice of

Chevalier said in return, and then we heard the outer door quickly close.

"I got it. I opened the damn thing, though it took me longer than it should've, but I got it," GC said in a triumphant whisper, excitement in his beady eyes as I looked down to see three Bible-sized black books on the rug next to him.

After a minute the door opened, and Cynthia, wearing her pink slip again, came around the desk.

"You need to leave now," she said. "Both of you."

"He got it open," I said, unable to contain my excitement. "We've got the codebooks."

"It's too late," Cynthia said, dismissing me with a wave of her hand. "We'll try again. Too much has gone wrong."

"I thought you said if he did it in ten minutes, we'd still have time," I said, feeling the need to prove myself, to make this night a success. "Can't we at least try to get it done?"

"No, schoolgirl, we can't," she said, her voice a harsh whisper. She looked at me with disdain. "Do you understand the international disaster this will be if we're caught? The timeline doesn't work. Get out now. And if you want to stay on this job, never question my decision-making again."

"Okay," I said, raising my hands in surrender. "Okay."

GC was already putting the codebooks back, locking the safe, and wiping it down. I gave a quick wave to Charles Brousse as we entered the reception area and opened the window. GC climbed out first, nimble and silent. As soon as he hit the ground, I started to climb down. I was trying to be as quick and quiet as the professional thief was. Now that the plan was off, I couldn't wait to get back to Phillip's car, safe and away from the building.

I heard GC hiss something at me, and when I looked down to whisper back, my left foot slipped on the third rung down. I scrambled to hang on to the ladder, but it started slipping to the right, sliding down the building. I felt myself in a free fall, trying to grab hold of a rung or the building, whatever would steady me, but it was hopeless. I held my breath so I wouldn't scream, and then the world went black.

# Chapter Ten

I opened my eyes and groaned, looking around at the dark leather back seat of a moving car. My head was pounding, and my first thought was that I had ruined everything and been thrown in a police car or the anonymous car outside the embassy. So I was very relieved to hear Phillip's voice.

"Ah, she wakes," he said, looking back at me. "You were only out a couple minutes, but I'm thinking a trip to the hospital is still necessary."

"No, no hospital please. I'll be fine," I said, sitting up, surveying the enormous bruise blooming on my elbow and the scrapes all over my legs in the light of the streetlamps we passed. There was a particularly nasty one on my left knee that was now dripping blood on the back seat. "What the hell happened? Did we get caught? Where's GC? Oh my God." I put my hands over my face as I remembered my foot slipping. "I can't believe I fell off the ladder."

"We did not get caught, and you did not kill yourself, thanks to GC, who broke your fall," Phillip said. "He carried you to the car and helped me get you inside safely. And his ride was pulling up next to the alley as I pulled away."

"No, I really don't need to go to the hospital," I said. "I just need to go home to take a hot bath and get a few hours' sleep. So . . . nobody got caught?"

"Things were cocked up from the beginning because those two chaps in the car showed up. The guard spotted them and was too concerned about it to take a break and drink champagne with Cynthia and Charles. We are going to have to try again. I'm just not sure you'll be a part of it. That's up to the general."

My whole body ached, and I felt so stupid I wanted to cry. I looked down at my saddle shoes. The bottoms were so worn, it was no wonder I had slipped.

"I should have never worn these old shoes. I saw no one on the way over; my cover story about being a co-ed didn't even matter. I'm an idiot."

Phillip was quiet for a moment. He glanced back at me in the rearview mirror, sympathy in his eyes.

"If it makes you feel any better, the bloody ladder was not secure, so first you slipped, but then the ladder went sideways, and it's a god-damned miracle Chevalier didn't hear anything. GC blames himself for the ladder. The whole night was a shambles from the start, wasn't it?" Phillip said with a sigh. "Now tell me your address because, against my better judgment, I'm taking you home."

We pulled up to my apartment in Georgetown, and Phillip helped me out of the car. I took careful steps. I opened the door to the sound of angry meows. There was a note on my kitchen table from Mary saying the cats had been fed and there was some macaroni and cheese in the fridge so that I would be fed too. I looked around at my apartment and tried to see it through Phillip's eyes. It was small, but now that my memories of my ill-fated marriage had started to fade, it had become a warm, comfortable oasis for me.

"This is a really nice flat, very cozy," he said, walking into my galley kitchen.

"Thank you," I said.

"Shall I help clean and dress that cut?" Phillip asked, looking at my knee and cringing.

"No, it's okay. I'm going to take a bath first."

"Do you want me to stay?" He blushed as soon as he said this, realizing how it sounded. "I'm sorry. I meant on the couch—nothing improper. Just to make sure you're okay."

"No, I'll be fine, but thank you." And I felt my own cheeks turn red.

"You should take the day off tomorrow, to rest and recover. I'll explain what happened."

"I'll be in. Maybe not at my usual seven a.m., but not too long after that."

"How did I know you were going to say that?"

We smiled at each other, and the quiet space between us turned into something I could feel as we looked into each other's eyes, something I could barely acknowledge to myself. What is it that makes the alchemy between two people suddenly change? How is it that one day you're looking at someone you hardly know in a completely different light from the day before?

Phillip took a few steps toward me and reached for my hand. I knew he was about to kiss me if I let him. And though a part of me wanted him to, I couldn't let my guard down with him or anyone else. Not yet.

"You should go get some sleep. I'm sure you're as exhausted as I am," I said, stepping back, breaking the spell.

"Right. Right you are. I'm knackered. And you definitely need to rest." Disappointment flashed in his eyes, but then his expression turned neutral, and I thought maybe I had imagined the moment because I was so tired.

I walked him to the door, thanking him again.

He walked down my front steps and, when he opened his car door, turned to me and smiled. "You handled yourself well tonight, Cavanaugh, despite everything."

"Thanks," I said.

I stood in the doorway and watched him drive away.

I woke at eight on Friday morning, after barely any sleep, and every bone in my body ached. Part of me longed to sleep the day away with my cats, but I was too eager to hear about when the next break-in attempt would happen and whether Donovan would let me be a part of it. I knew Cynthia wouldn't be taking the day off, so neither would I.

I put the coffee on, took some aspirin, and hobbled into the shower. By the time I left for the office, I felt less horrible than when I had first woken up, but definitely not my usual self.

I was at the OSS by a quarter past nine, hurrying to get to my desk. Maggie saw me walking by, called me into her office, and asked me to have a seat.

"Look what the cat dragged in," she said, looking me up and down. "Jesus, Anna. You look like hell."

"Thanks." I had tried to pull myself together, putting on my favorite dark-pink cotton dress with a long-sleeved ivory cardigan, styling my hair in a bun, and wearing a little more makeup than usual to hide my exhaustion—but nothing could conceal the bandage on my knee or the scrapes and bruises peeking out from my sleeves.

"I heard last night didn't go as planned."

"That's the understatement of the century. News travels fast."

"Only a few of us know what happened, but I was included in the briefing early this morning." She eyed me over her glasses, lighting a cigarette, cracking the window behind her.

"And you met the elusive Cynthia," she added.

"Yes, I did. She hated me."

"Yes, I heard that too," Maggie said with a laugh.

"I had these naive expectations of her being a mentor, giving me advice and rooting me on."

"Oh, that was truly naive of you," Maggie said, still amused. "I should have warned you. Cynthia is not a huge fan of women. Other than herself."

"That sounds about right."

"She's a difficult personality with questionable morals, but she's got moxie and she's one of our best. Her husband's flying in; that's going to put a wrinkle in things for her."

"Wait. Are you saying she's married?" I asked. It hadn't even occurred to me, seeing her with Brousse.

"Yes, with a child. Both her husband and daughter live in Chile. He's a British diplomat."

"And she never sees them?"

"Hardly. The spy trade is like a drug for her; she can't stay away from it," Maggie said. "And Brousse? He's just one of the many people she's targeted in the pursuit of intelligence for her country."

Something about her abandoning her child, living this secretive, nomadic existence, sleeping with men for secrets . . . it seemed so lonely and rudderless. I had hoped, when I met Cynthia, I would see something in her that I could relate to, something that validated wanting to do the type of work she did. But I was nothing like her. Nor did I want to be.

"What happens next, Maggie? Do you know if we're going to try again?"

She tilted her head, looking at me, eyebrows raised.

"Anna Cavanaugh, are you really sure you *want* to try again? Why don't you sit this next attempt out? There will be other opportunities . . . Speaking of which, Irene mentioned you might be interested in applying for one of the posts in London with her. Is that true?"

"I told her I would think about it. It would be my second choice. You know what my first choice is," I said, and she nodded. "I need to prove to him I'm capable, so I hope he'll let me be part of this next attempt after last night's disaster."

"None of what happened was in your control. Many factors contributed to last night's failed attempt—also, GC didn't secure the damn ladder properly, so that's not your fault either."

"I know. The night was a total 'cock-up,' as Phillip Stanhope says."

"He's right," Maggie said, stubbing her cigarette out in the porcelain French bulldog ashtray on her desk. "Anyway, it's up to Donovan to decide if you're included in the next attempt. And then, in terms of going into the field as an agent? That's above my pay grade—it's ultimately his decision too. But think about London. I need a few good women in the Cover and Documentation department over there. You'd be able to learn a great deal about life in the field, helping agents with their cover stories and fake identification papers. It could be a stepping-stone to becoming an actual spy yourself."

"I'll think about it," I said, though I doubted anyone from Cover and Documentation had made the leap to becoming a spy. "Thanks as always, Maggie."

The general was on the phone, the door to his office partially closed, when I arrived at my desk, two cafeteria coffees in hand, which I had fetched after talking with Maggie. It was a quarter to ten, and he was in back-to-back meetings beginning at ten thirty, so I was hoping I'd have a chance to speak with him about the Vichy plan before that.

I tapped lightly on the door, holding up the coffee, and he waved at me to come in, barely looking up from whatever document was in front of him. He was on the White House phone, so I hurried over and placed the coffee next to his hand. He looked up to give me a smile of thanks, and that's when he did a quick double take, looking me up and down. I had forgotten I'd cut my lip from biting it so hard when I fell, among my other injuries.

"Yes, yes, sir. I'll have Anna change my calendar," the general said. "I'll be there by ten thirty."

I was just about to shut the door behind me when he hung up and called to me.

"Shut the door and have a seat," he said. When I was sitting in the leather chair across from his desk, he took a sip of his coffee, eyes filled with worry. "How are you feeling?"

"I'm fine," I said.

"Like hell you are," he said, sitting back in his chair, crossing his arms. "Why didn't you stay home today?"

"Did Cynthia stay home today?"

"*Cynthia's* role is a little different than yours. And Cynthia did not fall off a ladder and nearly kill herself."

"It wasn't that bad, honestly."

"That's not what Stanhope told me. When the fall knocked you out, he said he and GC thought you were dead for a second."

"No, they didn't," I said, shaking my head. "That's nonsense."

"They *did*. Anna, look at you," he said, pointing out my various minor injuries, as if I wasn't aware of them. "What would your father say if he saw you?"

"He would say he was proud of me, proud of my moxie," I said, thinking of Maggie's words. "Although he wouldn't tell my mother about any of it."

Donovan looked at me and grunted, unconvinced.

"Sir, with all due respect, I am twenty-five years old. I'm not a child, even . . . even though people mistake me for one sometimes," I said, leaning forward in my chair, hands gripping my coffee cup. "I promise you, I am an adult and I can handle my parents. You gave me a job here for a reason, and if it involves being in harm's way, I accept that because I very much want to be here and . . . when you hired me to work here, you gave me a purpose I didn't realize I desperately needed. One I've needed for longer than you can imagine."

He took a deep breath and exhaled, then stood and walked over to the window and stared out at the Potomac.

"I need you to cancel my meetings this morning," he said. "I'm heading up to the White House, and I'll be there until at least lunchtime."

"Okay, sir," I said. "Is the White House meeting about the Vichy naval codes we didn't retrieve?"

"How'd you guess?" he said. "Roosevelt's not happy."

"What happens now?"

"What happens now? We try again—we have to," he said. "It seems those two men staking out the embassy were FBI, so we've got to deal with that. The plan is to go in again next Wednesday."

"And I . . . you're still letting me be a part of it?"

He turned, his arms still crossed, shaking his head.

"Yes," he said with a sigh. "I guess your plea has left me no choice but to let you continue to be a part of it. Besides, we don't have time to bring in someone else. And even though Cynthia wasn't too happy with you, the rest of the team is, including Huntington, whose opinion I value the most."

"Thank you, sir. I promise we will get it done," I said. "GC knows the safe combination now, and if they can drug Chevalier and the dog as planned, it will go much more smoothly."

"It has to," he said, frowning. "This is about getting those naval codes, but it's also about proving to the White House—and our UK allies—that the OSS is vital to the war efforts. We're still new, and we need to prove our value. If this can help the US and our allies in North Africa, it would be tremendous . . . for them *and* for us. Do you understand?"

"I do," I said. "Perfectly."

"Good. Now after you move my calendar around, I'm ordering—not suggesting—that you take the afternoon off. Go home and rest. You took a bad fall, and we've got a critically important week ahead; I need you rested and healthy."

I started to protest, telling him I could make it through the day, but he held up his hand.

"Okay, okay, sir. I'll go home. And thank you," I said, shutting his office door behind me.

# Chapter Eleven

*Anna—sorry for the ladder mess-up. It was my fault.
Glad ya didn't get killed. Here's some presents. Hope you're
feeling better. —GC*

I glanced at the barely legible handwritten note once more, smiling as I listened to my mother, on the other end of the phone, ramble about summer plans with her country club set on Cape Cod. It was almost seven o'clock on Friday evening, and after a nap, two baths, and more aspirin, I was under my favorite yellow cotton blanket on my sofa feeling somewhat human again.

I had found the note from GC on my kitchen table when I got home at two o'clock, next to a vase of fresh sunflowers, a can of coffee, and a bag of sugar. When I opened the fridge, I discovered butter and hard cheddar cheese, no doubt procured by GC on the black market, as well as six-packs of Coca-Cola and beer.

"Now dear, when are you coming home?" my mother asked, bringing me back into what had been a largely one-sided conversation.

"I'm not sure when I'm going to be able to come up for a visit, Mother. General Donovan has me extremely busy."

I heard her tsk into the telephone.

"I don't mean a visit. I mean home for *good*," she said. "Aren't you lonely down there? And it seems like you're working such long hours. A young woman like you shouldn't be working so hard."

*Unless it's to find a husband* was the subtext.

"Mother, I actually enjoy the work very much, and yes, it's long hours, so I don't have much time to be lonely. Also, I've made some friends. There are quite a few women my age working there—"

"I just ran into Sally Lafferty, from the Winsor School board of directors," she said, as if she hadn't even heard me. "She said you were the best French teacher Winsor's ever had and that she'd hire you back in a second. Wouldn't that be wonderful?"

I held back a groan.

There was a knock on the door, and I jumped up, relieved for an excuse to get off the phone and hoping it wasn't GC with more get-well-soon goodies from the black market.

"Mother, I'll call you Sunday night. Someone's at the door."

"Well, who is it?"

"I don't know, but I have to go . . ."

"It's your friends bringing you sustenance and cheer." I heard Julia's voice and smiled.

I said a quick good-bye to my mother and rushed to get the door, wincing at how sore my body still felt when I stood up from the sofa. Mary had called earlier with an offer to bring dinner, but I had declined because I knew how many questions she would have if she saw the state I was in. Now, instead, I'd have some explaining to do to my friends from the OSS.

When I opened the door, Julia and Irene were standing there smiling. Irene was holding two brown paper bags, and Julia was holding a large square cardboard box. Irene frowned as soon as she saw me.

"Oh, Anna, you look terrible," she said, examining me from head to toe. "Your lip is so swollen, and look at that bruise on your elbow. And where did all those scrapes come from?"

"Well, my goodness, Irene. What a thing to say as soon as she opens the door," Julia said, giving me a once-over before adding, "though I am very glad we came by, dear, because it looks like you could use some company at the very least."

"Thank you," I said, as I gave them both a hug, thrilled at the surprise visit. "I'm fine, honestly. I apologize for being in my pajamas."

"I told Maggie you canceled our dinner plans for tonight, and she suggested—very strongly—that we bring dinner to you," Irene said as I led them to the kitchen.

"Who are these gorgeous flowers from?" Julia said, putting the box next to them on the table. "Anna, is there something you haven't told us? Do you have a secret admirer we don't know about?"

"Oh no. No, definitely not," I said, thinking about GC and his gold tooth and elf-like looks. "It's . . ." I needed to change the subject. "What's in that box? It smells delicious."

"Because it *is* delicious," Julia said in her matter-of-fact way. "There's a small Italian restaurant near my hotel called Ciro's, and the owner makes this. It's called pizza Neapolitan—it's dough topped with creamy mozzarella cheese, baked fresh tomatoes, and Italian sauce. It will be the best thing you've ever tasted."

"And we also brought beer and Key lime pie for dessert," Irene said, emptying the bags she was carrying.

I grabbed some plates and napkins, and we took the beer and pizza Neapolitan out to the garden, where my friends admired its late-summer splendor as I lit candles on my little iron table.

The pizza was as good as Julia had promised it would be, and I hadn't realized just how hungry I was until we started eating. After we had finished almost the entire pizza, we sat back, catching up on some minor gossip about work, sipping our beers.

Then Irene asked the question I knew she would. "What happened to you last night, Anna?" She was pointing to the blood on my pajama pants that I didn't know was there. It was time to change the bandage on my knee.

"We're worried about you," Julia said. "So is Maggie. She was adamant we come over tonight."

"I'm . . . I'm not sure how much I can say," I said.

"Anna, Irene and I see nearly as much intelligence as you do," Julia said. "Meaning we already have an inkling of what it's about."

"What Julia is saying is, we know it has something to do with the Vichy French embassy," Irene said. "If you want to talk about it, if you need to talk about it, it will not go beyond us. We can promise you that."

I looked at both of them, feeling my eyes well up, trying to decide. I was tired and frustrated, and my body was still so sore. All of it was making me overly emotional.

"Okay," I said in a quiet voice. "But not out here. I've become paranoid for good reason, as I'll explain. Let's clean up, and I'll tell you what I can inside."

We brought everything inside and each got another bottle of beer. I put Artie Shaw on the record player, and once the three of us were settled in, I told them everything—about how I had volunteered to be part of the Vichy embassy break-in because I wanted to prove I could be a field agent, how much Cynthia disliked me, and how everything had gone wrong, including my mortifying fall. I even told them about the Georgia Cracker breaking in and leaving me get-well presents. The only thing I didn't tell them about was the quiet moment when I thought Phillip Stanhope was going to kiss me. That part of the night I was not ready to discuss.

I finished talking, and they both looked slightly stunned, like they were still taking in everything I had just told them. I felt lighter, unburdened by the secrets and stress I had been holding inside.

"Well, Christ, Anna," Irene said, taking a pack of Lucky Strikes out of her purse and lighting one. "I don't even know where to start. First,

I'm so relieved you're okay after that fall. Second, I don't know what I'm more shocked by—the fact that Cynthia stripped naked to distract the guard or that the OSS is hiring ex-cons and one *broke into your house* to leave you presents."

"Yeah, it's been a wild couple of days," I said as I pulled an ashtray out of the drawer in the coffee table and handed it to her.

"And how come you've never mentioned wanting to be a field agent to us?" Irene said.

"Because I thought you would both think I'm crazy?" I said.

"And we *do* think that," Julia said with a deep, solemn nod. But then she broke into a smile, and the three of us started laughing.

"Thanks," I said. "I don't even know if they'll give me a chance. And if they're looking only for Cynthia types, I do *not* fit that profile. But, yes, I want to go back to Europe, back to France, undercover. I know it's probably a little naive and idealistic given my background, but I want to try."

"Not all female field agents are like Cynthia," Irene said. "I don't know real names, of course, but I've seen details about them in intelligence reports. Many of them are chosen for their language skills and any international experience—so you've got that going for you."

"Irene's right," Julia said. "Language skills are key, and there is no one profile. They are young, older, married, unmarried. Some are mothers; most are not."

"Well, we'll see," I said. "Thank you for listening."

"I'm proud of you," Irene said. "I think of the day we met when you were going for your interview. I must admit I misjudged you that day as this wide-eyed, sheltered girl from Boston."

"Well *I* never misjudged you. I knew you had it in you from the start," Julia said, and Irene told her to shush, laughing again.

"What happens now?" Irene asked.

"It's going to be up to the general. If the next break-in attempt at the embassy is a success, that has to help, right?"

They both started to protest.

"No. No, you cannot be considering being a part of that," Julia said. "You need time to recover. Irene is right—you look absolutely terrible. Like you've been in a brawl at some skid row bar."

"Julia," I said, swatting at her arm.

"I'm sorry, it's true. Irene can be so blunt. I didn't want to make you feel worse by agreeing," Julia said with a shrug. "But now that you're going to put yourself in harm's way again, it is time for *brutal* honesty."

"You don't need to do this," Irene said. "Especially after taking such a bad fall."

"I know I don't need to," I said, "but I feel compelled to. To be a part of getting it right this time."

I told them about the general reluctantly agreeing that morning to let me participate in the second break-in attempt.

Irene and Julia looked at each other.

"All right. Well, if you're going to do this, will you at least tell us when it's happening?" Irene said, "so we can be there for you if you need us?"

"Yes, and we'll bring you more pizza Neapolitan—I need an excuse to eat it again," Julia said.

"Well, in that case, I will definitely tell you," I said, moved by their concern. "Thank you."

# Chapter Twelve

**August 26, 1942**

"You're fidgeting like last time," Phillip said as the elevator doors closed.

"I'm not," I lied. I kept fussing with a few curls that had fallen out of my ponytail, and I had even been cracking my knuckles in the car on the way over to the Wardman Park Hotel, something I hadn't done since final exams during my Radcliffe days.

It was Wednesday evening, the night of our second attempt to steal the Vichy naval codes. We had said only a few words to each other on the ride over, driving with the windows down on what was the hottest night of the summer so far. I was dressed in the same outfit as the week before, though no sweater this time, and I had chosen my very sensible black loafers—better for climbing ladders.

"You're sure you're feeling all right, then?"

"I promise you, I'm fine." That statement was mostly true. I had taken the weekend to rest and recover and was not quite healed but was getting there.

"It's like déjà vu," I said as we walked out of the elevator into the cream-colored hallway on the second floor.

"This better be the only part of the night that's like déjà vu," he said. Even though he was supposed to be the seasoned professional, tonight he looked as jittery as I felt.

"It will be. We'll get it right this time," I said, hoping that if I said it out loud, it would come true.

We knocked on the door to suite 215B and walked into a smog of cigarette smoke and humidity. There were at least twice as many technicians as the week before, along with a palpable tension in the air, because of the stakes of the operation and perhaps also because General Donovan himself was present tonight, conferring with Huntington in the corner of the room.

"Phillip, Anna," Donovan said when he spotted us. "The other three are in the bedroom getting ready to leave. Come with Huntington and me. I'd like a brief word with all of you."

We walked into the bedroom. Cynthia was pacing the room, a Virginia Slim in her hand. She was wearing her hair in victory rolls, and I was once again struck by her beauty and glamour. When she saw me, she gave me a once-over, her eyes narrowed. Brousse was dressed in a perfectly tailored gray suit, sipping a martini. GC was standing at the table, wearing a dark-gray one-piece work suit and double-checking his tool kit, which resembled a black leather doctor's bag.

Donovan cleared his throat, looking around the room at us.

"While you all understand the stakes, what you don't know is that if we don't get those codes tonight, Roosevelt is not going to give us another chance."

Cynthia started to speak, but Donovan shot her a glance and she stopped.

"I know what you're going to say, Cynthia, but this is it," Donovan said. "He wasn't thrilled with what happened last time, and he feels these black bag operations on American soil are far too risky from a foreign relations standpoint. We get it done tonight, or we fail. I believe we can do it—I believe in every one of you in this room."

I noticed GC stand taller when Donovan said this.

"Okay, let's go, then," Cynthia said, clearly irritated, picking up her purse from the nightstand by the bed and checking it. "I've got enough

Nembutal in here to put an elephant to sleep. Charles, grab the champagne. Chevalier had better be in the mood for a glass or two tonight . . . Don't fall this time, schoolgirl," she said, smirking as she walked by me and out the bedroom door.

Charles Brousse followed behind her, giving me an apologetic smile and whispering, "You'll do fine."

GC left a moment after them, saluting all of us.

"Glad to see ya back tonight, Anna," he said, nodding at me. "So sorry 'bout the ladder. Hope ya liked your presents."

"I did, GC. Thank you," I said, smiling at him sweetly. "But if you ever break into my house again, I'll make sure the general throws you back in prison."

GC gave a nervous laugh and hurried out of the room.

Huntington and Phillip looked at me, shocked. Donovan's face was red with anger, and he stepped forward as if he was going to go after him.

Phillip started to speak. "Anna, what the bloody—"

"Honestly, it's perfectly fine. I know he meant well. And sir, I'm sure it won't happen again," I said, looking at Donovan as I said the words. "Phillip, let's go find some coffee out there before it's our turn to leave."

∾

Phillip and I parked in a different location on Thornton Place NW than the week before. It was eleven thirty, but the air was heavy with sticky moisture, and the temperature was still at least eighty degrees.

Because GC knew the combination, he had assured us that, provided Chevalier and Alphonse were properly drugged, they'd be able to get the codebooks out to me quickly.

"Okay," I said as soon as Phillip turned off the engine. "I better go. I want to be there as soon as they have them in hand."

"Yes, and I'll keep circling the neighborhood," Phillip said. "If I see you before I'm parked back at this exact spot, I'll pull over and you can jump in."

"Sounds good." I put my canvas bag on my shoulder and was starting to get out of the car when I felt him grab my hand.

"You're going to be brilliant," he said, squeezing it, both our palms sweaty.

"I better be," I said, feeling my stomach churn from nerves. I let go of his hand, shut the door, and whispered, "See you soon."

Most homes on the street were shrouded in darkness like last time. In the corner window of an old green Victorian, I could see the silhouette of a young man sitting at a desk, his face partially illuminated by a small reading lamp. I saw him glance up from his reading and quickened my pace, hoping he hadn't spotted me.

And once again, I was back in the dark alley at the bottom of the ladder. I held on to it, pulled and shook it, to make sure it was secure this time. No sooner had I done this when someone from above signaled me with the flashlight. Making the sign of the cross, I climbed up the rungs. Cynthia was at the window, holding the three enormous leather-bound books in her hands.

"Already?" I said in a whisper.

"Yes," she said, and she even smiled at me in triumph. "Here, open your bag."

I did as I was told, and she placed the Vichy naval codebooks inside, kissing the third one before she did.

"Now hurry, fast as you can," Cynthia said. "I'll see you in a few hours."

She shut the window, and I hustled down the ladder, watching my feet, breathing a sigh of relief when I hit the ground. I cut through the alley and was back on Thornton Place, my heart beating rapidly from adrenaline as I scanned the street, saying a silent prayer that Phillip would be turning the corner any second.

"Are you lost, sweetheart?"

I jumped at the sound of a voice behind me and whirled around. A man was coming up the street, walking his dog, a large white standard poodle that didn't look friendly. He was in his midforties, his brown hair cut in a short military style and his eyebrows bushy.

My heart was beating even faster, and I clutched my canvas bag as tight as I could.

"I saw you come out of that alley," he said. He had an accent I couldn't place. "I thought, *Why in the world is that girl walking through alleys at this hour?* Can I help you find where you're going?"

*Think, Anna. Be calm and think.*

"Oh no, I'm not lost," I said. I tried to laugh, but I knew it came out forced. "I'm secretly meeting my boyfriend here; he's picking me up any minute. My parents can't stand him, so, um, yeah, we picked this as a rendezvous point tonight."

*Where the hell is Phillip?*

"Kind of an odd place. What made you choose Thornton Place? Do you live near here?"

The Ford sedan headlights were coming down the street behind the dog walker, and I waved to Phillip frantically. He was flying down the street, and when he pulled over, he nearly jumped the curb.

"Thank you for your concern," I said to the dog walker, whose face had turned mean and skeptical as I jumped into the car.

"Sweetheart, you're finally here," I said as I slammed the car door. "Go, go, go," I added in a harsh whisper under my breath. Phillip peeled away from the curb, a brimmed hat pulled over his eyes so the dog walker couldn't get a good look at him.

"Who in the bloody hell was that?" Phillip said, looking in the rearview mirror when we were a safe distance away.

"Damned if I know. He came out of nowhere," I said, taking deep breaths to calm myself. "Maybe just someone walking his dog before bed?"

"It's either the FBI again, because Hoover, the head, hates Donovan," Phillip said, gripping the steering wheel hard, "or it's the Germans."

"Are there really many German spies in the US?"

"More than you can imagine," he said. "Please tell me you've got the books. The general's right: there's no way we can attempt this again."

"Yes!" I said, letting him take a peek inside the bag. The book on top was marked *CHIFFREMENT SECRET*—the French words for *secret encryption*.

"Thank God," Phillip said, grinning from ear to ear in a boyish way. "Let's get these beauties copied."

We sprinted back to the suite at the Wardman and were met with quiet clapping and fist pumps. Huntington shook our hands as the team of technicians, operatives, and photographers grabbed the books out of my bag and got to work methodically tracking and photographing every single page.

Too excited and nervous to sit and watch, I asked a quiet, fastidious technician named Sam if I could pitch in and help, and he made me his assistant. Phillip was in the corner, in a serious discussion with Huntington for the first half hour after we arrived. But soon they too were laying out photographs of the codes to dry on any available surface. We placed them down the length of the sofa and spread them across the Oriental rug in orderly rows. The atmosphere in the suite was focused but grew more upbeat and jovial as we got closer to finishing.

It took two hours and forty-five minutes, making it a little before three o'clock in the morning when the last page was photographed. Huntington carefully placed the books back in my bag. Phillip and I were out the door of the suite, running to his car, wanting to get them back into Cynthia's hands and from there into the safe as soon as humanly possible.

"Remember, you're to go to the front door and give it three quick knocks," Phillip said as we pulled up to the embassy. "If Cynthia doesn't answer immediately, come back to the car. I'll be parked over there." He pointed to an oak tree less than a block up the street.

I nodded and, not even thinking, grabbed his hand and squeezed it as I got out of the car.

Cynthia opened the door before I could even knock on it.

"Is it done?" she asked in a breathless whisper. She looked disheveled and exhausted. Her hair was in a messy bun, strands of it sticking to the side of her face.

"It's done," I said, handing the books to her. She gave me a genuine, grateful smile.

"Okay." She exhaled. "Before he disappears into the night, GC's going to help me secure these in the safe and make sure we don't leave a trace behind. Tell them I'll be back at the suite soon."

She shut the door in my face, and I skipped down the steps, almost floating. I had done my part without a misstep.

When I got back in the car with Phillip, he had that schoolboy grin again.

"We did it," I said, pumping a fist in the air.

"Almost," he said. "We won't know for sure until Cynthia's safely back at the suite."

"Right."

"Would you like me to drop you at your flat?"

"I don't think I could sleep if I wanted to," I said. "Are you going home?"

"No, I'm going to go wait at the Wardman to make sure Cynthia and Charles get back and the bloody job is finished. Also, I need a stiff drink."

"Sounds like a plan. I'll join you," I said, noting he looked quite pleased at my answer.

~

There was a raucous hero's welcome when Cynthia and Charles arrived at the suite, only slightly muted because it was after four in the morning. Cynthia stood in the middle of the room and just stared at the hundreds of pages lying out to dry, unable to speak. She held her hands over her mouth, stunned, and then she looked around at everyone with tears in her eyes, and we all burst into a round of applause. Huntington gave her a hug and slapped Brousse on the back, laughing. There was no sign of Donovan, and someone said he was on his way home to shower before heading to the White House to deliver the good news.

A couple of the technicians started opening the bottles of champagne that had been delivered to the suite just before Brousse and Cynthia had arrived. When it appeared everyone had a glass at the ready, Huntington raised his hand and the room grew quiet.

"I know you all need to go home and get some sleep, but we need to celebrate this historic moment with a toast. Thank you all for your service in making this operation a success," Huntington said. "The impact of this intelligence on the Allied efforts has the potential to change the course of the war. And to Cynthia and Charles, I know this would not have been possible without your work over the past two years. You are a credit to us all."

Everyone toasted, and Cynthia and Charles clinked their glasses together and kissed. As I stood talking with the professorial technician I had assisted earlier and a few of the others, Huntington came over to me.

"Well done, Anna," he said, clinking my glass. "And you avoided injury this time."

"Thank you," I said. "I'm relieved."

"I think . . . ," he said, pausing for a moment as if he wanted to tell me something, but was checking himself, "you and Donovan and I need to have a discussion . . ."

"Oh, Huntington, I hope you're not getting the schoolgirl's hopes up about any future jobs," Cynthia said, nearly leaning on Huntington. She looked exuberant and more than a little tipsy.

"My name is Anna, Cynthia," I said, feeling my cheeks start to redden. "The operation is over. I don't need the nickname anymore. Not that I ever did."

"Okay, *Anna*." She said my name like an insult. "You did all right tonight, but let's not get ahead of ourselves. There was one very specific, small task that was required of you. That doesn't mean you're ready to graduate to spy. To do what *I* do. You don't know the risks and the sacrifices for the cause. I mean, look at you. Have you ever sacrificed anything in your pampered little life?"

"Well, my husband died trying to heal soldiers in Pearl Harbor. Is that sacrifice enough, *Cynthia*?" I said through gritted teeth. Her face softened when I said this. She hadn't expected that. Good. I'd had enough of this woman, even if she had just pulled off the biggest espionage heist on American soil ever.

"How dare you judge me? You don't know me. You have no idea who I am or what I'm capable of," I added, spitting out the words.

"Ladies, it's getting late, and we're all exhausted . . . Come, Cynthia. Charles is on the balcony having a cigarette. Let's go find him," Huntington said, putting a hand on Cynthia's shoulder.

Cynthia opened her mouth to say something more to me, but then, taking a sip of her drink, she just nodded and let Huntington lead her away.

Phillip had just walked up behind me, and I could tell by his face he had caught at least part of the conversation.

"Are you all right?" he said. "Please don't let her get to you. She's drunk and probably hasn't slept in weeks. I came over to see if I could give you a ride home."

"Yes, I'm fine," I said, though my face was burning. "And I'm so tired I can barely stand up anymore. I'd love a ride."

The sun was rising over DC, making the sky a golden pink as Phillip turned down my street.

"I'm just going to walk you inside your apartment because I have visions of GC sitting at your kitchen table."

"I highly doubt that, but thank you for your concern," I said, opening the front door to loud meows.

He took a quick look around as I fed the cats.

"All clear," he said, clapping his hands together. "I should go and let you sleep."

"Yes, I'm sure you're knackered too," I said using his British expression, and he smiled.

There was an awkward pause at the front door as we turned toward each other. The air between us felt heavy with things unsaid. Before I knew what was happening, he reached out to put his hand on my face. I closed my eyes for a second, smelling the soap on his skin. I put my hand over his and opened my eyes, and there was no denying the feelings between us. But I was feeling too confused and too tired to decide what that meant. All I knew was that I was afraid to trust someone with my heart, to trust myself.

"Phillip, I . . . I'm not sure I can do this yet," I said, my heart aching in my chest. I still had my guard up.

"Anna, I have to leave," he said, his face anguished.

"Yes, you should go. We're both tired."

I looked down, feeling embarrassed, pulling my hand away, but he reached for it and pulled me closer.

"You don't understand," he said. "I mean I need to leave DC. I'm going back to London."

"You are?" I said. My heart sank in my chest. "When?"

"Tonight," he said.

"Oh," I said. "That's . . . oh."

He let out a deep breath, holding both of my hands now. I started to pull away, but he held tight.

"Listen, I just found out two days ago," he said. "I thought I'd be here for at least another couple of months, but British intelligence has assigned me to some other joint initiatives with the OSS that they've got in the works. And to be quite honest, after tonight, my work here is done. It seems I've briefed everyone in the building on our methods. I've trained a number of blokes in Secret Intelligence that are far better than that Archie. My superiors wanted me to stay on just for this last operation—because it's such a critical intelligence coup. You have no idea how monumental tonight was."

"I know. I'm proud to be a part of it," I said, and this time I did pull away, walking to the window, looking at the sun nearly up in the sky now. "Well, you should go. I'm sure you have a lot to do."

The bittersweet ache of caring about someone and being separated from them was familiar, different from how it had been with Henri, yet the same.

"There's only one thing I haven't done nearly enough of here in the States, isn't there?"

He came up behind me, put his hands on my shoulders, and turned me toward him.

"What's that?" I said in a whisper.

"Spend time with you," he whispered back, both hands on my face this time.

I was too tired to overthink it, as I normally would have done. That's why when Phillip leaned into me, for a few short minutes, I let go of all my fears and doubts and kissed him back. I melted into his arms as we kept kissing. I had forgotten the dizzying warmth of a first kiss, so full of possibilities and questions.

A dog barked outside, breaking the spell, and we pulled away from each other for a moment, laughing.

"Oh, Cavanaugh," he said, wrapping his arms around me. "Whatever am I going to do about you?"

"Well, not much, Phillip Stanhope. You're leaving," I said, teasing.

He pulled a piece of paper out of his pants pocket. "This is the address of my flat in Knightsbridge, in London."

"Thank you," I said, looking at it. "I guess we'll write each other, then?"

"Yes," he said, nodding slowly.

I looked up at him.

"And that's . . . also just in case you ever end up there yourself."

"What?" I said, searching his eyes. "What aren't you telling me? Are they going to let me go into the field?"

"I didn't say that," Phillip said, lifting his hands in protest. "And I don't know anything for sure. But let's just say that, after tonight, I think your life at the OSS is going to change."

"Are you joking?" I said. "Because it's too late—I already have my hopes up now."

"Darling, I would never joke about something like that," he said, his voice low. "Now, may I please kiss you once more before I go?"

I looked up, studying his face and memorizing it. Then I nodded and gave him a sad smile as he leaned down for our first and perhaps only kiss good-bye.

# Chapter Thirteen

**September 2, 1942**

I felt restless in the days following the embassy break-in, wondering what would come next for me at the OSS and what I needed to do to get where I wanted to go. I also thought about kissing Phillip, more than I cared to admit even to myself.

It was a week before Julia, Irene, and I finally had time to have lunch together. At that point I was feeling desperate to talk to them and get their thoughts on everything that had transpired. As we all three leaned in, I told them about the second attempt at the embassy, Cynthia's behavior toward me, and the exhilaration I still felt about getting the naval codebooks and returning them.

"That Cynthia sounds like a peach. We should invite her out for drinks sometime," Julia said with sarcasm.

"I think she's jealous of you," Irene said in a matter-of-fact tone that made me laugh.

"Hardly," I said. "She's a breathtakingly beautiful super spy. Why in the world would she be jealous of me?"

"Because you're young and pretty, and it's clear that Huntington is considering you for other SI jobs. Also, she's used to being the only woman in the room. She prefers it that way."

"Maybe," I said. I thought of the jealous look on Cynthia's face when Brousse complimented my French.

"I agree with Irene," Julia said. "But women like that? Who don't help other women? Who only view them as competition? They are just terrible."

"That is definitely true," I said.

"There's something you're leaving out," Irene said, eyes narrowed, pointing at me with her fork. "I can tell. What haven't you told us?"

"Ah, you're good. I think you should consider being a spy," I said with a laugh. I had been feeling the afterglow of kissing Phillip since he had left my apartment at dawn on Thursday.

As I shared what happened when he drove me home, they both hung on every word, gasping at the end when I told them he had already left for London.

"I knew there was something between you two," Irene said.

"Well, you knew it before I did, then," I said. "Truly."

"He's so very dashing," Julia said, as she scraped the last of the cafeteria's best-selling chocolate pudding out of its little glass bowl. "And that British accent is just dreamy."

"But he's back in London. Now what happens?" Irene said.

"I don't think anything, to be honest," I said, though it hurt to say it. "I may not ever see him again. It's probably for the best."

"Why would you say that?" Irene asked, frowning.

"Exactly. Why would *not* seeing him be for the best?" Julia said. "He could be the love of your life."

"I doubt that," I said, laughing. "Ladies, I just . . . I don't know if I'm ready to take a chance, to really fall for someone. And also, I know where I want to go within the OSS if I get the opportunity—which I realize is still a big *if* at this point. I already had one man in my life stand in the way of me getting what I wanted. I don't want to risk having another do the same thing."

"Given what you were involved in the night you kissed, do you really think Phillip Stanhope would do that?" Irene asked.

"I don't know. But he's thousands of miles away, so I don't think it's something I need to think about right now," I said, pausing before adding, "I do have to tell you it was nice . . . to remember what it felt like to kiss someone, to feel that way again."

I felt my face flush. I was surprised how much I wished he was still nearby.

"Mm-hmm," Julia said, eyebrows raised, giving me a Cheshire cat grin.

"Oh, stop," I said, laughing. "I have been doing all the talking here. Julia, what's the latest on the Ceylon post?"

"I'm so happy I can finally share this!" Julia said, clapping her hands together. "Maggie told me Monday, and I submitted the final paperwork last night. If all goes well, I leave mid-October."

Irene and I whooped so loudly that people at the tables around us turned to look and laugh as we clinked our Coke bottles together.

"Irene has news too, don't you?" Julia said.

"Yes," Irene said. "Maggie's been busy this week. A lot of women received their overseas post assignments. I leave for London around the same time as Julia."

I hugged and congratulated them both but couldn't help but feel a combination of wistfulness and envy about their plans. I hadn't officially applied for the London post, despite Irene's urging, because I was banking on the general considering me for a field agent post in SI. But despite my involvement in the embassy break-in, he had given me no indication that he would be transferring me anytime soon.

"I can't believe my two best work friends are leaving me," I said, giving them an exaggerated pout. "I don't know what I would have done here without you, especially in those first couple of weeks. And I'm thrilled for you both, but I'm also going to miss you so much."

"Yes, well, when are you going to ask Donovan about what's next for you?" Irene said. "What are you waiting for?"

"I keep waiting for a quiet moment, but you know how his schedule is," I said. "There hasn't been one."

"Well, find one, even if you have to stay late," Julia said. "And please promise me that you will both write me regularly? I will write letters and share with you my many adventures with travel, exotic food, and handsome officers . . ."

We clinked our Coke bottles together one last time, and I felt a sense of melancholy as we gathered up our trays to head back to our desks. My friends would be leaving DC for posts around the globe, marking the end of the beginning of my time at the OSS. And I had absolutely no idea what would come next for me.

∼

After hearing Julia's and Irene's news, I was determined to find a time to talk to Donovan about my future at the OSS. But all week he was in meetings at the White House and elsewhere off-site, so I had barely had a chance to say more than a few words to him. On Friday, hoping to have my opportunity, I waited until after seven for him to come back from his meeting at the Pentagon. But I finally gave up and decided to meet up with Irene, Julia, and some of the girls from Research and Analysis who had gone out for cocktails.

I was in the back of a taxi, almost at the restaurant, when I rummaged through my purse and realized I had left my house key at the office. Cursing loudly, I asked the grumpy driver to turn around and take me back to headquarters. I slammed the door and told him not to wait. At this point, my friends might not even be at the bar by the time I got there; I was better off just going home.

Scotty was at the front desk and gave me a preoccupied nod as I hurried through the main hall, calling out to him that I forgot my keys, aggravated with myself for forgetting them. He was busy listening to whatever ball game was on the radio. There were just a couple of office lights on, and the empty halls were dimly lit and so quiet that all I could hear was the clicking of my heels on the tile floor.

As I got closer to my office, I could see that all the lights were on and hear voices coming from behind the general's partially open door. I half tiptoed to my desk and froze when I realized it was the general and Huntington talking.

"I really like her for it, Bill," Huntington said. "She's a perfect fit for the role, as you already know."

"She has zero training as a wireless operator," the general said. "She has no training whatsoever yet to prepare her for a field assignment."

"But she showed she's up for the challenge with the embassy break-in, and she's smart as a whip. We can get her trained in the UK," Huntington said. "Her French is flawless—even Brousse said she sounds like a Parisian. And I'm guessing her German is excellent, too."

I stood there frozen with goose pimples on my arms.

"She did fine with the break-in, but that's a far cry from being a spy in occupied territory," Donovan said. "She's untested."

"Look, we know it's much easier for a woman to go undercover in France right now. That's why the Brits have been sending more women, with some success I might add. And look how well our gal Pauline is doing. We'll send Anna to the UK and have her trained as a wireless operator and drop her into France by December's full moon."

"I don't know," the general said, letting out a big sigh.

"I know you had this in mind when you first mentioned the OSS at the funeral," Huntington said. "To have an OSS wireless operator in Paris within the Druids network, with Amniarix? It could be a big coup from an intelligence standpoint."

"I know she wants to go abroad, but I had hoped we wouldn't need her for this, Edgar," Donovan said. "Maggie and I thought we could send her to London or Bern, even Spain. Not to occupied territory."

"But we do need her and many more like her," Huntington said. "Desperately."

There was a pause in the conversation, and then Huntington added, "It's the family connection. That's why you're hesitant, isn't it?"

"Anna, turn the light on. Why on earth are you looking for your keys in the dark?" I jumped at the sound of Scotty's voice behind me and turned just as he flipped the light switch. "Did you find them?"

"Um, yeah, I did, Scotty. Thanks," I said, wincing. He seemed to have realized what he had done because he winced when he heard Donovan yell.

"Anna Cavanaugh, get in here right now!"

I bid Scotty good night, and he mouthed, "I'm sorry."

I walked into the general's office, cringing and holding up my key chain.

"Forgot my keys," I said, dangling them as evidence, as if that mattered. "And I'm sorry. I shouldn't have been listening in the dark, but then I realized you were talking about me . . ."

"Yes, we were," General Donovan said in an aggravated tone. "Now, let's test your eavesdropping skills. How much did you hear?" He put his feet on his desk, and there was a whiskey in his hand. Huntington was smoking a cigar and looked quite amused as he nodded at me.

"Starting with the part where Huntington said he liked me for it," I said, looking at Huntington. "Thank you."

"You're welcome," Huntington said.

"I'd go tomorrow if you'd let me," I said. I looked Donovan in the eye, swallowed hard, and attempted to make my case. "And look, I know you think I'm naive going into something like this. I probably am, but I'm very smart, and I'm willing to learn everything I need to know. And I understand it's dangerous—"

"That's the thing. You really don't know," Donovan said, interrupting me and speaking to me with a harshness I'd never heard before. "You've never been to a war zone. We are talking about occupied territory—this is not just some great adventure you'd be going on. We're in a deadly struggle with a brutal enemy. Last fall, nearly all of the Brits' SOE agents in France were rounded up, arrested, or killed. And as the French Resistance grows stronger, so does the Germans' determination to stomp it out, along with any of its Allied supporters. As an American with false French papers, you will be treated as a spy if you're caught. You'll be imprisoned or immediately executed. You will live with that danger every single day."

I sat there and absorbed his words, trying to grasp what living like that would feel like.

"You're right," I said, my voice quiet. "I don't really know. But neither did you when you first went to war. And I'm sure it was shocking and horrific. But you adapted. You gained more skills as you went along. I will, too."

He reached behind him, got another small glass from the bookshelf, placed it in front of me, and poured, not taking his eyes off me the whole time. Huntington remained quiet, smoking his cigar, letting the words between us hang in the air.

I looked at the picture of Donovan's beautiful daughter, Patricia, behind him on the shelf, and I felt that familiar heartache for this man I had come to admire so much. I took a sip of whiskey and pointed at it.

"I know you're conflicted about sending me because you're friends with my family and because you're a father and you . . . you lost Patricia—the most unimaginable kind of loss. I know you're thinking about what my father would go through if something happened to me."

I paused for a moment before speaking again.

"Sir, I would never, ever equate the death of my husband with your own loss. But now that some time has passed, more than anything, Connor's death makes me want to find my passion and purpose, to discover what's next for my *own* life. And working here at the OSS has given me that, but I want to do even more. I want to serve my country and help a country I've grown to love. Please give me this chance."

Huntington looked at me, nodding like a proud uncle. Donovan's eyes were a little misty, and I blinked because mine were too.

"She was smart and headstrong, Patricia. A little like you," Donovan said, clearing his throat. "You two would have been friends, I think."

"I bet we would have," I said, smiling at the picture of the girl with the same sparkling blue eyes as her father.

Donovan took a deep breath and stared up at the ceiling, his hands clasped. I sat there frozen in my seat, waiting for his answer.

"I told you before, being an agent, it's not a life many people are suited for, Anna," Donovan said. "But because you're so willing, and because you're such a good fit for the role, I'm going to give you a chance."

"Thank you, thank you, sir," I said, clasping my hands together, nearly bouncing in my chair, not quite believing he was going to let me go.

"Huntington will draw up a contract for you. But the basics are, after you go through training, you will serve for a year with an option to renew, and any information you obtain will be top secret. You will accept the personal risk to your life, and your salary will be $336 a month."

He could tell by my face how thrilled I was about it all, because he then added, "But let me be clear. If during training any of your supervisors over there do not think you are up to this assignment in the field? You'll be taken out of the field and reassigned to a position in the London office immediately."

"Understood," I said, nodding, taking a sip of the whiskey.

"Well, that settles it," Huntington said, looking relieved and pleased. "One less role I have to fill. You'll be just terrific, Anna. You're a smart girl, and smart people can handle any job. And I think you're more than ready."

I gave him a grateful smile, knowing he was the reason I was being given this chance.

"We'll have to work out your exact departure date, probably sometime late November," Donovan said. "The Brits have scheduled a three-week training program at that time, specifically for women field agents going into occupied territories. Huntington, why don't you go through the exact details of this plan you've been trying to sell me?"

Donovan poured some more whiskey for the three of us.

"Happy to," Huntington said. "Because the best cover stories are the ones closest to the truth, you'll be sent undercover as a Parisian college student, but this time a French one. You'll perfect this new identity during your three weeks of training outside London, writing yourself a new life history, memorizing the addresses of places you've never lived and the faces of brothers or sisters that don't exist. Part of this family history will include your 'cousin,' the spy you'll be working with, known as Amniarix. As I know you overheard, you'll be working with the Druids resistance network in Paris, infiltrating a group of German officers to gain intelligence."

Huntington went on to explain that the most important training would involve learning to be a wireless operator, in order to help the group communicate directly with the OSS and SOE in London, but I would also receive weapons training as well as training in clandestine activities like burglary. Then, provided I received a passing grade from my supervisors, I would be sent to London for a few days to meet with the OSS's C&D, their Cover and Documentation department, to receive my false identity papers and other supplies, including a French-made wardrobe.

"You'll depart for Paris from RAF Tangmere via Lysander plane in late December on one of the nights the moon is full, when pilots have the best visibility. The Druids network members will meet you at a designated safe house outside the city."

"You'll have plenty of time to go visit with your family before you head overseas," Donovan said. "Promise me you'll do that?"

"Oh, of course, sir. I have to see my parents and my sisters before I go," I said, my mind spinning with what my family's reaction would be, with all that I needed to do and all that lay ahead. And the fact that I was returning to France, under more extraordinary circumstances than I could ever have imagined.

I longed to ask whether I would be allowed to contact my friends in Paris, or if that was unthinkable because of the danger. But I held back, afraid it would give Donovan a reason to change his mind about letting me go.

"You look like you have questions," Huntington said.

"I do, but honestly, I don't know where to begin," I said.

"I'll be sure to answer all of them, but I think we need to call it a night," Huntington said, putting out his cigar in the tin ashtray on the desk.

"Agreed," Donovan said, looking at his military watch. "I'm meeting with Roosevelt at the crack of dawn. I'll have Louis give you a ride home, Anna. It's late."

"Thank you," I said. "And thank you for this opportunity."

"You're welcome," Donovan said. "Now please prove to me that I made the right decision."

"I will," I said, praying that I could.

"Congratulations, Anna," Huntington said, reaching out to shake my hand. "You're officially part of SI, Secret Intelligence, now. I hope you understand that your life's about to change forever."

*Yes, I do? No, I have no idea?* I had so many questions and thoughts, and a roller coaster of exhilaration and pride and nervous fear too. I started to answer and realized I was choked up, at getting this chance, this whole new life, the kind of opportunity I'd always dreamed of.

"Do you promise?" I finally said with a teary-eyed smile.

# Chapter Fourteen

**October 16, 1942**

There were so many women headed to new overseas posts in October that Maggie decided a farewell party was in order. She'd organized one at the Mayfair, a popular restaurant with the nickname "café of all nations," making it an appropriately themed venue for the OSS soiree. The restaurant's interior was painted with colorful murals of scenes from around the world, and on the wall above the bar hung flags of every country, though Japan's, Italy's, and Germany's were now absent.

I was sitting in one of the turquoise banquettes next to Julia, drinking a gin and tonic and listening to Frances Carroll and the Coquettes, an all-girl big band Maggie had somehow hired for the night, working her magic as usual.

I had begged Mary to come with me to the party, to finally meet my work friends, but she had passed, saying she would feel too out of place. The closer I got to leaving, the more I cherished the time I spent with my best and oldest friend over cups of coffee or beers in my little garden. She had been there for me in DC, and in life, more than just about anyone, and I knew I would miss her terribly.

It had been a whirlwind month, keeping up with my usual work responsibilities while also preparing to head to England for training in November. As I had promised the general, I had taken the train home the weekend before, to spend a few days with my family and explain to them that I would be going overseas for a new position. I told them as soon as I arrived Friday night. My mother cried, and at first my father appeared furious and told me all the reasons I shouldn't go. My sister Colleen was beside herself that I might miss her upcoming wedding, scheduled for April of '43. Bridget's reaction had been the hardest to bear—jealous and sad. She begged to go with me, though she knew it was impossible.

Remarkably, by the end of the weekend, they had all come around, and, while not entirely supportive, they had all at least accepted the news. Colleen admitted that her wedding was probably going to be postponed anyway, due to her fiancé Brad's inevitable naval deployment, and Bridget made me swear I would put in a good word with the OSS upon her graduation, so that she might possibly join me.

Donovan still hadn't admitted it, but I suspected he had called and talked to my father while I was out shopping with my sisters during my visit. When I was saying my good-byes, my father told me more than six times how proud he was of me and that it was an opportunity I deserved, while my mother was much calmer about it all and kept telling me she was sure I would return engaged to a handsome officer.

"I have to tell you, all month I've felt like a kid the night before Christmas," Julia said, sipping her Manhattan. "I just cannot wait to go abroad. I've never been farther than Tijuana. And where in the world is Irene? This is our final night to spend time together and celebrate." She strained her neck to look toward the entrance of the restaurant.

"I don't know. I thought she'd be here an hour ago," I said, scanning the crowded room, a little worried. Irene was not one to be late.

"I hope she gets here soon. It's already eight o'clock," Julia said. She turned back to me, lighting up a Lucky Strike. "What about you, my dear? How are you feeling about everything? Are you all prepared?"

"I'm so excited. In some ways I wish I was leaving on Monday like you two, because I'm in a holding pattern until late November.

Maggie and I are close to hiring my replacement, and I found two recent Radcliffe grads who just moved to DC and are going to sublet my apartment. They're even going to take care of my cats. I guess I'm just about ready, yes."

That's when I looked up and spotted Irene, holding a rum and Coke, making her way through the crowd. She was wearing a red wool princess coat with leopard trim and a matching hat and looked as impeccable as ever, except for her blotchy, tear-stained face.

"Oh, Irene, what happened to you?" I said, sliding over to make room for her.

"Sweetheart, tell us what happened," Julia said, reaching across and patting her hand.

"What happened was I married the wrong man," Irene said, her voice angry, and now there were fresh tears in her eyes. "Michael and I just had a horrible, ugly fight. He thinks he can *forbid me* from going to London. He says he never should have agreed to let me go in the first place."

"And what did you say?" I said, giving her a napkin to blot her eyes.

"I . . . God, I finally really told him how I feel for the first time . . . in months? Years? I said, despite the fact we were married in the church, our marriage is not a real marriage, we are not in love, and he knew it as well as I did. And that he can't 'forbid' me to do anything. I told him I am going to London no matter what. And he said if I went, then he wouldn't be here when I got back."

She took a sip of her drink and spilled some on the table. I felt sick for her because I knew exactly how she felt.

"What did you say to that?" I asked.

"I said okay," Irene said, nodding, getting a fresh napkin for her tears. "I said fine."

"Oh, Irene, you poor thing," Julia said. "Do you want to get out of here? To go somewhere quieter where the three of us can talk?"

"No," Irene said, shaking her head. "No, this is great actually. The music is terrific, and people are in such happy moods. Last week I met Ruthie and Gloria, two of the girls who are going to London with me. I know they're here somewhere. This is exactly where I need to be—with you two, right here."

"Well, let's get another round of drinks, then," I said, motioning to the waiter.

We talked about all our upcoming plans and tried to discuss things that would cheer up Irene. At one point, Julia had us both roaring with laughter, telling us stories of some of the ridiculous pranks she had played on her roommates in college. And the band played hit after hit as tipsy couples danced the jitterbug.

"I'm so happy we're going to reunite in London, if only for a few days," Irene said to me. After an hour she was in better form, her usually pale cheeks flushed from the warm, smoky humidity of the crowded restaurant and the two rum and Cokes she'd had.

"I'm thrilled about that," I said.

"Are you going to see that dashing British lad Phillip while you're there?" Julia said in her best British accent, which was in fact terrible.

"Of course she is," Irene said. "Right? Why wouldn't you?"

Now I could feel my cheeks turning pink because I wasn't sure of my answer.

"I want to," I said. "But then I think, it's such a short time, what's the point really?"

"The point is that you might get to kiss a handsome man again," Julia said, in such a loud and animated tone that the table next to us looked over at her like she was crazy, and Irene and I couldn't help but laugh. "There's a war going on. Does there *really* need to be any point other than that? You've got to seize those small moments of joy when you can get them."

"I think the real reason would be that you care about him," Irene said. "Don't you miss him?"

"I . . . I do . . . it's just—"

"Anna, you're just the person I wanted to see." Huntington had come up behind me and interrupted, which I was grateful for, since I didn't know what I was going to say.

"Can I have a quick word?" he said to me, smiling. I nodded, and he added, "Oh, and Julia, I've been meaning to tell you I have an old friend from Boston Latin who's an OSS officer stationed in Ceylon. His name is Paul Child, terrific fella. He's been there for several months. Please look him up if you want someone to give you the lay of the land."

"Paul Child. Let me write that down," Julia said, grabbing a napkin and rummaging through her purse for a pen. "I will certainly do that, thank you."

Huntington and I walked over to a corner of the bar, as far away from the music as possible so we could hear each other better.

"As of tonight, your ticket on one of the Pan Am flying boats that are now being used for military and diplomatic transport is booked. You depart from New York on November 28, the flight takes an entire day. Upon arrival in Southampton on the 29th, the Brits will pick you up and take you to Hampshire, England, where you will report for training," Huntington said, a huge grin on his face.

I was so excited and grateful I couldn't help but give him a hug, which took him by surprise.

"Thank you for believing in me," I said. "I know that Donovan would never have agreed to send me if it hadn't been for you."

"I know you're up to the challenge," he said. "And I wanted to also give you a word about training. It's critical you learn everything that's required to become a wireless operator, but don't worry about some of the other aspects if you don't master them. They are training you for something that's never been done; there are no experts in helping an occupied country build a resistance from within. Just have confidence in yourself, in your intellect and creativity, and you will figure it out."

His words were reassuring. I was still nervous and knew that my self-doubt might creep in when I least expected it, but I couldn't let it show right now, not to this man who believed in me more than I believed in myself.

"I'll do my very best, I promise you," I said. "Sir, I had one question, but to be honest, I haven't wanted to ask it in front of the general because I was afraid of him changing his mind about letting me go."

"What is it?" he said, amused.

"You must know I have friends there, in Paris, from my days at Sciences Po. My closest friend is Josette Rousseau, and I know for a fact she's living in Paris. I'm guessing it's too dangerous to contact her, although I miss her terribly and would love to see her. But what if I run into her on the street? Or her cousin Henri? Or anyone else?"

"Well, it's likely many of those people you knew were among the thousands who fled the city during the exodus, or they've been taken away because of their ethnicity or for some other horrific reason," Huntington said, studying me, his face serious. "Anna, you weren't supposed to receive these details until training, but since you've asked, I'll share them now. The Druids resistance network is run by a man I think you know. His name is Georges LaRue. Your friends Josette and Henri? They are part of that network."

"I'm sorry . . . what?"

I sat there and stared at him, opening my mouth to speak and then closing it again and just frowning, trying to absorb what Huntington had just said. When I learned about Connor's death, it was such a shock that I had a moment where I felt like I wasn't in my own body. This new revelation shook me in that same way; I felt light-headed.

Huntington must have noticed, because he pulled a stool out for me. I sat and downed the rest of my drink, thinking of Josette's letters from a very different perspective now. It almost seemed obvious in hindsight, but I hadn't been looking at them through the right lens.

"How did I not know this?" I said. "Did General Donovan know this about them in January at Connor's funeral? Is that why I'm here?"

"In January, we knew that Josette Rousseau had been accused of spying on the Germans in Dinard, because she *was* spying on them. That's why she was forced to leave the city and return to Paris. As it turned out, her cousin Henri and friend Georges were involved in resistance activities of their own there. The general was made aware of your personal connection with the three of them from your letters."

"How'd you get my letters? Oh, never mind," I said.

"We knew of your language abilities, your obvious intelligence, and your experience living abroad, and of course there was Donovan's relationship with your father, so long before your husband's funeral, we had targeted you as a recruit for all of those usual reasons. The connection to the network was . . . interesting. But when we hired you, the scenario of you working as an agent in Paris was truly the slimmest of possibilities.

"As the general said, he knew you'd want a post abroad at some point, and we planned on placing you somewhere in the world, but not for this initially. As you know, he was and still is worried about putting you in harm's way. Circumstances have changed though. The Allies are desperate for wireless operators in France, and I believe you've more than proven your worth."

"Thank you. Yes, circumstances have changed," I said, still trying to wrap my mind around this news as the bartender placed another gin and tonic in front of me.

"There's one other detail you should know . . . ," Huntington said.

"Yes?"

When he spoke, it was the last puzzle piece clicking into place. It hit me as both a stunning revelation and an inevitability. A whisper of a suspicion that had been flitting through my subconscious since Josette's first letter from Paris.

"Your friend Josette Rousseau? She *is* the spy code-named Amniarix. She works for French industrialists and is in contact with the German military command in Paris on an almost daily basis, reporting intelligence back to the Allies in whatever way she can. She has become one of the most valuable spies in Paris."

I sat there and stared at him, absorbing the news. It was shocking and yet so obvious at the same time. Josette was the brilliant spy Amniarix, the one I would be working with in Paris. Of course she was.

# *Chapter Fifteen*

**Beaulieu Manor**
**Hampshire, England**
**December 17, 1942**

*12/17/42*

*Dear Phillip,*
*How are you? I hope this note finds you well. I'm writing from somewhere south of London, for reasons you know I cannot say, but I'm sure you can guess. I arrived here a few weeks ago on a Pan American flying boat, which was quite a thrill. There were a few other OSS women with me, heading to Algiers and Bern, among other far-flung destinations. If you've run into Irene, you may already know I'm here. She's currently working at the OSS head-quarters on Grosvenor Street.*

*I've witnessed just some of the devastation left from the bombings during the Blitz—blown-out buildings and roads destroyed. It's taken my breath away to see it up close. I'm so sorry for what this war has done to your country and its people. I'm terribly sorry about what it's done to your family.*

*Speaking of the people, the Brits I have had the opportunity to meet so far are so kind, so brave and patriotic, even though your country has suffered through this war for far too long.*

*I'm writing to let you know that I will be in London on December 20 for two nights before moving on to my next destination. I will be working at the OSS offices at 72 Grosvenor Street and staying with Irene. She's billeted in an apartment overlooking Hyde Park. If you are also in town, please be in touch. I would like to see you before I leave . . . as I have no idea when I will be back in London again. I hope you are well.*

*Warmest,*

*Anna*

I stared at the note, pen in hand, agonizing over whether I should write *Fondly* or *Best Wishes* or *Yours*—or if I should just rip it up and throw it in the trash. It felt as awkward to read as it was to write. My heart still ached when I thought of Phillip and our moments together before he left DC. I kept thinking about Julia's advice to seize the "moments of joy" in war, and held on to that notion as a reason to reunite. But I questioned if Phillip really wanted to see me after all this time, or if he was even in the city. And I was in London for such a short time. I wondered if it was worth stirring up whatever was between us just to have to say good-bye again.

Now that I was over the initial shock about what Josette, Henri, and Georges were involved in, all I wanted to do was get to Paris and be a part of it, to have the opportunity to play my role as a wireless operator and spy and to do it well.

My hesitation about seeing Phillip had nothing to do with Henri, though I was curious about the young man I had left in Paris. Our time together was an innocent, hazy dream. Now I was a widow with a fake identity, and he was living underground in his own city and working for the French Resistance. There was nothing remaining between us.

There was a knock on my bedroom door and a call of "Bonjour! Ready?" from the other side. I recognized the voice of Nora, a fellow trainee also heading to Paris.

"Coming!" I said, placing the letter in an envelope and leaving it on my desk.

It was seven o'clock in the morning, time for our drills on the palatial estate of Lord Montagu of Beaulieu, deep in the idyllic New Forest district in Hampshire, south of London. In the Beaulieu family since the 1500s, the estate had been requisitioned and was now the home of the SOE's Special Training School 31, better known as Station 31. It offered a discreet location and ready-made accommodations for agents in training and the officers on the teaching and administrative staff.

I had arrived eighteen days ago, with twenty-two other women trainees who were preparing to be part of F Section, the SOE's French Section. I was the only OSS woman in the training group, though I was told that more would be sent in the new year, and that one American woman, Pauline Wakefield, had been sent two years ago, and had since become one of the most extraordinary Resistance organizers and leaders in France.

In early November, the Allies had successfully invaded French North Africa in Operation Torch, paving the way for an invasion of southern Europe. Three days later, the Germans had responded by occupying the so-called Free Zone in France previously controlled by the French Vichy government. Now the entire country of France was under occupation. All these developments made the need for additional Allied agents in France more acute than ever.

The grand property that was our training school for these three weeks was jaw-dropping in both its architecture and the natural beauty that surrounded it. The main house had been remodeled in the 1800s into a sprawling Victorian country manor. Beaulieu's vast acreage included the ruins of a medieval abbey, several cottages, meandering trails, and the winter skeletons of gardens that I was sure were gorgeous at the height of summer. I had expected to be living in sterile barracks on a military base, not staying in a castle with grounds that resembled the backdrop of an English fairy tale.

So far, however, being there had felt more like going through the looking glass in *Alice in Wonderland* than any fairy tale. I had entered this clandestine existence and created a new identity, and soon I would be back in a city I adored, but which I feared I would no longer recognize.

"Morning," I said to Nora, opening the door to my bedroom with a smile. Like me, she was dressed in a stiff, khaki First Aid Nursing Yeomanry uniform. FANY was an organization British women of a certain class joined to volunteer for military work, and their itchy, unattractive uniforms now served as part of the cover story for all women in training at Beaulieu.

"A ten-kilometer run this morning," Nora said in her breathy, high-pitched voice as we hurried down the home's original grand Gothic staircase to meet the rest of the women at the back of the estate near the kitchen garden. "And it's freezing outside. I think I might die, quite honestly. I'm still sore from the eighteen-kilometer bike ride yesterday."

"We'll get it done," I said, trying to buck her up. "Just think of the steaming-hot cups of coffee that will be waiting for us in the dining room when it's over."

Nora Khan was a striking beauty, with raven hair and olive skin. She had a sweet, dreamy disposition and a fascinating background, having been born in Moscow to an American mother and an Indian father descended from royalty. Raised and educated in Paris, she was clever and fluent in multiple languages and had been working as a writer of children's stories before the war. But since befriending her, I had worried because while she was an absolutely lovely person, she appeared too flighty, too fragile to be sent to occupied Paris.

"Anna! Anna, may I have a minute, please?" We were heading out the back door when I heard the voice of Violet Banks, the SOE administrator in charge of the women of F Section. I told Nora to go ahead and I would catch up with her.

"Anna, your evaluation will be the first one tomorrow morning," Violet said. "It will be at eight a.m., with myself and Lieutenant Faraday, in his office."

"Oh, thank you, I will be sure to be on time," I said, my stomach doing flips, wondering if being first meant anything.

"Good luck today," she said, her expression serious. "Remember to do absolutely everything your instructors say."

It was an odd thing to say, because following instructions hadn't been an issue for me thus far. I nodded that I would and said good-bye.

I hurried down one of the many estate paths in the back of the main house, arriving at the kitchen garden just as the last few girls were also getting there. Our instructor, Stanley Taylor, a man built like a fire hydrant, was a detective on loan from the Scotland Yard murder squad. He nodded and checked off my name as I ran up.

"Where the bloody hell is Tatiana?" Stanley Taylor said with a growl, a vein bulging on the side of his shiny bald head.

"Here! Bonjour to you too, sir," Tatiana Marchand yelled, as she came bounding up one of the garden paths. "Though you know I'd still be done before this lot if I started a half hour after them, wouldn't I?"

"Don't get too cocky, Marchand," Taylor said, though he cracked a smile. "All right, ladies, get on with it then—a ten-kilometer loop, same as last week."

"You're not that fast," I said, laughing as I started to jog alongside Tatiana.

"You know I am," she responded in French with a sly grin, taking off ahead of me. Tatiana was also being sent to Paris and, like Nora, had become a friend. She was a natural athlete, with a slender physique and long, light-chestnut-colored hair she always wore in a braid.

The sky was the color of slate, there was frost on the branches of the Meyer lemon trees that lined the garden's path, and the air smelled like crushed leaves. While some of the training was worthwhile, I wasn't sure if this daily morning regimen was worth a damn. But, despite the cold, I had grown to enjoy our mornings in the ancient forest, even if it included wading through muddy bogs or navigating obstacle courses. The camaraderie with the other women and the breathtaking countryside made it worthwhile, and it also helped me miss Mary, Irene, and Julia a little less.

"Evaluations tomorrow. Are you ready, my friend?" Tatiana asked after I caught up with her. She wasn't even breathing heavily. "Reply to me in French like you're supposed to. No more English; you need to get used to *being* French."

"*Plus prête que jamais*," I replied. "As ready as I'll ever be" in French, because she was right. My stomach felt queasy, and I didn't know if it was from lack of food or my worry about passing the evaluation. The intense three-week training in spy craft had ranged from the routine and boring to the somewhat ridiculous. I could now make a cast of a key using a bar of soap, detect ways I was being followed, pass a message in a crowded place surreptitiously, and pick a lock, though I'd never measure up to GC's abilities.

"I'm sure most of what we learned will be useful, but I truly hope I never have to plant a bomb in a dead animal," I said, grimacing at the memory of what we had all dubbed "dead rat day" the week before.

"I must admit I rather enjoyed learning how to be an arsonist," Tatiana said, jogging with her hands on her head as she wrapped her braid into a bun.

I glanced at her, eyebrows raised. Tatiana, a self-dubbed Parisian "baguette girl," excelled in every aspect of spy craft, as if she had always been destined for the role. Born to a French father and an English mother, she was from the Marais neighborhood, where her father had owned a thriving boulangerie on Rue des Rosiers, before they had been forced to flee the mass arrests of Jews in Paris in July. Tatiana and her mother had made it to England, but her father and brothers had stayed behind for too long and been arrested.

"At least I'm confident about operating a wireless—"

"You're brilliant at the wireless," Tatiana said, interrupting me. "You're the best one of us by far."

"Thank you. My only worry? I'm a terrible shot," I said, voicing my biggest concern. "I don't think anyone here did worse than I did."

Unlike some of the other women in our group, I had never hunted, so this was my first experience ever handling a gun, and I had not taken to it at all. We had been taught to use Colt .32 and Liberator .45 pistols, as well as the lightweight Sten submachine guns that were popular with the Resistance because they were easy to assemble and clean. They were supposed to be the easiest to use, but not for me. It didn't matter the weapon, shooting felt awkward and foreign, despite spending extra time at the shooting ranges and on the course where paper Nazis would move toward you on pulley strings. I watched with envy while Tatiana and other trainees took to shooting like it was second nature.

"Nora was nearly as bad as you," Tatiana said under her breath. "I think it was a tie."

"Shhh . . . and thanks," I said. Poor Nora. I turned around to make sure she wasn't close and spotted her, a small figure with the other stragglers, at the opposite end of the cow pasture we had just run through.

"I think you'll be fine regardless of the fact you can't shoot a gun to save your life," Tatiana said.

"Again, thanks," I said, my voice heavy with sarcasm.

"I'm serious, Anna. We are not going to Paris to shoot Nazis, as much as I would love to. We're going there to blend in as common Parisians and to aid the Resistance. They're doing what they think is best but don't really know how to train us, do they?"

I nodded, thinking of Huntington's words before I left, about being trained for something that had never been done before.

"I'd like to think my skill as a wireless operator matters more than anything else we've learned," I said through my coughs, the cold air tightening my lungs. "And I don't think they can afford to *not* pass us; they need us too much. Let's wait for Nora. She's at the back of the pack."

"She better hurry. I'm desperate for a cigarette," Tatiana said, letting out a dramatic sigh.

# Chapter Sixteen

"Anna, it's like you are purposely trying to miss the target. Are you?" Nora said to me, hiding her mouth behind her hand, trying to be polite and not laugh.

It was late afternoon, and the sun was starting to set. After our sessions were over for the day, I headed to one of Beaulieu's firing ranges to practice in the freezing cold, but it did me little good. Per our instructor's last lesson, I had just crouched down and aimed a .45 at the target, a bull's-eye with Hitler's face in the middle, twenty yards away. I shot twice, and, once again, the recoil from the second shot made me fall on my back into the mud, and I had to scramble to get up and try to fire again. All four of my shots had missed the target completely. I swore under my breath.

"No, I'm not, Nora," I said, feeling the dampness from the mud seeping into my uniform. "I'm just hopeless. Have you seen Tatiana handle a gun? She was running through the paper Nazi course and hit every single one coming at her."

"You heard them: we're not even going to be carrying guns over there. You'll never have to shoot. Anyway, Lieutenant Faraday told me to come and find you. He's giving a final training on the wireless for the few of us who could use some help, and he asked for you to come and assist. I think he wants you to help me specifically, speaking of hopeless."

"Happy to," I said. "I could use the boost to my ego after missing this damn target more times than I hit it."

We went up to the main house to one of the drawing rooms that had been converted into an SOE training classroom. It was a stunning space with vaulted ceilings and a stone fireplace. When we arrived, Lieutenant Faraday didn't even see us, as he was leaning over Tatiana and her wireless radio, trying to walk her through instructions.

Faraday, one of the officers in charge of the training program and a favorite among the women trainees, was in his fifties, with weathered skin and silver hair cut close to his scalp.

The half dozen female trainees in the room were wearing head-phones and concentrating on the wireless radio sets in front of them. The radio sets consisted of coiled masses of wires, dials, and plugs in inconspicuous brown leather suitcases. They also included tiny quartz crystals used to set the radio frequency and an aerial and ground wire. The sets weighed forty-five pounds each, which made them awkward to transport, though it would be necessary at times in order to avoid detection.

While I had no discernible knack for shooting firearms or blowing up railways, after just two weeks of training, operating the wireless felt like second nature to me. This had been an enormous relief, as sending intelligence and receiving orders via wireless would be my main role with the Druids network. I could transpose Morse code into the cipher required for radio transmission at a rate of twenty-five words per minute, the fastest of all the trainees.

The ciphers were poem codes—based on verse written by Leo Evans, our brilliant young cryptographer in charge of wireless training. We were each given an original poem that we had to memorize as the underlying base for our ciphers, which were written on a silk handker-chief that could be easily hidden in our hair or clothing. I found the coding and decoding reminded me of the word games I'd loved as a child.

When tested by my instructor, I was able to quickly create a schedule, or "sked"—of days and times to send messages—and I kept the transmissions to less than ten minutes every time. The receivers in England would expect me to keep this schedule.

The only part of operating the wireless that did not come naturally to me at all was waiting for the replies. It tested my patience. I had considered taking up smoking because the waiting could be so agonizing.

In training, our coded messages were sent to Station 53 in Buckinghamshire, one of four receiving stations in England, where young women FANYs wore headphones and sat at wireless receivers awaiting messages from agents scattered all across Europe. They would jot down the chirps of the signals on paper and take them to the FANY cipher clerks to be decoded. Then the text would be read by either the SOE or OSS in London, and the answers would be coded and sent back.

I was warned that replies would often take more than an hour, which seemed like a torturous amount of time to wait while hiding in the occupied zone. The Germans now had trucks roaming the streets of Paris, packed with sophisticated detection equipment to pinpoint the sources of signals sent on frequencies not used by their own radio operators. Being a wireless operator was becoming a more dangerous job by the day.

"Ah, Anna, thank you for coming," Faraday said when he looked up. "Will you please sit with Nora and, um, help her in any way you can?"

Nora's back was to him, so he raised his eyebrows and gave me a doubtful look, like she might be beyond help.

I dragged a chair over to Nora's desk and sat down next to her.

"They are never going to let me go. I'm terrible at the wireless," Nora whispered to me, her eyes filled with worry.

"Nonsense. They need you—they need all of us—and you'll figure it out," I whispered back, not knowing if it was true. "And you'll probably be assigned as a courier anyway. You just need to be good enough for them to pass you in training."

"Anna, thanks for coming to help out," Leo Evans said. He was skinny with spiky hair and large ears. He kept tugging at his hair at the top of his forehead, so now it was sticking straight up in the air. "Nora just informed me she will not lie to the Germans if she's caught and forced to transmit under duress. When they force her, possibly torture her, to transmit, she will not use a fake security check to let us know she's in danger."

If caught and forced to operate the wireless under duress, agents all had a "bluff" check that only London knew about—it would be a warning that would come before the agent's true check.

"Okay . . . Nora, why won't you do that?" I looked at her, frowning. "If you're in danger . . ."

"I won't do that because it would be a lie, and it doesn't feel right to me, because lying is against my religion," Nora said, crossing her arms. Leo looked at me like he was about to lose his mind.

"How is being a spy, living a lie, all right with you, but using a fake security check is not?" Leo said. "I am just trying to understand your logic . . ."

"Me too . . . What the heck are you going to do if you're caught?" I asked. Leo was pacing in front of us, looking at Nora as if she had lost her mind.

"I've already thought about that, and I'm just not going to transmit anything for them, no matter what," Nora said, her face stoic.

Leo swore under his breath and put both hands on his head and looked up at the ceiling.

"Anna, this is madness, please help me convince her," he said, pleading. Then, as he looked back at Nora with compassion in his eyes, I realized he was smitten with her. "There is nothing wrong with lying about a damn security check. If you don't . . . you could be tortured, Nora."

I leaned on the desk, squeezing the bridge of my nose, trying to think.

"How about this?" I said. "What if Leo gives you a new, top secret security bluff, one that *only* the two of you know. Would it feel less like outright lying then? Because then it's technically just a secret that nobody else knows about but you two?"

Nora had uncrossed her arms, thinking about it. "All right, I guess that would be better," she answered.

"Brilliant, Anna," Leo said, throwing a fist in the air in triumph. He ran over to get paper and scribbled down a new security check, making sure I couldn't see it. He also gave her a two-page list of messages to encode, advising me to help her with them but "not too much." Nora worked through the list, using the silk handkerchief that listed her ciphers based on a lovely poem Leo had written for her that was far more sentimental than the limerick he had written for me. Though she was slow, she was able to get them done with only a little assistance from me.

I brought the first page of the list over to Leo while Nora continued to work on the second half. Leo grabbed them from me and sat down to review.

"Damn," Leo said in a quiet voice so Nora couldn't hear. "I was hoping she'd repeat all her old mistakes so I could write her a bad report to possibly keep her from going into the field. They're all correct so far."

"I thought they were, but I wanted you to double-check," I said.

"She's not cut out for this at all, is she? What was that nonsense about not wanting to lie?" Leo looked up at me, conflicted.

"I have no idea. Nora is an enigma sometimes."

"You're going to Paris. I wish there was a way you could look out for her. There's something vulnerable about her that doesn't suit this life. I'm not sure what they were thinking."

"They still might not let her go," I said. "She's terrified of most of the weapons, and she's been told by more than one instructor that she still offers up way too much information when questioned."

"Oh, they'll send her," Leo said, sitting back in his chair, watching Nora across the room with her elbows on the desk, rubbing her forehead as she worked through the messages. "I know you all are nervous about these evaluations tomorrow, but unless someone has completely cocked it up—and I don't think any of you have—you're going. We're desperate for organizers, couriers, and wireless operators over there, but especially operators. Right now, we're down to two wireless operators for all of France."

"Oh, I didn't realize things were that dire," I said, my worries about being kept back lifting a little.

"Oh yes," Leo said. "Still, if she's meant to be a proper agent? Then I'm Winston Churchill."

"She's with a different network there. That's all I know."

None of us were allowed to share details with each other about what we would be doing once we were in the field. I only knew Tatiana and Nora would be in Paris because Violet had told me, so if our paths did cross there, I wouldn't acknowledge that I knew them.

"Leo," I said, "if there's any way I can look out for her over there, I will."

"Thank you," he said, giving me a grateful smile. "I'd just like to take her out for a pint when all of this is over, you know?"

"Yes," I said, smiling back. "I'll go check to see if she's done with the rest of the list."

"Good." He nodded. "Pray she hasn't gotten a single one right."

# Chapter Seventeen

That night, after dinner with the rest of F Section and a cold shower, I fell into my bed exhausted, dropping off to sleep as soon as my head hit my pillow. Sometime after midnight, I awoke to loud shouting and footsteps in the hall outside my bedroom door. When I sat up to turn the light on my nightstand on, three uniformed men burst into my room, shouting in German.

*"Raus! Raus! Achtung!"*

A blinding light was shoved in my face, making it difficult to see, and I could smell cigarette smoke and musk and sweat. The quilt was stripped from my bed, and two of the men grabbed me and lifted me up by the elbows, squeezing so hard I cried out in pain. I caught a glimpse of their uniforms in the darkness—greenish gray, with braided lightning bolts on their collars—and recognized them as the Nazi secret police, otherwise known as the Gestapo.

They forced me to put my hands on my head and escorted me down the staircase through the darkened hallways of the grand house. I was barefoot and wearing only my pajamas, so before we even stepped outside, I was shivering, from either the cold night air or the terror I felt. Possibly both. There was not a soul in sight as we walked across a frosted field to one of the smaller cottages on the property.

Another uniformed officer opened the door of the darkened cottage, and I was shoved into a chair in the kitchen. I heard a click and winced at the brilliant spotlight directed at my face, making it difficult to see my captors' faces. There had to be at least eight or nine of them. My hand shook uncontrollably as I held it up to my face to try to block the light.

"*Du wurdest erwischt. Wie lautet dein Name?*"

The officer leaning against the wall at the back of the kitchen shouted this in loud, awkward German, informing me that I had been caught and asking my name. I felt my body relax and blinked back tears of relief when I recognized the officer's voice as none other than Lieutenant Harold Faraday. The SS officers that had escorted me were two of the Beaulieu's groundsmen.

*Get ahold of yourself, Anna. This is a drill, a test—nothing more.*

"My name is Anna Cav . . ." I made my first mistake as soon as I opened my mouth. I closed it, took a deep breath, and started over, reciting my new name and cover story, in perfect French.

"My name is Alexine Chauffour. I grew up in Saint-Malo. I came to Paris to stay with my cousin Madeleine Chauffour because she promised me a job working with her."

"What does your cousin do?" another "SS officer," otherwise known as Vincent Philby, asked.

"She is a translator and one of the top staff persons for the French industrialists' syndicate. Their offices are on Rue Saint-Augustin."

"Where do you live in Paris?"

"We are currently living in a student hostel at 93 Boulevard Saint-Michel until we can find better accommodations."

"Why is your cousin living at a hostel if she is from Paris? Does she not have a family home?"

"She does. Her family's home, my uncle Remy and my aunt Corrine's home, is on Avenue Foch. When *les boches* . . . ," I stuttered. *Ugh.* "When the Germans took it over, they went to their villa in the South, in Aix-en-Provence. My cousin stayed behind for the job."

It was my second slipup of the night. Tatiana had been referring to the Germans as *les boches*, an unflattering French slang expression for them. I didn't know the French I needed to express that the Germans were appropriating private homes for their own use. I cursed silently, knowing I should have expected that question.

The small kitchen filled up with cigarette smoke, the brilliant light never left my face, and the questions were fired at me in constant, rapid succession from the different "Gestapo officers" in the room as I struggled to stay focused. My mouth was parched, but I knew asking for a glass of water was out of the question. I was disoriented and exhausted, and I lost track of time. It felt like I had been sitting there for hours but couldn't know for sure.

"What are the names of your parents?"

I opened my mouth, started to speak, and closed it. I froze for a moment, realizing I had nearly just blurted out "Dick and Deidre Shannon." I could feel my usual mental acuity slipping. Their tactics were working. How much longer were they going to make me do this? Hadn't I proven myself yet?

"My parents are Albert and Louise Chauffour," I said in French. Then I closed my eyes, and, without realizing it was happening, I nodded off for a second, my head dipping to my chin. One of the "SS officers," a groundsman, slammed a wooden spoon on the table to wake me up, and I nearly got whiplash jerking upright in my chair. The spoon broke in half, the top of it bouncing off the table and onto the tile floor.

"I'm sorry," I said, still speaking in French, holding my arms over my face, covering my eyes from the spotlight. I continued to speak in loud, frustrated French. I was short-tempered from exhaustion and done with this charade. They had made their point, and I think I had proven myself up to the task. "Are you not satisfied with my performance? For God's sake, it's starting to get light outside. How much longer is this going to last?"

No one said a word for a few seconds, then the spotlight was shut off, and Faraday walked up to the table and sat across from me, clearly not amused at my outburst. He nodded to the rest of the men in the room, thanked them for their participation, and instructed them to leave. I heard one of the men leaving comment, "Of course the American would call bollocks."

Crossing his legs, Faraday lit a cigarette, and neither of us spoke until everyone had filed out. He placed his Gestapo officer's visor cap on the table. A chill ran through me now that I saw the silver skull on its brim up close.

"Well, that's one way to end a critical training exercise, isn't it?" Faraday said to me, eyebrows raised, his voice calm but irritated.

"I'm . . . I'm sorry," I said, shivering again, because now that everyone was gone the cottage felt drafty. "It was just, I knew it was all of you, and you *knew I knew*, and it seemed absurd to keep going on for hours longer. What more did you need from me?"

"I needed you to finish the exercise and not question it. I need you to do what needs to be done to complete your training," he said, his voice tight. "I'm disappointed in you. Do you think this is all a bloody game, Anna? Every agent candidate must go through this mock arrest and interrogation. These are the kinds of things that could save your life."

I thought of Violet Banks's pointed advice about following instructions and silently groaned, because now I knew she had been referring to this.

"I know," I said. "And I do not think this is a game—far from it. I shouldn't have done that. Please don't say this is going to keep me from going into the field. I am counting the days. I am sorry I interrupted the exercise that way; it was inappropriate and wrong."

He took a drag of his cigarette and studied my face. His expression was somewhere between wholly irritated and mildly amused. He blew out a trail of smoke and sighed.

"I know you must be knackered," he said, his tone softer now. "Go get yourself sorted and get something to eat. Miss Banks and I will see you in a couple of hours for your evaluation, and we'll discuss everything then."

I thanked him and got up to go, desperate for warm clothes and a glass of water. As I opened the door to the cottage, Faraday put a green wool military blanket on my shoulders, and I wrapped it around myself as I tiptoed barefoot across the field as fast as my freezing, dirty feet could carry me.

~

When I got back to the main house, I ran into Tatiana in the hallway outside my bedroom. She looked me up and down and gave me a sympathetic nod.

"Ah, you've finished your interrogation, I see," she said in a whisper. It was still before six in the morning. "Mine was three nights ago. How did it go? Are you feeling okay?"

"I will be after a change of clothes and some coffee."

I told her what had happened, and when I got to the part where I asked if we could end it, she burst out laughing.

"*Sacrebleu!* Did you really do that?" she said, her hands over her mouth. "Good for you. I wish I had. It got to be ridiculous after four hours."

"Yes, but I was an idiot to say it out loud," I said. "Faraday was not happy. All I had to do was go along with it. My evaluation is in a little over two hours, and now I'm more nervous than ever that they're going to hold me back from going."

"Nonsense," Tatiana said. "Go get some real clothes on. I'm cold just looking at you. And good luck."

After I had taken a quick, cold shower, washed the mud off my feet, and put on a clean uniform, I felt human again. I grabbed a slice of bread and jam for breakfast, even though my stomach was queasy with anticipation of my evaluation.

The door to Lieutenant Faraday's office was open when I arrived. He was talking to Violet Banks.

"I will take her out for a quiet lunch," Violet said. "I'll tell her there is no shame in stepping back now and that nobody needs to know."

My heart sank.

"And if she refuses to step back?" Faraday said. "She's mediocre with the wireless, isn't she? She can't shoot and is terrified of weapons of any kind. Taylor described her as 'not overburdened with brains.'"

I didn't think I was mediocre with the wireless, but I definitely couldn't shoot. If they were talking about me, better to just get it over with.

"Hello?" I knocked on the open door to Faraday's office, my cheeks burning.

"Anna, come in," Violet said to me with a polite but not particularly warm expression on her face. Violet was meticulously dressed, per usual, in a well-tailored brown tweed suit and sensible shoes, her chestnut hair in a low bun.

"Have a seat," Faraday said. On the oversize, intricately carved desk in front of him there was a file with my name on it, marked *OSS*.

I sat on the opposite side of the desk in a high-backed red velvet cushioned chair, next to Violet, who was sitting in its twin.

"Well," Violet said, looking at me, arms crossed, "I think we should start with the interrogation drill last night."

Faraday nodded, handing her my folder.

"A couple of missteps: speaking English at the start of it and referring to the Germans as *les boches* might get you shot. But the worst part, of course, is what happened at the end, isn't it?"

"I apologized afterward, and I'll say it again: I'm sorry," I interrupted. "I shouldn't have ended the drill like that. I was tired and not thinking clearly. I'll learn from it."

"Yes, well, you'll have to," Violet said. "As Faraday told you, this isn't a game. You're supposed to be dropped into a war zone a few days from now. We're trying to train you to give you the skills to stay alive."

I paused, considering my words, and then I said what I'd been thinking since I arrived at Station 31.

"With all due respect, they *might* save my life, and I appreciate all of the training I have received," I said. "But can we be honest? None of us really knows what's going to work, do we? Because this war is the first time this has ever been done—sending women undercover into enemy territory. There's no training manual. The instructors, the trainees—we're all making it up as we go along. In the end, it's a giant leap of faith."

Faraday and Violet looked at each other.

"Now let me ask you," Faraday said, "should we, meaning the SOE and OSS, put our faith in you? Should I report to General Donovan and Edgar Huntington that you are prepared and well-suited to go?" He thumbed through the folder that Violet had passed back to him. "You can't shoot worth a damn, and your defiance at the end of interrogation is troubling. You've also been described as 'rather impatient at times.'"

He paused, still reading. I just sat there, holding my breath.

"But on a positive note, you've been described as a 'brilliant' wireless operator. One of your instructors says that you are 'always decisive, with an analytic mind' and that you form 'good relationships with others' though you are sometimes 'prone to perfectionism and self-reproach.'"

I felt the tension drain from my shoulders at his praise for my wireless abilities, because now I knew they hadn't been talking about me before I knocked. And the instructors' evaluations were pretty spot-on. Faraday and Banks were both looking at me, waiting for me to respond.

"I swear I have learned my lesson from the interrogation. And no, I can't shoot a gun; that is very true," I said, biting my lip. "But I won't need a gun to blend in as a Frenchwoman, which is the most critical aspect of this job. And I can be impatient, but I think I am prepared. And I'm comfortable operating the wireless," I said. "I've been told more than once that I'm the best wireless operator in this training group."

My words hung in the air, and I prayed they would let me go.

"As Faraday and I have discussed at length, we need you in the field now. We simply do not have time to shape you all into perfectly trained agents, if there is such a thing . . . ," Violet said.

"Okay," I said, waiting for the "but."

"Follow orders and the protocols you've been taught, but also trust your instincts, because overall they seem to be good," she continued. "And I see you've formed some fast friendships here. Women bond quickly in these strange circumstances."

"That's true," I said. I was grateful for my new friends, though I found myself missing my parents, my sisters, and my friends from home even more than when I had first arrived. I longed for my talks with Mary in my garden, my lunches with Irene and Julia, even my mother's nagging. The homesickness hit me at unexpected times. It would help to see Irene in London and to reunite with Josette.

"I know your friendship with the spy Amniarix, Josette Rousseau, will be an asset," Violet said, as if reading my mind. She accepted a cigarette from Faraday and leaned over as he lit it for her. "But I would discourage you from getting romantically involved with anyone."

"You don't mean with a German officer? Never. Not in a million years," I said, horrified at the thought and thinking of Cynthia. It had clearly worked well for her; she had seduced Brousse and many more men before him. But trading sex for secrets was not something I could ever imagine doing myself.

"No, I wasn't referring to the German officers, though it wouldn't be unheard of. Some female agents use 'Mata Hari' games, as they're called," Violet said. "I was referring to affairs with other Resistance fighters. Romantic attachments in the field can cloud your judgment. Things can get . . . messy."

What was she saying? There was nothing to know about Henri. And then I thought perhaps they knew about Phillip; that would be more likely. In any case, I felt my face growing warm.

"Understood. No romance in Paris," I said, holding my hands up. This made them both smile.

"It is a hardship in the City of Love," Faraday said with sarcasm. "You'll go to London on Sunday for two nights to get everything you need from the OSS's Cover and Documentation group. I understand you'll be staying with a friend, so no accommodations needed?"

"Yes, Irene Nolan, a friend from the DC office, is now in London," I said, exhaling with relief. We were moving forward.

"Perfect. As you know, our plans are dictated by the moon, or Charlotte, as we refer to it in intelligence documents. Tuesday evening looks to be clear and crisp—a very pregnant Charlotte will be making an appearance—and that's when you're scheduled to fly. I'll arrange a driver to take you to RAF Tangmere on the evening of December 22," Violet said.

"Thank you, for everything," I said, standing up and shaking their hands. "I promise you I will take your feedback and do my best."

They were letting me go. I would be in France by this time next week. There were no more hoops to jump through, just my own inner demons to contend with, the "self-reproach" I was prone to. I got up to leave but realized I had a couple final questions for them.

"Josette's code name is Amniarix. What is mine?"

"Ah yes, excellent question. I was going to tell you before your departure from Tangmere, but since you've asked, it's Peacock," Violet said with a smile. "Like Amniarix, it's for the receiving stations that will be decoding your messages in London. They will know you only by this code name."

"Peacock . . . Why?" I asked, amused but frowning.

"Neither of us had anything to do with the choosing," Faraday said. "But it seems the higher-ups are partial to animal code names as of late."

"Okay, Peacock it is," I said. "And will anyone else in this training group be going with me on the twenty-second?"

"Yes, of course," Faraday said. "But exactly who that is remains to be seen."

# Chapter Eighteen

**London, England**
**December 20, 1942**

*11/2/42*

> *Dear Irene and Anna,*
>
> *My dear friends! I miss you and hope you are both well. I am not sure where you are in the world, Anna, so I am sending this to Irene in the hopes that she will share this letter with you at some point.*
>
> *Hello from far-flung Ceylon! I work nights and half days on Sundays, and while the work is incredibly tedious, there is much to love about being stationed here. One plus is the natural beauty of this area of the world. Oh, how I wish you could both see this place. It is absolutely to die for—just breathtaking and exotic in every possible way. Palm trees and tropical flowers and brightly colored birds and monkeys—monkeys!—and papaya trees.*
>
> *Also, I adore so many of the people stationed here. They are so interesting—biologists, engineers, cryptologists, and anthropologists from so many different countries.*

*There is a group of us that go out and try a new restaurant at least once a week—the spices are so unusual, and so many delicious new dishes. One of the members of this group is Paul Child, that friend of Huntington's I was supposed to introduce myself to. He is forty years old, short, and bald, with a mustache and nose that I wouldn't describe as handsome. I also don't care for mustaches—not that that matters, because he's far too old for me. He is in charge of visual development for the R&A department, and he calls himself an artist and a poet, a furniture maker and a Francophile. He is very sophisticated and a tad arrogant.*

*You would not even believe what I did yesterday. I went for a ride on an elephant! Yes, an elephant! I went with another gal stationed here. I had never even seen an elephant in real life before. They are majestic creatures, and it was one of the most glorious experiences of my life.*

*My dear friends, I miss you both very much, and I hope that this letter finds you well. Be safe and take care of yourselves in this crazy, dangerous "bubble" of wartime. I'm sure you are both working as hard as ever, but even if you can't go for an elephant ride, don't be afraid to seize other moments of joy when you can. In these dark times we have to embrace the moments of lightness, for after all, that's what will get us through.*

*With love, your dear friend—*
*Julia*
*Xoxo*

Irene put the letter down on the coffee table, next to the cream-colored wax candles we had just lit. Julia had sent it in early November, but Irene had just received it.

My train from New Forest had arrived at London's Paddington Station two hours earlier. I had spent the entire train ride writing letters home—a few to my parents, separate ones to Colleen and Bridget, and a couple more to both Mary and Julia. Irene would mail them for me after I left for France.

When I stepped off the train at the station, Irene and I had had a joyful, teary-eyed reunion on the crowded platform just as the air raid sirens' "all clear" signal sounded across the city. She had handed me my requisite helmet.

After a light British dinner of beans on toast at a quintessential English pub, we were sitting under wool blankets drinking tea on her sofa in her cozy, one-bedroom flat, in the Mayfair section of London, close to Hyde Park. I had shared only the broad details about training, showing her some of my scrapes and bruises and entertaining her with stories of our morning drills with Stanley Taylor. I told her of my friends and other instructors without mentioning any by name. It was a comfort to spend time with her before leaving for the Continent.

My last day at Beaulieu had been frenzied, with final briefings, packing up, and good-byes to friends, especially Tatiana and Nora, as well as the many instructors and staff, including the sweet cryptographer Leo Evans, who was heartbroken we were all leaving, or at least that Nora was leaving. I still did not know if either of my friends would be joining me on my moonlit flight to France, but I was hopeful that Tatiana might. It was still a question mark as to whether Nora would be allowed to go to the Continent at all.

"Ah, I miss Julia," I said, picking up the letter to reread it one more time. I pictured our ever-cheerful friend riding an elephant among the palm trees. "Especially her laugh."

"Me too. She had quite a bit to say about Paul Child, though he's 'not her type,'" Irene said, a look of amusement on her face as she sipped her tea. Even in her nightclothes she looked perfectly pulled together, with red slippers to match her plaid flannel pajamas, and her thick blonde hair in two identical braids. Warm pajamas and sheets were two of the things we had been instructed to bring from home. I was wearing flannel pajamas from home as well, although I was going to have to leave them here with Irene, as I'd be getting a whole new wardrobe for France.

"I noticed that," I said, smiling. "Why talk about him so much if he's really not your type?"

"Exactly. It's curious," she said. "Now back to you. Training's done and you're going into the field. You'll finally be in France in *two days*. Are you excited? Nervous? Do you feel ready?"

"I don't know if you could ever be totally prepared for something like this," I said. "I got the impression at training that the instructors realize that too. I'm nervous and excited and thrilled for this chance and just hope I don't screw up."

"Have you thought about what would happen if you got caught? Or worse?"

I shivered at the memory of interrogation night, the cold and utter terror when I was dragged out of bed, before I knew it wasn't real.

"I've thought about it . . . but then I've kind of tried to put that fear in a box in my mind—put it away—because if it consumes me, I'll be useless over there."

"I'm so proud of you, Anna. It's amazing. And no offense, but you've surprised me, doing this."

"No offense taken, and thank you. I've surprised myself," I said, sipping my tea and smiling at her. "I'm proud of both of us. You, moving to a new country by yourself? Now you need to tell me all about life in London . . ."

"Okay, but one more question first: Did you try to get in contact with Phillip Stanhope while you were at Beaulieu?"

"No," I said, sinking back on the couch and looking up at the ceiling, thinking of Phillip's eyes and our kiss the night he left. "I wrote a letter to tell him. One of the instructors heading to London could have dropped it off for me a couple of days ago, but I changed my mind and threw it away."

"Why? Don't you want to see him?"

"Yes? No?" I said, grimacing. "I want to, but then, what if he doesn't want to see me? What if he's got a sweetheart here?"

"I doubt he has a sweetheart, and think of Julia's philosophy," Irene said, pointing at the letter. "What exactly are you afraid of? Is it the fear of losing someone . . . again?"

She'd never been afraid to ask pointed questions.

"Honestly? No. With Connor it was over long before he left. When we got married, I still had dreams to pursue, but he made it clear he wanted me standing in his shadow, the dutiful wife and future mother to his children. The truth is, I'm not sure I want to see Phillip because I *do* care about him. If I see him, those feelings might get stronger. But I'm about to leave for the type of opportunity I've wanted quite literally my entire life, the type I wasn't able to pursue during my marriage. It's not the right time to get too attached . . . to anyone."

"Okay," Irene said. "But I still think you should try to see him and not overthink it. You care about him, and you're leaving, but that's the story of thousands of other people in this war."

"I'll sleep on it and decide in the morning," I said. "Enough about me, how has it been here for you?"

"It was an enormous adjustment at first," Irene said. "I was on the verge of tears at least once a day and could hardly sleep."

"Oh no," I said, surprised given how relaxed and serene she had seemed since I had arrived. "Were you very homesick?"

"That's the thing—that wasn't it at all," Irene said. "But getting used to living in what's essentially a war zone? The air raid sirens, the destruction, bringing a helmet everywhere you go—that made me a nervous wreck the first couple of weeks. That and the pressure of the job in Cover and Documentation. It's a terrible responsibility. One mistake could cost someone their life."

"Well then, please make sure you get mine right," I said, laughing, though I couldn't deny being nervous at the thought of the Gestapo arresting me because of a faulty identification card or British-made clothing tag.

"Oh, trust me, my friend, I am quadruple-checking everything for you. And the pressure is no longer getting to me. I'm feeling much better."

She took a cigarette out of the pack on the coffee table and shrugged. "It's like anything, though; after a while you adjust, because you have to. These Londoners? They are remarkable—their attitude and their courage. Much of their city is destroyed, many of the men are at the front, they have lived on a bland, barely sustainable diet of rationed food . . . and yet they get on with it and even manage to enjoy life once in a while."

"Americans have no idea how easy we've had it," I said, recalling my mother's recent complaints about the sugar rations. I paused for a moment. "You know I have to ask: Have you heard anything from Michael since you left?"

"Oh yes, Michael," she said, saying his name as if tasting something bitter. "I received a letter from him shortly after I arrived—very apologetic about his outburst the night of the going-away party. Telling me he didn't mean it when he said I shouldn't come back, begging me to work things out. Of course, mentioning the church and our parents too, to trigger my strong Catholic guilt."

"And . . . ?" I said. "What do you want?"

"I know for sure now that I don't want to go back. For me, it's over. I'm happier here than I have been at home for a very long time. I love living *alone*, believe it or not, not coming home to tension and bitterness."

"No, believe me, I understand," I said.

"And I really adore living in London. The work is fascinating, and the people in Cover and Documentation are all top-notch. You'll meet them tomorrow. David Bryant, the head of the OSS London? He's a fantastic guy, a few years older than us, played football at Princeton back in the day. Since it's so near Christmas, we're all planning on heading to a nearby pub at the end of the workday, so that will be fun . . ."

"That *will* be fun," I said. "I could tell you were doing well as soon as I saw you. There's a lightness about you, like a weight has been lifted."

"That's *exactly* how I feel. Now that I've decided what I want to do, and now that I'm here? It's a huge relief."

"But have you written him back to tell him?"

"Yes . . . I just haven't mailed it yet." She cringed when she said this.

"Irene, you've got to," I said.

"I know, I know. I'm just putting off the inevitable. I'll mail it after this week. With the full moon, there are seven evenings where the pilots leaving out of Tangmere have enough visibility to fly to the Continent and see the improvised landing zones without their lights on, so everyone in the OSS—and SOE—is working overtime through Christmas. On that note, we should really go to sleep. Busy day tomorrow."

With the mention of sleep, I couldn't help but let out a huge yawn.

"I could fall asleep on this sofa right now."

"Nonsense. I borrowed a decent mattress from the widow who manages this building. Let me get you settled."

# Chapter Nineteen

**December 21, 1942**

On Monday morning, we made the short walk from Irene's flat to the OSS headquarters in London, at 70-72 Grosvenor Street. It was a bland, five-story office building down the street from the US embassy, chosen for both its location and its inconspicuous facade. The first floor was Special Operations, Secret Intelligence, and Research and Analysis. The second floor housed Sabotage and Counterintelligence, also known as X-2, and the third was Communications and Propaganda. On the fourth floor were Country Units, assigned to collect intelligence that would support all the OSS missions into occupied Europe.

After Irene had given me a tour of the offices and introduced me to several of her new friends, we headed behind the headquarters building to the Cover and Documentation department, also known as C&D.

C&D was in a former residence, three stories high with leaded windows. The carved moldings and tiled fireplaces inside gave a hint of the elegant home it had once been before the war.

"So, this is the print shop for creating forged documents," Irene said, taking me inside a garage, its entire expanse filled with heavy presses. A sharp, sour smell of ink permeated the air. "Here we reproduce all sorts of counterfeit identification documents: perfect passports, workers' identification papers, ration books, and, in your case, your *Ausweis*, the identification card the Germans require in occupied France."

"Amazing," I said, running my hand over the cold metal of one of the presses.

"Isn't it? The whole operation is," Irene said, clearly proud of London's headquarters. "We've got retouch artists, photographers, and printers to create these documents and a whole team, including myself, that checks for inconsistencies. The engraving plant is in what used to be the kitchen. There's a fully staffed tailor shop in the attic, where we'll get you outfitted with an entire French wardrobe—either from clothes made here by our team or collected from refugees."

"Ah, this must be the famous Anna."

Two men walked into the garage. The one who had spoken, in an American accent, I guessed to be in his early thirties. He was broad shouldered, with thick dark hair and a cleft chin. He looked like an ex-football or ex-rugby player. The other man appeared to be around the same age, taller and thin, with dark-framed glasses that almost clashed with his white-blond hair.

"David," Irene said. Her whole face lit up at the sight of them—or rather *him*. And the huge smile on her face matched the ex-football player's, who I knew now must be David. "And Willie. Come over, you two, and meet Anna."

I shook hands with David Bryant, head of the OSS in London, and Willie Renick, director of the C&D department.

"Lovely to meet you both," I said, shaking their hands.

"And you as well," David said to me. "Welcome to OSS London. Willie here will be getting you everything you need. Along with Irene, of course. Please feel free to come see me if there's anything else I can do for you while you're here."

"Thank you. Irene's told me so much about you," I said, and Irene shot me a look because the only thing she'd told me was that he was an ex-football player.

"Did she now?" David said, pleased. "All good?"

"Of course all good," I said, nodding.

"And I'll see you both after work at the Running Horse pub tonight?" he asked, looking into Irene's eyes.

"Yes, of course," Irene said, her cheeks turning a bright pink.

*Uh-oh,* I thought, just as Willie Renick shot me a pointed look, as if he knew what I was thinking. I had noticed David was wearing a wedding ring when I shook his hand.

"So, Anna," Willie said, rubbing his hands together, "we will have your documents ready for you to review later today. We've even done up some new, fake transcripts from Sciences Po."

"And do you know what I'll be bringing for luggage?"

"We do," Irene said. "You'll have a worn French-made suitcase for your clothing and incidentals, as well as a small, battered brown leather suitcase, also made in Europe, to hold your wireless."

"Sounds good," I said. Something about the things I would carry with me to France made my arms break out in goose pimples. I had been so focused on getting through training, it was now sinking in that the following evening I'd be on a plane to France, reuniting with my old friends in such a strange and different capacity. The world had turned upside down since we had seen each other last. How would Josette feel about why I had returned? What would Henri be like now, and how would he react when he saw me? I kept trying to imagine life in Paris under occupation.

"Do you have any questions?" Willie asked.

"Yes, you have that look on your face I know too well, like you have a million of them," Irene said to me.

"No, honestly, though I know I will have some," I said.

"Well, good," Irene said. "Let's go grab a quick cup of what the English call coffee in the basement cafeteria next door, and then we'll head up to the attic to get you outfitted," Irene said. "We will see you this afternoon, Willie."

I thanked him, and we said our good-byes.

"So, David Bryant . . . ?" I said in a quiet voice after we had fetched our watery coffee and before we stepped back inside the rear building.

"Yes, he's been so helpful since I've been here," Irene said. "Probably the first friend I made."

"Irene, be careful there," I said, being as honest with her as she would be with me. "He's married, isn't he?"

She stopped walking and looked at me, blushing again.

"How did I think you of all people wouldn't notice?" she said. "I know he's married, and I promise you, nothing has happened between us, but I can't lie, not to you. I think he's handsome and charming and so smart. His wife, Alice, is back home in America working for an armory in Massachusetts. Things between them haven't been good for a long time—at least according to him. So . . . we have that in common."

"I just don't want you to end up hurt, that's all," I said.

"I know," she said, squeezing my hand. "Thank you. Now, let's get you looking like a shabby but fashionable Parisian student."

The "clothing depot" was up a steep, rickety staircase that led to the top floor. The attic was two large rooms with sloped ceilings. A half dozen women sat at sewing tables, some sewing by hand, others using machines, chatting with each other. A record player filled the room with soft music, and despite the stuffy quarters there was a feeling of warm camaraderie in the air as they glanced up from their work to greet us.

Every wall was lined with racks bursting with clothes. Sections had large signs above them, like "Farmer," "Clergy," and "Student."

"Gemma has been working on assembling your wardrobe," Irene said, introducing me to one of the women sitting at the sewing tables. She was in her late fifties with curly white hair, a round, soft face, and thick glasses.

"Pleasure to meet you, miss," Gemma said, her eyes crinkling when she smiled. "You'se one of the first ladies we've outfitted here, so it's been quite fun."

"Is that so?"

"For France, yes," Gemma said. "There was one other last year."

Gemma fetched a large box of clothes that was hidden by the "Student" section of the racks and brought it over.

"A bicycle will be your main form of transportation," Irene told me. "While some Frenchwomen dare to wear pants, you want to be discreet and blend in, so, among other things, Gemma has made you a couple of long wool split skirts, called *culottes*—basically pants disguised as skirts. You're going to have to try them on so that Gemma can hem them. You don't want to be tripping over yourself."

I spent the next couple of hours with Gemma and Irene going through the box of clothes, trying things on so Gemma could pin and hem them. There was a shabby navy-blue windbreaker that had come over with a refugee, a knee-length black-and-white polka-dot rayon dress with the zipper and hooks on the left side to look French-made. They had also found me one pair of shoes and one pair of boots, both with cork soles.

While they worked, the ladies of the C&D tailor shop entertained us with stories of their children and talked of their husbands away at war, always keeping an eye on the latest piece of clothing they were working on as they chatted. Gemma was a gifted seamstress, and she and Irene had put together a student wardrobe that was practical and discreet, shabby but with a hint of the understated elegance that all Frenchwomen seemed to possess, even poor university students. No detail was too small. Buttons were threaded in two parallel lines rather than crisscrossed, and labels that were the exact replicas of those of French clothing makers were stitched on with care.

"My mother gave up on teaching me how to sew," I said to Gemma as she pinned the polka-dot dress I was wearing. Irene had left me in Gemma's hands to take care of some other things in the office downstairs. "You're a marvel, Gemma."

Gemma blushed and waved her hand at me. "Oh, it's nothin' really, dear," she said. "Just takes practicin' and patience."

"True. I wasn't patient when I was learning, and neither was my mother," I said.

"Do you miss your mum? Your family?" Gemma asked. She was kneeling next to me, pins in her mouth, holding on to the dress hem and measuring how much length needed to be taken off.

I felt an ache in my chest when she asked. Since arriving in England, I'd done my best to keep my mind focused on what was ahead, on what I needed to learn. But feelings of homesickness ultimately washed over me sometimes, usually when I awoke in the middle of the night and let my mind wander to dark places. I would be spending my first Christmas away from my family as an American spy in Paris. I thought of my parents and Bridget and Colleen and Brad sitting around the fireplace at our house in Yarmouth, on Cape Cod, joking and laughing and playing board games, a safe, comfortable distance from the war that was raging on.

"Sometimes," I said. "But then I think about why I'm here and doing what I'm doing. It will be worth it. There will be other Christmases to spend with them."

She took her pins out of her mouth and looked up at me and smiled. "God willing," she said, her eyes sympathetic. "You're a brave young woman. Your parents should be very proud."

*If they actually knew what I was doing.*

It was hard to consider myself brave when all I had done so far was train and prepare.

I was about to reply to Gemma when the sound of Irene's voice echoed from the stairwell.

"Can someone please help? I have more honey biscuits from the cafeteria than I can carry."

Pippa, a shy young seamstress with dark-brown braids, ran to the stairs to take the biscuits off Irene's hands. She brought them over to a table in the corner of the room and placed them on a plate next to a large green teapot. The women took turns going downstairs to refill the pot with fresh tea over the course of the day.

"Ah, you look very French indeed," Irene said to me, nodding at the black-and-white polka-dot dress.

"Thank you. It's all thanks to Gemma's hard work," I said with a smile, and Gemma, pins back in her mouth, just waved her hand at me again like I was speaking nonsense.

"I just saw David, and he wanted me to pass on the message that you've been summoned to report to the SOE's F Section later this afternoon."

"Oh, did he say why?" I asked, frowning.

"He did not," Irene said, handing me a biscuit while Gemma finished up. "I'm guessing it has to do with your travel plans. You're to go to the flat in Orchard Court that F Section has been using. We'll arrange for someone to give you a ride over—it's just off Baker Street."

"Oh, okay," I said. "That makes sense."

"Are you nervous?" Irene asked, watching my face.

"No, not really. Well, maybe a little," I said. "More curious why they need to see me today."

"Well, after you're done, you can meet me at the pub as planned," Irene said. "We'll have a toast to Christmas together while we can."

# Chapter Twenty

Late that afternoon, a heavyset doorman with thick eyebrows, wearing a dark wool suit and black hat with silver trim, met me in front of the nondescript flat at Orchard Court, the base used by the SOE's F Section in London's West End. He greeted me as if he was expecting me but didn't ask my name, and I didn't volunteer it. We went through the gilded gates of the lift, and when we entered the second-floor flat, he ushered me into the black-and-white-tiled bathroom. It was small, and the enormous black bathtub and onyx bidet left little room to move. I looked at him, confused.

"Apologies, as it's a small flat, miss, isn't it? We've got no space for a waiting area," the doorman said. "If you'll please wait here, Miss Banks will see you in a few minutes."

"Oh, I didn't realize it was Violet Banks I was seeing. Thank you," I said.

He nodded and shut the door. I sat on the edge of the hideous tub and tried to guess what she wanted to discuss. Minutes later, I heard the door to the flat shut, and the doorman knocked and motioned me to follow him through the flat to what at one point must have been the bedroom but now was a simple office with a large oak desk and three chairs.

Violet Banks was sitting at the desk smoking a cigarette, wearing one of her signature tweed suits and smart-looking court shoes. She gave me a small, tired smile, and there were dark circles under her eyes that contrasted with the rest of her complexion, which was paler than usual.

"Anna, come in and have a seat please," she said.

"Is everything okay, Miss Banks?" I asked, trying to read her face, which was impossible. Had they changed their mind about sending me? "Are the plans still on for tomorrow night?"

"Yes, everything is going ahead as planned," she said. "And you will be pleased to know that I have arranged for Tatiana and Nora to be on the same flight to France that evening."

"Oh, thank you," I said. "That is great news."

"Yes, I thought you would appreciate that. You'll be landing in a field about one hundred miles southwest of Paris. Upon landing, all three of you will be taken to a nearby safe house, leaving separately for your assignments from there."

She paused and exhaled cigarette smoke.

"I know this probably goes without saying, but you are to have no contact with each other in Paris; it's far too dangerous. I'm aware of your concerns about Nora, of everyone's concerns about her, and while I share them, I spent a great deal of time with her toward the end of training, and I believe she is up to the task."

"Okay," I said, thinking of my friend, praying Miss Banks was right.

"Tatiana, we both know, is more than capable," she added, and I laughed at this because it was true. Of all the trainees, Tatiana seemed born for the role—fearless, but with an easygoing manner that made people like and trust her.

"Yes, I have no doubt Tatiana will do just fine," I said.

"We'll have you picked up at OSS headquarters tomorrow evening at seventeen hundred hours for Tangmere. At the base, you'll receive your wireless radio and some other critical gear and supplies."

There was a knock on the door. It was the doorman.

"He's here, ma'am," he said, peeking his head in the door, his expression pained. "I'd prefer to not make him wait in the lavatory."

"Perfect timing, Park. Yes, I would prefer you didn't either. Please bring him in." Then, turning to me, she said, "I think you have all the information you need from me. There's someone here who wants to see you before you leave for France."

*Phillip,* I thought, feeling my face redden and my heartbeat quicken in my chest. I turned to the door just as Park was opening it fully. My mouth dropped open at the sight of General Donovan, wearing a belted gray trench coat over his uniform.

"Well, hello, Anna," General Donovan said with a huge smile, amused at my shocked reaction. I jumped out of my chair, and he opened his arms and embraced me in a long, tight hug.

"I have to see to some other things at headquarters, so I'll leave you to meet in private. I know there's a few things General Donovan wants to discuss with you," Violet said. She was standing up and holding her purse, seemingly embarrassed by such overt American-style affection.

"Yes, thank you for taking such good care of her while she's been over here," Donovan said.

"It's been my pleasure, sir," she said, and I could tell she was sincere. "I will see you tomorrow evening, Anna."

"Oh, you'll be at Tangmere, too?" I said.

"Well, I have to see all of my girls off . . . even the American ones," she said, smiling, but there was worry in her eyes. "I wouldn't miss it."

After we said our good-byes and I shut the door, Donovan took his coat off, laid it on the back of Violet's chair, and sat down.

"It's quite a surprise to see you here, sir," I said.

"Yes, well, I have several meetings this week with Churchill, among others, but I wanted to make time to meet with you too."

"Thank you," I said. "It's an honor."

"Of course. We didn't get a chance for a proper good-bye in DC," he said. Then, clearing his throat, he got right to the point: "I received your training evaluation. It was positive overall, as you know. I understand your shooting abilities are lacking, but we aren't sending you in to be an assassin, so I'm not worried about that. They were unhappy with your disruptive behavior the night of the mock interrogation, as I'm sure you know."

"Yes, I know," I said with a sigh. "I'm really sorry about that. I was overtired and got too emotional."

"It was 'so very American of you,' was how I believe Faraday put it. Acting like a bit of a maverick is what I think he meant. You have to obey orders and follow plans when you're out in the field, but I'm not here to chastise you about things you already know."

"Okay," I said. "And I do know. Again, I'm sorry. So . . . why *are* you here?"

He leaned back in the desk chair and put his fingers together in a pyramid. "A few reasons, Anna. One, I will keep your father up-to-date, as I know you will not be able to write to your family for some time. And he asked me to deliver this directly to you." He reached behind him into his coat pocket and handed me an envelope.

"Thank you," I said, looking down at my father's familiar handwriting, imagining him sitting at his desk in Cambridge, cigar in one hand, pen in the other as he wrote to me. "Does he have any idea what I'm really doing here?"

"As you are well aware, your father is no fool," Donovan said. "And he's been able to glean enough information from various sources in the papers, from myself, and from other friends in the government to understand more than most about the OSS's mission. We talked before I left, and of course he pressed me for answers about your assignment over here. He's well aware that the work of the OSS is clandestine. He knows you're working out of the London office, but given your language skills, he guessed you might be doing more than just office work during your time abroad."

"I see," I said with a sigh. My father *wasn't* a fool. I knew before I left that he was suspicious about what I'd really be doing in Europe. "For what it's worth, I have written several letters, and I'm leaving them with Irene to mail to my parents at intervals, so they'll hopefully worry a little less."

"Ah, that was wise—thinking like an agent." He pointed to me, pleased.

"I thought so, thanks."

"The other reason I'm here." He paused, his eyes studying me, serious and caring.

"Yes?" I asked, knowing by the look on his face whatever it was wasn't good.

"We've just confirmed that French Resistance members were executed by the Nazis at the end of November. We are still trying to find out the exact details and the identities of those killed, but we believe some SOE agents were among them. And we know at least one wireless operator was in the group."

I swore under my breath, and a chill went through me. Now I knew why Violet had looked stressed and exhausted.

"My thoughts exactly," Donovan said, leaning forward. "Anna, you need to understand, the casualty rate for wireless operators now? It's even higher than when we first discussed this role. The Brits are saying the average life expectancy for wireless operators is . . . six weeks. *Six weeks.* The Germans have become very adept at tracking down signals in their trucks; you will have to be extremely careful about where you transmit and when. You can't be careless; you can't be a maverick."

"Sir, now that I've been here, I promise you, I understand that more than ever," I said.

He paused, looking at me. I sat and waited for him to speak.

"I'm giving you one more chance to change your mind," he said.

"No. Absolutely not," I said, shaking my head.

"You could stay here in London and work at headquarters. There is no shame in not going."

"No," I said, trying not to sound rude, but I was frustrated now. "Sir, I've made it this far. I'm going to France. Does Violet Banks know we are having this conversation?"

"Yes," he said. "She would have talked with you about it herself if I hadn't come to town."

"I'm not changing my mind because of the danger. Have you ever changed your mind about anything because of the danger?"

He looked up at the ceiling and let out a deep breath. "No," he said. "And I knew this would be your reaction."

"I can do this," I said, pleading with him. It was just like our conversation in DC, although this time the stakes were even higher. It was on the eve of the day I was supposed to leave, and I knew he could make the call—he could order me to stay in London, and that would be that. I decided to put everything I was feeling out there, to try to make him understand how much this role meant to me.

"I will *not* get caught," I said. "I won't. I can't begin to tell you how good it feels to be recognized for being smart and talented at something. I have thought about this more than I can say. What if this is what I'm meant to do? What if all my life has been leading to this, so that I can contribute to putting an end to this war in some small way? My late husband, Connor . . . Everyone always talked about his brilliance, how he was 'destined' for great things. Everywhere we went. It was so . . . annoying, since I'm being completely honest here. Because the truth is, I was—I am—at *least* as smart as he was, but nobody except maybe my best childhood friend, Mary, had expectations for me beyond being Connor Cavanaugh's wife. Even my own mother, for God's sake."

He nodded, fingertips on his lips as he watched me, thoughtful.

"Please," I said, realizing I was begging but beyond caring. "I want to do this for my country. But I need to do this for myself."

Another pause, and I held my breath, waiting for his answer.

"Okay, Anna Cavanaugh. You've once again made your case," he said. "I didn't think you'd change your mind, but I wanted to give you the chance. You've got creativity and smarts—more than most. That goes far in the field when you're living in the fog of war and making it up as you go along. We're all amateurs at this kind of guerrilla warfare, even the Brits, despite what they say."

"Yes," I said, on the edge of my seat, thrilled that I had his blessing. "I've realized that since training."

"And now that we're both being completely honest? I wish you weren't so capable, because then I'd have a real reason to hold you back. My only reservation, aside from your mock interrogation rebellion, is that I can tell from the report and my own observations that, at certain times, you doubt yourself. Maybe it's because you spent some time in someone else's shadow? But I can tell you there's no time for that in the field."

"Yes, sir," I said.

"I'm sure you can overcome that," he said. "I've sent several women to the Continent, but with the exception of Pauline Wakefield, you're one of the first women the OSS is sending into occupied France, because of your personal connections with the spy Amniarix and the Druids network. So I'm letting you go, and now you *really* can't let me down."

He smiled.

"I promise you, I won't."

"I know you won't. One thing to remember: the Allies are particularly interested in what new secret weapons the Krauts are building. This remains a blind spot for us, and it's frustrating as hell."

"Okay, weapons blind spot. Anything else?"

"I know you learned this in training, but I have to say it: anything you hear on that front, anything that seems remotely important, you need to get it to London right away, through wireless if possible, or through the network of safe letter boxes throughout Paris. However you can."

"Got it."

"And now, a little going-away present."

He reached into his trench coat and pulled out a small black velvet box.

"What is this?" I said as he placed the box in front of me on the desk. "If this is a going-away present, that means you knew I would still want to go."

"Oh yes," he said, laughing. But then his face got serious. "It belonged to Patricia. I bought it for her on a trip to Paris years ago. You'll see why I want you to have it."

I opened the box and gasped. Inside was a gold-plated peacock brooch, resting against the velvet interior. The peacock's body was a brilliant blue enamel, its gold-plated wings adorned with sparkling rhinestones and blue and emerald gems.

"A peacock, like my code name. It's lovely," I said, smiling and rubbing the wings with my finger, moved that he would give me a pin that had belonged to his late daughter.

"It's not expensive—costume jewelry, really—so it's appropriate for a Parisian college student to own," he said. "Obviously, you'll have to wear it with discretion over there. In other words, never wear it when you are working undercover with the Germans."

"Understood. And thank you," I said, holding it up to the light to admire the stones.

"Patricia loved peacocks for some reason," he said, his voice soft. "In Catholicism, peacocks represent renewal. In Buddhism, they symbolize wisdom and long life. Even if you can't wear it often, I thought you should have it. For luck."

"I will cherish it," I said, feeling my own voice catch. "Thank you for giving me this opportunity."

I walked around to the other side of the desk and hugged him.

"Just keep yourself alive, for the love of God," he said in my ear before we both pulled away. "Or your father will kill me."

"I'll do my best," I said with a small laugh, wiping my eye.

He looked at his watch and grabbed his trench coat.

"Sir, I'm meeting Irene and some other folks at the pub. Care to join us for a quick pint?"

"I wish I could, but I've got a date with the prime minister," he said with a groan. "He's in a nasty mood, so say a prayer for me."

"Will do," I said, laughing.

He was already at the door. After all, Prime Minister Winston Churchill was expecting him.

"And Anna?" He turned and looked me in the eye. "Please do take care."

"I will, sir. Thank you again. For everything."

# Chapter Twenty-One

*11/29/42*

*My dear Anna,*
*Of course, I was initially upset when you informed us*
*of your decision to go abroad with the OSS, as the news*
*was a shock to your mother and me. I've since talked to*
*Donovan at length, and while I am still not happy about*
*your decision to go, I do understand it much more than*
*when we said good-bye.*

*Having only daughters, I thought I would be spared*
*seeing one of my children go off to war. My memories of*
*the dangers and tragedies of my time as an officer in the*
*Great War are still raw, still fresh, even after all these*
*years. I can only pray that you stay safe and that your own*
*experiences overseas are different than mine.*

*As I write this, I'm looking at the huge oak tree in*
*the backyard, the one that used to hold your beloved tree*
*house. Do you remember the summer you were seven,*
*when you stayed up in that tree house, insisting it was*
*your pirate ship? You'd drag the atlas up there and map*
*your imaginary journeys through every ocean in the*

*world. Your yearning for an adventurous life was obvious even when you were young.*

*I thought that a year in Paris would satisfy your wanderlust, though I had my doubts. And then when you came home and married Connor, I imagined the two of you might travel the world together, and I'm sorry that wasn't to be.*

*A parent's first instinct is to protect their children and keep them safe—yes, even when they are grown women. But now, after all you've been through, I need to balance that instinct with my wish to see you follow your dreams, because you deserve to do that. I don't want to protect you from the life you're destined to lead.*

*You are so very bright, Anna, I'm not sure you even understand what you are capable of accomplishing. I'm sorry if I haven't told you that enough. In our conversations in the past year, I have sensed your restlessness and desire to do more. Now Donovan has given you this opportunity, and while I will worry the entire time you are gone, I also couldn't be prouder of you.*

*Stay safe, my dear, and please send letters whenever you can. Donovan has also promised to keep me updated. I know you will do great things, and I hope you find the kind of big, adventurous life you've always wanted.*

*Love,*
*Father*

I reread the letter from my father one more time before putting it in my coat pocket, feeling a mixture of warmth at his pride and that now-familiar ache of homesickness as I walked through the streets of London. He had written it the day after I left the US, and I was so grateful to have received it before leaving for France. I arrived at the

Running Horse pub at dusk. The London night air was cold, the sky clear and filled with stars. I could see through the window that the pub was packed with patrons, clusters of them spilling out onto the street, standing at high tables, smoking cigarettes and drinking bottles of beer. London was a melting pot thanks to the influx of Allied soldiers, and the pub reflected that with the number of men in American and Australian military uniforms.

A young soldier opened the door for me, and I braced myself as I navigated my way through the smoky, sweaty sea of people, searching for Irene. It was one of the oldest pubs in London, with a dark wood interior and checkered tile floor, which was sticky under my shoes thanks to spilled beer. A British soldier at the end of the bar was playing an accordion, and the crowd in the corner near him was singing along to Christmas carols.

I finally spotted Irene squeezed into a booth at the back of the pub with a group of friends I recognized from C&D. David Bryant was seated right next to her, knee to knee. Irene was laughing at something a raven-haired girl named Florence was saying, and David just kept looking at Irene with complete adoration. I was once again struck by how much more relaxed Irene was here, how happy she seemed, despite the war. It was obvious that her marriage had been weighing her down at home. But there was the uneasy truth that she was still married, as was David, and she was going to have to deal with that sooner rather than later.

Saying "Excuse me" every few seconds, I had almost reached the table when I felt someone grab my elbow and whisper in my ear. "Excuse me, are you the American OSS agent Anna Cavanaugh?"

A warmth washed over me at the sound of the familiar voice with the posh British accent, and I whipped around to find myself nose to nose with Phillip, looking into his eyes. I broke into a smile and gave him a hug, even happier to see him than I imagined I could be.

"You're here," I said, breathless, my face flushed from the heat of the room and his presence. It was a surprise to see him in a British Army uniform, and he looked more handsome than I remembered.

"Well, yes, darling, it is my hometown," he said.

"Did you know I would be here?"

"I hope you won't be angry at Irene if I admit that, yes, I was informed that you would be here. And once I knew, nothing could stop me from seeing you."

I turned and saw Irene watching us. She mouthed, "Are you mad?"

I shook my head and mouthed, "Thank you," and she gave an exaggerated wipe of her brow to show her relief.

"Follow me," Phillip said. "There's a table by the window opening up. Let's try to snag it before those chaps that have their eyes on it get there first."

I gave Irene a quick wave, and she held up her beer bottle and toasted me. Phillip took my hand in his, and it was as if no time had passed since we'd said good-bye in DC. It felt so natural, it made my heart ache. I had truly missed him.

We were able to get the table by the window, and I was relieved it was far away from the carol singers.

The waitress brought us two bottles of beer from the bar, and Phillip sat across from me, reaching for my hand, and, for a minute, we were content to just sit there, holding hands across the table, delighted to be in each other's company for this short time. I took a deep breath and tried not to think about the future or the past.

"You look smashing, Anna," Phillip said in a soft voice. "I'd almost forgotten how gorgeous you are."

"You're being far too kind. Or maybe you've already had too much to drink?" I said, laughing, feeling my cheeks glowing red. "I feel bedraggled, to be honest. It's been a long day. If I'd known you were going to be here, I would have at least changed my dress."

I smoothed out my plain suit dress and ran my fingers through my curls, self-consciously trying to tame them.

"Not too much to drink at all. I got here right before you," he said.

"Phillip, I'm so sorry I didn't contact you myself," I said. "I realize how foolish it was not to. It's wonderful to see you."

"I understand why you didn't, truly," he said. "You're here until when? The twenty-sixth or the twenty-seventh?"

"I leave tomorrow," I said. He looked into my eyes, both of us wistful.

"Ah, even sooner than I thought," he said, holding my hand even tighter. "And I have to report to a base in the Midlands tomorrow. I'll be there overnight. I thought I would at least see you once more when I got back."

"I believe we are star-crossed," I said.

"We are, darling," he said. "But we will just have to enjoy this evening together to the fullest." He was quiet, studying my face as if to memorize it. "Seeing you again is better than any Christmas present."

"And I'm so grateful to Irene for ignoring my stubbornness," I said.

"Now, tell me, Cavanaugh, you got what you wanted: Donovan is sending you into the field, one of only a handful of OSS women, I'm told. The SOE is way ahead of the Americans on that front. All this time I was hoping you'd take a position at the OSS London offices, living in relative safety. Though I knew that if you had your way, you'd be heading to France."

"Yes," I said.

"And here you are. I can't decide if you are the bravest woman I've met or the craziest. This is not a normal life you're about to embark on. It's damn dangerous. I hope you understand that."

I knew he was saying this because he was worried and being protective, but I still felt myself getting defensive, especially because I felt like I had just had this same conversation with Donovan.

"Not very long ago, I was living a normal, easy, boring life where I married the wrong man, after being pressured by my family. That life made me feel like I was suffocating. War isn't easy for anyone. Since I started at the OSS, I've felt more alive than I've felt in years. I have to do this."

"I know," he said with a sad smile. "I know because I feel the same. And full disclosure? I will also be going to the Continent sometime in the next few weeks."

"You can't say where or when, can you?"

"No, you know I can't."

"Well, let's toast to another star-crossed encounter in the future," I said, and we clinked our bottles together.

"I will drink to that."

We stayed at the pub for another beer, and Phillip suggested we have supper at the Long Bar, in the basement of the historic Criterion restaurant in Piccadilly Circus. It was a grand, gilded cavern with neo-Byzantine architecture, and I felt like we were in another world.

We never stopped talking through supper. I learned more about what I had known was an upper-class upbringing. He was the youngest of two brothers and a sister, and he'd gone to school at Eton and then studied classics at Oxford. He'd spent many summers in Biarritz, France, where his family had a second home. I told him all about my younger sisters and my parents, my time at Radcliffe, and our cottage on Cape Cod. And I finally shared a little more about my marriage to Connor.

"Before he left, I told him the marriage wasn't working," I said. We had finished supper and were waiting for the bill. Phillip was smoking a cigarette, looking at me intently. "For a long time, I felt sick with guilt over telling him that. A part of me still does, but then it wasn't like he didn't already know. It was obvious to both of us."

"You've been through quite a lot, haven't you?" he said, putting out his cigarette and reaching for my hand, stroking the top of it with his thumb. "And yet here you are about to embark on something many people would never dream of. I'm sorry I said you might be crazy. To be doing what you're doing—and as a woman? Well, it takes a certain kind of courage. Most women I know would have chosen the comfortable life in Boston."

"I don't know about that," I said, thinking of Julia jetting off to Ceylon and Irene being brave enough to come to London, of Tatiana and Nora and all the women I had met at Beaulieu—and, of course, Josette. "I think there are many women running in to help in this war effort in one way or another. It's just that nobody ever hears about them."

"Can you stay out a little longer?"

"Yes," I said, knowing the thrill of spending time with Phillip combined with the adrenaline of heading to France would help get me through tomorrow even if I was exhausted.

"Thank God." He smiled, and my heart melted and ached at the same time as I tried to remember everything about his face—the scar on his forehead, and the way his eyes crinkled when he smiled.

"Where are we going?"

"It's a surprise," he said, giving me a wink as he paid the bill.

It was cold but not freezing, so we walked through the busy streets of London, and I was content to have his arm around me the entire time. After about ten minutes, I could hear music coming from a few blocks away.

"Where exactly are you taking me?" I said, looking up at him as we walked. He stopped in the middle of the street and turned toward me, both arms around me now.

"After I left you in DC, I thought that if we were ever reunited in these crazy times, I would take you dancing. I just want to dance with you. Will you please indulge me on our first and last night together in London, darling?"

"I will, but I must warn you: I haven't danced in a very long time," I said. His face was inching closer to mine, and I could smell cigarettes and after-dinner mints on his breath. "I'm afraid I may have forgotten how."

"Doesn't matter. Just follow my lead," he said, and then he pulled me closer and kissed me. I heard a passing GI whistle at us, but I ignored him and leaned into Phillip.

We broke apart, smiling and laughing as we continued on to our destination, the Royal Opera House. Phillip explained it had been converted into a massive dance hall called Mecca at the start of the war. There was a small line out front, but it moved quickly. Inside, the reception area was packed with young people—it seemed every Allied nation uniform was represented.

Phillip held my hand tight as he led me into the Mecca dance hall, and I couldn't believe the sheer size of it. It was a cavernous space with multiple levels of balconies on both sides. Several hundred couples were dancing, and in the middle of them all was a raised stage where a large orchestra played, accompanied by two groups of singers, one composed of women in long, diaphanous pale-pink dresses, and behind them a chorus of men in dinner jackets and bow ties.

"Ah, it's Teddy Foster's Big Band. They are brilliant. Not Glenn Miller, mind you, but sounding better all the time."

We made our way onto the dance floor, getting as close to the band as we could manage just as they started playing their next tune. It took a few minutes, but I started to get over my self-consciousness and enjoy twirling and swinging around the dance floor with Phillip as if neither of us had a care in the world. We danced through two more songs, and then a slow ballad came on, and Phillip pulled me into his arms.

I put my head on his chest and closed my eyes, feeling happier than I had in a very long time. But it was a bittersweet happiness, as it was approaching midnight and I knew we would have to get back to the reality tomorrow would bring.

"Ah, Anna," Phillip whispered in my ear. "If I could whisk you away for a weekend holiday, to a remote cottage in the English countryside right now, far from this war and the world, I would."

I lifted my face from his chest and looked into his eyes, his expression of longing mirroring my own.

"And I wouldn't hesitate to go," I said, taking it for the fantasy that it was. We both had too much more to do in this war to go anywhere right now. "I'm sorry this night has to end so soon."

"Me too, darling," he said, kissing the top of my forehead.

We danced to a couple more songs and then grabbed a taxi back to Irene's flat, where Phillip walked me to the door. There were no lights on, and I realized she still wasn't home, so I was grateful she had given me a spare key that morning.

Whether it was the late hour or the drinks and what might be our last good-bye, as soon as we shut the door, we wrapped each other in a tight embrace, kissing with a passion I had never experienced in my marriage. We stayed like that for several minutes, and then, with Phillip's hands on my face, I pulled away from him, finally catching my breath.

"I'm sorry, but . . . Irene will be home any minute," I said. "I wish . . ."

"I know," he said with a frustrated sigh. "It's time for me to go."

"Thank you for tonight," I said. "It made me realize what I've been missing. And it will be a memory I'll cherish."

We held each other and didn't say anything for a minute.

"Anna, I have to tell you something," he said.

"Yes?"

"You should know, the reports about Operation Torch in North Africa, they are very positive. Things have gone well for the Allies," he said. "And it's thanks to the Vichy French naval codes we acquired. We made history. You and I and the team made history."

"Despite the fact that I literally fell on my face the first time? It wasn't much, my part of it," I said, laughing.

"Yes, despite that fact, and you were much more a part of it than you realize. We had been left in the lurch by that wanker Archie."

"Thank you for telling me," I said, feeling a sense of overwhelming pride. I needed this news before leaving. It was like a navigation point, a sign that I was going in the right direction, that I was meant to be right where I was at this moment.

"Just trust your instincts in Paris working with your friend Josette, and for God's sake be careful. I know you'll be incredible."

"Wait, you assumed I'd be going to France. But . . . how do you know I'm going to Paris?" I looked at him, surprised.

"Yes," he said, holding me in his arms. "I'm privy to more intelligence than you think, and I needed to know where in the world you were going to be, so I would have made it my business regardless."

"I really have no idea how long I'll be gone," I said. "And I'm guessing you have no idea how long you will be gone . . . when you go."

"That's true," he said, tucking one of my curls behind my ear. "I think you are a wonder, Anna Cavanaugh. And even though this might be our last good-bye for some time, I am not giving up on the two of us finding our way back to each other someday."

"Neither will I," I said. I missed him before he was even gone. And despite our promises, I knew that never seeing each other again was a strong possibility.

He leaned down and gave me one long, slow, final kiss good-bye, wiping the tear trickling down my face.

# Chapter Twenty-Two

*December 22, 1942*

I fell into a restless sleep after Phillip left, waking up every hour until I finally got up and wrote one more brief letter to my father that Irene could send for me from London. At 4:00 a.m., I still hadn't heard her key in the door and was getting a little worried, though I had a feeling where she was. At 5:30 in the morning, the sound of the front door woke me.

She walked into the bedroom and started tiptoeing around my mattress.

"I'm awake. You can turn on the light."

"So sorry to wake you," Irene said. She was wearing the same dress, but her hair was no longer pinned up in victory rolls. Instead it was down in a wild blonde mess around her makeup-free face. "Please, before you say anything, I know this is so unlike me, and I can explain . . ."

"Sit down, my friend. You remember what I told you about Paris and Henri? I am definitely not one to judge. You should know that," I said.

"You weren't married though," Irene said, biting her lip. "Neither was he."

She looked me in the eyes, and I nodded. "Yes, that's true," I said. "That complicates things in every way."

She sat down on the mattress next to me.

"You really care for him?" I asked.

"I completely adore him," she said, falling onto the mattress and looking up at the ceiling. "But . . ."

"But it's time to stop delaying the inevitable?"

"Yes, it's time," she said with a sigh. "I am sending Michael a letter tonight. And David is doing the same, sending one to his wife. My parents may disown me, but I can't live like this anymore, clearly. And even though Michael has not been the best husband, I know it's not fair to him to go on like this."

"You'll feel better once it's resolved," I said.

"I know I will. I'm sorry it had to come to this. I should have done something about it long ago," she said as she sat up. "Now please tell me all about your night with Phillip to get my mind off the dreaded letter. And then we've got to head to C&D to gather the last of your things before you go."

As I got dressed, I told her everything, happy to relive the details, still so fresh in my mind.

"And how do you feel now that you know you're not going to see him again, at least not for a long time?"

"I'm so glad you told him I was here, because, though it hurt to say good-bye, and my feelings for him are stronger than before . . . I believe in the possibility of love again. I haven't felt like this since before I got married—since Henri, if I'm being honest."

"You're welcome," Irene said, running a brush through her hair. "Let me go freshen up. We can have breakfast and head into the office in a couple hours."

Gemma the seamstress must have worked all night to have my French clothes altered and ready, because when we arrived at C&D, they were already all packed neatly in my battered French suitcase. She had done the sewing and packing with such maternal care, I had to give her a hug of thanks, and she wished me luck.

The day went by quickly, as I reviewed all the materials for my life in France with a new identity. Willie Renick had all my necessary counterfeit identification documents ready for me. My personal Ausweis identity card was complete, and it felt strange to see a black-and-white photograph of me with the information for my alter ego, Alexine Chauffour. It had travel stamps that reflected my cover story of being Josette/Madeleine Chauffour's cousin from Saint-Malo.

"Here's your suitcase to hold your wireless," Willie Renick said, knocking on the door and walking into Irene's modest office in C&D. "Violet will have that for you at Tangmere." He opened the compact, worn-looking brown leather suitcase and showed me that there were two secret compartments in the lining.

Irene and I were enjoying one last cup of coffee together in her office when David Bryant knocked on the door and gave me a sheepish smile.

"Your car is here, Anna." He was a bit disheveled and looked as tired as Irene and me, which was no surprise.

"Already?" Irene said, looking at him and then at me. "I can't believe we have to say good-bye again. Are you sure I can't convince you to stay?"

"You know you can't," I said. "But I'll be back. It was nice to meet you, David." I stood up and reached out to shake his hand. Looking him in the eye, I added, "Promise me you'll be good to my dear friend here, okay?"

I hoped his intentions were sincere, but having just met him, there was no way to know for sure.

"I promise you, Anna," he said, never meeting my gaze.

"Let me walk you out to the car," Irene said, her face scarlet.

We said our good-byes to David and, each of us holding one of my suitcases, made our way outside to where a gleaming black Rolls-Royce was idling.

"That wasn't necessary," Irene said. "Though it's appreciated."

"Just . . . take care of things at home," I said. "And make sure he does too. If not, things could get ugly and even more complicated fast."

"I will, and trust me, I will make sure he does too."

It was already dusk, clear and cold, and Charlotte was rising. When the young officer in the front seat of the Rolls spotted us walking toward it, he jumped out to help us with the suitcases.

"I can just put those in the back for you, miss," he said. "My name's Robert Taylor. I'm a new SOE liaison. I'll be taking you down to Tangmere."

Robert Taylor was so young looking I guessed he might have lied about his age to enlist. He brought my luggage around to the back of the car, and I turned to Irene.

"I wish it was a certain other SOE liaison driving me," I said. "Thank you again for telling him I was here."

"Of course," she said.

"When you write to Julia next, please send her my love and tell her why I won't be writing for a while."

"I will," Irene said, reaching out to give me an enormous hug. "And I'll send those letters you wrote to her, Mary, and your family you left me too."

"Please take care of yourself, my friend—take care of your heart."

"You too, and be safe. I hate all the good-byes in this damn war," Irene said, rubbing her finger under one eye to wipe a tear. "I better go inside now before I ruin my makeup."

"I'll be in touch when I can."

"You better be."

I climbed into the car, wiping my eyes, and turned to see Irene waving from the curb as we pulled away.

❧

"Miss? Anna? Please wake up, we're almost there," Robert Taylor said in a quiet voice as he tapped on my shoulder ever so lightly. Just beyond London's city limits, I had fallen fast asleep with my face mushed up against the passenger-side window. I sat up and squinted at the darkened landscape outside.

"Did I snore?" I asked, cringing. I rubbed my face and could feel an indent on my cheek from the door.

"No, miss," Robert said, chuckling.

"Are you lying?"

"Not at all," he said. "You've been out for about an hour and a half."

"I'm sorry. I haven't slept that well since I got here. I didn't mean to be rude."

"Oh, it's fine—not rude at all," Robert said. "I'm taking you to the cottage at Tangmere. They use it as a base for what they call the Moon Squadron—the fliers. It's just past the guardhouse."

Minutes later we pulled up to a traditional but sizable English cottage. It was brick with multiple chimneys, its windows and doors trimmed in white, and it was covered in vines in various places.

We pulled over and parked, and Robert Taylor brought my suitcases to the front of the cottage just as Tatiana opened the door.

"*Bonsoir!* Ah, finally, our American friend is here," Tatiana said in French, calling out to whomever was inside. "Come on inside. The fire is warm, and we are just about to have tea and go over details. It's a beautiful night for a moonlit flight, no? Are you excited? You look like you could use a cup of tea, or coffee. I know you like your coffee."

My driver seemed to lose his ability to express himself in the presence of this vivacious woman speaking rapid French. He handed off my bags, and I thanked him as Tatiana pulled me inside.

In the light of the cottage I noticed her long chestnut hair was now blonde and cut to just above her shoulders. She had parted it on the side and pinned the front section of it back with a barrette, which flattered her face.

"Your hair," I said. "I love it."

"Yes, Violet's suggestion," Tatiana said in a whisper, rolling her eyes. "I was not so happy, but I understand. It wasn't that long ago I was in the Marais selling baguettes. What can you do?" She shrugged. "Remember, we are not allowed to mention names to anyone here tonight—not even the pilot or the squadron leader."

I nodded. I remembered.

The inside of the cottage was charming, with whitewashed stucco walls and low ceilings with dark, rustic beams. We walked into a room that had been transformed into a makeshift operations center, with a black telephone and a scrambler and several large maps of the continent of Europe pinned to the walls. There was a roaring fireplace, and a proper porcelain tea service had been placed on the table in front of it, as well as a serving tray of mini sandwiches and pastries.

"My dear friend," Nora said as she and Violet came in through a door on the opposite side of the room. She gave me a warm embrace. "I'm delighted you're here and we're all flying together. I just found out hours ago."

"Welcome," Violet said, after Nora broke away. She smiled and greeted me with a quick hug as a man walked in behind her.

"This is Hugh Firth. He leads the RAF 138, a special duties squadron. We're going to have tea as he takes you all through some basic instructions."

"It is a pleasure to meet you," Hugh said in a baritone voice. He was middle-aged with a long face that accented his bushy brown mustache. "Let's get started, shall we? Air Ops in London just called to tell us that the coded BBC radio message notifying the reception committee of your impending arrival has gone out, so they know you're coming tonight. The pilot is preparing the Lysander plane now."

We sat around the table, and Violet poured us tea as Hugh Firth took us through the details. Lysanders were one-engine monoplanes that required only one pilot and could fly at a low enough altitude to go undetected by enemy radar. Using only maps, a watch, and a compass, the pilot would navigate by moonlight to the small, improvised airstrip in Avaray, in the Loire Valley, about one hundred miles southwest of Paris.

"The pilot will be guided in by lights from a reception committee of Resistance fighters," Hugh said. I could feel my stomach starting to get jumpy from nerves, and I regretted nibbling on the scone in front of me. "The *chef de la Résistance* is in charge of all incoming and outgoing flights. He, along with his team, will be on the ground to meet you, and you'll have to move very quickly."

"From there, you'll be taken to a designated safe house to meet your network contacts," Violet said, lighting up a cigarette and offering one to Tatiana, who happily accepted. "Over the next twenty-four hours, you'll all leave there separately."

"Do you have any questions for me?" Hugh asked, looking at the three of us.

Nora looked wide-eyed and worried, fidgeting with her teaspoon, while Tatiana smoked her cigarette and looked slightly bored, like she'd done this type of thing a million times. My reaction was somewhere in the middle, anxious and excited to get on with it, but with undeniable nerves too.

"I know Violet needs to speak with you about a few matters," he said after it was clear we had no questions. "And I have to go make a call to London."

Hugh left the room, and Violet walked over to a small wooden desk in the corner by the fireplace and took out three small paper packets, handing one to each of us. I opened mine to see four small glass prescription bottles.

We had gone over these four medical remedies in training. One bottle contained sleeping pills that, if stirred into a person's coffee or cognac, could knock them out for six hours. Another contained Benzedrine tablets, which could help you stay alert for hours or even days. The third vial was filled with yellow pills that would induce cramps and diarrhea if you needed a good cover story. And in the final vial were three large white pills, and just looking at them made the churning in my stomach worsen.

"The L pills," Nora said in a soft voice, holding the bottle with the white pills in front of her face, her olive skin pale.

"Yes," Violet said with a grim nod. "The capsules are coated in rubber and filled with cyanide. If merely swallowed, it would pass through your body harmlessly. To release the cyanide, you must bite down on it. If bitten and swallowed, it would be the last pill you'd ever take, killing you in two minutes. Keep it with you, hidden, at all times—sew it into your sleeve if you have to. If you ever find yourself imprisoned or being tortured with no possible escape . . . well, you will have it with you." Her voice wavered, and she paused for a second. "I pray to God you will never have to use it."

We were all quiet, looking at the bottles. I thought about the unimaginable horrors that would lead someone to bite down on that little rubber-coated pill.

"Now that we've gotten that over with, I want to speak with each of you individually," Violet said. "I'd also like to review the personal items you're bringing one last time. We don't want even a trace of England or America going with you. Nora, let's start with you, shall we?"

Nora and Violet went to fetch Nora's suitcases by the front door, and I heard them ascending the staircase.

"Good," Tatiana said in a whisper, moving over to sit next to me on the sofa. "I need to talk to you alone, and I was afraid I wouldn't get the chance."

"Oh, what about?" I said as she lit up another cigarette.

"I'm worried about Nora. I'm surprised she's here, to be honest," Tatiana said. "I asked her where she's going to be in Paris, what network she's going to be working with."

"Tatiana!" I said in a harsh whisper. "And did she tell you?"

"Naturally, she did—I knew she would. Remember, it's against her religion to lie," Tatiana said with a shrug. "So I know, and I think you should know too. We'll both know where she is, and if we are ever in a position to help her, we can."

"Violet would murder you for this," I said.

"Yes, however *we* both know that Nora is not equipped for this role. But they are desperate for wireless operators . . ."

"They're sending her to be a wireless operator?" I said, covering my face with my hands. "Are you joking?"

"I would not joke about this."

I sighed. And I thought of my conversation with Leo, about keeping an eye out for Nora if I could.

"My brothers and father are in the prison camps in Poland somewhere. I couldn't save them from . . . from that, and it haunts me every day," Tatiana said, her voice trembling. "We need to look out for each other over there. You and I, we need to look out for Nora; she's not as strong as us. I know you feel protective of her too. Let me tell you what I know? Please?"

It was a rare moment of emotion, and I couldn't argue with her.

"I'm not sure what good it will do, but tell me."

"Good. She's been assigned to Alliance, the largest network in Paris. Her cover story is that she's a children's nurse," Tatiana said. "She will be living at a flat at 98 Rue de la Faisanderie in the 16th arrondissement."

"I can't believe she told you all of that," I said, rubbing my hands over my face. "But then again, knowing Nora, I can."

"Maybe it won't do us any good," Tatiana said. "But even if there's a small chance we can help her in some way?"

We heard footsteps on the stairs, and Tatiana went back to where she had been sitting. Nora walked in the room looking calmer, more serene than she had been minutes before.

"You're next, Anna," Nora said.

I took my suitcases upstairs and found Violet in one of the bedrooms, sitting at a small table by the front window. There was a wireless radio set, the one that would belong to me.

"Anna, have a seat," she said with a smile. "Oh, but before you do, please open both of your suitcases. I'll go through the things in the one for your clothes, and we'll put the wireless in the other case."

Violet went through every piece of clothing and my personal items, examining every button and label on my clothes, checking my French cork-soled shoes and my French-made toiletries to make sure there was not a hint of my American identity among my belongings. The silk handkerchief that contained my ciphers was now tucked discreetly inside my bra, but I took it out so she could inspect it. She also reviewed all my identification papers and permits, even the French francs I would be bringing with me. Finally, she placed the wireless radio set in the suitcase. When she was satisfied, we had a seat at the table by the window.

"I know Donovan told you about the recent tragedies in occupied France."

"Yes, he did." I swallowed hard. "But it didn't change my mind."

"Somehow I didn't think it would," Violet said. There was pride in her voice as she added, "Not one of the female trainees from Beaulieu has changed her mind. You can't teach courage—or ambition. You all had it when you got to Beaulieu. That's why you were chosen. Follow plans and protocol, and take extra precautions regarding your wireless schedule, your locations, and the time you spend transmitting. You are ready, Agent Peacock."

"Thank you for saying so," I said, proud at her words and still getting used to my new code name.

"Oh, I almost forgot, this was on my desk at the SOE when I got in this morning. It's from Phillip Stanhope . . . for you."

"Thank you," I said. My heart hurt to see my name in his handwriting.

"Just make sure you rip it up when you're done reading it," she said, giving me a knowing smile.

# Chapter Twenty-Three

The full moon watched over us as we said our last good-byes to Violet and climbed the ladder to board the Lysander. My suitcases were jammed beneath our hinged wooden seats, and the rear cockpit was as cramped and uncomfortable as promised. The young pilot, Fitz Williams, performed his last checks. We could see the silhouettes of Violet Banks and Hugh Firth waving good-bye to us as the Lysander, or "Lizzy," turned its nose to the runway and departed for Avaray, France. I opened Phillip's letter just as we were taking off. Hugh Firth had been right: your eyes do adjust to the moonlight.

22/12/42

*My dear Anna,*
*I stayed up half the night thinking, and I was compelled to write you this letter and only hope you receive it before you leave. I was contemplating what our lives would be like if we had met during a different time, when things were calmer and we would have the time together I so wish we could have now.*

*There was so much I wanted to say to you last night when we said good-bye, but I did not. Why? Mostly because we British are a tad reserved with our emotions.*

*And, of course, we were saying good-bye once more, with no guarantees in this war. You called us "star-crossed," and perhaps we are, although there is something about that word I dislike, for it evokes a feeling that we are doomed to always be this way.*

*I know you lost your husband, and I don't pretend to know how that feels. When I am with you, I feel you holding back, protecting yourself from heartache, and that I understand completely. I only hope you someday realize that if you continue to keep walls up around your heart, you'll have only lived half a life.*

*Of all the star-crossed lovers in history and literature, I'd like to think we are most like Odysseus and Penelope in Homer's* Odyssey. *They were apart for twenty years through trials and tribulations, but he found his way back to her. That is my wish—to find my way back to you in the madness that is wartime.*

*Take care, and for the love of God, be safe. I will be thinking of you and of course worrying about you . . . until we meet again.*

*Yours,*
*Phillip*

Reading the letter both warmed me and made me miss Phillip even more. But it also calmed my nerves and took my mind off the present dangers of our late-night flight across the channel to the Continent.

I folded it and put it back in my pocket, feeling heartbroken I couldn't keep it. I wanted it for posterity, because despite it all, I knew it was quite possible I might never see Phillip Stanhope again. I was grateful to the man who had brought the possibility of love back into my life. He hadn't said he loved me, but I could feel it in his words.

And I hadn't even realized how much I needed to feel that until I read the letter.

It was such a small airplane, you could feel it move with the currents of air around it. Every dip and bump made me grip my seat tighter. I could hear Nora softly muttering prayers. Tatiana was next to me, her face pressed up against the window as if she wanted to lean out of it to better see the coastline of her country as we approached.

We remained quiet for some time, lost in our own thoughts.

"There they are, ready for us," Fitz said, finally breaking the silence as the Lysander flew ever lower. He pointed to small pulses of flashlights down below us that I recognized as Morse code signals.

And then we could see tiny pinpricks of light, like little beacons of hope, illuminating a small makeshift runway. I heard Tatiana gasp and whisper, "*Ma patrie*"—my homeland.

We were landing in France, my heart's second home, and I was filled with pride and excitement about being back here and what I was about to do. I blinked back tears, because joining the OSS, getting myself here, had been my decision alone. No matter what happened next, for good or for ill, this part of my life story belonged to me.

We gripped our seats as we landed with a bump and taxied down the runway. As soon as the Lysander was at a standstill, the pilot moved with speed and precision, collecting packages filled with supplies—guns and money—and throwing them out the door of the plane. He then grabbed each suitcase and flung those out the door too.

"Come on, come on," Williams said, waving us out the door. Tatiana went first, followed by Nora. I thanked him and peered out to see a half dozen Resistance fighters, all of them carrying Sten guns and working as fast as the pilot had to load the supplies and our suitcases into a black pickup truck. With them were two men with luggage, waiting to embark. A hulking man wearing a black beret was shouting orders.

In one of my fists was Phillip's letter, now ripped into tiny pieces. I took a deep breath and let them go in the wind, and they scattered down the runway as I stepped out of the plane onto the ladder, nearly stumbling on my newly hemmed culottes when one of the Resistance members grabbed my hand to assist me.

The driver of the truck did not even put the headlights on as we drove on bumpy dirt roads past fields dotted with the silhouettes of sleeping cows or sheep. Tatiana, Nora, and I huddled together against the frosty air as the half dozen Resistance fighters sat on the edges of the truck bed and scanned the darkness, searching the night for any sign of the enemy. I found myself doing the same, feeling a paranoia I guessed would become second nature.

After about fifteen minutes, we took a sharp right, arriving at an arched iron gate. We pulled up to a sprawling, ancient stone farmhouse with wooden shutters, and one of the Resistance members helped us jump out of the back of the truck. Only one of the men remained with us, while the rest headed back to the airstrip to pick up more arrivals. The man was broad chested, handsome, and swarthy in a movie-star kind of way.

"My name's Bernard Fairfax," he said, walking backward and holding his arms out wide as we walked up a winding stone path to the front door. "Welcome to the best safe house in France. The owners, Monsieur and Madame Terrier, are wonderful hosts."

"You're SOE?" Tatiana said.

"I am," Bernard said with a proud nod. "After Cambridge, I spent a year at the Sorbonne, so I'm fluent in French. I've been working with the Resistance network in this region for about six months, also as a wireless man, among many other things."

"You are not going to be joining us in Paris? That's unfortunate," Tatiana said in a flirtatious tone I'd heard her use before, when she wanted a favor from one of the instructors at training.

He stopped, turned to her, and then smiled.

"No, I am not," he said. "So let's make the most of this evening." He held out his elbow for her, and she smiled back at him and took it.

Nora just looked at me, eyebrows raised, as the front door opened. When I had pictured the safe house in my mind, for some reason I had envisioned a spartan apartment or cottage with some somber Resistance fighters standing around until it was safe for us to leave. But, this being France, we walked into a festive party atmosphere, with at least two dozen Resistance fighters socializing in a large open room with a roaring hearth and low, beamed ceilings. The air in the room was almost too warm, and it smelled of men's sweat and cigarettes, mingled with a savory cooking scent. Both French and English were being spoken, making it clear that many of the people here were also agents from abroad.

"Good evening! Good evening, welcome." A white-haired man came up to the door, kissing us on both cheeks and speaking in French. A skinny, short-haired brown dog barked and jumped up and down at us in greeting.

"Shush!" he said, leaning down and scooping the dog up. "I am Guy Terrier, and Colette, come here please . . . ," he called, and a slight woman with kind eyes hurried over. "This is my wife. Welcome to our home."

We made our introductions, and Colette went to fetch us mugs of mulled wine as Guy told us to make sure we had something to eat. I gratefully accepted the wine and was standing by the fireplace to warm up when I heard a familiar voice cry out in French from across the room.

"Is it possible? Is it really *you*?"

The room quieted, and I looked up from the fire. She was wearing a red wool coat and black culottes and looked thinner than I remembered, but she was just as striking. Small and lithe, she had always reminded me of a pixie with her large, round dark eyes, alabaster skin, and thick, shiny chocolate-brown hair.

*Josette.*

I gasped as we pushed through the crowded room to embrace each other. A few of the revelers cheered for us, then everyone returned to their conversations as the two of us held on, laughing and crying at the same time. With certain friends, time folds in on itself. No matter how long it's been since you've seen each other, the friendship remains the same as it's always been, like no time has passed at all.

"Look at you!" she said when we pulled apart. "You look the same. Your hair is a little longer—so beautiful. But I don't know whether to kiss you or kill you, *mon amie.*"

"Kill me? Why would you do that?" I asked, wiping my eyes, still laughing.

"You are *here*," Josette said, looking at me with wonder, hands on my shoulders. "These are dangerous times, and yet . . . have you gone crazy?"

"No," I said, laughing again. And then, turning serious, I said, "Josette, I was given the chance. How could I ever say no? I'm here for the same reasons as everyone else in this house."

Her eyes teared up again, and she just shook her head, taking my face in her hands. "You have no idea how grateful I am to have you by my side during this madness," she said, giving me another tight hug. "My brave, dear friend."

I brought her over to meet Tatiana and Nora and Tatiana's new friend, Bernard, who had not left her side since our arrival.

"Hello, Bernard, good to see you again," Josette said, giving him a cool look.

"And you," Bernard said. He stood up straighter and looked a little sheepish.

"The contact from my network is here, and he said we're heading out soon," Nora said, her voice nervous. "Even though it's getting close to the midnight curfew. Tatiana isn't going until midday tomorrow. When are you leaving?"

I looked at Josette.

"Just after dawn," Josette said, studying Nora as if unsure what to make of her.

"Oh," Nora said, frowning.

"Be safe," I said. "And take care of yourself."

"Thank you for helping me with the wireless," Nora said, hugging me. "I wouldn't have made it here without your help."

I felt a pang of guilt, remembering how Leo Evans and I had agonized about Nora and her poor wireless skills, wondering if it might have been better if she had failed.

"Now, come with me," Josette said, grabbing me by the elbow.

We made our way through the crowd of mostly men, though I was encouraged to see a few other women in the party besides the ones I knew. Josette stopped to introduce me to one named Pauline.

"Pleasure," Pauline said, shaking my hand. She was tall, with an oval face and almond-shaped gray eyes. She spoke French with a strong accent.

"You're American?" I said. "Ah, you're Pauline Wakefield, aren't you? Your reputation precedes you."

"I am, and I'm surprised to hear that it does," she said, giving me a warm smile. "I worked for the SOE for the first couple of years of the war. Now that the OSS is in the game, I'm working for my own country again. I'm curious, where did you train?"

I told her how I had trained with the SOE in Beaulieu and that the OSS would be sending others soon.

"Happy to see they're finally sending more women. We blend in so much better over here these days. Always good to see you, Josette. I'll be leaving after we receive all the supplies we're supposed to—more ammo and guns finally." Then, dropping her voice, she added, "I've got to get my men out of here soon. This many Resistance and so much wine in one farmhouse? It always makes me nervous. People start to share too much. Stay safe, my friends."

When she was out of earshot, Josette whispered, "Pauline is one of the best agents in the Loire Valley. She and Bernard have organized a very large Resistance group here, hundreds of men strong. Bernard's a bit arrogant but fantastic with both the wireless and explosives. And Pauline is an excellent shot, so she's been training the men here and also serves as the group's courier. It's rumored that the Germans have a bounty on her head."

Josette found a door at the rear of the house that led outside to where the large barn was, and I breathed in the fresh night air and smoothed my hair back. Voices were coming from somewhere nearby.

"Where are we going?" I asked.

"More people want to see you," she said, pulling me along.

"Josette, who?"

"She has arrived," Josette said in a loud voice as we got closer to the barn, where I could see the silhouettes of two men smoking cigarettes in the moonlight.

We got closer, and I recognized one of them as Georges LaRue, a professor at Sciences Po and now the head of the Druids network I would be working for.

Then my eyes focused on the other figure, and I couldn't breathe. It had been over three years, and he had filled out, more a grown man now than a college boy, but he had the same shock of jet-black hair, the same strong, handsome cheekbones and aquiline nose.

*Henri.*

"Henri. My God. It's you," I said, my heart beating in my ears. I was more nervous than I had been the entire flight over.

"Bonsoir, Anna," he said, looking into my eyes, his smile tinged with sadness. He shoved his hair off his forehead with his hand, a habit I remembered well. "Welcome back."

He bent down and kissed me on both cheeks in a formal, awkward way, smelling like smoke and the cedar-and-spice cologne I remembered so distinctly as my mind flooded with memories: The two of us sitting next to each other with our group of friends on the banks of the Seine, walking through the streets of the Marais, or studying together at an outdoor café. And my last beautiful day in Paris, taking photographs throughout the city and spending one passionate night together in his bed, tangled in the sheets, not falling asleep until almost dawn. That year in Paris, I had felt like the best version of myself, and Henri was one of the main reasons why.

I knew it was more than just the mulled wine that was making my face warm and my stomach flutter. It had been so long since I had seen him I had convinced myself it was a lifetime ago. But now it felt like yesterday, even though I was now a widow and a spy, and he was an ex-POW and Resistance member hiding in his own city.

With just a glance and an awkward, polite kiss on both cheeks, the feelings I had for him so long ago came rushing back. I felt like the wind had been knocked out of me. How could I still be feeling this way after such a long time apart? And what did that mean about my feelings for Phillip?

"Anna," Georges LaRue said, kissing me on both cheeks and giving me a warm hug, as I tried to get a grip on myself. Georges LaRue was tall and boisterous with reddish-blond hair that I remembered as always looking unkempt, and tonight was no exception. He wasn't what you would call handsome, but he was exceptionally brilliant and had been one of the most popular professors in the math department at Sciences Po.

"It has been a long time, but we are so happy you are here to help. How were your travels? What did you—"

"Do you have the wireless radio with you?" Henri said to me, interrupting Georges, his face serious, almost cold, now that the niceties had been exchanged.

"Henri, you are being rude. She just arrived; let her relax for a moment, please," Josette said, swatting his arm. "Go get another glass of wine."

"Yes," Georges said, giving him an annoyed look. "Let her enjoy the welcome party at least."

"Of course I have it with me," I said. "It's in a small suitcase inside."

I composed myself, because it was clear that whatever feelings he might once have had for me were long gone, which was no surprise. And I felt foolish about my own butterflies, the warmth of my emotions, and I hoped they weren't obvious.

"Georges, you know it's better if we leave now while it's still dark," Henri said. He looked at me and added, "We'll leave now and bring the wireless with us to the next safe house, just outside Paris. We will meet you both at our flat on Rue Fabert, our Paris safe house, tomorrow evening. You can make your first communication to London. There is no time to waste."

Georges looked up at the moon and appeared to be thinking. "Henri is right, of course," he said. Josette started to protest, but Georges held up his hand. "As much as I enjoy these parties, the sooner we leave, the better."

He leaned down, took her face in his hands, and kissed her on the lips, making it clear that she was more to him than just another member of the Druids network.

"Let's go," Georges said. "Anna, you can show us to your wireless inside."

"No. If my wireless radio is going tonight, I'm going with it," I said. "We can discuss you helping me move it to different locations once we get to Paris. But I cannot let you take it tonight. It's mine. It's my responsibility."

"Anna, you must let us take it. It's unsafe . . . ," Henri said, frowning at me.

"No . . . I'm taking it," I said, stammering a little, my cheeks still flushed, and I was glad for the darkness. "I'm here to be your network's wireless operator. I was finally given my *own* wireless radio an hour before I got on the plane tonight, and I am not letting it out of my sight."

Henri started to argue with me, but Georges stopped him. "I understand," Georges said. "And Henri, I know you do too and you're just worried about these two getting caught transporting the wireless. Josette, you know the precautions you need to take?"

"You know I do, *mon chéri*," she said.

Henri swore under his breath but said nothing more.

"Okay," Georges said, giving Josette another, longer kiss. "Be safe. Come on, Henri. We will see you ladies tomorrow night."

We stood for a moment and watched them walk away, and I felt an ache in my heart.

"He didn't want you to come," Josette said in a whisper.

"What?" I said, feeling sick at the words.

"Henri. When he learned the OSS and SOE had told us they could send you, our amazing American friend, to work with me and to be our wireless operator, Georges and I thought it was a fantastic idea. But Henri didn't want you to come; he thought it was crazy." She looked me in the eyes. "He says it's twice the worry. He hates that I'm working *and* spying on les boches. But he cannot deny I'm terrific at it. And now you'll be helping me. So it's twice the worry for him."

"I thought maybe he just didn't want to see me again," I said.

Josette laughed. "Henri not wanting to see *you*, Anna Cavanaugh? Don't be ridiculous," Josette said. "He was in a POW camp for six months. He has been through so much. Just give him time. He's still the same sweet Henri inside."

# Chapter Twenty-Four

*December 23, 1942*

Josette and I shared a bed in a closet-sized bedroom on the second floor of the farmhouse, and I woke up just as the sun was rising, once again too filled with anticipation about the day to sleep. After I got dressed, I went to find Tatiana to say a quick good-bye. I asked a Resistance fighter who had slept in front of the hearth if he had seen her—and he gave me a smirk and told me to check the last bedroom in the rear part of the house.

I tapped on the door and heard Tatiana's voice.

"Tatiana, it's me. I'm leaving," I said. She opened the door, looking paler than usual, and her newly blonde hair was a nest of tangles. In the room's small bed, Bernard was lying shirtless and sound asleep.

"Ouch," Tatiana said, holding her palm to her forehead.

"Um, did you . . . have a good night?" I said, eyebrows raised, nodding at Bernard.

She gave me a mischievous smile and glanced back at him. "I did," she said. "Some of it's a little foggy, but I did."

"I just came to say good-bye," I said, giving her a hug.

"I hate good-bye," she said. "I wish we were working together in Paris."

"Me too," I said, and I meant it. I was fortunate to be working with Josette; it would make this odd life less lonely.

"You remember the address I gave you for our friend, just in case?"

"I do," I said. "Who knows, maybe she'll do just fine."

"Who knows." We gave each other a doubtful look.

One of Pauline's men drove Josette and me to the train station, ten minutes away. We bought our tickets, and I carried the wireless suitcase while Josette carried my other one, along with the small leather satchel she had brought with her. The platform was crowded and dirty and smelled of urine. I did a double take and my breath caught at the sight of three gray-uniformed Gestapo patrolling the crowds, randomly singling out passengers and asking to see their identification. It was difficult not to stare. They almost looked like they were play-acting to me.

Josette and I stood together, not speaking, although at one point she gave me a look, communicating with her eyes that I needed to relax. I was feeling jumpy, fidgeting in their presence, and I knew I needed to act calmer. Despite the cold air, I felt sweat dripping down my brow. There was an announcement that the train would be arriving in five minutes, and I exhaled; it was almost time to board. Then I heard a voice behind us.

"You two, show me your papers." A young Gestapo officer with a scowl on his face was pointing at us. He spoke French with a guttural German accent. My pulse started racing.

"Good morning. Yes, here you go. How are you this morning, sir?" Josette said, giving him a huge smile and handing over her fake Madeleine Chauffour papers to him. I pulled my own out of my wool coat and gripped them tightly so he wouldn't see my hand shaking. He handed Josette's back to her and then took mine, staring at my face for a few seconds. I gave him the best fake smile I could muster.

"Where were you visiting, Alexine?" he asked.

"Um . . . our . . . our aunt and uncle, in Avaray," I said, telling him the story we had concocted before bed.

"Yes, you cannot get roast chicken in Paris these days," Josette said, batting her eyelashes in a way that almost seemed comical. "They offered to have us over for an early Christmas dinner."

"Next time, maybe you can invite me, no?" the soldier said, looking at her with a flirtatious grin. He handed me back my papers without looking at me again.

"Maybe we can," Josette said with a dazzling smile.

I could hear a train approaching, and I thought he was going to let us go, when he looked down at our suitcases.

"What are you carrying in those big suitcases?" he asked, pointing at mine.

"Oh, we are girls, we like to bring many things with us," I said, groaning inside. I was going to have to do better.

"Don't you know? We have a *wireless* in this one," Josette said laughing, holding up the case she'd been carrying. The one without the wireless.

I looked at Josette and nearly choked but recovered enough to turn my cough into laughter, watching his face, terrified of what he was going to say next. But he just smiled and rolled his eyes as the train pulled into the station.

"Foolish girls," he said, waving us away.

We found two seats in the back of the train car, but there were German soldiers on board too, so I didn't dare discuss what had just transpired. The air in the car was stifling, smelling of stale cigarettes and body odor. My heart was still hammering in my chest, and I clasped my hands together in my lap because they wouldn't stop shaking.

We rode in silence for a while. I took deep breaths to calm myself and looked out the window to watch the French countryside go by. Most of the people on the train were somber, wearing well-worn clothes and "armistice shoes" with cork or wooden soles. Many of the women still managed to look fashionably well put together—a few wore ornate homemade hats, or nicely tailored suits that had clearly once been drapery in a former life. One woman in a gray hat with a black bow dabbed her eyes with a handkerchief as she read the translated version of *Gone with the Wind*. No matter how hard I tried, I knew I would never have the effortless style of a Frenchwoman.

"Are you okay?" Josette whispered in my ear after we had been riding for about an hour.

I nodded. I had finally stopped shaking.

"It gets easier, I promise you."

"*You* make it look easy," I said. "I don't know how you do it. How you've done everything that you've done. It's incredible. I was a fumbling idiot."

"You were fine, just a little fidgety. Don't be so hard on yourself," Josette said, shaking her head. "Remember, les boches don't think much of women, especially 'foolish girls.' It's amazing what you can get away with when men don't think you've got a brain in your head."

The train pulled into Gare du Nord in the 10th arrondissement of Paris, and we walked out one of the many doors flanked by Greco-Roman-style columns. I looked up at the outside of the station; its columns and the statues atop them were filthy and blackened. The large roman-numeral clock in the middle of the arched glass facade said the time was three in the afternoon, an hour ahead of the real Paris time.

"Paris is on Berlin time now," I said, looking at Josette. "I had forgotten."

The street in front of the station was filled with people on bicycles or *vélo-taxis*, cyclist-powered rickshaws. I saw one delivery truck and a horse-drawn carriage carrying crates of wine.

A black Citroën Traction Avant car with two small Nazi flags affixed to its rear bumper drove by. When one of the Gestapo officers inside looked out the window at me, glimpsing the silver skull on his cap made me shiver.

"It's a little quieter than I remember," I said in a soft voice. "Not as many cars."

"Yes, it is a bit quieter," Josette said. "Very little petrol, so just a few German cars on the road. And even most of the songbirds are gone.

Many of them died when all of the oil and gas tanks were set on fire. A black smoke spread out across the entire city, poisoning them. It's why the buildings are black with soot."

"I was going to ask about that."

"I know we have our things, but do you mind walking to the apartment on Rue Fabert?" Josette said. "It's on the Left Bank and will take us about an hour, but—"

"That sounds perfect," I said, interrupting her. She didn't need to convince me. "I need the fresh air after the train. And I've missed this city."

The streets hummed with bicycles and horses and the occasional German automobile or military truck. As we walked, the clickety-clack of so many women's cork-soled shoes created a kind of quiet, rhythmic music. Despite the cold, Parisians were sitting outside the many cafés we passed. It appeared that the ingrained French café culture at least was surviving the war.

One café was packed with gray-uniformed German soldiers, all smoking and drinking and talking loudly in their native tongue. I held my breath at the sight of them, and I wondered at what point seeing them everywhere would start to feel normal.

"We've been invited, along with Georges and Henri, to a Christmas Eve party at the American Hospital tomorrow night," Josette said in a quiet voice after we had passed by the Germans. "Dr. Sumner Jackson is the American doctor in charge of the hospital and a member of the Resistance. He's become a very loyal friend of ours."

"I look forward to meeting him," I said. "And what time are Georges and Henri meeting us at the apartment this evening?" I asked, nervous at the thought of seeing Henri again after our first awkward reunion.

"Probably around nineteen hundred hours."

"Where are they living?"

"Right now, they are staying with an art curator, a member of the Resistance named Zoé St. Clair. They are sleeping in her attic, with artwork she is hiding from the Germans. There are literally Braques and Picassos under their mattresses."

"You are joking."

"I am *not*. But they move around quite a bit. Some nights they stay in the safe house. That is where you and I will stay, as long as we know it's secure."

"So we won't actually be staying at the student hostel?"

"For now, no. We will stay there occasionally, and if the Germans ever check up on us, the girls there know what to do."

At certain intersections, there were German street signs—large white stacked wooden arrows with angry black lettering, ugly gashes on the landscape of the city. When we reached the opera house, a chill ran through me at the sight of the enormous Nazi flags flying in between each of its magnificent columns.

"That's for a German music festival," Josette said, rolling her eyes. "The bastards even have one flying on top of the Eiffel Tower."

Near the opera house was a boulangerie with a line out front that was several blocks long. Many of the people in line were mothers with children, some were elderly. All of them looked exhausted, and many looked far too thin to be considered healthy.

"People wait in line for hours for food," Josette said. "If you have a family, getting enough to eat consumes most of your time."

"That is just horrible," I said, my heart aching at the sight of a fair-haired toddler in a shabby brown coat whimpering to his mother.

"It is," Josette said with a nod.

"And my God, you've dealt with this for years. People must be so tired."

"And angry, and disgusted," Josette said, bitterness in her voice. "In the early days, most of the French just hoped it would all be over quickly and were too fearful to do anything. That has changed, though."

"Has it truly?"

"I know it has," Josette said with conviction. "The will to resist, the hope of winning—people want their country back. What finally changed many people's minds? The treatment of the Jews here—like our friends, Simone Monteux and her family. Monsieur Drucker. Too many others.

"First, they took away their businesses and imposed quotas on Jewish doctors and lawyers and students. Then, they made them register and wear horrid yellow stars on their clothing—the humiliation. They couldn't go to theaters or restaurants. They couldn't *cross the Seine*, for God's sake. And then in the spring of '41 they started arresting them . . . just taking them away."

"Where?"

"Different places, none of them humane. In June, they took hundreds to Drancy, a horrible internment camp north of the city, hardly any food and no running water. One of the worst times was last summer in mid-July, they rounded up thousands of Jewish families and held them captive in the Velodrome d'Hiver, the bicycle stadium," Josette said, blinking fast and staring ahead at something I couldn't see.

"Henri, Georges, and I did what we could to help a friend who had been smuggling Jewish children out of the city, to hide them in remote villages. But many children refused to leave their parents. And their parents couldn't force them to go. Jewish families, some with little babies who were terrified and screaming, were crowded onto buses by *French* police and imprisoned by the monstrous Gestapo in the velodrome. They were kept there for five days in the most oppressive heat and given barely any food. One water source for thousands of people. The toilets broke after a day. The naked cruelty and . . . evil—it was unimaginable. But the unimaginable was happening. In *my city*. I went there . . . to the velodrome . . . I heard the screams of people inside, like they were going mad. I will never, ever forget those screams for the rest of my life."

She stopped and looked at me; now I was blinking back tears too.

"What happened to them all?" I asked, horrified by the picture she had painted with her words.

"After those five days, those who survived were sent to prison camps in occupied Poland," Josette said, wiping a tear off her cheek, frowning. "I keep thinking, if the Nazis treat Jewish people with such inhumanity here, for all Parisians to see, how will they treat them when there is no one watching?"

We had reached the Pont de la Concorde, which stretched across the Seine. Ahead of us was the Palais Bourbon, the seat of the French National Assembly and the symbol of the French government. We stopped to take in the sight of an enormous white banner with the words "DEUTSCHLAND SIEGT AN ALLEN FRONTEN"—"Germany triumphs on all fronts"—that had been hung across its classic portico facade, a humiliating reminder to the French people every day.

I clenched my fists, sick with anger at the sight of the banner, at all of it. I was especially upset by the stories of the families we knew. Our friends.

"I'm telling you all of this because we are living and working side by side with the enemy. At times it can feel terrifying, and we must constantly be on guard. They have executed more Resistance members than I can bear to say," Josette said, looking me in the eyes. "But you will adjust; I know you will. And your anger, and the solidarity in what we're doing? Those are the things that must be stronger than your fears."

"I understand," I said, in a whisper.

At the OSS I had learned some of what had been happening in occupied France, as I had read many of the briefings that crossed Donovan's desk. But nothing had prepared me to see the terrible reality of the city and its people held hostage.

"I haven't even asked yet: What day do I start going to work with you? With the Germans?" I asked once we started walking again.

"We will go see them at the Hotel Majestic tomorrow morning," Josette said. "Just for a half day, because it's Christmas Eve."

"Good," I said. "I'm ready for the real work to begin."

# Chapter Twenty-Five

A half hour later, Josette and I arrived at the safe house on the Left Bank. The nondescript apartment building at 26 Rue Fabert was in the 7th arrondissement, and like most of the buildings in Paris, much of its cream-colored stone exterior was dirty and blackened with soot. The building's concierge was Madame Chevrolet, a grumpy older woman whose hair was wrapped in a royal-blue turban. She was very skinny, with deep lines in her cheeks and thin, painted-on black eyebrows. Madame had a ratty-looking terrier named Bijou, or Jewel in English. As she and her dog walked us up several flights to our apartment on the top floor, nasty little Bijou growled at me the entire way.

"Will you be expecting anyone else, mademoiselle?" Madame Chevrolet asked Josette in French as she opened the door to the apartment for us. I was adjusting to the rhythm of the language again, of speaking French rather than English, and I was thankful to Tatiana for making me do so during training.

"Yes, madame, this evening. You know who they are," Josette said. We put our suitcases down, and Josette moved to shut the flat's door, but Madame cleared her throat, and Bijou growled again as if on cue.

"Oh yes, sorry," Josette said, reaching into her pocket and handing Madame a stack of francs.

"*Au revoir,*" Madame said with a grim nod, as she picked up Bijou and left.

"That dog hates me," I said, taking off my shoes and sinking into the small green sofa.

"Bijou hates everyone—you are not special," Josette said with a laugh. "We pay Madame to be our lookout, to make sure nobody breaks in or sees our comings and goings. I'm afraid if we didn't pay her, she'd accept money from the Germans. Her only true loyalty is to Bijou."

The small apartment was clean and sparsely furnished, with hardwood floors, high ceilings, ivory-colored walls, and original moldings. The living room had two floor-to-ceiling windows facing the street, their exterior adorned with the ornate, wrought-iron balconies typical of many Parisian buildings.

Josette showed me to the bedroom and bathroom so I could rest for a while and freshen up. The bathroom mirror revealed the dark circles under my eyes and my haywire curls. Tired and disoriented, I felt like a fish out of water. The reality of being in occupied Paris, of being back with Josette and Henri, still felt surreal.

*Henri.* I hoped things would at least become friendly again . . . not strange. It bothered me, the way his smell, his touch, still had such an effect on me after all this time. And it made me think of Phillip, with some guilt in my heart. I wondered where he was now and hoped he was safe and that we would see each other again someday.

I splashed water on my face to wake myself up and focused on setting up the wireless radio on a small table in the corner of the bedroom. As planned in London, the first communication would be at exactly 8:30 p.m., short and sweet, just letting London know I had arrived and was safe within the Druids network.

I heard the door to the apartment open and Josette greeting Henri and Georges, so I left the wireless to join them. Georges looked even more disheveled than the last time I'd seen him, wearing the typical high-waisted pants and threadbare dark-colored coat of most Parisian men. Henri was dressed similarly but wearing a tweed newsboy-style cap that made him look even more roguishly handsome. Once again, he kissed me in a formal, forced manner, and I tried to ignore the quickening in my heart when I felt his lips on my cheek.

They had brought some food, and Georges opened a cabinet and took out a bottle of wine and four glasses.

"Real coffee is still impossible to come by in Paris, even for me," he said as he poured wine for all of us. "But this being France, wine can be found . . . if you know where to look for it."

"Is your wireless radio set ready to go?" Henri asked, once again so intense and serious. I searched his face for the young man I once knew, who had laughed easily and enjoyed life to the fullest.

"It is," I said. "It's in the bedroom. I have about twenty minutes before I'm supposed to send my first message."

"Can you show me?" he asked.

I led him in to the wireless, pushing down the thoughts of our last night in his bedroom, the last time we were alone together. I focused on the radio and explained my plan, in an effort to prove to him that I knew what I was doing.

"And you know how to do this—the coding?"

"That's why I'm here," I said, taking a sip of wine for courage.

"Good." He nodded. "We need more and better communications with the Allies. Also, more weapons and agents. Your SOE has been slow."

"I'm with the American OSS, not the SOE," I corrected him, though it was probably all the same to him. "You must know that the Allies are very serious about helping the Resistance here now. That's . . . that's why they're dropping more agents, sending more supplies."

He shrugged, studying the wireless. "That is what we hear," he said. "But we haven't received nearly enough guns to train, or enough agents and money to truly organize. We have men rising up to join, but not enough supplies. It still feels like broken promises. In this message, can you ask when the next arms shipment for us will be?"

"Yes," I said, happy to finally be of service. "Of course. Let me just code it." I took out a small notebook and wrote it out and then put it through the poem code. It was on the silk handkerchief that Leo had given me at Beaulieu, though I didn't even have to give it a glance, I knew it so well. I would burn the paper later and hide the handkerchief in my bra again. I looked up and blushed, realizing Henri had been watching me work. I glimpsed the small brown leather case on a strap around his neck.

"Oh, your camera," I said. "You're still taking pictures?"

"When I can, when it's safe," he said with a shrug, lifting the camera case. "Some pictures I take to share with the Allies; some I take for history, for posterity. Josette kept it for me, when I . . . when I was away."

A pause. He was looking down at his camera and not at me.

"Henri, I . . . I'm sorry for all that you've been through," I said, biting my lip, wanting to say so much more, about us, about my feelings. Instead I just added, "Going to war, being imprisoned . . . and now hiding in your own city. There are no words for how sorry I am."

"Thank you. I'm also sorry, for your loss," Henri said. He looked me in the eyes, and for a moment the veil over his emotions was swept away, and I saw heartache and anger and something I couldn't define. "You're a widow, and yet you are here. I still don't quite understand how . . . or why. When I saw you come down the hall just now, it was like I was seeing a mirage . . . a dream of a simpler time."

"Yes, those were simpler days," I said, giving him a small smile. "I miss those days, and I've missed this city so much."

He looked down for a second, and when he looked up, he was smiling, *really* smiling at me like he used to, and I felt my heart surge because it was the Henri of old.

"Anna . . . I . . ." He started to speak, but then Georges called out from the other room, breaking the spell.

"Come, let's get something to eat," Henri said, and just like that, the emotional veil was up again. "It's almost time to use that thing."

At eight thirty, the aerial and ground wires were set, and Georges and Henri went to keep watch from the roof. I set a radio frequency using one of my tiny quartz crystals. I broadcast my first message, leading with my safety check to identify myself. I hadn't eaten dinner, as my stomach was in knots and I was overheated from nerves, even though the bedroom was chilly. I sent the Morse-coded message out into the atmosphere, in less than five minutes as required. But then there was the agonizing wait for a response. I pictured the FANY operators taking down the combination of chirps and then hurrying to the cipher clerks to have them decoded.

Sipping my wine in the darkness, I scanned the street below for the antenna-equipped German radio detection vans that patrolled the city, and I hoped to God one would not turn the corner onto Rue Fabert.

Forty minutes stretched into fifty, and I waited in front of my wireless with my headset on, fixated on the radio's coiled mass of wires and plugs, my hands clasped in prayer that I would get a response soon. My stress was rising, as the longer I kept the frequency open waiting for a reply, the bigger the risk of being caught. In training, I had learned that the Germans tracked every signal sent on frequencies not used by their own radio operators. If they detected my transmission, they would immediately begin work on finding my location. Their ability to precisely locate clandestine radios was getting faster all the time.

It had been a solid hour when I heard a tap on the door and looked up to see Henri.

"Nothing yet?"

"Nothing," I said, taking off one headphone so I could hear him. "I checked my code three times; I know it's correct."

"You need to shut it down, pack it up, and try again tomorrow. It's been long enough; les boches can triangulate radio signals very quickly these days."

"No, we need to establish first contact," I said. "They need to know I made it and I'm safe. And I need to know they heard me. Just five more minutes; it can take them over an hour sometimes. The process is complicated."

"Anna, no," Henri said, his voice strained. "It's too dangerous."

"But I have to . . ."

*"No,"* Henri said, his anger flashing. "You just got here; we cannot risk it. Do you even know what you're doing with that thing?"

"Of course I do," I said, furious at his condescending tone.

"Anna, I am afraid Henri is right," Georges said, coming up behind him in the doorway. "We'll have the wireless ready for you at the hospital tomorrow night. Shut it down; it's been too long."

I sighed, frustrated that I'd failed to do what I'd been sent here to do, on the first try. I nodded, removing the crystal, folding up the wires and hiding the suitcase under the bed.

"Let's go, Henri. We have to go to La Caravalle for a meeting before curfew," Georges said. "Anna, it's not your fault, it could have been a bad signal. It happens."

"I know," I said, still blaming myself.

"Come," Josette said, grabbing my hand and pulling me up from the table. "Tomorrow night you can try again. You didn't eat earlier, and we have a long day ahead of us tomorrow."

I nodded and followed her out to the living area. Georges kissed Josette good-bye, and Henri put on his hat to leave.

"Good luck tomorrow, on your first day of work at the Majestic," Georges said. "Get any morsel of information you can from les boches, but be careful."

As Henri was shutting the door behind them, he turned back and looked at me.

"I'm sorry for my anger," he said, taking off his hat and shoving back his thick hair, his face flushed like mine. "But you're new to the way it is now in Paris. I just want to keep us all safe."

"I'm sorry too," I said, "Good night, Henri."

He shut the door, and I turned toward the small sofa where Josette was sitting. Her legs were tucked underneath her, and she was wrapped in a blanket, balancing a glass of wine on her knee.

"Come sit, my friend." She patted the couch. "Why do you have that look on your face?"

"Because I failed on the first try, at the job I was sent here to do," I said with a sigh, sinking into the couch next to her.

"And it was probably not even your fault. Why are you doubting yourself? I'm sure it will work the next time."

"It better—it has to," I said, taking a sip of wine, trying to keep things in perspective. "Or Henri might try to get me sent home."

"It *will*," she said, looking at me with an expression of mild amusement. "And as I said, Henri is still Henri. Just a little bit broken . . . and more cautious than before."

"I understand why he's cautious about being detected. I should have listened to him the first time," I said. "I was being stubborn."

"Yes . . . but I wasn't talking about that," Josette said, eyebrows raised.

"Then what were you talking about?" I frowned at her.

"I meant he is more cautious than ever . . . with his heart."

# Chapter Twenty-Six

On my first night in Rue Fabert, we went to bed shortly after midnight, after hearing the sirens signaling that curfew was in effect. Those were followed by police cars with loudspeakers trolling the streets, announcing the same. Just before bed I looked out the window to see all of Paris in a cold December darkness. The coal was rationed, so Josette and I slept in the double bed under what she told me was "as many blankets as Georges could find." More than once I woke in the night to the sound of more sirens, and close to dawn gunshots rang out somewhere close by.

We awoke early on Thursday, drinking "coffee" made from roasted barley and chicory, a poor excuse for the real thing. I felt haggard and out of sorts, having spent half the night awake and restless, knowing that today I would be spying on the enemy under my assumed name for the first time and feeling the gravity of what I was about to do.

On our way out the front door of 26 Rue Fabert, Bijou growled at us, and I was pretty sure I heard Madame Chevrolet do the same. Before we had gone to sleep, I had rehearsed my cover story as Alexine to Josette several times. She had discussed the various German officers she met with most frequently, and what our work for the French industrialists required. Over the past few months, she had provided the Allies with incredibly valuable information about locations of German plants and commodities, among other intelligence. Huntington and others spoke of the spy Amniarix with reverence and respect for what she had already accomplished. But Josette had explained that, far from being satisfied with what she had done so far, she was frustrated because she still had not discovered anything valuable regarding a critical intelligence issue: the new weapons the Germans were building.

"Two pairs of ears are better than one," she had said to me. "And I know your memory for details is brilliant."

We decided to walk to the Hotel Majestic on Avenue Kléber in the 16th arrondissement. Formerly owned by the French government, it was now the headquarters of the German military high command in Paris. We crossed over the Seine via my favorite bridge, the beautifully ornate Pont Alexandre III, and headed down the Champs-Élysées. I was adjusting to the sights and sounds of this darker, sadder version of Paris—the Nazi flags and German signs, the many German soldiers and their black Citroën cars, the proliferation of bikes and horse-drawn carts, and the long lines of Parisians waiting with ration cards in hand at the boulangeries and charcuteries and crèmeries we passed.

"We won't stay long here today," Josette said. "I've been instructed by the industrialists to take any new German orders for the French firms we represent and to drop them at their offices by lunch. Everywhere is closing early."

"Okay," I said, feeling queasy from nerves.

The Majestic was a Belle Epoque–era building, and its grand entrance was guarded by two young Gestapo officers in shiny black boots, peaked caps over their white-blond hair.

Josette squeezed my hand as we walked up the steps.

"Just do what I do and take in everything," she said in a whisper, giving me a wink. "We'll write it all down when we get back to Rue Fabert. They love having us around because we are young and pretty, and as I said, they underestimate us because of that too. We are just stupid girls. How could we be dangerous?"

"I'll remember that," I said with a nod. I smoothed out my polka-dot dress and black cardigan under my charcoal-gray coat. That morning I had tamed my curls and swept my hair up in front with a barrette. I had also borrowed Josette's red lipstick. She was wearing a floral dress under her red wool coat and had a jaunty black felt hat that I adored.

"Okay, *Alexine*?" Josette asked.

"Okay, dear cousin *Madeleine*," I said, swallowing hard. "Let's go."

Blond soldier number one clearly recognized Josette, as he gave us both a warm smile and opened the door to let us through. His counterpart put his arm up in front of me and asked to see our papers, scowling at the first soldier like he was an idiot. When he took a cursory glance through Josette's papers and a much longer look at mine, I prepped myself for a barrage of questions, but he nodded and let us pass.

The lobby of the former hotel was gorgeous, with marble floors, gilded moldings, and a border of painted murals that framed its high ceilings. Josette nodded to the officer sitting at reception and greeted the bellman at the elevator by name.

We arrived at the fourth floor, and I clasped my hands together tightly to keep them from shaking. I took a deep breath as the door opened. We stepped out into a large open space that spanned the entire length of the hotel, with several desks arranged in perfect rows of three across, most of them occupied by German officers. There were also several more uniformed men milling about, talking in small groups of two or three. I noticed that almost all eyes were on me and Josette. I dug my fingernails into my hands and gave a small, forced smile at the faces of the enemy.

"Madeleine, I see you have brought your new associate today." A tall, dark-haired man with the palest blue eyes I had ever seen walked up to us, a serious expression on his face. He spoke stilted, guttural French, and I had to stop myself from cringing. "May I see your papers, mademoiselle?"

"Yes, this is my cousin, Alexine Chauffour," Josette said in German with a warm smile, though the dark-haired man's face didn't change. "Alexine, this is Officer Herbert Keppler. He is the head of this entire division."

243

"It is a pleasure to meet you, sir," I said in French.

"Do you really speak German as well as your cousin does?" he asked, looking down at my papers and back at me, not entirely convinced.

"Yes, I do," I replied in German.

"You know you are all getting to be too much work for a little thing like me," Josette said to him. She had taken on a whole different demeanor. Josette was headstrong and smart, while this Madeleine character was a wide-eyed, flirtatious ingenue. I had caught a glimpse of her at the train station. It was an impressive transformation.

"I have been desperate for help," Josette continued, "and here she is. She arrived like an angel on the night before Christmas Eve. The French industrialists hired her on the spot."

"And you are from Saint-Malo?" Keppler asked me, just as another officer called Josette over with a question regarding something he was working on.

"Yes, sir," I said, trying to contain my nerves as Josette left me on my own to talk with him. "I grew up there, sir."

I was trying to inhabit my role of Alexine, a native French girl, born and raised in Saint-Malo.

"And your parents' names?"

"Albert and Louise Chauffour. My father is the brother of my uncle Remy, Madeleine's father."

"Are they still there?"

"They are in Aix-en-Provence, staying with Madeleine's parents."

"Did you attend university?" he asked, firing questions at me, perhaps trying to catch me in a lie. It was hard to know, but I tried to stay focused and not miss a beat.

"Yes," I said. "In Toulouse."

"Do you have any brothers or sisters?"

"Two younger sisters, Sylvie and Giselle. They are also staying in Aix-en-Provence."

He studied me in a way that made me want to squirm, but I kept smiling at him and batting my eyelashes.

"You have the most extraordinary blue eyes," Keppler said, with a small smile now, still fixated on me.

This was unexpected, and though Josette had told me that many of them were unabashed in their flirtatiousness, I didn't think this would be the case for someone of his stature. Not on my first day.

"Um . . . thank you, sir. I could say the same about yours," I said. I didn't have to fake a blush. It wasn't a lie. His eyes were a startling pale blue, like a Siberian husky's. Looking into them made me so uneasy because there was something cold about them, lifeless. It had been the right thing to say because he seemed pleased, but I felt my stomach turn when he smiled.

"Officer Keppler." Josette came back over to us and tapped him on the shoulder. "I was going to introduce Alexine to some of the men. Are you still closing the offices by lunchtime as planned?"

"Yes," Keppler said, "but please, before you ladies leave, you should have a glass of champagne with us. It is Christmas Eve, after all."

"Of course," Josette said, taking me by the arm and leading me away. Josette brought me around the floor, introducing me to the various officers working at their desks. Some of them started to speak with us in terrible, broken French and were visibly relieved when they realized that like Josette I also spoke German fluently, though her German was stronger than mine from speaking it regularly.

I started to feel myself relax, and my hands stopped shaking. They were just men, after all—a few of the younger ones were shy, even. There was a heavyset, bald officer with a monocle. He was definitely one of the more lecherous, openly staring at my chest. Others were flirtatious, commenting on my "pretty curls" or my "beautiful smile."

"And I have saved the best for last," Josette said with a smile and sweep of her arm, as two young men jumped up from their desks to shake my hand. "Alexine, these are my good friends Franz Becker and Otto Wagner. Unfortunately for us, they have recently been promoted."

"Yes, both of us were just assigned to a very critical new special project upstairs. We start after the holidays," Franz said, pumping my hand up and down. "It's so nice to meet you." He was tall and thin with light-brown hair and a few freckles across his nose, with a smile that reached his eyes, unlike Keppler's.

"Yes, nice to meet you," Otto said. His round cheeks were bright pink, and his hands were thick like bear paws. He was shorter than Franz, stocky, with curly blond hair cut very short.

"Nice to meet you as well," I said. "Congratulations on the promotion."

"You know I am very happy for you both, even though it means I won't be seeing you as often," Josette said with a pout.

"Now you'll just have to go out for drinks with us more," Franz said.

"Yes, and you too, Alexine," Otto said with an enthusiastic nod. "To Les Deux Magots, one of our favorites."

"I believe Otto loves Paris even more than Berlin," Franz said, teasing him.

"There is a lot to love about Paris," I said. "What is the new project you will be working on upstairs?"

"Oh, that is top secret, mademoiselle," Franz said, shaking a finger at me and speaking in French so terribly, it was clear it was on purpose. He botched the pronunciation of *mademoiselle* so badly that Josette burst out laughing.

"Yes, we will go out for drinks, and hopefully help you improve your dreadful French," Josette said.

"Madeleine, come here, I need help translating this order for your bosses," Keppler called out to her from across the room, a look on his face of annoyance . . . or jealousy? It was hard to tell, but we nodded to Franz and Otto, and I followed Josette over to see what Keppler needed.

I spent the rest of the morning as Josette's shadow, assisting her in the translation of documents when necessary and gathering the orders for goods such as steel and rubber that we would take back to the French industrialists. At exactly noon, Berlin time, a crate of Pommery champagne was delivered to the floor, and champagne flutes appeared out of nowhere.

"A welcome to our beautiful new assistant, Alexine Chauffour," Keppler said, holding up his glass. "I know it is difficult to be away from family on this Christmas Eve, so a toast to all of you for your service."

My nerves came rushing back at the mention of my alias. I restrained myself from downing the entire glass of champagne as I felt goose pimples break out up and down my arms. I had survived the morning, but no matter how normal some of the Germans seemed, we were flirting with the enemy. If they discovered our game, we could be killed.

I looked up and saw Keppler walking over to where Josette and I were standing by the windows. Josette was talking to Franz and another officer. Rather than interrupting them, Keppler came and stood far too close to me, and I could smell his odd citrus cologne.

"Funny," he said, studying my face with his cold eyes. "You're both quite pretty, but . . . you don't look like cousins. In fact, there is no family resemblance at all."

I shivered and prayed he didn't see. "That's because I favor my mother's side of the family," I said.

"Ah, your mother Lucile Chauffour?" he asked, watching my reaction.

"My mother . . ." I hesitated and laughed to cover it up. "My mother Louise. She has the same eyes as me. The same hair also."

It had to be a test. Why else would he mention her name again?

"Ah sorry, your mother Louise. I read your papers quickly. As they say here, *Joyeux Noël*, Alexine."

"Joyeux Noël, sir."

He smiled and tipped his champagne flute at me. I did the same to him, praying he didn't notice the slight tremble in my hand.

# Chapter Twenty-Seven

"Trust me, Anna, I do not think he suspected anything," Josette said to me as we dragged two rusty bicycles from behind 26 Rue Fabert. "Don't worry. I think he's a little crazy, and his mind is full of suspicious ideas. Many of them are like that."

"I'm not so sure," I said, still feeling uneasy.

"The best news I received this morning was that Franz and Otto's promotion involves a new project upstairs," Josette said. "I have to find out what they're working on. Those 'secret' offices? *That* is where the most valuable intelligence lies."

After the champagne, Josette and I had left the Hotel Majestic, dropped the orders off to the French industrialists' offices, and headed back to the apartment at Rue Fabert to freshen up and get the bikes. It was a twenty-minute bike ride to the Christmas Eve party at the American Hospital located on the outskirts of Paris in Neuilly-sur-Seine. I was in no mood for a party, emotionally exhausted from my first day playing the role of Alexine, but I needed to get a message to London after my failed attempt. According to Georges and Henri, the hospital was a safe place to transmit from, and there was a wireless available for me to use.

It was dusk, and many of the cafés were lit up and bustling with customers trying to muster some Christmas Eve cheer before the clock struck midnight. I saw more than a few Parisian women sitting at tables with

German soldiers, drinking and laughing, celebrating the holiday. I mentioned it to Josette when we reached an intersection close to the hospital.

"Many women have had affairs with Germans. Often it's the only way to get black-market food or clothing for their families," Josette said, her expression sour. "It is called 'horizontal collaboration.' It disgusts me, but then I ask myself, If I had a starving child at home, what would I do?"

"I . . . I think I would do anything to save my child," I said, remembering the quiet whimpers of the underweight children I saw standing with their mothers in the lines for food.

"I think I would too," Josette said with a sigh. "The only problem? Now there are even *more* babies here, with German fathers."

We arrived at the American Hospital on Boulevard Victor Hugo, just as my feet and fingers were starting to feel too frozen to bike anymore. The hospital reminded me of a comfortable, welcoming hotel you'd see in New England, with a center building and two matching wings.

Josette had explained that Dr. Sumner Jackson had created an "underground railroad" that had already helped many Allied servicemen escape. With Henri, Georges, and Josette's help, he would often interview these men to gain any intelligence for the Allies about German troop movements.

A young American nurse greeted us when we arrived and led us down a long corridor lined with doors on either side, spotlessly clean tile floors, and white walls, the strong smell of cleaning products not quite overpowering the less pleasant odors. The nurse explained that many of the patients there had been sent from the German POW camps to be treated because their field hospitals were overwhelmed.

We entered a festively decorated cafeteria packed with male patients, most in hospital gowns and robes, sitting at long, dark wooden tables with plates of food in front of them and small glasses of red wine. They were smiling as they listened to a group of nurses on a makeshift stage in the front of the room who were giggling as they tried their best to get the group to sing along to Christmas carols.

Seeing the little Christmas tree on the stage, I felt a wave of melancholy wash over me. I imagined my family, in our house on Cape Cod, and I hoped they weren't too worried about me. I thought of my friends scattered from the war—Mary in DC, Irene in the UK, and Julia in the tropics. And I thought of Phillip, as I had often since the night we said good-bye. Where was he now? Josette, as if sensing my homesickness, put her arm around my shoulder.

"It's wonderful to have you here," she said. "It must be difficult to be so far away from home on Christmas. I miss my family, and they are only a few hours away."

"It's good to be here," I said. "And even the way it is now, this city still feels like a second home."

Georges and Henri were standing near the stage, huddled and talking with a tall, gray-haired gentleman in a white coat. We made our way over to them when the little concert ended to rousing applause from the audience.

"Ah, just who we were waiting for," Georges said. "Anna, this is our dear friend, Dr. Sumner Jackson."

"Lovely to meet you, Anna," Dr. Jackson said. He was wearing dark-framed glasses, and his untamed, wiry eyebrows were escaping over the tops of them. "I hear you're from Boston. I'm from Maine. Red Sox fan?"

"Of course," I said with a laugh. He was the kind of person that emanated warmth. I liked him immediately. "American Hospital—what does that mean?"

"Well, since the war started, it means we're a designated Red Cross military hospital, serving both civilian and military patients. You're only the second American woman I've met in your line of work in France."

"Yes. I recently met her—the first," I said.

"I also just met another recent SOE arrival from London," he said. "A spitfire of a girl with bleached blonde hair. She's helping with the underground railroad we've set up."

*Tatiana.* For some reason, it was comforting to know what she was up to and that she had been here. I wondered how Nora was doing.

"I think I know that one, too," I said with a broad smile.

"The wireless is ready for you upstairs," Henri said to me in an abrupt tone. "Don't you need to try again very soon?"

"Yes, in twenty minutes, at 6:00 p.m. Thank you so much for the reminder," I replied, not hiding my sarcasm.

"Josette, I want to talk to the two RAF fighters," Georges said. "To see if there's any intelligence we can get from them. Will you come with me?"

"Of course." Josette nodded. "Henri, will you show Anna where the wireless is set up? Be her lookout."

Henri just nodded, an annoyed expression clouding his face.

"Thank you all for your work," Dr. Jackson said. "And please do have something to eat while you're here. The struggle to feed hundreds of patients gets harder every day. We converted part of the garage into a secret pig sty last year—that means pork for Christmas Eve dinner tonight, and our resourceful cook boiled vegetables in enormous cauldrons in the courtyard."

We thanked the doctor, and then Henri silently led me up several flights of stairs to a small room with sloped ceilings on the top floor of the hospital. The suitcase containing the wireless was on a table next to an arched window, which provided the only light in the room. Henri took a wax candle out of his pocket, placed it on the table next to the wireless, and lit it with a match.

"That's the door to the roof," he said, pointing to a black metal door on the opposite side of the room. "Do you need help getting that antenna out through the window?"

"Yes, thank you," I said, as we unpacked the wireless and set up the two antennas, cracking the window to stick the one outside. My palms were sweaty, and my heart was beating hard in my chest, from nerves about failing and, if I was being honest with myself, about standing so close to Henri. "Cautious with his heart," Josette had said . . . though I had chalked that up to Josette's own romanticism, nothing more.

"Where did this wireless set come from?" I asked. It was a slightly different, older version than mine.

"It belonged to one of the radio operators who was captured by the Gestapo," he said in a blunt tone.

"What happened to him?"

"They held him prisoner on the top floor of a mansion at 84 Avenue Foch, their headquarters. Then they tortured him, and when they couldn't get anything out of him, they shot him."

"Oh, that's horrific," I said, gritting my teeth and wrapping my arms around myself.

He turned his head, and in the flickering candlelight, I caught a glimpse of an angry, twisted scar beneath his right ear that he hadn't had years before. I let out a small gasp at the sight of it and was about to ask what happened when he stepped back from me and took out a cigarette.

"I'll head outside and keep watch for the boche vans. It's time to start, no?"

"What? Yes. Yes, you're right. It is," I said.

He nodded and went out on the roof. I put the headset on and chose the radio frequency I'd be transmitting on, plugging in the required crystal. Using the tiny Morse key, I started with my safety check and then transmitted my message. All in less than five minutes, as planned. And once again I sat back, took a deep breath, and prayed for a response.

After fifteen minutes, I heard the door to the roof creak open behind me, and Henri looked at me, asking me with his eyes if I'd received anything back. I just shook my head, frustrated and embarrassed because he looked as aggravated as I felt. Each minute felt like an eternity, and I just sat there, fidgeting and hoping I would hear something soon.

A half hour later, Henri peeked inside again, and he was about to say something when I heard a crackle on my headphones and held my hand up to stop him.

My hand shaking, I wrote down the incoming message, removing the crystal and shutting down the wireless as soon as it was clear there was no more to come. I took the piece of silk handkerchief out of my brassiere in case I needed my ciphers, but I was able to decode the message without even glancing at them.

> MESSAGE RECEIVED PEACOCK. PLEASE ADHERE TO PLANNED SKED TIMES MOVING FORWARD. SOE AND OSS HAVE URGENT NEED FOR INTEL REGARDING NEW SECRET WEAPONRY. NEW REPORT STATES IT IS BEING DEVELOPED ON GERMANY'S BALTIC COAST. TELL DRUIDS EXPECT A LARGE DELIVERY WITH THE NEXT FULL MOON. SAME LOCATION. STAY SAFE.

I read it out loud to Henri and let out a cheer, jumping out of my chair.

"I did it," I said, ripping up the paper into tiny pieces, feeling giddy with exhilaration. "It really worked. I knew I could do it, but after last night, well, thank God."

"Yes, you did it," Henri said with a real smile that went all the way up to his eyes this time. "Your code name is Peacock? I like it."

He nodded to the peacock pin I was wearing.

"Yes, I wore it for luck tonight. It's a gift from the head of the OSS," I said, so relieved and thinking that Donovan would be proud of me in this moment. "Of course, I won't be wearing it much while I'm here . . . never around the Germans."

"I think that's wise," he said, still smiling.

"Aren't you happy? You'll be getting more arms next month."

"If they succeed with their plans, yes," he said, pacing the room.

"They will," I said. "I promise you, they are committed to helping the Resistance from within now. They know they have to. Especially if there is ever to be an Allied invasion, they will need help from inside France."

"You speak with the naivete of someone who has not lived under occupation for years," he said, his tone matter-of-fact this time, no bitterness.

"You're right," I said. "I don't know anything about what you've gone through."

He stared at me for a few seconds, frowning, his cheeks flushed from the cold.

"No, you don't," he said. "I'm going to smoke another cigarette outside before we go downstairs."

I quickly packed up the wireless equipment in its suitcase and headed outside, pushing the heavy metal door to the roof with both hands. It was a clear night, and I could see the silhouette of the Sacré-Coeur basilica atop Montmartre in the distance. I wrapped my arms around myself, this time from the chill, and looked out into the beautiful, suffering city.

Henri stubbed out his cigarette before walking over to me, taking off his jacket, and putting it around my shoulders. We were standing inches apart.

"You know, I assumed I would never see you again. Not that I didn't want to, but . . . I heard you were married," he said, saying the word *married* as if it tasted bad.

He turned, and we were face-to-face, and he was so handsome now it almost hurt to look at him.

"Why did you come? Why are you *really* here? Paris is a terrible, dangerous place, and you're doing a job that may get you killed. I still don't understand why you would come back."

"I . . ." I couldn't believe how much being near him still affected me; my heart was beating so fast I was sure he could hear it. The butterflies I'd had every time I was with him years ago were back as if they had never left. "I'm here because I finally convinced the OSS I could do this job, and I want to do something that matters in this war. And . . . and because when I was living in Paris, I felt more alive than I ever had before in my life. And, despite the danger, I feel like I am meant to be here and nowhere else."

He was quiet for a moment, looking at me like he was trying to solve a puzzle.

"That way of thinking is so American," he said. His tone was cynical, but his smile was real.

"Well . . . I guess it is." I just shrugged.

"It's taken most Parisians years of suffering to want to do something. Some still just want this all to go away without having to *do* anything. The wealthiest Parisians go about their days as if the war is not even happening. They simply ignore the horrible things the Germans have done. Worse, many of them are using the Germans to get more money for themselves."

His face was so close I could smell the cigarettes on his breath, and I wasn't sure who reached out first, but we were holding each other's hands. The emotional wall he had put up for the past couple of days was starting to crumble.

"Oh, Anna . . . ," he said, rubbing my face with his hand, his dark eyes looking into mine like they had so long ago. He let out a long sigh. "After all this time, here you are again, and . . . you? Don't you understand I now have someone else here to worry about?"

I didn't know what to say. Our feelings for each other were still there, and I was stunned to realize it. And my heart ached because I also cared for Phillip. I hadn't stopped thinking about our last kiss and his letter, the one I had scattered to the wind. I cared for both him and Henri, in ways that were different and yet very much the same.

I bit my lip and was reaching out to touch the scar under his ear when we heard footsteps on the stairs and stepped away from each other.

"*Salut!*" Georges called out as he and Josette came bursting out onto the roof together.

"Did you have any luck?" Josette said, gritting her teeth, a pleading look on her face as she held her hands up as if in prayer. "Please tell me you got through to them."

"I did," I said with a smile as I relayed the message to them.

"Perfect," Georges said, clasping his hands together. "Well done, *Peacock*. You both have to get whatever you can out of your friends at the Majestic as soon as possible. Those friends of yours—what are their names? Otto and Fritz . . ."

"Franz, and yes Georges, we will," Josette said, rolling her eyes. He leaned down and kissed her hard on the lips, and she pushed him away, laughing.

"Is it time for us to go, then?" Henri asked Georges, stealing a glance at me.

"Yes, it is," Georges said. We went downstairs with them and bid them good-bye at the entrance to the cafeteria. This time when Henri kissed me on both cheeks, his lips lingered with the second kiss.

"Merry Christmas," he whispered in my ear, and I just nodded when we looked into each other's eyes.

"Come on, Anna," Josette said. "I'm quite hungry, and they have real *pork*. Oh, how I miss real food. And there are some patients here that would love to dance with the pretty new American."

I stole a glance back at Henri, who was walking away as we headed into the cafeteria to join the party, where the nurses and patients were jitterbugging.

"Mon amie, you must remember, we are working and at war, and times are difficult, but we are not dead," Josette said to me, leading me toward the buffet and giving me a knowing sideways glance.

"What are you saying?" I said, frowning at her but amused.

"It is obvious you two still care about each other," Josette said. "Right now, there is enough to fight against in Paris. Why fight how you feel as well?"

# Chapter Twenty-Eight

**February 12, 1943**

I had only been in Paris for just under two months, but London was already impatient for more intelligence from me. With nearly every message I received via the wireless, they were pressing hard for more information about the Germans' secret weaponry. We continued to provide critical information regarding factories and troop movements, among so much other intelligence, which I knew was also extremely valuable, but it was the weaponry—the scope of it, where it was being built—that mattered most to them. And it was information we still hadn't been able to provide.

Josette and I were frustrated, but as much as we tried to "coincidentally" run into them in the elevator or lobby, we had hardly seen Otto and Franz since they had started working in the offices upstairs. It was a Friday afternoon, and we were planning to once again linger in the lobby after work in the hopes of catching them and inviting them for a drink at a nearby café.

I considered all of this as I sat at my desk in the Germans' Hotel Majestic offices and translated documents from the French industrialists regarding recent sales of steel and rubber to the German military. My arms broke out in goose pimples, and I looked up to see Keppler watching me from across the room with those icy-blue eyes, as he often did, without apology. I knew it helped to encourage him in at least a mildly flirtatious way, in the hope that the more naive and flighty I seemed, the less he would suspect. But from that first day, my gut told me he was suspicious of me, this cousin who had dropped into occupied Paris. Smiling, I gave him a small wave, and he just nodded back.

When I wasn't working at the Majestic with Josette, I had been maintaining my schedule with the London offices, communicating with them on the wireless about all the Druids network's activities, rotating between our apartment on Rue Fabert, the American Hospital, and also the hostel on Boulevard Saint-Michel.

It had taken me some time to adjust to this odd new life, to the Nazi presence everywhere and my constant paranoia, to the freezing nights huddled next to Josette under blankets, and to a mostly bland, repetitive diet of whatever food we could get with our ration cards. Watery potato and leek soup, cabbage, and beets were constants in our meals. The occasional supper at a café was slightly better. Many café owners had to rely at least somewhat on the black market to stay in business, so that contributed to their menus' variety.

"Are you leaving soon, *Fräulein*?" Keppler was now standing right in front of my desk.

"Yes, sir, just waiting for my cousin," I said, giving him a smile and batting my eyelashes while groaning inside. I tried not to say Josette's cover name out loud too often, for fear of getting it wrong. "She should be back soon."

"Did you finish that translation?" He pointed down to my desk.

"I am nearly done; I promise it will be finished before I leave."

"Your work has been excellent so far. Your translation skills are most impressive," he said. He leaned on my desk, one hand next to my work, his eyes either on the documents in front of me or on my chest—it was hard to know which, but either way it made my skin crawl.

"Thank you. That means a great deal coming from you, sir," I said, turning red from the discomfort of his proximity.

"What are your plans for this evening?" He looked into my eyes, and I swallowed hard, thinking of something to say other than the truth. I was about to answer when I heard Josette call to me.

She was walking toward us with Franz and Otto, and I breathed an imperceptible sigh of relief. "Look who I found in the elevator."

I stood up to greet them, and the young soldiers saluted Keppler.

"It's good to see you again," I said. "I had only just met you and you both disappeared upstairs. I told Madeleine that her friends had forgotten about her."

"Mademoiselle, *never*," Otto said, pretending to be aghast. Something about his round cheeks made him look cherubic. "In fact, we were planning on coming to see you both today to invite you to a party tomorrow night at a very grand residence on the Avenue de Malakoff."

"It's being given by a wealthy American woman," Franz added, his eyes on Josette.

"Yes, excellent idea. You should both come," Keppler said. "You've been working very hard. Sometimes you have to play."

I looked at Josette, and she nodded at me.

"Sounds lovely. Thank you for the invitation," I said. It was the opportunity with Franz and Otto we had been waiting for, but I hated that Keppler would be there too.

"We would love to attend," Josette said, and again I was struck by her transformation into the flirty ingenue. I had told her that, after the war, she should consider becoming an actress.

"Excellent. I have some business to attend to, but I'm pleased that I will see you there," Keppler said, leaving the four of us, much to Franz and Otto's visible relief.

We made plans to meet them in front of the apartment building on Avenue de Malakoff, and though I knew it wasn't a real date, it felt like one, and that made me feel guilty. Guilt over socializing with German soldiers, guilt over my lingering feelings for Phillip, wherever he was in the world. And, if I was totally honest with myself, guilt out of disloyalty to Henri. There was an undeniable ache in my heart for him alone.

We had barely seen Henri or Georges since the first week of January, and even then it had been for a brief rendezvous in a "safe" café or at the house on Rue Fabert. The third week of January they had gone back to Avaray to receive their much-needed shipment of arms and ammunitions, but they had returned empty-handed, angry, and frustrated. The message from London had said that poor visibility due to clouds and rain had prevented any full moon drops and they would attempt again in February.

Tonight, Josette and I would be meeting both of them at La Caravalle, a music hall in Montmartre; its owner was also a Resistance member and he allowed the basement of the club to be used for clandestine training, among other purposes. All day I'd had that nervous, fluttery anticipation of seeing Henri that I had felt years ago.

After another hour, I finally finished translating and grabbed my coat and purse to leave. Josette and I were waiting by the elevator when Keppler called to us.

"Yes?" I said. "Did you need something else?"

"No, but . . ." Keppler paused, frowning. "This is a rather formal party tomorrow night. Do you both have something appropriate to wear?"

The question felt odd, but being "students" we both dressed simply for work—culottes and skirts, simple blouses and well-worn sweaters, the occasional dress.

"Oh sir, *of course* we have something fashionable to wear," Josette said, and she actually winked at him. "After all, we are French."

Keppler gave us a genuine laugh as he bid us good night.

# Chapter Twenty-Nine

"We actually don't have anything fancy to wear to this party," I said to Josette. "Do we?"

We had taken the overcrowded, rancid-smelling metro into the Montmartre area of Paris and were sitting at the cozy Café Tabac a couple of blocks from La Caravalle. It was a cold, drizzly Friday evening, and the area was teeming with Germans. Montmartre was home to the famous Moulin Rouge cabaret theater, several nightclubs and cafés, as well as numerous brothels, and all these businesses were thriving thanks to the Germans.

"Well, we can't afford haute couture, but I have an old friend, Catherine. She works at the fashion house Lelong," Josette said. "She is a courier with one of the larger resistance networks. She will let us borrow dresses, I am sure of it."

"Will her bosses know we are borrowing them?" I asked, frowning.

"Of course not. Don't be ridiculous," Josette said with a mischievous smile. "She would be fired on the spot. But her brother is a designer there. He'll be able to find us some, and nobody will even know they're gone."

I was about to ask how we were going to walk out of House of Lelong with two "borrowed" dresses when a blonde woman dressed in a camel-colored coat and veiled black beret walked into Tabac and headed straight for our table. Now, when Josette and I went to a café, we always chose tables in the back of the establishment, preferably up against one of the walls so we could have a view of the entire place.

The blonde pulled up a rattan chair from one of the tables nearby and sat down with us.

"Tatiana," I whispered in shock when she took the veiled beret off. "Your hair is even blonder now, and a little shorter too? I almost didn't recognize you."

"It's hard to find a good hairdresser in Paris these days," she said with a shrug, leaning in to kiss me on both cheeks. "So good to see you, my friend. And you as well, Josette."

She looked as pretty as ever, but her face was thinner, and there were dark circles under her eyes. She pulled a pack of Gauloises cigarettes out of her pocket and offered us one, even though women weren't given cigarette rations.

"The owner knows me, so I promise you he won't care if we smoke," Tatiana said, sensing our hesitation. Josette took one from her, lit it, and inhaled with pure contentment.

"How did you know we would be here?" I asked, frowning.

"I happen to be a very good spy," she replied, winking at me.

"I don't need to tell you that you shouldn't be here," I said, still keeping my voice very low, reminding her that agents in different networks were not supposed to contact each other. Tatiana shook her head and gave me a grim smile.

"Come on, Anna, do you really think all those old men in London know what's best for us here?" Tatiana said with a smirk.

"Honestly?" I said, eyebrows raised. "Probably not."

"They tried to train us, but this work? This entire *life*? It is all an improvisation."

"That is true," I said, giving her a small smile, and Josette nodded in agreement. "Oh no, are you here because something happened to Nora . . . ?"

"No, thankfully," Tatiana said, looking up at the copper ceiling and blowing a stream of smoke. "I have seen her, though I haven't spoken to her. She's far too honest. I'm afraid she'd do something foolish if she saw me."

"So, she's all right?"

"She is with that network as a wireless operator and constantly moving. So far, she is safe and has not gotten herself killed. So that is good news, no?"

"That's a relief," I said.

"Speaking of the wireless, I need your help," Tatiana said, getting to the point. "There are more Allied soldiers coming through the underground network every day. But Maurice, our network's wireless operator, is gone."

"Where?" Josette asked, looking as alarmed as I felt.

"He was taken three nights ago by the Gestapo," Tatiana said. Her voice filled with anguish, she added, "He's in solitary confinement at Fresnes Prison, which I have heard is hell on earth."

I shuddered. It was a grim reminder of the deadly game we were playing.

"I have heard the same. Filthy, rat-infested cellblocks," Josette said, and she swore under her breath and visibly shivered.

"I am so sorry, Tatiana," I said.

"And of course I was having an incredibly passionate affair with him," Tatiana said, letting out a big sigh and already lighting up another cigarette. "So that makes it all worse."

"And now you need my help getting messages to London?" I said.

"I do," she said. "I could leave them with Dr. Jackson at the American Hospital. He's the hero of the underground network here. Many American and British soldiers have made it out of Paris alive because he convinced the Germans they died in his care."

"No problem," I said. It would increase my workload. It would increase my chances of getting caught—every second I spent on the wireless did—but that couldn't be helped.

We discussed when she would leave the first messages for me, paid our bill, and rose to leave, as Josette and I were due to meet Georges and Henri.

"Stay safe, my friend," I said to Tatiana outside Café Tabac, giving her two kisses good-bye.

"You too, mon amie," Tatiana said, looking slightly mysterious with the black veil over her face. "And do me a favor. Have a drink and let yourself have a little fun, for God's sake. This is still *our* city. The Talmud says living well is the best revenge. Enjoying life right now? It is its own kind of resistance."

∾

La Caravalle was a well-known French music hall in Montmartre, famous for the jazz musicians and bands it attracted. The groups played terrific American big band jazz and swing music, but since Germany had banned American music, all the clubs now referred to the music as specifically "French jazz." The club's owner was a supporter of the Resistance, and had often let Georges and Henri hold meetings in the basement, recruiting and training new members of the Druids network and others.

Josette and I arrived at the club a little after seven. The interior was dark and cavernous and smelled of stale, cheap wine. It was already half full of patrons, many of whom were still wearing their coats, because it definitely wasn't heated. A six-person band was warming up on a stage flanked by navy-blue velvet curtains.

We made our way backstage and descended a wrought-iron spiral staircase so steep I had to hold on to both railings. Josette knocked six times on the door at the bottom, and Georges opened it with a smile as young men started streaming out, saying bonsoir to us as they passed. A few of them had an odd bulkiness to their coats, hiding the guns and ammunition they had just received.

"Oh no, did we just ruin the party?" Josette said in mock offense.

"No, we were finishing up," Georges said, putting his arm around her and kissing her on the cheek.

"There is not much more to do in terms of training until we get more weapons. We could only outfit a dozen of them," Henri said. He looked in my eyes, genuinely happy to see me as he kissed me on the cheeks, and I felt a familiar warmth rush through me from being so close to him. "Hello, Anna. Anything else from London?"

"No, I'm sorry to say," I said. "Just that they'll try to fly again next Saturday if the weather is clear."

"These new men need to feel like the Allies are on our side," Henri said, his frustration evident. "I was counting on last month's shipment."

"Let's go get a drink upstairs, my friend," Georges said, clapping Henri on the back. "Nothing more we can do tonight."

I was the last one to go up the spiral staircase, and Henri reached back and grabbed my hand. What is it about a small gesture as simple as holding a hand that can make you unable to think of anything else?

"These stairs are treacherous," he warned me with a smile as we made our way up them together.

The four of us found a table in a corner far enough from the stage that we didn't have to yell to hear each other. The band onstage was dressed in matching suits and playing to a club that had filled up quickly.

"Are there Germans here tonight?" I said when we sat down, scanning the crowd for uniforms.

"There are Germans everywhere, *ma chérie*," Henri said. He was sitting close to me, our legs touching under the table. "It's harder to tell them apart when they're not in uniform."

"Speaking of not wearing uniforms, wait until you hear where Anna and I are going tomorrow night," Josette said. She told them all about the party we'd be attending.

"Finally, we might be able to get some more intelligence out of Franz and Otto," I said.

But instead of being excited, Georges's and Henri's expressions were serious. Henri was frowning, worried.

"I wish there was some way we could go with you," Georges said. He scratched his forehead, clearly thinking of alternatives. "The Majestic offices are one thing; a party where there's drinking and . . . Do they think they are taking you out on a date?"

"Yes, of course," Josette said in a gentle tone, putting her hand on his. "But we need them to. From the messages Anna has received, it's clear London is desperate for information. We have seen very little of Franz and Otto, and now we have a chance to discover what they know—the party and the drinking will help. They'll be inclined to talk more."

"No Mata Hari games, though?" Georges said, and a storm crossed Josette's face.

"Georges, never. Why would you even ask me that?" she said. Dropping her voice, she added, "I would never, ever sleep with a boche. You know that. I would rather die!"

"I just had to ask the question," Georges said, his voice tight. "I knew it would come to this, this going out with them. But I don't have to like it."

"Yet you have been pressuring us to get this information as much as London has," Josette said in a harsh whisper. "We *must* do this."

There was an awkward silence at the table, and I took a long sip of my wine as the audience started clapping and a statuesque woman dressed in a black lace cocktail dress walked to the microphone at center stage. The band started to play again. The woman started to sing a ballad in French. Her voice was slow and sweet like honey as couples headed to the dance floor in front of the stage.

"Come on, Anna, let's dance," Henri said, grabbing my hand again and pulling me up from the table. The air in the club was a smoke-filled haze, and the lights were so low we had to be careful navigating our way through the tables.

When we reached the dance floor, he put his free hand around my waist and pulled me close. I caught my breath as I reached up and wrapped my arm around his neck like a question mark, careful not to touch his scar and feeling light-headed at our closeness. And then I thought of dancing with Phillip my last night in London, and my heart hurt. Life and love were complicated, and war made both monumentally harder.

Henri represented the path not taken, and these past few years thoughts of him had led me back to the brief period of time I had lived here, when I had felt most happy and free and in control of my own life. And though for a long time I had been racked with guilt over our brief affair, deep down, I had come to realize that I had no real regrets about it.

"I thought they needed a moment to themselves," Henri said in my ear.

"I agree."

"And I wanted to dance with you again," he said as he pulled me tighter. "Do you still know how to tango?"

"I might remember." I laughed. "I haven't tangoed since that night in the amphitheater on the Seine. I'm guessing that doesn't happen anymore?"

"Not since les boches arrived."

"It will happen again."

He pulled away slightly and looked in my eyes. "Will you dance with me there when it does?" he asked, our faces so close I could feel his breath.

"I will," I said.

And then his lips were on mine in a soft, slow kiss, and for a moment the dance floor melted away and so did the years. I let myself get swept up in it, and my worries and the war outside disappeared.

He then kissed my forehead as we continued to dance, my head on his chest, and I could hear his heart beating as hard as mine was.

"I am also worried about you going to this party tomorrow," he whispered. "I wish I could go with you. To protect you. Always remember what these men are capable of. Please be careful."

"We will, I promise." I thought of Tatiana's wireless operator, and a shiver went through me. Henri sensed it and pulled me closer, leaning down to kiss me one last time before the song ended.

# Chapter Thirty

**February 13, 1943**

On Saturday afternoon, Josette convinced me to tint my legs to create the look of silk stockings with her bottle of Elizabeth Arden iodine, a beauty necessity among certain women in occupied France. We had also gotten our hair done at one of the few operating salons on the Champs-Élysées. It was such a luxury to have my curls washed and styled. They were pinned up in front, off my face, and fell softly down my back. Josette's hair was styled in victory rolls that framed her face and accented her large eyes.

We arrived at the House of Lelong at 4:00 p.m. Catherine Dior, Josette's friend who worked there, was about the same age as us, with thin lips and a long nose. Her light-brown hair was in a chignon, and she was dressed in a striking burgundy velvet suit. She ushered us through the hallways, past rooms that were bustling with seamstresses and designers draping fabrics on mannequins, sitting at sewing machines, or carefully hand-beading dresses. We entered a large storage closet that smelled sweet and sour like new fabric with a touch of closet must. There were shelves of sewing materials stacked in cardboard boxes up to the ceiling. Catherine pulled out a tape measure without a word and quickly started taking our measurements.

"Thank you for doing this, old friend. How are things with your network?" Josette asked as Catherine wrapped the tape measure around her waist.

"Same as everyone's, I think," Catherine said as she wrote Josette's measurements on a little pad of paper. "There are not enough supplies, not enough wireless operators. We wait impatiently for an Allied invasion I fear might never come."

"It will come," Josette said. "Maybe not in the timeline people hope, but it has to come."

"I believe that too," I said, though I shared her concern that the Allies were not moving quickly enough.

Catherine gave us a doubtful look, told us she'd be back in a few minutes, and hurried out the closet door.

"And she knows what we're looking for?" I asked Josette.

"Yes, I left her a note early this morning, and she's happy to help us; however, she's busy and wants us in and out quickly to avoid getting caught."

"Of course." I nodded, pausing for a moment. "Is everything okay now between you and Georges?" I had been waiting to ask her the question.

"Yes." Josette sighed. "I love him, Anna. I am mad about him. He is passionate and brilliant and a little bit crazy and he makes me laugh. But at this moment, things are quite difficult. There is so much to be done. So much pressure and fear, and, well, also we don't get much time alone together."

She twisted her mouth and raised her eyebrows, her pale cheeks turning bright pink. I understood immediately what she meant.

"Oh. Oh . . . If you want me to stay at the hostel some night so you . . . so you can have some time alone? I am happy to do that."

"Thank you," she said. "And what about you and Henri? I was so happy to see you dancing last night. He has needed some sweetness and light in his life."

"After all this time," I said, shaking my head, "I can't believe the feelings are still there."

Now it was my turn to blush.

"But they are," Josette said, smiling.

"They are," I said, thinking about our kiss on the dance floor, hoping it wouldn't be the last, and then feeling a wave of guilt about Phillip, because I did still care for him. And if he showed up in Paris tomorrow? I had no idea what I would do. "Josette . . . I have to tell you something."

"Yes?"

"After Connor died, I felt so much guilt and sadness, because marrying him was a mistake, and he and I both knew it. I had no interest in men and definitely no interest in marrying again. But right before I came here, I met someone."

"Oh?" Josette asked, eyes wide with surprise. "Well now, you must tell me everything."

I told her all about Phillip Stanhope, thinking about his green eyes and that smile, describing our brief time together in DC and London and ending with the letter I ripped up on the plane.

"And you are feeling guilty now about Henri?" Josette said, reading my mind.

"Well, yes," I said, biting my lip. "Even though the future . . . Everything is so uncertain now."

"Anna, my friend, you think too much." Josette smiled at me. "Sometimes you just have to let yourself live in the moment, don't you think? You and Henri were happy last night, at a time when happiness is in short supply."

I was about to reply when Catherine came through the door, carrying a pile of dresses so high we couldn't even see her face.

"Get undressed. My brother is coming to help," Catherine said as we helped her set the pile of dresses down.

"Oh no, my friend, we wouldn't want to impose," Josette said. "I'm sure he's much too busy."

"Not too busy to help you spy on Germans," Catherine said. "These dresses will be your suits of armor going into battle. You must look *perfect*."

We both got undressed, Josette stripping down to her underwear in seconds. I took my time, feeling odd standing half naked in a storage closet.

There was a knock, and a man's voice said, "Caro?"

Catherine opened the door and introduced her brother, Christian. Dressed in an impeccable dark wool suit, he was older than us by at least ten years and balding, with the same nose as his sister.

"Caro was right. You are much shorter than the models, but at least you're both very pretty," Christian said, looking us up and down, arms crossed and fingers on his chin. "This shouldn't be so hard."

I had my arms crossed in front of my chest, feeling awkward and somewhat mortified to be in my underwear in front of these strangers. However, Josette, Christian, and Caro acted like it was the most normal thing in the world to do.

He sorted through the pile and took out an olive-green dress with a peplum skirt and held it up against me.

"Absolutely not. This color is horrid on you," he said. He made a sour expression and pointed in my face like he was scolding a toddler. "You should never, ever wear it. Promise me?"

"I promise," I said with a solemn nod.

Josette stifled a laugh and I felt myself relax. We were in the best of hands. To Christian and Caro, we were simply models that needed to be dressed to perfection, my modesty was the least of their concerns.

"I was thinking this one for Josette?" Catherine said. She was holding up a cap-sleeved scarlet-red silk dress with a V-neck and a thick black patent leather belt.

"Beautiful," Josette gasped. Christian nodded in approval, and Catherine helped her slip it on. It was way too long, but she looked regal in it.

"Good," he said. "That fabric is from the curtains at Théâtre de la Michodière. I was designing costumes for a show there recently." He took a few pins out of his breast pocket and fastened the hem at midcalf. "One of the seamstresses can fix the hem in no time at all."

"Now you," he said, turning to me. "I know the one, the black taffeta with the bateau neckline and fuller skirt."

Catherine dug through the pile and helped me put it on and zipped me up.

"Ah, it is gorgeous," Josette said. "So romantic looking."

Catherine and Christian looked at me and made me turn around a few times.

"Yes," Christian said, as he kneeled down to pin the hem on mine. He stood up and gave us a warm smile. "Beautiful, both of you. My work here is done. Caro will get these altered for you quickly. And you'll make sure they have appropriate hats and shoes?"

Catherine nodded.

He kissed us both good-bye.

"Thank you for what you are doing for France," he said, his face serious, his eyes kind. "Be careful tonight, *mesdemoiselles*. I hope you get what you need to help the cause."

⁓

When we walked out a side entrance of Lelong, I felt like Cinderella going to the ball, as we bid our fairy godmother, Catherine Dior, good-bye and promised her we would return the dresses promptly the next day.

Despite the chill, we decided to take a horse and buggy to meet Otto and Franz in front of the building as planned. When we pulled up in the buggy, our friends were speechless at our transformation, until they started complimenting us to the point of embarrassment.

"You will be the most beautiful girls at the party," Otto said, holding his elbow out for me to take as we headed inside the grand building.

"I highly doubt that," I said, laughing.

They looked handsome and had taken extra care, their dress uniforms neatly pressed. Franz had slicked back his hair, and Otto's looked freshly trimmed.

The lobby of the building had high ceilings, ornate moldings, and marble floors.

"What is the name of the woman giving the party?" I asked as we headed up to the fifth floor in the elevator. We were speaking German, because their halting French made it difficult to have real conversations.

"Her name is Florence Gould," Franz said, and I felt the color drain from my face. "She is a very wealthy American; her husband is heir to a vast fortune."

*I knew her.* My parents had introduced me to her and her husband, Frank Jay Gould, at a fundraising gala at the Park Plaza Boston for Save the Children years before. Frank was the well-known son of railroad millionaire Jay Gould, and he owned several hotels and casinos in the South of France. I distinctly remembered Florence because she was the event's chairwoman and a former opera singer, vivacious and beautiful and *much* younger than her husband. We had talked with her quite a while that evening. I prayed she had forgotten me.

I had known we were going to an American's party. How did I not think to ask whose it was before now? In my mind I saw General Donovan shaking his head at me in disappointment. It was a foolish mistake.

"Are you all right, Alexine?" Otto said. "You look pale."

"I'm fine," I said, faking a smile and patting his elbow. Josette gave me a nervous sideways glance.

"Gentlemen, help us take these wool coats off so we can make a proper entrance," Josette said.

"You're a princess, Madeleine," Franz said with reverence as he took off her coat, as if he couldn't believe he was lucky enough to go to a party with a woman like her.

"And Alexine, you look like a Hollywood movie star," Otto said with a gasp.

"What do you know about Hollywood movie stars?" I said, teasing, using the acting skills I never knew I had until now.

The elevator stopped, and the door opened. I took a breath and composed myself as Franz pushed open the caged door.

Florence Gould's apartment was palatial, taking up the entire floor of the building, with a marble entryway, shining parquet floors, and glittering chandeliers throughout.

The party was packed with revelers dressed in their finest, and I recognized a few of the officers from the Hotel Majestic. We made our way through the crowd, getting appreciative looks from the men and reactions from the women that ranged from warm and curious to blatantly jealous. Franz and Otto went to get us drinks at a small bar that had been set up next to an incredible buffet of caviar, foie gras, smoked salmon, decadent Brie cheese, and real bread—so many of the delicacies that had all but disappeared from Parisian life.

"The food," Josette said in a quiet voice, gazing at it as if admiring a beautiful painting. "I have not seen so much food like this, in one place, in years. It's like a mirage."

"I am guessing Florence Gould has many friends in the black market," I said, bitterness in my voice. I watched as people around us laughed and ate to their hearts' content. And I thought of the gaunt little girl I had seen in one of the boulangerie lines earlier in the day, with large brown eyes and legs that looked like toothpicks under a dark-blue wool coat she had outgrown. I felt ill with anger.

Josette looked at me, the anger in her eyes reflecting my own. The very rich of Paris were insulated from the tragedies of wartime; to them, it was an exciting inconvenience.

"Who is this woman named Gould? Do you know her?" she asked in a whisper.

I was about to whisper back when Franz and Otto returned with champagne for us and generous glasses of cognac for themselves. Good. The harder they drank tonight, the more likely we would be to finally glean information from them.

"Ladies, I almost didn't recognize you," Officer Keppler said. I noticed many of the women in the room eyeing him with interest and admiration. "You look quite beautiful."

"Thank you," I said and then forced myself to add, "and you also look quite handsome this evening."

"Thank you, Alexine," he said, looking me in the eyes. "Where did you find such a dress?"

I looked up to see Florence Gould making her way through the crowded room, looking at me as if she recognized me but couldn't quite figure out why.

*Compose yourself, Anna. You are Alexine Chauffour from Saint-Malo.*

I bit the inside of my cheek to remain composed. I couldn't control my cheeks turning red, but there was much that I could control.

"Herbert Keppler," Florence Gould said when she reached us. "Thank you so much for coming tonight. I had to come over and say hello and introduce myself to your friends." She was studying my face. "Or maybe reintroduce myself? I'm sure we've met before. You're American, yes? You're Dick and Deidre Shannon's daughter . . . Anna, isn't it?"

"Bonsoir, madame, I am . . . I am afraid you are mistaken," I said, in the best French-accented English I could muster. I gave her a warm smile and held out my hand. "My name is Alexine Chauffour, this is my cousin Madeleine. We work for the French industrialists, often with Officer Keppler at the Hotel Majestic."

Josette greeted her warmly as well, gushing over her beautiful home. Florence was flummoxed, dark eyebrows knitted as she looked at me. She was in her late forties now but still very attractive, with deep-set green eyes and glossy chestnut hair cut in a flattering bob that framed her face.

"I . . . I could have sworn . . . ," she said. "I apologize, you are the spitting image of a young woman I met in Boston . . . Her family is very well-known in Boston society. Is it possible you are related?"

"No, I'm sorry," I said, shaking my head. "I am from Saint-Malo. I have no American relations."

Keppler did not take his eyes off of me during this exchange, and the look in them had gone from flirtatious to something much darker. Franz and Otto just looked puzzled. Otto's glass was already empty, and he headed to the bar for another.

"Do you have these parties often, madame?" Josette asked, taking a sip of champagne that was more of a gulp. "We felt privileged to be invited by German officers."

"I do have these parties quite often. I am so happy you could attend," Florence said, although I could tell she was still trying to work out the fact that I wasn't who she thought I was. "Your dresses are incredible. Are they from Rocha?"

"No, Lelong," I said. "Perhaps you know of the designer Christian Dior?"

"Everyone knows Dior," Florence said. "He is quite gifted, one of the up-and-coming designers in Paris."

We talked a little more about fashion, Florence boasting about how the black-and-white beaded dress she wore was haute couture by Balenciaga, and how well connected she was with all the designers. At this turn in discussion, Keppler stopped watching my every move and left us to talk to a group of officers cloistered nearby. I started to breathe again.

"I have to go and mingle with my guests, but please enjoy yourselves and feel free to tour the apartment," Florence said, searching my face, and I knew she still wasn't convinced she was wrong.

Josette and I didn't dare look at each other as we got another glass of champagne and searched the party for Otto and Franz. They were smoking cigars on one of the balconies, and we went outside to join them, grateful for a break from the humidity of so many bodies and lit fireplaces.

"Ah, I told you that you would be the most beautiful girls at the party," Otto said, throwing an arm around me. I wasn't sure how many cognacs he had had so far, but it smelled like at least three. "Right, Franz?"

"Agreed," said Franz, who was more composed. "What did you think of Florence Gould?"

"She is quite . . . something," I said.

"She has many affairs, you know," Otto said.

"Oh?" Josette said. "Where is her husband?"

"He stays at their mansion in Juan-les-Pins," Otto said, enjoying sharing this gossip. "She stays in Paris and has affairs, including with a few German officers."

We talked for a while longer, and as Otto finished his cognac, I knew this was the moment.

"What in the world are you doing upstairs now?" I asked him. "Is it so important, really? Don't you want to work with us downstairs again?"

"It is very important work," Franz said, pride in his voice. "Perhaps the most important work in the war right now."

"Really?" Josette said, her voice flirtatious and teasing as she batted her eyes at Franz. "I highly doubt that."

"It is," Otto said. Then in an exaggerated whisper, he said, "We are working on the plans for the most astounding new weapons."

"No!" I said. "You cannot be serious . . . you both are working on these new weapons?"

"We are," Otto said, his face so close to mine I nearly had to cough from the smell of cognac. And then, dropping his voice low, he added, "They can fly over vast distances, much faster than airplanes. And they're being designed and tested at Peenemünde on the island of Usedom."

I had taken a sip of champagne at that moment and nearly spit it out when he said it. I was glad it was too dark to see the goose pimples on my arms. *This.* This is the information we had come for. Finally.

"Otto, the ladies will grow bored of this talk," Franz said, his voice tight. "It's time we all went inside; it's too cold out here."

"Oh no, I find it fascinating. Don't you, Alexine?" said Josette. "Much more interesting than the work we are doing."

"I can hardly believe it's true," I said. "I think Otto is exaggerating to try to impress us."

"It is absolutely true," Otto said, bragging as a hiccup escaped his lips. "Stay late some night, and I will show you more."

"I would love to," I said.

"Oh yes, I would love to see more. German engineering is incredible," Josette said.

We went back inside, and Otto took ahold of my hand. I let him hold it, but I knew at some point soon he would want more, and I would have to make it clear I wasn't *that* type of girl.

In order to keep up appearances, we stayed at the party for two more painful hours. I was careful with how much champagne I drank, and I made myself have some bread and cheese to fill my stomach. More than once, I caught Florence Gould talking quietly with various women, pointing or nodding toward me, not even trying to hide it.

"Ready to go soon, *chère amie*?" Josette asked, and I nodded.

We were sitting by a fire with Franz, Otto, and a few other officers we knew from the Majestic. I looked up and caught sight of Florence in the hallway ducking into what I now knew was her bedroom at the opposite end of the apartment.

"Just one moment, and I'll be ready," I said. "I'm going to have a word with our hostess."

I walked down the hall as fast as I could without being obvious, knocking on the door of her bedroom and letting myself in before she finished saying, "Who is it?"

She was powdering herself in the mirror above her gigantic mahogany dresser. The ruby and diamond bracelets dripping off her wrists sparkled in the light.

"Darling, I was just freshening—"

"You know who it is, and you must promise me not to tell a soul," I said in English, my voice a whisper as I tried to temper my seething anger. "I have worked too hard to get here and do some good in this war to have an American acquaintance mess it up for me."

Florence gasped and started to speak, but I held my hand up for her to stop.

"I am Alexine Chauffour from Saint-Malo. And you are going to make sure that every German at this party knows that. No more gossiping, no speculating. Do you understand?"

"Ah . . . um . . . well, yes," Florence said, stammering. "I . . . I won't. I promise."

"I don't understand. You were the chairwoman of that Save the Children event. Do you not see the hungry children in the streets every day? And when you hear the gunshots at night, who do you think the Germans are shooting at? They aren't hunting for deer in the streets of Paris."

Florence just looked at me for a moment before nodding. "I promise you I will not say a word," she said, her lip trembling ever so slightly. "You are Alexine Chauffour. And I hope you succeed at . . . at whatever it is you are doing here."

"Thank you," I said. "The Germans are the enemy; please try to remember that. They would kill you in a heartbeat, like they've killed many others."

I was about to open the door when she called to me.

"Wait," Florence said, holding a hand to her chest. "I . . . I am sorry. Not all of us can be so strong in these times."

Now it was my turn to pause before speaking. "Anyone can be strong if they want to be. You've chosen a different path. Here's your chance to do some good." I left the bedroom, resisting the temptation to slam the door behind me.

"There you are," Josette said, standing up when I went back to the fireplace to find her. Keppler had joined the group, and as usual he was staring at me with an interest that made me squirm. "Are you ready to go?"

"I am," I said, satisfied that Florence Gould would keep my secret now.

"Oh, please stay, just a little longer?" Otto said, grabbing my hand and squeezing it, though he didn't get up from his chair because he was too drunk to stand.

"No, I'm sorry, it is time. It's almost curfew, after all," I said. "But thank you for a lovely evening."

"Can we escort you out?" Franz asked, much more sober, and gazing at Josette with an adoration that was vulnerable and sweet.

"No, that is not necessary," said Josette. "We will see you next week, I hope?"

"Good night, ladies," Keppler said. I felt my skin crawl as he walked up and stood so close to me I got a whiff of his strange citrus cologne. "It's funny that Madame Gould mistook you for an American, isn't it, Alexine? Named Anna something?"

"Yes, that was so very funny," I said, forcing a smile on my face as he watched my reaction.

"Anyway, I have friends in the Gestapo," Keppler said. "They know who all of the Americans in Paris are, whether the Americans want them to know or not."

I couldn't even look at Josette. It was an odd and cryptic thing to say. And I took it as a warning.

"Well, clearly I am not one of them," I said, trying to laugh but not entirely succeeding.

"Alexine, an American?" Otto started laughing, the kind of silly, snorting laugh that's only possible after six cognacs or so. "That is absolutely ridiculous. *American?* Look at her! She is as French as could be."

At that moment I could have kissed that round-cheeked German officer out of gratitude. Franz just shook his head at him and started laughing too. Keppler seemed annoyed, but even he cracked a smile, and I took that as our cue.

"Au revoir, my friends," Josette said, grabbing me by the elbow.

"Until Monday," I added with a smile and a nod as they said their good-byes to us.

We grabbed our coats, made our way out of Florence Gould's bizarre party, and dashed into the night.

# Chapter Thirty-One

**February 14, 1943**

After the party, Josette and I took a vélo-taxi to the women's hostel, and within seconds of taking my dress off and piling on blankets, I fell into a deep, dreamless sleep. I woke up Sunday morning with a feeling of accomplishment and hope that we were finally making progress. I was sure as soon as I shared this new intelligence that evening from Rue Fabert, it would only whet London's appetite, and they would be pushing for more about the mystery weapons that were being tested in the Baltic Sea.

We discussed the various ways we could orchestrate another evening of socializing with our German officer "friends" soon, as we walked down a narrow side street near the Sorbonne late Sunday afternoon to meet up with Georges and Henri at Le Chat Noir, a bar owned by a friend in the Resistance.

When we arrived, the owner, an older gentleman with a thick white mustache and heavily lined face, directed us to a stone staircase that looked like it had been carved into the floor. It descended into a basement bar that was not much more than a musty cave that smelled of mildew and stale beer. The stone walls were a pale copper hue, and they were decorated with vintage theater posters.

Aside from the bartender, Georges and Henri were the only ones there, sitting in the back corner at a rickety round wooden table, sipping small glasses of red wine. They waved us over. I sat down, and Henri greeted me with two kisses and got up to get glasses of wine for Josette and me. Josette went to find the ladies' room, and Georges leaned over and started talking fast in a whisper.

"Anna, since we're alone for a minute, I have an enormous favor to ask."

"Of course," I said. "How can I help you?"

"I'd like to bring Josette back to Zoé St. Clair's. To stay the night," Georges said, as he lit a cigarette and gave me the sheepish look of a teenage boy. "She's too embarrassed to ask you herself. Henri will go to Rue Fabert with you, and of course he'll keep watch when you contact London tonight. And I see you are blushing already, so let me tell you he has already said he will stay on the sofa in the living room. He's not being presumptuous about you two; he wanted me to make sure you knew that."

"I told Josette I would understand if you needed time alone," I said. He was right, I was blushing. The thought of Henri staying overnight with me at Rue Fabert brought a mix of emotions that were hard to process. "Of . . . of course. That's fine."

"Thank you," Georges said, giving me a huge smile as he patted my hand. "Thank you so much."

When Henri and Josette returned to the table, in hushed voices we shared all the events of the evening at Florence Gould's party. When we told them about Otto's boast about the testing site location, Georges raised his fist in the air and let out a whoop that made the bartender jump. Henri was also thrilled, but his reaction was more measured.

"Do you understand what this *is*?" Georges said, slamming his glass down and nearly tipping over the wobbly table. "This may be one of the greatest military secrets of the war. It is crucial information for the Allies."

"I do," I said, feeling cautiously optimistic. "But I know we need to get much more."

"Yes, they are not going to be satisfied with just the location," Henri said in agreement. "As soon as they get this from you, they are just going to push for more details."

"We were just discussing that on the way here," I said. "We'll make plans with the two Germans again soon. And fortunately, Otto really likes to drink cognac."

"He's also quite attracted to Anna," Josette added.

"Why wouldn't he be?" Henri said, giving me a small smile. But then his eyes clouded with concern. "But Georges is right: you're both going to have to be more careful than ever."

"I agree," I said. And I shared Officer Keppler's comments after Florence Gould recognized me.

"Be careful there," Henri said, pointing at me. "Keppler is a high-ranking German officer because of his family's Prussian roots, and he is very well connected within the Nazi party."

"And he's not a fool, so consider what he said a warning," Georges said. "If you feel he truly suspects you, we will have to move you two out of the city for a while—"

"Oh no, we can't," I interrupted him, frustrated at the thought. "We're finally getting somewhere, we can't stop now."

"Anna, Georges is right, I'm afraid," Josette said. "I want to get this information as much as you do, but if we think our cover is about to be blown, we need to get out."

I looked up at the black chandelier above the table. "I don't want to give up when I feel like we're finally getting close."

"Trust me, I understand. Oh, another thing." Georges reached into his coat pocket and handed me an envelope. "This is a message from Tatiana. She asked that you send it to London tonight. It's regarding another downed Allied pilot hiding at the hospital."

"Did she say anything about our friend?" I asked. Nora had been on my mind. I had taken my bike and gone by the apartment she was staying at in the 16th arrondissement, just to make sure she was okay. But there had been no sign of her.

"No, nothing," Georges said. "I only saw her for a minute."

We stayed at the bar for another hour, and more people trickled in, filling up the tables around us. I was feeling cautiously celebratory and couldn't wait to pass on the new intelligence. At seven o'clock, I told Henri it was time to go to Rue Fabert, to prepare for my scheduled communication with London.

Georges said he would take care of the bill, and Henri and I kissed our friends good-bye. Josette whispered a thank-you in my ear.

"Are you ready?" Henri asked, holding out his hand.

"Yes," I said. "Let's go. I've looked forward to this all day . . . Oh . . . sending this news, I mean."

My face burned.

Henri just grabbed my hand and laughed.

~

Our concierge, Madame Chevrolet, was wearing a teal-colored turban, and her drawn-on eyebrows were thick and black as if to match her grouchy mood. Bijou went insane when he saw us, barking like a tiny lunatic, and Madame finally scooped him into her arms when he jumped up and tried to take a bite out of my finger.

She walked us to the door of our apartment, and Henri took some francs out of his wallet and handed them to her before she even cleared her throat. With Bijou squeezed under her right arm, she counted them in silence, nodded, and bid us good night.

And then Henri and I were alone in the apartment, and while I felt nervous about that fact, I had to push those feelings down and focus on the task at hand. I took off my coat, fished my peacock pin out of my purse, and fastened it to my blouse. Henri caught me doing this, and I just shrugged.

"For luck," I said. "I'm going to get ready."

"Okay, call me when you're going to start."

I coded my message about the Peenemünde test site and then Tatiana's news about the Allied pilot, with a plan to burn the paper after I was finished, as usual. I knew the message was correct. I had barely had to look at my silk handkerchief since I arrived, but tonight I pulled it out and triple-checked my message for accuracy. It was too important.

Henri came in and put his hands on my shoulders as I was setting up my antennas and getting the crystal out.

"I am going to be on for longer than I'd like," I said with a sigh, rubbing my hand over my face. "But it can't be helped. These two messages are going to take time, and then I know London is going to take a little longer than usual to respond because they don't receive this kind of intelligence every day."

"I'll keep watch from the roof," he said, squeezing my shoulders and kissing me on the cheek. A thrill went up my spine.

At exactly 8:35, starting with my safety checks, I began my radio transmission to the station in London, sweating from nerves but exhilarated about what I was about to share. I was fast but careful, keeping track of the time as I kept track of my coded message. I was twenty minutes in, three-quarters of the way done sending it, when I heard Henri open the apartment door and call my name.

"The trucks—a caravan of roofless lorries with antennas," he said, breathless as he burst into the bedroom. I jumped up. "They are here! You need to shut it down. Shut it down now!"

And then the power went out, and we were standing in darkness. One glance out the bedroom window revealed the Gestapo had cut power to the entire block; we heard the screech of cars coming closer. Henri started cursing as he helped me take down the antennas.

My hands trembling, I ripped up the paper I had been using into tiny pieces and swallowed them, nearly choking on the dry scraps, then I almost tore my blouse yanking my peacock pin off. Henri helped me pack up everything as fast as I could. There was a knock at the door, and I was considering that we might have to jump out the window when I heard Bijou's bark.

Madame was standing there holding a candle in one hand and Bijou in the other.

"Follow me if you don't want to be captured," she said. "The Gestapo's cars and trucks are surrounding the block. They will be searching every building for you."

I ran back to the bedroom and grabbed the wireless suitcase, Henri threw his camera around his neck, and we followed her in silence down several flights of stairs until we reached the basement of the building. It was damp and its low ceiling was a maze of pipes. Madame stopped walking abruptly and looked down, holding her candle to the floor until she saw the outline of a trapdoor. She put Bijou down and handed me the candle, feeling around until she found a ridged edge and pulled open a door in the floor. From the dim light I could see it was a circular space large enough to stand up in and about twelve feet in diameter.

And then I coughed and held my arm over my face; the smell coming out of it was overwhelming and vile.

"This used to be for animal waste, but it was cleaned out years ago," Madame said. "Henri, you jump down first, and then help her down. It's only about three meters to the bottom."

Henri jumped down without hesitation, his feet landing with a thump. He started coughing uncontrollably. Once he was in, I passed him the wireless suitcase and sat on the edge of the opening. I turned and lowered myself slowly, and he grabbed me by the waist and lowered me the rest of the way. Madame passed us a candle on a small tin holder and a box of matches and threw down an old wool blanket.

"I will come get you when it's safe," Madame said, closing the door and leaving us in the pitch dark, in a stone hole that smelled like rotting dog manure.

I held my hands over my face to try to block the smell, although I could already feel it seeping into my clothes and hair.

"We can't risk lighting the candle," Henri said, as he started to cough again. "Even though it might get rid of the stink."

"I don't think anything could get rid of this stink," I said, my voice muffled from my hands.

"I agree," he said. "This might be the most foul-smelling place I have ever been in. And remember, I was in a men's prison."

"What are the chances Madame Chevrolet leads the Gestapo right to us?" I asked. "She's the type that might be getting paid by both sides."

"I thought of that too," Henri said, cursing under his breath. "I guess we will find out."

I spread the blanket out so we didn't have to sit directly on the dirt floor and wrapped my arms around my knees, resting my chin on top of them.

"Are you scared?" Henri asked, sitting so that our arms were touching.

"Am I scared?" I said. "Of course. I was terrified in the apartment. But now . . . I thought I would be paralyzed with fear, but instead I'm just trying to figure out how we can get out of this."

"That's why you're good at this work," Henri said.

"Do you think so? That I'm good at this work?" It warmed me to hear him say it.

"Yes," Henri said. "I knew you would be. I still wish you had stayed away, somewhere safe."

"But then we wouldn't have seen each other again," I said softly. I could sense his face close to mine.

"That is true, ma chérie," he said with an exaggerated sigh, putting his arm around my shoulders.

"Why'd you bring your camera?" I asked, feeling it resting between us.

"I took some photos the other night, of a number of Gestapo officers outside their headquarters on Avenue Foch, to pass along to the Allies. The film is still inside."

"Ah," I said in a soft voice. "I always knew you were brilliant, Henri. But I never realized how brave you were until now."

"I am just doing what needs to be done," he said. "I love my country. I want it back." He was quiet for a moment before adding, "And what about you, my courageous American friend? Choosing to come here? I don't think you give yourself enough credit."

"I haven't done enough yet to get credit," I said. "I still feel like an imposter."

"You're definitely *not* an imposter," he said, kissing my hair.

We sat there listening in the darkness, and I prayed our hiding place would not be discovered.

"Can I ask . . . how did you get that scar on your neck?"

He didn't say anything for a few moments, and I was about to tell him it was okay not to tell me when he started to speak in a whisper.

"In prison, I had a friend named Ollie. He was very small, even shorter than you, with big ears and glasses. But he was so quick-witted and kept up the spirits of many of the prisoners with his jokes and stories.

"One day a new prisoner arrived at the camp—a large, brooding bully of a man covered in hair like a gorilla. We nicknamed him the Boar because he was big and ugly and a nasty person. One night we were heading back to our cells, and he started a fight with Ollie over nothing at all, really—he just wanted to pick on someone. I thought he was going to kill my friend, he was so much bigger. I jumped in the middle of it, and the Boar whipped out a small, very sharp knife and jabbed me with it. I lost so much blood."

"My God," I said. "I'm so sorry."

"It was a blessing in a way," Henri said, putting his hand on the scar, remembering. "My uncle had been trying to bribe whoever he could to get me out. The injury was an excuse to get me to the American Hospital. Dr. Jackson saved my life, in two ways."

"I didn't realize that. I had been meaning to ask how you got out."

I leaned against his chest, staying close, happy to breathe in the scent of his cologne, as it masked the horrible odor of the cave, if only slightly.

I thought of the terror my parents and sisters would feel if they knew where I was at this moment. I closed my eyes and said another silent prayer that we'd get through the night without being captured by the Gestapo.

The moment I closed my eyes, we heard shouting and banging up above at street level, and I froze and looked up as if I could see through the trapdoor.

"Des bottes allemandes," Henri whispered. German boots.

"They're here," I said. We waited.

The Gestapo stomped up the stairs of 26 Rue Fabert. I was sure they banged on every apartment door in the building. I could barely breathe from the smell and the fear that washed over me as we waited to see if they would make their way down to the basement. Twenty minutes later, the sound of the boots got closer, and the Germans were right over our heads, tromping all over us. I bit down on my hand, waiting for them to notice the outline of the door in the floor.

If we were discovered, I knew they would torture me to force me to send messages to London under duress, to get the names of other agents in Paris. The cyanide pills were upstairs in a hidden pocket in my coat. It was the first time I had thought about them since I had arrived.

Minutes passed, and then a voice hollered that they were clearing out.

One of the officers in the basement started swearing, saying it had all been a waste of time.

Henri and I didn't speak; we just leaned against each other and waited. I finally started to breathe again, my heart still hammering in my chest.

Finally, after at least an hour, we heard footsteps and the patter of paws. There was a knock on the trapdoor, and Madame lifted it up.

"Are you alive down there?" she asked. "The power is back on."

"We are, madame," I said, as Henri lifted me out and passed me the wireless. "Thank you for saving our lives."

"You'll be well rewarded for your efforts, Madame Chevrolet," Henri added.

"I better be," she snorted, picking up Bijou. "Les boches offered me one thousand francs for the names of anyone in the Resistance."

⁓

Thanks to Madame, we had avoided capture, but the apartment at Rue Fabert was, as they said, "burnt"—safe no longer. And I was beyond frustrated—I needed to know if London had received my intelligence, but I would have to bide my time and be even more careful about where and when I communicated with them.

The bathroom shower was freezing cold, but I had never been happier to take one in my life. As the water splashed down on me, I couldn't stop shivering from the cold of the spray and from the terror we had just avoided. After Henri and I had both showered, we heated up bland potato soup and poured big glasses of red wine from Georges's supply.

Henri poured me another glass of wine after dinner, and we sat down on the sofa together, my feet resting on his legs. His hair was wet, and he had managed to find a change of clothes that belonged to Georges. The cream-colored button-down shirt was two sizes too large and hung on him in a way I found undeniably attractive. It was unbuttoned at the top, giving me a glimpse of his toned chest.

"You can never use the wireless here again," he said, and I could see the wheels turning in his head, thinking of all the angles of what came next.

"I know."

"This will be our last night here, for any of us. Georges and I will have some of the men move your things tomorrow. You can stay at the hostel for now. We will try to find one or two other safe houses for you and Josette."

"You don't think they will come back here tonight, do you?" I said.

"I do not," he said. "But Madame promised to stay up and keep watch."

"That is unusually kind of her," I said, frowning.

"Well, that was after I paid her two thousand francs," he said, smiling.

"Of course," I said, shaking my head. "I should have known."

We were both quiet for a moment, looking into each other's eyes. He put his hands on my legs, and his touch felt electric.

"Henri, I have to know that London received that intelligence about the weapons site," I said, running my hand through my damp curls, failing to tame them.

"Yes, but after what just happened, you must stick to your schedule to be safe," he said. "You'll try again at the hospital this week."

"I know," I said, nodding, thinking about how close a call we'd had. "I hate that I have to, though."

"You are very impatient," he said, teasing as he took a sip of wine, "but I understand why."

He sat up, reached into the back pocket of his pants, and pulled out his wallet.

"More francs for Madame Chevrolet?" I asked, and he shook his head.

Instead of francs, he pulled out a small black-and-white photo, trimmed to fit in his wallet, ragged and worn at the edges. I leaned over to look at it, and my breath caught. In the photo, I was smiling, on the verge of a laugh, not looking into the camera but at someone to the right of me. The picture brought me back to a carefree evening—I could smell the warm summer air, and I could picture Josette and all our friends, laughing together.

I opened my mouth to speak, though I wasn't sure what to say, and he stopped me.

"Please, before you say anything . . ." He held up his hand before placing it on mine. "This photo of you is from the night of your going-away party. I took so many photos that day, but this one is my favorite, my best. Because to me, it perfectly captures that evening, for eternity. It captures an expression of life—the joy of just being young and free on a beautiful night in the city. I've kept it with me through everything. I've kept it with me to remind me of what life can be, and it gives me hope for nights like that again."

"I don't even remember you taking this one," I said, blinking back tears, moved that he had kept a photo of me with him, despite everything.

"Anna, I kept it in my wallet, even though I had lost hope of ever seeing you again," he said, his voice soft. "But it was such an incredible night—you took my breath away that evening. You . . . you still do."

I looked at him and squeezed his hand.

"Thank you," I said. "I have often thought of what would have happened if I had decided to stay here."

"Me too," he said.

I nodded. The air between us felt thick, heavy with emotion and wistfulness for what might have been and a romantic tension that I couldn't deny.

"We should get some sleep soon," I said.

"Yes, we should." He gave me a nod, looking into my eyes as he put his glass down.

He pulled me toward him, so that I was sitting on his lap on the couch, and we kissed, long and slow, and then more heated, his hands under my shirt and mine in his hair. He let out a soft groan, and I was breathless, my heart beating so loud I was sure he could hear it as he started to unbutton my blouse. Torn about what should happen next, I pulled away and stumbled backward as I got up from the sofa. There was an expression of disappointment and hurt on his face.

I thought about all that had just happened. About the dark, dangerous place we could have ended up tonight, instead of here. There was nothing guaranteed but now. Connor was my past, and I had no idea if the future was with Henri or Phillip or someone else—or in a Gestapo prison. All I knew was that I wanted nothing more than to have the war and the world melt away for a while. So I took a deep breath and reached for his hand.

"Come with me," I said.

He took my hand, his eyes searching mine. "Anna, are you sure?" he asked as he stood up from the sofa.

"Yes," I said. "I'm sure I want you to come to the bedroom with me right now and not leave until morning. After what happened tonight, I . . . What in the world are we waiting for?"

We started kissing again, and I laughed as he scooped my legs out from under me and carried me into the bedroom.

# Chapter Thirty-Two

**March 19, 1943**

My last night at 26 Rue Fabert had been both a nightmare and a dream. The terror of hiding from the Gestapo, the thrilling rush of relief when they had gone, and then, afterward, the passionate, dizzying hours Henri and I spent together in bed, until sunrise. It was a night full of such heightened emotions that I knew it would be etched on my mind like a tattoo. Decades from now, I would remember it all in vivid detail and tell my granddaughters how I had lived as a spy in occupied Paris in the war, experiencing danger and adventure and, with Phillip and now Henri, something like romance that, if given the chance, might turn to love.

The raid marked a turning point in my strange new life, in ways that were both sweet and bitter. Henri and I were now together, both as comrades in the Resistance and lovers in life. With a future so foggy with uncertainty, we lived in the present, stealing moments together whenever we could—in the basement of La Caravalle, in the attic at the hospital. Every moment I was with him was a thrill. His touch, his smell—all of it was intoxicating to me, and I would count the hours until I would see him again. It gave us both desperately needed happiness, a distraction during the dark days and nights.

But the raid had also made me hyperaware of the constant imminent threats we faced in Paris. From the moment I had heard those

German boots above my head, a trapdoor away from being caught, my paranoia increased a hundredfold. In hindsight I had been naive, thinking that our safe places would always remain safe, that the sprawling expanse of the city itself made us safer. I had underestimated our enemy, and I vowed to learn from it.

Despite the constant dangers and arrests, the growth of the Resistance in both size and scope was also very real. This was in large part due to the Vichy France puppet government instituting the Service du Travail Obligatoire, or STO, in February. This required French men of military age to do two years of compulsory labor service in Germany. Thousands of young men all over France went underground to avoid this fate. Realizing it was time to take a side and do something, many joined the Resistance.

The once-scattered, chaotic resistance networks were now coalescing, thanks in part to clear, unwavering signals of support from the Allies. During the full moon on February 20, Georges and Henri had finally received their shipment of guns and ammunition, and they reported that several more SOE and OSS had arrived in the French countryside and that even more agents and supplies would be delivered in the months to come.

You could feel the rising anger of Parisians who had lived under brutal occupation for so long. And with that anger came the powerful combination of pride and hope. It manifested itself in small ways—in the enormous *V*s for victory being drawn by anonymous graffiti artists in bright white chalk on buildings and walls all over the city, and in the style of Parisian women's dress—they wore short skirts, bright colors, and outrageous turbans, displaying their loyalty to French fashion like a badge of honor, an act of resistance in itself. Some Parisian teens who were supportive of the Allies now carried two fishing rods because the words *deux gaules*—two rods—sounded like de Gaulle, the exiled leader of the Free French Forces.

And the tide of fury and unrest was becoming apparent in larger ways as well, in strategic and more violent acts of resistance. In the weeks following the raid, there had been an increase in assaults on and murders of German soldiers, not through any organized resistance, but by individual citizens. And now the growing resistance networks were becoming increasingly successful in their acts of sabotage on railways and bridges throughout France, crippling the German supply lines.

All this enraged Hitler, and hundreds of French hostages were executed in brutal acts of retaliation. Large, garish yellow Nazi posters with thick black borders were posted all over Paris, listing the names of those recently killed, and they sent a chill through me every time I saw one. In the metro and the parks, signs and placards declared:

ANYONE COMMITTING ACTS OF VIOLENCE AGAINST THE GERMAN ARMY WILL BE SHOT. ALL CLOSE MALE RELATIVES OVER 18 YEARS OLD WILL BE SHOT. ALL FEMALE RELATIVES WILL BE CONDEMNED TO FORCED LABOR. ALL CHILDREN, UP TO 17 YEARS OLD, MALE OR FEMALE, WILL BECOME WARDS OF THE STATE.

But despite what felt like ever-rising danger, my solidarity with my friends and my passion for the cause now overshadowed my fear the majority of the time. During my time in occupied Paris, I had grown to understand that being fearless was not living without fear, but pushing through and doing what needed to be done in spite of it.

The week after the Rue Fabert raid, I was relieved and triumphant when London communicated that they had received my message about the location of the testing site for the new weapons. They were ecstatic and "making plans" based on the intelligence. And, not surprisingly, they immediately pushed for more—they wanted confirmation of the location, they wanted details about the testing site, they wanted drawings and dates and timelines.

One night, Otto and Franz had invited us to go out to dinner with them at the upscale restaurant Maxim's, where we had a meal that was so delicious I thought Josette would weep with joy. Then on several evenings we had met them for drinks at the Ritz bar, the most popular spot for German officers in Paris. But, despite teasing and flirting and wide-eyed questions, we still had not been able to get any of the other information out of them that we desperately needed.

It was now mid-March, and on a dreary, gray Friday morning, Josette and I were taking our time biking to the Hotel Majestic, stopping to talk at every street corner, discussing our frustrations and debating what to do next. On her bike, Josette looked like a girl on a French postcard with her red coat and black culottes, her hair peeking out from underneath her black hat.

"I would rather die than sleep with Otto Wagner," I said to her, unable to hide my frustrations as we waited at an intersection to cross, "but I now understand why some female agents play that game. After the Gould party, I thought it would be easy to get the other intelligence we needed from him. We're running out of time."

"I know," Josette said, her voice tight and worried. "I had also thought it would be easier than this." She let out a string of curse words that made an old woman in a plaid kerchief walking by give us a dirty look.

On an island in the Baltic Sea, the Germans were testing an "astounding" new weapon. And someday soon, the last test would be conducted and the weapon would be used against the Allies. It could be tomorrow—that's what weighed on my mind every minute of the day. If we confirmed what we already knew and found out everything London wanted to know, we could possibly save thousands of lives. If we ran out of time and they started using the weapon . . . I wouldn't be able to live with that kind of guilt. The thought of these weapons being successful made me physically ill.

We biked along in silence for a while, riding directly under the giant Nazi flags along the Rue de Rivoli, lost in our thoughts.

"I just need another real opportunity, not at a public place where too many people could hear us talk," I said at the next crowded intersection.

"Do you think Franz suspects what we're up to?" Josette said. "I noticed the last time we were at the Ritz, he was counting how many cognacs Otto ordered."

"I honestly doubt it. I think he's just afraid of Otto making a fool out of himself," I said, but then my paranoia kicked in and I thought about Franz and how he had seemed more pensive lately. He adored Josette, bringing her little gifts of black-market chocolate, always finding excuses to stop by her desk. "Although I'll keep that in mind next time we're with them."

"Alexine! Alexine!" I heard someone almost screaming my alias and looked up to see a very thin, raven-haired woman in a dark-green coat waving at me frantically from across the Champs-Élysées. She was unusually striking, and it took me a few seconds to place her.

*Nora.*

Josette and I hurried across the street with our bikes, and Nora wrapped her arms around me in a hug so tight it made it hard to breathe.

"Oh, my friend," Nora said in her high-pitched, breathy voice, "it's so good to see you after all of this time."

She broke away, greeting Josette with two kisses. Up close, it was clear her time in Paris had taken its toll on her. I knew I had lost weight from the ration diet, but Nora was emaciated, and the circles under her eyes were so dark it looked as if she'd been punched.

"How are you?" I said, afraid of the answer.

"I am . . . doing the best I can," she said, her eyes tearing up. She dropped her voice to a whisper, as there were German officers on the crowded street. "You would be proud of me—my wireless skills have improved. I'm working for three different networks."

*"Three?"* I said with a gasp. "How can you do all that yourself? That's impossible, you must be on the wireless all the time."

"More than I would like, yes," Nora said, resigned. "But how can I say no when people's lives depend on it? I move around a great deal, staying in different places, to stay safe. Although I'm getting more nervous by the day." She scanned the streets around us. "Sometimes? I feel like I'm being watched. And with the recent arrests . . ."

Josette looked at me, her eyes wide with alarm.

*I feel like I'm being watched.* I loved Nora, but I wanted to shake her for calling to me in the middle of a crowded street.

"You keep going. I'll catch up with you," I said to Josette, and she gave me a wave, riding away before I finished the sentence.

"We shouldn't be talking here," I said to Nora, grabbing her elbow and whispering into her ear. "And you should get out of the city if you think you are in danger. I have some ideas. I will leave you a message in the letter box at 11 Avenue Foch, the home of Dr. Jackson. Do you know it?"

She nodded, blinking back tears. "I'm so sorry, Anna," she said. "It is just so good to see you."

"I know, my friend, you too, but we need to be very, very careful." I gave her a very quick, tight hug because at this point, if we were being watched, it was too late, and my heart broke for her.

"I have to go. Please stay safe, Nora. I promise I will be in touch soon." I got back on my bike and rode away.

∾

"Do you actually think someone is watching Nora?" Josette asked me in a low voice. It was the end of the day, and we finally had a moment to ourselves, standing in front of the gilded mirror and marble sinks in the ladies' room at the Hotel Majestic.

"I'm not sure. She doesn't seem well," I said as I put on a fresh coat of lipstick. "My guess is she's cracking from the pressure and just *thinks* she is. I'm going to talk to Tatiana. I think we need to get her out of the city for a while."

"It was risky and foolish for her to call to you in public like that," Josette said in a quiet hiss. "What was she thinking?"

"Nora thinks with her heart more than her head," I said. "She was just desperate to see an old friend."

We walked out of the ladies' room and almost straight into Otto.

"Were you waiting around for us?" I teased.

"Of course not," he said, laughing. "What do you take me for? I was, however, heading to your offices to find you. I have an invitation for both of you."

"Oh, to what?" Josette asked.

"Me, Franz, and the other men we live with at 17 Avenue Foch are having a party tomorrow night," he said. "We would like our two favorite Parisian girls to attend. Can you come?"

"Hmm . . . do we have any better offers?" I asked Josette.

"I don't know . . . we might," she replied, putting her finger to her lip, as if thinking of what other glamourous invitations we might have.

"Now you're teasing," Otto said. "Please come."

"We will be there," I said with a smile. "Thank you."

"Be where?" Officer Keppler walked up behind Josette and me, standing so close to me our arms were touching, and it was all I could do not to flinch. Otto saluted and I forced a smile. Keppler had been in Berlin for a couple of weeks and had just returned. I had enjoyed the break from his creepy behavior.

"To the party, Officer Keppler. You are coming, yes?" Otto asked.

"Yes, I will be there," Keppler said.

The four of us exchanged a few more pleasantries about Keppler's trip to Berlin, and Otto bid us good-bye.

I went to gather my things, relieved the day was over. I was reaching for my purse in my bottom drawer and didn't even see Keppler until he was standing right in front of my desk.

"Oh, you startled me," I said. He had gotten his hair cut in Berlin and looked like he was wearing a new uniform as well, or at least his old uniform had been cleaned and pressed. If Hollywood ever cast a handsome yet sinister German officer, he would look just like Officer Keppler.

"Alexine . . . I missed seeing you while I was away. You are fond of Herr Wagner?" he asked, referring to Otto.

"Yes, I mean . . . he's a good friend," I said. He *missed* me? I still believed he was suspicious of me.

"I don't think *he* feels you are just friends," Keppler said, watching me.

"Oh, I think he understands. We're just friends," I said, nodding too vigorously because I didn't think he understood at all and my vagueness was on purpose.

"Otto Wagner is not good enough for a beautiful girl like you," Keppler said. "You need someone more sophisticated."

He was looking me in the eyes in a way that made me want to run from the building and never come back. I didn't need someone, least of all him. But I had to play this game.

He ran his finger down the length of my desk as he often did, which felt oddly intimate, and all I wanted was to swat his arm away.

My cheeks grew warm more out of anger than embarrassment, as I tried to decide what to say next. I kept it simple. I wanted to encourage him a little, but not too much.

"Thank you for the compliment, sir," I said, giving him a small smile and forcing myself to keep looking in his eyes.

"You may call me Herbert," Keppler said, a smile playing on his lips, though his eyes were still dead. "Especially if we are to become better acquainted. I will see you at the party tomorrow evening."

# Chapter Thirty-Three

An hour later, Josette and I arrived at Le Chat Noir and went to our favorite table in the downstairs cave.

"Please do not mention to Henri or Georges what Keppler said to me at the end of the day," I said to Josette after we had ordered our drinks.

The bartender brought over our glasses of wine, and Josette waited until he left to respond.

"Anna, we must tell them," Josette said. "Keppler is one of the highest-ranking German officers in Paris. He has many friends in the Nazi party, in the Gestapo. We can manage Otto and Franz without a problem, but you getting too much attention from Keppler makes . . . What if he suspects us? Or, even worse, what if he does in fact have feelings for you?"

"I think the second possibility would be much worse," I said with a groan, putting my head in my hands. "But it will just worry them more, and we *have* to go to this party. So please don't say anything?"

"Don't say anything about what?" Tatiana said as she pulled out a chair, glass of wine in hand. She sat down at our table and pulled a pack of cigarettes out of her pocket, handing one to Josette without even asking. Two young women sitting at a nearby table eyed the pack with longing, so she offered it to them and they each gratefully accepted a cigarette. She was dressed in the same camel coat and black veiled hat we had seen her in at the café in Montmartre, and her white-blonde hair still surprised me. I thought how different she was from Nora, how this former baguette girl from the boulangerie seemed born for this life as a spy, and she never would have known if it hadn't been for the war.

"I'm glad you're here," I said after Josette and I greeted her with kisses. "You'll never guess who I saw today."

I told her about seeing Nora and the condition she was in. Tatiana's face darkened.

*Merde!*" She cursed loudly and banged on the table when I mentioned Nora was working for three networks. Several patrons looked up from their tables to see what the fuss was about.

"You need to keep it down," I said in a low voice.

"She cannot handle three networks," Tatiana said in a harsh whisper. "Who would be stupid enough to have her do that?"

"The networks that are desperate for wireless operators," I said with a shrug. "They have no choice."

"Speaking of the wireless, that's why I am here," Tatiana said. She had already slid an envelope across the table to me so I could stuff it in my purse. "We have a few more downed pilots coming through the American Hospital this week."

"Got it. I'll pass this information on," I said.

"But what are we going to do about Nora?" Tatiana asked.

It didn't matter to either of us that we weren't supposed to be in contact with her, never mind helping her. Tatiana had been right. The men in charge of us overseas had no idea what our lives would be like here. We would decide what was best for ourselves, what was best for our friend.

"I think she needs to be moved out of Paris," I said. "She's worried she's being watched. She's not in good shape."

"She could go work for Bernard and Pauline. They could use her, I'm sure of it," Tatiana said.

"How do you know for sure?" Josette asked.

"I've had to go to a few of the full moon supply drops in Avaray. I see Bernard sometimes," Tatiana said with a shrug and a mischievous smile, and it was clear she more than just "saw" Bernard.

"But who will take over for her?" I said. "I could maybe handle one more network, but not three."

"When Georges and Henri went to the supply drop in Avaray this week, they were told that a large number of SOE and OSS would be arriving in the next few months, including some more wireless operators," Josette said.

"I could make a direct request to London for a replacement for her," I said. "I'll say it's extenuating circumstances; they can notify the networks she's working with of the change in personnel. She'll just have to hold on for another month."

"But can she?" Tatiana said, lighting another cigarette and passing two more to the next table. "I don't know . . ."

"She has to. I'll try to boost her spirits in the message I'll send her via Dr. Jackson's drop box. I'll tell her we've got a plan and to stay strong," I said.

I spotted Georges and Henri making their way down the stone staircase. Henri looked at me, and my heart leaped. It had been almost a week since we had seen each other. Tatiana saw my expression and turned around to see why I was beaming.

"Well, well," she said, looking back at me with a knowing smile of her own. "It is very good to see that look on your face, mon amie."

"What look?" I said, raising my eyebrows, feigning ignorance.

"Ha!" Tatiana said, giving me a smirk. "You know exactly what I mean." She stubbed out her cigarette and got up from the table, giving us kisses good-bye. "I need to go. Stay safe, and I'll be in touch soon. Please let me know if you hear anything about Nora."

"And you do the same," I said. She nodded to Georges and Henri, who were navigating through the crowds from the bar to our table, and disappeared up the staircase.

Henri and Georges squeezed in next to us on either side, and I felt a rush of contentment and warmth as Henri wrapped his arm around my waist.

"I've missed you," he said into my ear, pulling me into a kiss. As an American, I felt it was too long for being in public, but no one batted an eye.

"Okay, lovebirds," Georges said, teasing, "we have things to discuss."

"And we have some good news to share," I said. Josette and I first told them about Nora and our plans for her, followed by some interesting bits of intelligence I'd be sharing with London.

"But we've been saving the best news for last," Josette said, rubbing her hands together. "We have an invitation to a party at 17 Avenue Foch Saturday night, with several officers who work in the secret offices upstairs from us at the Majestic. It's the chance we have been waiting for."

"And that London has been waiting for," I said, sharing Josette's excitement, although Keppler's behavior remained a nagging worry.

Georges and Henri looked at each other.

"What?" Josette asked. "We thought you would be happy about this."

"A party on Avenue Boches," Georges said with a groan.

Avenue Foch was a wide, tree-lined boulevard in the heart of the 16th arrondissement and considered one of the most prestigious addresses in all of Paris. The Germans had taken over several of the magnificent nineteenth-century villas that were empty because families had fled or, in the case of several Jewish families, been arrested and sent to the camps.

"At least it's not number 84," Henri said, referring to the mansion that was the Gestapo's French headquarters.

The prison on the top floor of 84 Avenue Foch was where they tortured prisoners, many of them Resistance members, for information—pulling their fingernails out, or submerging them in a bathtub until they were nearly drowned, among other unspeakable acts of terror. Dr. Jackson, one of the few non-Germans still in his family home on Avenue Foch, had mentioned hearing screams when bicycling home from work. I thought of the night in the basement of Rue Fabert, how those screams could have been ours.

"I don't like this at all," Henri said, scraping the table with his finger, frowning. "I have a bad feeling."

"We have to go," I said, feeling tense and disappointed by their reaction.

"You both know we do," Josette said, looking at me in disbelief. She leaned over the table and dropped her voice to a whisper. "We haven't gotten anywhere in a few weeks. We need more about the island and the weapons. I feel like it's the first real chance we've had in a while."

"Because it *is*," I said, also talking low. "Every day we don't get this intelligence is another day closer to when those weapons will be ready to use."

I put my hand over Henri's, and he looked up at me, his eyes filled with worry. I could not tell him about Keppler.

Georges ran his fingers through his hair, making it stick up in odd directions even more than it already was. He sighed.

"You're right, of course," Georges said, looking at Josette and me. He then looked at Henri and shrugged. "They have to go."

Josette planted a kiss on Georges's cheek.

Henri sighed and gave a small nod.

"I'm not happy about it, but I agree," Henri said.

We promised we would be careful and discussed our excuses for leaving if things got uncomfortable or anyone grew suspicious of us. It was comforting knowing that Dr. Jackson's home was close by.

Josette and Georges got up to get us a second round of drinks.

Henri lit a cigarette and put his arm around my shoulder.

"As I've said, you are a very brave woman," he said. "Not many women would do these things."

"I don't know about that," I said. I thought of all the women I knew who were being brave in ways large and small: the fearless Tatiana smuggling Allied pilots out of the city, and Nora, who was pushing herself, working for three networks despite how scared she was. I thought of the mothers who stood in line for hours for food for their children, and even Madame Chevrolet, who had been loyal to us in the end. If the Allies did finally triumph in this war, it would be largely because of the work of women in the shadows.

"I will be at La Caravalle tomorrow all day, meeting with many new members of the network, organizing them and figuring out what roles they're capable of playing," he said. "But I'm staying in room 424 at the Hotel Esmeralda, near Notre-Dame, tomorrow night. It's owned by an old friend. Please meet me there after the party?"

"Definitely," I said, putting my hand on his face, thrilled at the thought of having another whole night alone with him. "I wish I didn't have to go tomorrow. Thank you for understanding why I must."

"Just be on guard, more than ever," Henri said, tucking a curl behind my ear as he looked at me. "This is where les boches live. You're going to a party in the lion's den."

# Chapter Thirty-Four

**March 20, 1943**

"We can't leave tonight until we have something more about the weapons," I said to Josette, fidgeting with my hair and trying to calm my nerves. "I don't want to disappoint London again."

The cold night air stung our faces when we exited the Porte Dauphine metro station, emerging from its charming art deco entrance located in a small park just down the street from Avenue Foch.

"Yes, you've said that to me at least four times today already," Josette said, her tone somewhere between teasing and annoyed.

"I know," I said. "I'm sorry."

"Don't worry, I understand," she said and grabbed my elbow. We huddled close and walked quickly, bracing ourselves as the wind whipped down the street. "So you'll focus on Otto, and I'll work on Franz and anyone else from their office who might have too many cognacs and be in the mood to flirt and boast about their work."

"And hopefully Keppler will be too busy mingling with the other high-ranking officers to pay much attention to me," I said.

"Don't count on that," Josette said, giving me a sideways glance.

"I know," I said, taking a deep breath and blowing it out. "I'll handle him if I have to."

We both couldn't help but stare when we walked by 84 Avenue Foch. There were several sleek black Mercedes and Citroëns parked in front of it. Two armed Gestapo in dark leather trench coats stood at the entry of the mansion's gate. The windows on the top floor were all darkened, and I said a silent prayer for any prisoners who might be trapped up there.

Ten minutes later, we reached the wrought-iron gate of 17 Avenue Foch, and we could hear a party already in full swing. The two of us stood for a moment under the lamplight and braced ourselves as if going into battle. I smoothed out my polka-dot dress underneath my wool coat—no Lelong couture tonight. I noticed my iodine-tinged legs were blotchy from the cold.

"Let's go, *Madeleine*," I said. "Let's get this done. And I need to get inside before my legs fall off. I can barely feel them."

"Mine too, *Alexine*," Josette said.

We rang the doorbell, and a young woman opened it. Her brown hair was in a tight bun, and she was dressed in a light-gray military uniform. The "gray mice" in Paris were female German military personnel who had a very low opinion of Frenchwomen. She tilted her head, took a drag of her cigarette, and looked us up and down without a word.

"We're here for the party," I said in German. "We were invited by our coworkers at the Hotel Majestic, Otto Wagner and Franz Becker."

"I suppose you can come in, then," the woman replied with a shrug, rolling her eyes as she left the door open for us, turned her back, and walked away.

Ignoring her rude behavior, we stepped inside, and I gasped. The mansion was as grand as Florence Gould's apartment and several times larger. It had parquet floors, intricate moldings, and shimmering gold-covered walls. Not knowing what to do next, we left our coats folded neatly in an alcove by the door and made our way into the crowds. We passed German officers who gave us appreciative smiles and greetings, and a few more gray mice who did not. There were other Frenchwomen at the party as well, including a few faces I recognized from the Majestic.

"I was afraid you were not going to come," Otto said as he walked toward us. Seeming genuinely thrilled to see us, he had a cognac in hand as he greeted us both with kisses on our cheeks. He smelled like peppermint and alcohol.

"We wouldn't miss it," I said. "This house, it's . . . fantastic."

"You both look beautiful," he said, his eyes lingering on me longer than Josette. "Franz is in the study. But let's get you both some champagne first."

The bar was set up in a grand room with a roaring marble fireplace, near where a six-piece band was playing. Otto got us flutes of champagne and another cognac for himself, and judging by the number of guests teetering or talking too loudly, the drinks had been flowing steadily for a while.

It was so packed with people we had to squeeze through the room single file. I was behind Josette and just about to step out of the room when Keppler appeared in front of me.

"Alexine, one of the loveliest *Parisian* girls I know," he said. "You are very late."

"That is the French way," I said, smiling as he kissed my hand. I was disciplined enough not to recoil. Was I imagining his emphasis on *Parisian*? "We are always fashionably late."

"Is that what they call it?" Keppler said with a smile, taking a sip of his wine. "So happy you came. There may be dancing later. Will you dance with me?"

"I . . . um . . . yes, if there is dancing," I said, though touching him, being so close to him, was going to require my best acting performance yet.

"Good. Tell me, do you know how to tango?" Keppler asked, watching my reaction. I froze for a second.

*Is it a trick?*

"I . . . I do," I said, nodding way too many times. "My mother made me take dance lessons as a child."

"In Saint-Malo?"

"Yes, in Saint-Malo," I said. Wanting to end the conversation, I added, "We were just going to join Franz in the study."

"Ah, of course, and Otto, I suppose," Keppler said. He touched the dimple on my right cheek with his hand, and it took so much restraint not to smack it away. "No matter. I will find you later."

"I will see you soon." I nodded and turned to leave, walking as fast as I could without being obvious.

I took a large sip of champagne, rattled by Keppler, not knowing if he was just flirting or if his underlying motives were more sinister. I went into the study and found Franz smoking a cigar by the fireplace. Josette was sitting on the arm of his chair, and Otto was on a burgundy sofa opposite them. It was a dark-paneled room, with empty bookshelves that had the ghostly outlines of books that must have sat on them for years. There were several officers and Frenchwomen milling about, flirting and laughing, but it was still far cozier and quieter than the main room.

"Otto and I were taking bets on whether you would come," Franz said, his freckled cheeks pink as he looked at Josette.

"I was just saying we don't see you two enough these days. We had to come," Josette said, her eyes on him as she turned on her charm. "How many of you live in this palace?"

"A dozen of us," Otto said, pleased when I sat next to him on the sofa. "And sometimes more, when others come from Berlin for meetings."

We talked with them about the differences between Berlin and Paris, what they missed about that city, what they loved about ours. Josette and I treaded lightly around any topic that might turn controversial, and we never shared our real thoughts.

After an hour, another officer, tall and pale-skinned with white-blond hair, joined us by the fire. Franz introduced him as Bruno Richter.

Bruno explained that he also worked upstairs, and I knew I had to seize the chance.

"So, is it true what Otto and Franz told us before, that they are building this astounding new weapon on Usedom in the Baltic?" I asked Bruno. He looked at Otto and Franz with concern, and Otto waved his hand.

"Alexine and Madeleine work downstairs. We can trust them with anything, right, girls?" Otto said.

Franz looked less comfortable about the discussion.

"You absolutely can," Josette said, patting Franz on the shoulder. He reached up and squeezed her hand and held it, and his demeanor seemed calmer, happier. He had given her the chair and was sitting on the floor next to her.

"Yes, Germany's top scientists and engineers are on that island," Bruno said, quite pleased to brag about it to us. "They have built not one, but *two* super weapons: a long-range rocket and a pilotless jet aircraft armed with bombs."

"No," I said, shaking my head, ignoring the nausea I felt at the thought of what these weapons could do. "What you are saying cannot be true. It's science fiction."

"It is absolutely true," Otto said. "It is top secret and one of the most important efforts in the war."

"Franz, is what they're saying true? It sounds far-fetched," Josette said. She was still letting him hold her hand, and I was sure that was why he was happy to answer.

"What Bruno says is true," Franz said, "and they successfully tested the rocket in October. It has a horizontal range of over three hundred miles."

"Fifty of these stratospheric bomb rockets could destroy all of London," Otto said. "They're going to aim them at most of Britain's large cities next winter."

I couldn't even look at Josette because I knew she was feeling the same way I was. Sickened by these boys talking about their weapons as if they were pretending on the school playground.

"I am sorry, it just sounds too outrageous. You must be exaggerating," I teased, nudging Otto and taking a large sip of champagne because inside I felt like screaming.

"Exaggerating?" Otto said, downing the last of the cognac in his glass. "Come over here, I will show you that I am not exaggerating in the slightest." He grabbed my hand, pulled me up from the couch, and brought me over to the desk in the corner of the study. His briefcase was leaning against it, and he pulled out several documents and spread them on the desk. And suddenly there it all was, everything we had been wanting to discover, right in front of my eyes.

I looked at them, taking photographs in my mind of the mother lode of German intelligence laid out before me. One was a drawing of a huge rocket, with a shocking amount of detail, including its size, range, fuel, and launch speed. It even included information about the planned locations of launch sites on France's coast. The other document was a map of the testing site known as Peenemünde on the island of Usedom.

"This is . . . well, it's fascinating," I said, leaning in to read some of the smaller details about the rocket's fuel supply—eight hundred liters of petrol—as well as its deficiencies. I said *click* to myself as I made another mental photograph, details to save for later, when I could copy them down on paper. I put my hand over my mouth and hoped I didn't look as ecstatic as I felt.

*Breathe, Anna. Act interested, but not obsessed.*

"It is," Otto said, his chest almost puffing out with pride. "German engineering is so far ahead of the rest of the world."

"Come here, you have to see all of this," I said to Josette. I needed her eyes on them as well, in case I missed any detail. Josette came over with Franz, who had an odd expression on his face but didn't seem alarmed like he had been at Florence Gould's party. Bruno had moved on and was sitting in the corner of the room, next to the brunette who had rudely greeted us at the door.

I looked around to see if any of the other Germans in the room had noticed what we were doing, but they were all too busy trying to keep the interest of the various women they were flirting with to pay the four of us any attention.

"I am sorry for teasing you," I said to Otto. "I'm so proud of both of you for being involved in such strategic, important work."

"Me too," said Josette. "It's truly incredible."

"These other documents deal with how to access the site. It's very closely guarded," Otto said, happy to continue to impress us. "In addition to a military pass, three other special passes are required to gain access, all color coded."

I wasn't sure what had changed with Franz, but this time he let Otto keep talking as Josette and I took it all in, asking questions and encouraging him to tell us more.

"Otto, my friend, I think you have impressed the ladies enough for the evening," Franz said suddenly, eyes darting to the fireplace. "Perhaps you should put those papers away now?"

Keppler had entered the room. He was giving a tour of the home to two men wearing the distinct black-and-red uniforms of the Gestapo. I shuddered and noticed that even though Otto had appeared slightly drunk, he managed to scoop up the documents and file them into his briefcase in seconds.

I excused myself to find a bathroom, nodding to Keppler as I walked past him, relieved he didn't call me over. I had no desire to be that close to any Gestapo. I wanted so badly to flee the party at that moment, to get what we had just seen down on paper.

A woman in a floral dress pointed me toward a door at the end of the main hall, just off the kitchen at the back of the house. I squeezed by a couple deep in drunken conversation and slid open the pocket door, stepping into a salmon-colored bathroom. I was about to latch it and was startled when Otto slid it open and stepped in, then shut it behind him. I knew what he was hoping would happen next, and I took a breath, trying to figure out how to avoid kissing him, hoping he wasn't about to reveal an ugly side of himself that I had not yet seen.

"Otto . . . I—"

"You must be quiet and listen very carefully to what I'm about to say, Alexine—or whatever your name is," Otto whispered to me in perfect English, holding his finger up to his lips. My knees almost buckled from the shock, but I stayed upright.

"You speak English?" I said.

"Before the war, my parents sent me to the London School of Economics," he said with a half smile, "because they didn't want me to be educated by Nazi professors."

"My God," I said. I had been thinking our tactics were so clever, but Otto was playing the game with us the whole time. "You shared all of this tonight on purpose?"

"Yes," he said, "and I hope your memory is as good as the men in your office say it is, because Franz and I just gave you some of the most important intelligence of the war so far. You need to get it all down on paper and get it into the right hands as soon as possible."

"You've known all along," I whispered, mystified and angry at myself that I didn't suspect it before.

"It was a hunch," he said. "And then at the Gould party, I knew my instincts had been right."

"How . . . why are you doing this?"

"As you know, I am an officer of the Wehrmacht, the German military. There are some of us, like me and Franz, who don't believe in what the Nazi party—what Hitler—is doing," Otto said, his voice soft but thick with emotion. "I saw them burn the Jewish residents of my town to death. The Nazis are evil war criminals. The world may never forgive Germany for their acts."

His eyes were watering, and now mine did too, for this young, compassionate man who had the courage to do what was right.

"Thank you," I said, "for being so brave, for sharing this with me."

"I had to. But there's more you need to know," Otto said. "Keppler."

"Oh no," I said, a wave of fear washing over me. "Does he know?"

"No. If he did know for sure, you'd be in the prison at 84 Avenue Foch already," he said. "He suspects you might not be who you say you are, though your work for him has been impeccable, so that has been in your favor. Also, he is attracted to you, if you haven't noticed, so he'd like it not to be true, because he thinks of you as a possible mistress."

"I think I'm going to be sick," I said, feeling the color drain from my face.

"No, what you're going to do is make plans to get far away from him. Keppler is ruthless, his Gestapo friends even more so. Now that you have the intelligence you wanted, you have to get it in the right hands and disappear. He has people watching the hostel where you live, so you cannot go back there tonight. You need to get out of Paris as soon as you possibly can."

I groaned and put my hands over my face, thinking about the times Georges and Henri had come to the hostel, wondering if they had been spotted. Paris was such a large city, I had thought that if I was paranoid enough, I would—we would—remain anonymous and unseen. We should have taken even greater care about where and how we met, especially after the raid at Rue Fabert. I thought we had been cautious enough. I was wrong.

"I cannot thank you enough," I said, giving him a hug. "You are saving my life, and hopefully many other lives, with this information."

"Just please, get the intelligence to London and go into hiding," Otto said, holding me tight and letting out a small sigh. "I . . . I need for this to matter."

"I will make sure it does."

We decided that he and Franz would escort Josette and me from the party to the metro station down the street. I would go to the Hotel Esmeralda with Josette and get everything down on paper, and from there we would come up with a plan to get the intelligence to London as fast as we could.

We slid open the door to the bathroom, and Keppler was standing in the hallway a few feet away with his Gestapo friends and a couple of gray mice, who looked at me like I had validated their opinion that all Frenchwomen were whores. Keppler frowned at us. Otto took my hand and led me down the hall past the group, and I looked down and away from them, as if I was embarrassed to be caught in the bathroom with a man. We called to Franz and Josette that it was time to go, and I went to fetch my coat by the door, glancing back down the hall to see that Herbert Keppler was walking toward me.

"Leaving so soon?" he said, his eyes never leaving mine.

"Yes, I . . . I am not feeling well," I said. "That is why Otto was in the bathroom, to check on me. He thought I had fainted in there."

"I am sorry to hear that," he said. He seemed genuinely relieved to hear the excuse for Otto's presence. "We didn't even get to dance."

"I promise we will dance another time," I said. I had gotten much better at faking smiles and lightheartedness.

He helped me put on my coat and then leaned in.

"I will hold you to it, my dear," he said. It sounded more like a threat than a promise, his hands on my shoulders as he kissed me on the cheek. I knew he felt me shiver.

# Chapter Thirty-Five

We said a grateful good-bye to Otto and Franz at the entrance of the metro, thankful for their courage in sharing such extraordinary intelligence with us. I was frantic to get everything down on paper while it was still fresh in my mind. For the entire crowded, foul-smelling train ride, I kept going over the map and the drawing of the bomb in my mind, reciting the data from the documents to myself, willing the train to go faster. Josette and I didn't speak the entire way, and when I saw her lips moving, I knew she was doing the same.

The Esmeralda was a small, dodgy hotel in the shadow of Notre-Dame cathedral. We stormed inside the front door, partly to get out of the cold but mostly because we had work to do. I rang the bell at the front desk four times, and a slight young man with thick, wire-rimmed glasses emerged from the back room, yawning, annoyed to be woken from his nap.

"Please, sir, do you have a pencil and some paper?" I asked. "I'm staying in room 424, and I would like to borrow a pencil and paper. I will return the pencil and reimburse you for the paper."

He looked at me and Josette, eyebrows raised, trying to decide what to make of us. We had run all the way from the metro. My curls were wild, and my cheeks chapped from the cold. Josette looked only slightly less crazed than me.

"Please," Josette said, holding up her hands in prayer. "It's rather urgent."

He sighed, went into the back room, and returned with a stack of paper and two pencils. We thanked him and ran down the hall to the caged elevator. As soon as the elevator door closed, I started sketching the weapon on the top sheet, though it was awkward without a hard surface.

"Do you want to start with the map, and then we can both fill in the blanks for each other?" I asked.

"Perfect," Josette said, grabbing a pencil from me.

Room 424 was at the end of the hall near the stairwell. I banged on the door, and when Henri opened it, I leaned into him and gave him a hard kiss on the lips.

"What . . . ?" He laughed when I pulled away. "Josette . . . Does Georges know you're here?"

"He doesn't, but I know he'll come here when I don't arrive at Zoé's house," she said.

"We got it," I said, taking off my coat and sitting down at the small table next to the window. The room smelled of mildew, and the walls and ceiling were paneled with dark wood, making me feel like we were trapped in a hope chest.

"We got everything we wanted," I said to Henri. "Did you bring my wireless?"

"Yes, but what exactly did you get?" he asked.

Josette sat across from me, and we got to work sketching out what we remembered, while I told Henri about the intelligence revelations. He was as exultant as we were, pumping his fist in the air and planting a kiss on my forehead. But his face darkened when he learned of my exchange with Otto in the bathroom, and about Keppler's suspicions.

"I'm afraid you will both have to get out of the city after we get this information in the right hands," Henri said. I looked up at him, and our eyes met, both of us sad at the prospect. "You can stay at Guy and Colette Terrier's at first, and then we'll find you a safer place from there. Pauline and Bernard are building an army. They could use your help as couriers, and with the wireless, of course."

"That's where I was going to suggest Nora go," I said. "It makes sense."

Henri poured us glasses of wine and gave Josette a cigarette, then he paced the room while we worked. I continued to get down all the details I could remember—size, fuel, launch speed, and deficiencies. Josette was working just as furiously, recreating the map of the testing site, and we went back and forth, asking each other to verify details, comparing notes and drawings. After an hour and a half, there was a knock on the door, and Henri looked through the peephole.

"Georges," he said, opening the door.

"Josette!" Georges came rushing into the room, and when she stood up, he scooped her into his arms, lifting her off the floor. "Thank God. I was so worried. I thought something had gone horribly wrong." He looked over her shoulder at the scattered papers in front of us on the table.

"What is all of this?"

For the second time we explained what had happened that evening, letting both men really examine Josette's map and my drawing of the weapon, and the details we had included on those pages and subsequent ones.

"I cannot believe what I am seeing," Georges said. He whistled through his teeth and looked up at the two of us with astonishment. "You have done it. Do you even realize what you have here? This might be the most important intelligence discovered in this war."

I felt goose pimples on my arms and blinked back tears, exhausted, exhilarated, and overcome. Josette started laughing and came over to give me a hug.

"I could not have done this work without you, *ma chère*," she said into my hair. "Thank God, we finally got it."

The four of us took a moment to toast and celebrate.

"I don't even understand, how did you do this? How do you remember things like this?" Henri asked me, frowning at the drawing in front of him. It was exactly as I remembered it on the table at Avenue Foch.

"I don't know. I always could," I said. "And I know it's right."

"You're extraordinary, Anna." And then, looking at Josette's detailed map, he added, "You are both extraordinary."

"Oh, can you take photos of these pages?" I asked, looking at his camera. "So we have a copy of them on film?"

"I can if I can get more film," Henri said, cursing with frustration. "I just finished the roll that's in here. It's getting harder to come by these days."

"I have to go off schedule and send a message tonight to tell London what's coming," I said. "But how are we going to get these papers to them quickly? They need to see this intelligence now."

Georges was pulling at a tuft of hair, pacing.

"Wednesday night," he said, "I am scheduled to meet with Gabriel Comtois, one of the leaders of the Alliance network. He has forged documents to give me for some of the latest recruits. We are meeting at the Passy metro, at exactly 9:30 p.m. I will let them know what we have for them ahead of time. They are the biggest resistance network in all of Paris; they can get the documents to the right people in London very fast."

"I have to go to Pauline and Bernard's that evening, to meet with the new Resistance sector leaders, the people we will be working with in Nice, Toulouse, and Lyon," Henri said. He nodded at me and Josette. "When I'm there, I'll let the Terriers know you'll be arriving Thursday to stay with them and hide out for a while. After the intelligence is passed on, you shouldn't spend another minute in this city."

"I'm scheduled to be on the wireless that night at the hospital," I said. "And Josette, you were going to come with me to help Tatiana.

There are new underground patients coming through, at least two Allied pilots. But Georges, I'd like to go with you—"

"Or I could go with you," Josette said, interrupting me, looking up at Georges. "You should stick to your schedule at the hospital, Anna, no?"

"Nobody needs to go with me," Georges said, annoyed. "That's ridiculous. It's just a handoff of papers on a staircase. I've done it dozens of times before."

"No, I have to go with you. Please let me come," I said. "I'm sorry, Josette, it's just, *this*?" I pointed at the papers. "This is the reason I'm here. I feel responsible for getting these into the right hands."

Georges didn't say anything for a moment. He took a long drag of his cigarette and blew out the smoke, thinking. "Okay." He sighed. "You may go with me."

"I understand why," Josette said, nodding at me and then Georges. "You must both promise me that you'll come back in one piece?"

"Of course we will," I said with a smile.

~

Sometime well after midnight, when we were sure we had everything down on paper that we could possibly remember, Georges and Josette left and got a room down the hall from us. It was decided that Josette and I would stay at the Esmeralda for now, and someone in the network would be sent to retrieve our personal belongings from the hostel and deliver them in the next couple of days.

After they had left, Henri and I fell into bed together, kissing and laughing, undressing each other and making love until I finally fell into a bone-weary, exhausted sleep.

I dreamed that I was standing in the middle of a medieval village square next to a cathedral. The sky was filled with dark, fast-moving clouds, and Henri and Josette stood next to me. Josette was calling for Georges, who was somewhere we couldn't see. Suddenly Phillip appeared, across the square, in front of the cathedral. And as soon as he saw us, I knew he knew about Henri.

"Just stay safe, Anna," Phillip called out to me, his voice echoing off the buildings around us. "Stay alive."

Then gunshots rang out, and I couldn't see where they were coming from, but I knew they were aimed at us, and we started to run. A second round, even closer now, and I screamed but no sound would come out.

I woke up gasping and sat up in bed, hugging my knees, taking deep breaths to calm myself. Henri sat up and took me in his arms, and I leaned against his warm bare chest.

"I'm sorry to wake you," I said. "Just a bad dream."

"Do you want to talk about it?"

"No," I said, wrapping my arms around him.

"I'm here. And tonight, you are safe with me, my love," he said.

*My love.*

"My mind is just restless," I said. "I wish we could get that intelligence to London tonight. What if we get it to them and it's too late to make a difference? What if they're almost finished testing?"

"But based on everything you've told me, we've still got time."

"I hope so."

We sat in each other's arms for a moment, listening to the distant sounds of sirens blaring somewhere in the streets.

"Promise me you will come visit me soon—after I leave the city Thursday?"

"Nothing would keep me away from you, Anna," he said.

I lay back on his chest, and he kissed my forehead, stroking my hair until I fell fast asleep again.

# Chapter Thirty-Six

*March 24, 1943*

Josette and I had made our plans and decided we would leave Paris first thing Thursday morning.

On Wednesday night, I would go with Georges to the Passy metro station, to make sure our precious intelligence was handed over to the Alliance network. Then Georges and I would meet up with Josette at the hospital, and she and I would leave there at dawn for the countryside, hitching a ride with one of the men in the Druids network who drove a supply truck, because it would be safer than taking the train and having to show our papers.

We continued to go to work at the Hotel Majestic, knowing we needed to keep up appearances and do everything we could to ease Keppler's suspicions until we could get the intelligence in the right hands and leave Paris. It was excruciating being so close to him, now that we knew he was suspicious enough that he'd had men spying on *us* for some time.

Just before five on Wednesday, I found myself watching the clock, relieved that it was almost time to leave the hotel for the last time. I signaled to Josette across the room that it was time to go, and she gave me a slight nod and a warning look with her eyes.

"Alexine, are you leaving so soon?" Keppler was standing behind me, his hands on my chair, fingers touching my back.

"Oh, yes, sir, you startled me," I said, turning to look up at him, trying to sound breathless and flirty.

"No more of this *sir*, remember. You should call me Herbert," he said with a leering smile.

"Yes . . . Herbert . . . we have a hair appointment tonight," I said. "It's so hard now for women to find a hairdresser in the city, but Madeleine discovered one that is open, and we're going right after work."

"That is a shame. I wanted to invite you for a drink at the Ritz." He had taken his hands off my chair and was leaning on my desk, sitting so very close to me that I could smell the cigarette he had just smoked and the cloying citrus cologne I had grown to detest.

"Oh, well, thank you," I said, keeping my voice calm and light-hearted. "How about tomorrow night?"

He paused before answering and then smiled, his cold eyes looking into mine, trying to convey a connection and intimacy I had to pretend to share, and it made my stomach turn.

"Perfect. Tomorrow night, then," he said with a nod. He got up to leave, putting his hand in my hair, fingering a curl on the side of my face before walking away. "Don't change your hair too much. It's beautiful as it is."

"Thank you . . . Herbert," I said. He nodded, obviously pleased I had called him by his first name unprompted.

⤳

Twenty minutes later, we bid good-bye to the guards at the Majestic for the last time, and I breathed in the chilly evening air in relief, suppressing the urge to run down the street.

"Maybe you're the one who should become an actress when this is over," Josette said when we were far enough away from the hotel to talk. She gave me a sideways glance, eyebrows raised. "That was a nice performance for Keppler."

"Do you think he believed it?"

"I think he did, based on his reaction."

"I pray we never see that man again," I said, shivering at the thought of him touching my hair, his hands on my back.

"I know," Josette said with a deep sigh. "Me too."

We walked to a discreet hair salon Tatiana had told us about, located down a narrow cobblestone alley in the Marais neighborhood. The hairdresser was a tall, skinny woman with angular features and long arms. She reminded me of a crane, the way she moved around the salon. She gave Josette a bob that framed her pixie face, and colored her hair a lighter, sandier brown. My dark curls were a little harder to disguise, but she cut my hair to just above my shoulders and suggested a deep auburn hair dye, convincing me it would work better than anything else would.

"Wow," Josette said as we stood looking in the mirror together when we were finished. "You have red hair."

"It's not really *red*, though," I said, cringing and leaning in close to look at the color. It was a little brighter than I expected. "I prefer to call it auburn. And honestly, with your new hair, I might not even recognize you from across the street. She did a perfect job."

We generously tipped our hairstylist and left the salon after dark to meet Georges and Henri at a tiny café a few blocks away.

"Thank you for going with him tonight," Josette said, hooking arms with me as we rounded the corner.

"Of course."

"I would be too nervous to go with him. Too emotional if anything . . ."

"Nothing is going to happen. We will be back at the hospital before you know it. Like he said, it's a routine handoff of papers. Georges has been doing this work for a long time now. I'm guessing he's one of the best network leaders in France."

I said a silent prayer that I was right and all would go according to plan. It had to.

"I love him dearly," she said, her voice breaking a little. "The best thing about this war has been falling in love with him."

"I thought the best thing about it was reuniting with your best American friend?" I said.

"Well, that too, naturally," she said with a laugh.

We arrived at the front of the Boot Café, on the border of the Marais and Bastille neighborhoods. Its wooden exterior was a deep blue, the word *Cordonnerie* in big black letters above its door, a nod to its origins as a cobbler's shop dating back to prerevolutionary times.

It was small and cheery, with a black-and-white tile floor and a rustic wood-beamed ceiling. Henri and Georges were smoking cigarettes at a table next to the bar, and we squeezed our way past patrons and waiters to join them.

"Your hair," Henri said, kissing me on the cheek and tugging one of my curls. "I love it."

"Thank you. I'm not sure I do," I said, looking in the mirrored wall behind him, frowning at my reflection.

"Your hair could be emerald green and I would love it," Henri said.

"And look at you, Josette," Georges gasped, putting his hand on his chest when Josette took off her hat. "It's like I'm having an affair with another woman. This is very exciting."

Josette gave him a playful smack on the arm.

"Do I smell *real* espresso?" she asked, eyeing the bar. "How do they have real espresso? I might cry with joy."

"They do," Georges said. "Just don't ask how. And I would order now, before they run out."

Josette and I ordered, and when the cups of espresso arrived, I put my face over mine, breathing in the heavenly smell.

"How I long for my old Paris, my city filled with espresso and runny cheese and real warm, crusty bread," Josette said with a deep sigh, holding the cup under her nose with her eyes closed.

"And if we are going to get that Paris back, we have to talk about what we're doing tonight," Georges said, amused but ready to get on with it.

"Do you have the papers with you?" Henri asked, leaning in, dropping his voice, and grabbing my hand. "I have to leave soon, but I wanted to make sure you were ready."

"The papers are in my purse," I said with a nod. I had not let the intelligence out of my sight since we had written everything down.

"Good," Georges said. "And you're ready for our little mission?"

"I am as ready as I can be," I said, feeling my stomach churn at the mention of it. "Are you armed?" I asked Georges, and he looked surprised.

"Yes. Always," he said, his face serious.

Josette turned pale at this, and Georges put his arm around her, reassuring.

"I've got to go now, or I'll be late," Henri said, looking at his watch. "I'm hitching a ride on one of the trucks out of the city." He looked at me. "Will you walk outside with me for a minute?"

I nodded and grabbed his hand. We stood in the street, holding hands. I was fidgeting and couldn't stop tapping my foot. He seemed to be searching for words, and I was feeling so many things—determined, paranoid, uneasy—but more than anything, I felt heartsick, because our time in the same city was coming to an end, and I had no idea when circumstances would change again.

"I can tell you're nervous; it's understandable," he said. "That's what will help keep you safe."

"Yes," I said. "I'm a little nervous, but I'll be fine. I need to see this through."

"Oh, I know you do." He smiled at me.

"Will I see you later, at the hospital?"

"I am going to try to return late tonight, yes," Henri said. "It may be the last time we see each other for a while."

"I know."

He put his hands on my face and leaned down to kiss me.

"Anna . . . ," he said, still holding my face. "After all this madness is over, would you . . . would you ever consider staying . . . in France? With me?"

I thought about what he was saying, about what that kind of future might be like, and my heart swelled. I also thought of my star-crossed romance with Phillip Stanhope, and seeing him in my dream a few nights ago and so many nights before that. The war had barely even given Phillip and me a chance to begin, but here was Henri, hoping we would have the chance of a happy ending, despite the odds.

I missed my family and friends from home often, of course, and it hurt to not be in contact with them. But it occurred to me that I had recovered from my homesickness weeks before. And the reason I had was that, despite being in a dangerous, occupied city, I was with these cherished friends in a place that felt something like home too.

Henri was looking at me, worry in his eyes because I hadn't answered yet.

"I would stay in France with you," I said, smiling, and he let out a breath and started laughing, kissing me again.

"Yes! Thank God," he said. "That is the best news."

"It's something for us to look forward to," I said, feeling the warmth and comfort of his presence, and of what might be for us, but also that nagging dread of what we might have to endure before we got there.

"Be safe tonight," he said, blowing me a kiss as he walked away backward. "We will say a proper good-bye at the hospital later."

Then he ducked around the corner and was gone.

At fifteen minutes past nine o'clock, Georges and I were walking across the Pont Passy, a viaduct bridge that spanned the river Seine, connecting the 15th and 16th arrondissements. To the right was a gorgeous view of the Eiffel Tower, a beacon of hope in the darkness. I never tired of the sight of it, and something about it tonight, standing majestic even now, gave me courage.

The Passy metro station, the rendezvous point with the Alliance network contact, was at the other side of the bridge on a platform at the top of a three-story stone staircase. I clutched my purse against my waist, reaching in to feel the papers every so often, to make sure they were still intact. The temperature had been dropping since we left the café, and the wind off the river whipped around us, stinging my face and making my teeth chatter.

Georges had smoked cigarettes the entire way, and we didn't talk much, both of us lost in our thoughts about the task at hand. When we were about a hundred yards from the station, we reviewed our plan.

"The tiny alleyway that you can hide in is there, just around the corner from the staircase," he said, pointing to the left. We headed over to it together, and he stomped out his cigarette. It was two minutes until nine thirty, and my stomach was in knots.

"If you see anything, or anyone, whistle to me. I'm to go up and meet him on the staircase, on the first landing from the top."

I took my prized intelligence papers out of my purse and handed them to him. At exactly nine thirty, he saluted me and headed up the staircase, where I lost sight of him. I had to remind myself to breathe as I waited, crouched in the alleyway, holding my hands tightly to keep them warm and stop them from shaking.

Five minutes later, Georges appeared again at the bottom of the stairs, the papers still in his hands.

"He wasn't there," he said in a whisper, letting out a string of quiet curses.

"So we leave and try again tomorrow?" I said, distraught that our contact had not shown.

Georges looked at me, his face in shadows. "This is too important," he said. "I'm going to go up to the landing one more time."

"No, you waited the required five minutes," I said. "Remember protocol: if it doesn't happen on time, it doesn't happen at all." It was one of the rules that had been drilled into me at Beaulieu.

"To hell with protocol. Anna, you know more than anyone what we have here," he said, his voice harsher than I'd ever heard before. "I am going to try again one more time; he's probably just taking extra precautions."

My gut was saying to tell him not to try again, but I wanted desperately to get what we had to London.

"I want you to leave the papers with me, then," I said, putting my hand out. "If he shows, you whistle to me, and I'll come hand them off."

"Anna, I—"

"No, I insist. At least take this precaution if you're going back up. Please."

He sighed and looked as tense and frustrated as I felt. He handed me the papers.

"I'll be whistling in a minute, you'll see," he said, but I had a feeling of dread as I watched him walk away. I stepped out of the alley and opened my mouth to tell him to come back but shut it again. We had to try to get these out tonight.

As soon as he turned the corner and headed up the staircase for the second time, I heard sirens approaching and the terrifying sound of dozens of jackboots coming from the top of the staircase Georges was ascending. He was walking right into the arms of the Gestapo.

I melted back, deeper into the narrow alley, terrified that they had seen me too. Kneeling down, I gagged on the smell of stale urine and my own fear as I listened to the Germans shouting in their guttural accents. There were sounds of a struggle, shuffling feet, grunting, and cursing coming from the stairs—then two gunshots rang out, followed by more shouts of fury. There was a loud cracking sound, and I heard a man howl in pain, and I knew from the tone that it was Georges. I had to bite my fist to keep from screaming or vomiting. Had he been shot or just beaten with something . . . or both? Was he seriously injured? I knew they had him now. I was furious at myself for letting him go back up a second time, and devastated that there was nothing I could do to help him get away now. I wasn't armed, and it sounded like there were over a dozen of them. If I tried to help, I would just get captured too, with the papers in hand.

The shouting stopped. The struggle was over. In my mind, I saw Georges LaRue being shoved into the back of one of the Gestapo's cars, and then I heard the sound of them driving away. I took a deep breath, sat down against the wall, and wrapped my arms around my legs. I couldn't stop shaking as I looked up at the sky and it started to rain.

# Chapter Thirty-Seven

I stayed in that filthy alley, trying to stop my uncontrollable shivering, for a long time after the Gestapo left with Georges. I had to get to the American Hospital to warn Josette and Henri and figure out our next steps. But first I had to get ahold of myself.

Georges had been captured and possibly injured, and I had been helpless to stop it from happening. And with the horror of Georges's capture came the devastating reality that we had failed to deliver the Usedom intelligence to someone who could get it to London quickly enough for it to make a difference.

My throat hurt, and the rain was now soaking through my wool coat and puddling in my boots. I stuffed the intelligence papers deeper in my purse and covered them with my scarf, hoping it would protect them enough from bleeding into each other. I didn't dare take the metro or hail a vélo-taxi, and it was going to take me a good hour to walk to the American Hospital. I had to start out soon to make it there before curfew.

Walking out of the alley, catlike, I took deep breaths to calm myself. The Gestapo had not left anyone behind to wait for me when I crept out of the shadows. I thanked God for that.

Twenty minutes later, I started to feel less panicked but still stayed alert and kept a brisk pace. Some cafés were open, brightly lit and filled with patrons, including German soldiers. People hurried by each other in the rain, and a few cars passed, including a police car with sirens that made me freeze for a second. But nobody paid attention to me as I walked with my head down and arms crossed, still freezing and ever wetter.

I turned down Rue de la Faisanderie, knowing the street name was familiar, but having trouble remembering why, which I blamed on the state I was in. It was only when I saw three of the black Citroën cars pulled up onto the curb a block ahead that I remembered and felt sickened. They were all parked in front of 98 Rue de la Faisanderie, Nora Khan's address in Paris.

It was quite possible that she wasn't even there, as she said she had been moving often to stay safe. That's what I prayed for as I ducked into a side street a few doors down from her address and flattened myself up against the side of a boarded-up pâtisserie, waiting in the darkness to see what happened next.

I heard the door open and peered around the corner. I had only heard the sounds of Georges's capture, but this time I saw a half dozen men in leather trench coats and jackboots, and watched in horror as the tallest among them dragged my dear friend Nora out of the building by her hair, cursing at her in German the entire time. A glimpse of Nora's face in the streetlamp revealed her stoic expression, much to the consternation of her Gestapo captors. She was silent and looked almost serene, showing no signs of the sheer terror or physical pain she had to be feeling.

The bravery of my sweet friend made me start to cry, and I wanted to scream at them to get away from her, but like with Georges, that would only lead to my own capture. And I had the papers in my bag that I still had to get to London. Helpless again, and filled with a combination of rage and fear, I punched the wall I was pressed up against, cursing into the night sky as I watched one of the black cars drive away with Nora in the back seat.

The fact that Nora and Georges had been captured on the same night could not be a coincidence. The Gestapo had new intelligence about the resistance networks in Paris. They were rounding us up.

I walked the two miles to the American Hospital, taking a route far away from Avenue Foch, walking as fast as I could without looking like I was running. The rain had stopped by the time I entered the front lobby and rushed up to the young American nurse at the front desk.

"Well, what in God's name happened to you?" she said, coming around the desk to meet me. "You're white as a ghost, and, oh sweetheart, you're soaked. Get that wet coat off. Let me get you some warm blankets."

"I need to see Dr. Jackson. It's urgent," I said, hoping that Josette was with him, but dreading it at the same time.

"Dr. Jackson just finished talking with our new 'patients,'" the nurse said, giving me an understanding look. "I'll take you to him."

She wrapped a gray wool blanket around my shoulders as we made our way up to Dr. Jackson's office on the second floor. I heard Josette's voice followed by a laugh that I was sure was Tatiana's coming from behind the open door, and I hated that I was about to burst their happy bubble with my news.

I walked into the office. Dr. Jackson was at his large oak desk, and Josette and Tatiana were sitting on the opposite side of it. They looked up at me, their smiles disappearing when they saw the condition I was in.

"Please bring a fresh change of clothes. Her lips look a little blue; we need to warm her up," Dr. Jackson said to the nurse, jumping up and putting his arm around me as he helped me sit down in the only open chair in the room.

That kind gesture, that feeling of being safe and among friends, broke a dam in me, and the tears started streaming down my face again as I let out a sob.

"Oh no. Where is Georges?" Josette said, standing up from her chair, hands on her mouth. "Anna, where is he? Please tell me he's downstairs."

"Josette, I . . ." I looked up at her. She had turned pale, and I struggled, knowing the words I was going to say next would rip her world apart. "The contact . . . he didn't show. I told Georges not to go up the metro stairs one more time, that it didn't feel right, but getting this intelligence out was so important he insisted . . . The Gestapo, they came out of nowhere. They . . . they have him. They captured Georges. I'm so—"

"No!" Josette screamed through tears, pointing at me in fury. "No! How could you, Anna? How could you let this happen? You promised me you would both return safe. You should have never let him go back up those stairs. This is your fault! I will *never* forgive you for this."

"Wait, Josette, wait," Tatiana said, her hand on my shoulder. "This is not Anna's fault. This is a horrible thing that happened, but it is not her fault."

"No, it's not," Dr. Jackson said. "Josette, take a deep breath, please. Blaming Anna won't make things better."

"I can't even look at you right now," Josette spit at me. "I need to get some air."

She stormed out of the office, and I heard her running down the hall.

"Tatiana, they got Nora, too," I said in a whisper. I explained how I'd seen Nora being arrested when I was walking back.

"Merde! Merde!" Tatiana said, kicking the chair she had been sitting on and knocking it over. She covered her face with her hands. "This is a nightmare. A horrible nightmare."

"It is. But now we have to make a plan," Dr. Jackson said. His eyes showed his worry, but his demeanor was calm, and I was grateful for that.

"Do you think they're taking them to 84 Avenue Foch?" I said, horrified at the thought of Georges and Nora being tortured in the hellish fourth-floor prison.

"I don't know," Dr. Jackson said, taking his glasses off and rubbing his eyes. "But at this moment? We have to make sure they don't find you or Josette or Henri."

"I know," I said, feeling panicked again. "If they knew of Georges LaRue, about his meeting tonight, how much more do they know about us? About who we are?"

"Assume they know everything," Dr. Jackson said. "Take all precautions. We've got to get the three of you out of the city as quickly as possible. Despite the fact that the hospital is in the shadow of one of the Gestapo's buildings, we have not yet aroused their suspicion. Remember, we are protected under the Geneva Conventions as a Red Cross military hospital."

"You're *supposed* to be protected. They are rounding up people, shooting people in the streets . . . Do you think the Nazis really give a damn about the Geneva Conventions?" Tatiana said, swearing again as she lit a cigarette.

She walked over to the cabinet behind Dr. Jackson's desk and took out a bottle of cognac and three glasses. Dr. Jackson raised his eyebrows at her boldness but didn't object as she lined up the glasses on his desk and poured us all a drink.

I reached into my purse and breathed a sigh of relief when I pulled out the papers; they were a little wet and torn at the edges, but other than that they were intact.

"When he went back for the second time, I told him to leave them with me," I said, taking a gulp of the cognac and feeling it burn my throat on the way down. "We still have the intelligence we were supposed to pass along."

But Dr. Jackson and Tatiana didn't even hear me; they were looking at the drawing and the map, like they couldn't believe what they were seeing.

"My God," Dr. Jackson said. "This is extraordinary."

"Anna, how did you even . . . ?" Tatiana said and swore again. "The Germans are building *this*?"

"They are," I said. "And after what happened tonight? No couriers, no go-betweens—nobody is delivering this to London but *me*. Though I don't know how the hell I am going to do that. I can't dare use the wireless to ask for help. I need to go quiet on that for a while."

Dr. Jackson and Tatiana looked at each other, and Tatiana nodded.

"What?" I asked.

"Two of the Allied pilots here?" Dr. Jackson said. "We are smuggling them out in a Red Cross supply truck tonight. They're heading to Tréguier on the coast, where there will be a safe house . . ."

"And a boat," Tatiana finished his sentence. "A fisherman has agreed to help them navigate the mines planted along the coast and take them to Plymouth, England, tomorrow."

"Is there room for Josette and me?" I asked.

"There's definitely room on the boat. It will be tight and uncomfortable in the back of the truck. We'll make it work," Dr. Jackson said.

"And the driver has been given plenty of money to bribe officers at any checkpoints," Tatiana said. "Leaving in the middle of the night is safer—not as many boches on the roads."

"Can you have Bernard radio London, so they know that we're coming?" I asked Tatiana.

"Yes, after what's happened this evening, I should also leave Paris tonight, somehow," Tatiana said.

"What time do we leave?" I asked. The clock on the wall in his office said it was just past midnight.

"The truck will be here in two and a half hours," Dr. Jackson said.

"What if Henri is not back from Avaray?" I asked, anguished at the thought.

"You have to go," Tatiana said. "Whether he's back or not. You have to get this to London. It's all that matters." She pointed at the papers.

I swallowed the last of my cognac and nodded. Because as much as it hurt, I knew that she was right.

# Chapter Thirty-Eight

Tatiana went to find Josette and talk to her, to see if she could calm her down. While she was doing that, Dr. Jackson helped me put together bags that included a change of clothes and basic toiletries. There would be no returning to the Esmeralda. My wireless would have to be left behind as well, but Dr. Jackson assured us that everything at the hotel, including the wireless, would be picked up and hidden safely somewhere in the hospital, provided the Germans didn't get to the Esmeralda first.

By 1:30 a.m., I was in the cafeteria with Tatiana, forcing myself to eat the bread roll and cold cabbage soup she had managed to find for me in the kitchen.

"Josette is upstairs resting. She is looking for someone to blame," Tatiana said in a quiet voice. "Deep down she knows it's not your fault; just give her time. She's heartbroken and terrified by what might happen to him."

"So am I," I said, putting my head in my hands. "It's awful."

"Be strong, mon amie," Tatiana said. "You have a long journey ahead."

"I know," I said. "I will."

"So, what made you . . ." Tatiana looked up at the entrance behind me and gave me a small nod.

I turned around. There was Henri, and by the anguished look on his face, I knew Dr. Jackson had told him everything. I ran and jumped into his arms, and felt myself get choked up, the tears falling again.

"I'm so sorry," I said. "I'm so, so sorry."

"Shh," he whispered in my ear as he held me tight. "It's not your fault. Once Georges LaRue makes up his mind to do something, nobody can change it. Not even you."

"I'm going to check on our pilots," Tatiana said after greeting Henri, knowing we needed to talk alone. "I will see you upstairs."

"Did Dr. Jackson tell you the plan?" I asked Henri as he sat across from me, where Tatiana had been sitting.

"He did." He reached across the table and held my hands in his.

"And?"

He paused for a moment, looking down at the table.

"I am going to go with you and Josette to Brittany tonight," Henri said. "To make sure you get on that boat to England. But . . . Anna . . . I cannot go with you there."

"What do you mean you can't go?" I said. "It's not safe for you here; you have to come with us. With me."

"It hasn't been safe for me in my own country for a long time," Henri said. "I will stay out of Paris for now, hide out somewhere in the Loire Valley. Bernard and Pauline are connected to the resistance networks in that region and beyond it. And I'll try to find out what I can about Georges's whereabouts, and your friend Nora too, to see if there's anyone we can bribe, anything at all we can do to get them out."

Now it was my turn to be quiet. How could so much change in one night? My life in Paris, with these friends who felt like family, had been far from easy the past few months. But we had been lucky enough, and wise enough, to embrace those moments of happiness we had—dancing at La Caravalle, the four of us laughing and having drinks at Le Chat Noir. In a few short months, this life as an agent in occupied Paris that I had been living had gone from surreal to oddly comfortable. I was horrified and heartbroken that Georges and Nora had both been captured. I hated that it was all coming to an end.

"There's nothing I can say that would convince you to go with me, is there?"

"No," he said with a sigh, looking in my eyes. "You . . . you will come back to France though, yes?"

"As soon as I can, hopefully on the next Lysander," I said. "I'll join you in the Loire Valley."

"Oh, thank God," he said, pushing his hair off his forehead and then leaning down to kiss my hands. "I thought you might not want to come back, after all, after tonight."

"Henri Rousseau, if you thought that, then maybe you don't know me as well as I thought you did," I said.

Minutes later, I was sitting on his lap and enjoying our last moments alone when I heard someone clear their throat from across the cafeteria and looked up to see Dr. Jackson.

"It's time?" I asked as he walked over.

"It's time," he said. "The truck is here. He pulled around back near the courtyard so you won't be visible from the street when you get in."

When we got to the rear lobby next to the courtyard, Josette and Tatiana were there. Josette had her head down and was clutching the small satchel the doctor had given her, not even looking up when we arrived. Also waiting were two young men around my age who I guessed were the pilots, and a short, heavyset man with a salt-and-pepper beard, wearing a black cap low over his face so you could barely see his eyes.

"Anna, Henri, this is David Sullivan and James Peterson of the US Army Air Forces," Dr. Jackson said, introducing us.

"You're Americans," I said with surprise. "I assumed you were RAF pilots."

"No, ma'am," James said, reaching out to shake my hand. Tall with sandy-colored hair and freckles, he looked like he had just walked off a farm in Iowa. "Nice to meet you. You can call me Jimmy."

"So great to meet an American girl over here," David said, pumping my hand up and down with enthusiasm. He was shorter, with dark brown hair with an untamed cowlick in front.

The man in the cap grunted and muttered something in French about needing to get on the road.

"And this is Siméon, your kind and courageous driver," Dr. Jackson said, putting a hand on his shoulder.

Siméon revealed a hint of a smile from underneath the cap, and, with barely a nod to us, he went outside to start up the truck.

With our satchels, some canteens of water, and small parcels of Red Cross–issued biscuits and raisins for the journey, we boarded the supply truck. It was going to be tight; the five of us would have to squeeze in and find space amid cardboard boxes of medical supplies. The Americans went in first, followed by Josette, who quietly said good-bye to Tatiana and thanked Dr. Jackson, wiping tears from her face as Henri helped her climb in back.

"Please be safe, my friend," I said, giving Tatiana a tight squeeze.

"You too. I'm not sure I'll rest until I know that you are," she said, and I was surprised to see her eyes glistening. "I am going to get a ride out right after you leave. I'll make sure Bernard lets London know when you're coming."

"I'll pray for Nora and Georges and see if I can do anything to help them from London. And I will be back."

"I know you will. This life . . . it's like a drug, isn't it? You can't imagine going back to how you used to live before."

I looked in her eyes and nodded. She wasn't wrong.

"I will miss you. Thank you for not following the rules and for staying in touch with me."

She laughed and hugged me again. Henri had already climbed in and told me to hurry, so I gave Dr. Jackson a quick hug.

"I'm honored to know you," I said. "Thank you for everything you've done for us and everything you do for the cause."

"Anyone in my situation would do the same," he said, waving his hand in protest, embarrassed at my praise.

"Not everyone," I said, shaking my head.

"Be careful. Get that intelligence in the right hands."

"Nothing could stop me."

I took Henri's hand and climbed into the truck.

# Chapter Thirty-Nine

For a five-hour truck ride in cramped quarters, being physically and emotionally exhausted turned out to be a blessing. When we first started out, David and Jimmy talked almost nonstop, asking the three of us questions—too many questions—about where we were headed and what in the world I had been doing as an American girl in occupied Paris. I gave evasive answers, but they kept pushing, and I was about to tell them they needed to stop for their own safety when Siméon pulled the truck over, leaned into the back, and told them to shut up or he would leave them on the side of the road.

It was quiet in the truck after that, and at some point in the next hour, sitting with my knees tucked under me and leaning against Henri's shoulder, I fell into a deep sleep. Henri jostled me awake a few hours later. Both Jimmy and David were fast asleep, and Josette looked like she had just woken up. I stretched and tried to shake the pins and needles out of my numb, stiff legs. It was stuffy and smelled like sweat, and I longed to open up the back and get fresh air.

Josette pushed a few boxes aside and scooted her way over to where Henri and I were sitting. I had been straining my neck, trying to get a glimpse of where we were.

The safe house where we were meeting the agent who would bring us to England was in the middle of Tréguier, a small medieval port town on a hill above the river Jaudy, which provided easy access to the

English Channel. Josette and I and some friends from Sciences Po had once spent a warm spring weekend there. I had been charmed by its narrow, ancient streets with houses constructed with exterior timber frames and plaster or brick. They reminded me of gingerbread houses, and they were painted in decorative color combinations of ivories and yellows, burnt reds and chocolate browns. I remembered it had felt like stepping into a fairy tale village.

"Do you remember the last time we were in Tréguier?" she asked me.

I nodded, relieved she was speaking to me again.

"I do," I said. "We went to that *crêperie*, and the weather was so nice, and there was a street festival . . . for one of the saints maybe?"

"It was a perfect day," Josette said in a soft voice. "I miss crêpes so much."

"You miss *all* food," I said, grinning.

"That is true," she said, as she reached over and hugged me.

"I'm sorry," I said, feeling my voice crack. "I swear, I tried to convince him not to go back up."

"He never would have listened to you," Josette said, giving me a tearful smile when she broke away. "Or me. Or anyone. I'm sorry for blaming you."

"I'll do everything I can to help get him free," I said. "I promise you that."

"I know you will," she whispered, squeezing my hand. "Thank you."

Siméon finally stopped the truck, and I popped my head up again to see that we were parked next to the Cathedral of Saint-Tugdual, a massive, towering Gothic structure, incongruous with the little village of half-timbered houses that surrounded it. I looked at Henri's watch to see that it was almost seven thirty in the morning.

"The safe house is a blue-and-white one, just across from where we are, down the side street there," Henri said, pointing out the windshield, standing but bent over because the ceiling of the truck was too low for his height. "I am just going to go make sure it is in fact still safe, and I'll come back to get the rest of you."

"Do you want me to come with you?" I asked, feeling tense and claustrophobic and paranoid.

"No, you should stay. I think we're safe, but just in case," Henri said.

He squeezed by me to get out, kissing me on the cheek as he shoved aside some boxes. When he did, I caught a glimpse of his gun, hiding in his inside coat pocket, and I tensed up, my heartbeat quickening. Just as Siméon opened the door, I grabbed Henri's hand.

"Wait," I said, and when he turned around, we were nose to nose. I put my hands on his unshaven face and kissed him on the lips. "I love you."

He gave me a look of surprise, and then his whole face lit up, dark eyes sparkling as he jumped out of the truck.

"*Je t'aime aussi,*" he mouthed as he walked away backward, putting his hands to his chest and then stuffing them in his pockets like he didn't have a care in the world. *I love you too.*

"*Je vais aller pisser,*" Siméon said with a grunt as he pulled down the back door of the truck again.

"Our driver's quite charming," Josette said, and I just rolled my eyes.

"What did he say?" Jimmy the pilot asked.

"He said he's going to go take a piss," I told them.

The two pilots laughed.

"Tell me again, how do you know French so well?" David asked. His cowlick was askew, making him look like a little boy who had just woken up from a nap.

I told them about going to Sciences Po in Paris with Josette and how both of us were also fluent in German. I asked them more about where they were from and what they had been doing before the war. Jimmy was supposed to take over his family farm in Nebraska, though he had fallen in love with flying and had a talent for it. David had planned to go to dental school after college, but that was on hold.

"Where the hell did Simian go?" David asked, getting up to look out the windshield.

"It's *Siméon*," I said. "He's not a monkey."

"But he's very hairy like one," David said. "Don't you think it's odd he hasn't come back yet?"

"Hey, do you hear that yelling?" Jimmy asked, frowning, also getting up. "Is that German?"

I listened and froze. I couldn't see him, but I could hear him. It was Henri. He was yelling very loudly. In German.

*"Wohin gehen wir? Wo bringst du mich hin?"*

*Where are we going? Where are you taking me?*

"He's warning us," I said.

Josette and I looked at each other in terror.

"Are either of you armed?" I asked the men.

"No," Jimmy said, turning white.

"Both of you, over here, grab the bottom of the door," I said, double-checking to make sure my purse strap was secured across my chest, the papers safely inside. "On the count of three, we have to pull up this door, get out of this truck, and make a run for it. Josette and I will go toward the church; you two go in the opposite direction. Do not stop until you find shelter somewhere. Many French hate the Nazis. Someone will take you in and help you hide."

I counted to three, and we lifted up the gate of the truck and jumped out. The sky was full of rolling gray smoke clouds, and a chilled wind was whipping off the river. Henri was on the opposite side of the square in front of the church, a couple hundred yards away. His hands on his head, he was flanked by two Gestapo agents and a German officer. The streets were otherwise empty of people. Out of the corner of my eye, I saw someone peeking out from behind a curtain in one of the houses in the square. The two pilots disappeared down a cobblestone side street, but I hesitated, wanting to do something to help Henri get free.

"Run! Get away! Go!" Henri screamed at us, and we started to run, but I turned around again at the sound of an officer's voice.

"You stupid whores! You thought you were a step ahead of *me*?" the German officer hollered at us, and I gasped when I recognized the voice of Keppler. I stood frozen to the spot, filled with hatred, knowing he was responsible for this. Josette grabbed my elbow, both of us paralyzed.

"You run and he dies, *Anna Cavanaugh*," his voice bellowed across the distance between us.

"Run! Get out of here. Don't listen to him, Anna," Henri yelled, his voice hoarse with anguish. "Get away now!"

Everything happened so fast, and at the same time it was like time slowed down as I was witnessing it. Henri elbowed the agent to the right of him in the head so hard he knocked him down. He wrenched the gun out of the man's hand, shooting the other officer in the chest. He turned the gun on Keppler and took aim, but he was a half second too late. Keppler's gun was aimed at Henri's forehead, and he pulled the trigger, looking at me with a sick smile.

"No! No! Henri! *No!*" I screamed so loud it rang in my ears. I fell to my knees, and it felt like a punch to my gut as I watched Henri's body hit the ground. I knew he was gone.

I stumbled upright and started to run to him, screaming and crying and swearing at Keppler, a ringing in my ears from the gunshots. Within seconds, Josette grabbed me by the arm and pulled me in the opposite direction, down one of the side streets. I fought her, crying and cursing, but somewhere inside my survival instinct kicked in. I knew I had to let her lead me away, or we'd die.

I couldn't stop sobbing as I fought the urge to go back to him, though I knew he was dead. I wanted to be with him. I didn't want him to be alone. But Josette held on to my hand, pulling me along, and we kept running, past the cathedral, down one of the narrow cobblestone streets. The streets and alleys of the medieval village were a maze, and we turned down one and then veered left down another, hoping to keep the Germans off our trail. I heard the dreaded sirens, and I knew Keppler must have more Gestapo with him.

"Where do we go?" Josette said in a gasp, her voice sounding as devastated as I felt. "What if the village is surrounded?"

"I don't know . . . ," I said. It felt hard to breathe as the dizzy, cold clamminess of shock washed over me. "Henri is gone . . . he's . . . I can't breathe . . ."

"Anna, I know," Josette said, her voice breaking in a sob, pulling me on. "But we have to escape . . . what are we going to do?"

The sirens were getting closer, and I could hear jackboots on the cobblestone. Somehow, we kept running, and I slipped and fell down, crying out as I banged my knee and forced myself back up. We were just about to turn a corner down another ancient alleyway when I heard someone speak.

"Mesdemoiselles," a woman's voice called out from the cracked door of a house across the alley. "Come, come inside. Please, let me help you. Better to hide than to run until they catch you."

# Chapter Forty

*It was springtime in Paris, on a warm sun-filled day after the war, and I was walking through the Tuileries Gardens admiring rows of vibrant red and purple tulips. Henri was a mathematics professor at Sciences Po, and I worked as a translator for the American embassy. We had two little girls named Jeanne and Elise. Jeanne had my curls, and Elise had her father's dark eyes. They'd learned English as well as French and loved to spend summers in America, on the beaches of Cape Cod with their American grandparents.*

*I put my hand up to shield my eyes from the bright sun, and I finally spotted Henri sitting at a wrought-iron café table under one of the pink-blossomed Judas trees. Our daughters were playing hide-and-seek nearby. I called out to him and waved, but he didn't hear me, so I called to him again . . .*

I swallowed the scream in my throat as something woke me up and my dreaded new reality came rushing back into my consciousness. I started to cry. *Henri is dead. Gone forever.* He had been mine for a dark season, and now, was this really happening? In the instant he was shot, my life had turned surreal again, surreal and bitter, after a few brief months of sweetness with the spice of danger. I had somehow believed the Nazis' terror would never get close enough to destroy us. How wrong I had been.

I looked up to see that what had woken me was a wizened old woman with long, untamed white hair. She was standing above us and holding an ancient rifle, pointing it in my face, the finger of one of her knotty, blue-veined hands on the trigger.

"Madame, madame, please," I said, raising my hands. Josette bolted awake at the sound of my hoarse voice. "Please, your daughter? She said we could stay . . ."

Morane Gallou, the young mother who had saved us, came sprinting up the stairs yelling in Breton, a Celtic language unique to Brittany. She hurried over and held out her hand to the old woman. The old woman frowned at Morane and cursed at her in Breton but relinquished the gun. I finally exhaled.

"Go downstairs. Dinner is ready. Bleuenn is waiting for us," Morane said to her, in French this time for our benefit. The old woman shuffled to the attic stairs, gripping the rough wooden railings tightly as she made her way down.

After calling to us in the street, Morane had ushered us into her home and up to her slant-ceilinged attic. We had sat on a blanket and waited, overcome with emotion and still in shock, while she kept watch from her downstairs windows. I couldn't stop shaking, reliving the moment Henri had been shot over and over in my mind, crying uncontrollably. Josette was curled up in a ball, rocking back and forth, paler than I'd ever seen her. I didn't remember falling asleep, but we must have after a few hours.

When her mother had gone downstairs and was out of view, Morane looked at us, pointed a finger at her head, and twirled it around, her thick, dark eyebrows raised.

"I'm so sorry about that," she said. She spoke with a distinct Brittany accent and was a handsome woman with sharp cheekbones and full lips, hair in a messy bun. "She's not right in the head anymore. I took the ammunition out and hid it from her a long time ago. Did you sleep a little?"

"A little, thank you," I whispered, and Josette just nodded, rubbing her face with her hands.

"I was just out for a walk with my daughter, Bleuenn, to talk to some of the neighbors and find out if the Gestapo were still searching for you. It seems they have searched all of the houses closest to the cathedral. They are now knocking on doors on the opposite side of the city. I doubt they will be able to search every single home in Tréguier. But if they come here, you will go in there." She nodded to a tall pale wood armoire in the opposite corner, where the ceiling was less slanted. "You can both fit inside, hiding among my husband's clothes."

"Thank you for your kindness and your courage," I said, my voice breaking on the word *courage*. It was still hard to speak without crying.

"Yes, we . . . I can't thank you . . . ," Josette said, putting her face in her hands.

"Oh dear, you've both been through a terrible time, haven't you?" Morane said, coming over and putting her arm around both of us. "I've covered all the windows and locked the doors. Come, please try to have a little something to eat with me, my mother, and Bleuenn. You must be starving. Yesterday I did some sewing for a nearby farmer, and she gave me some real eggs—a rare treat."

"Thank you for everything," I said, helping Josette off the floor. I had no appetite at all, but I knew we had to eat to stay strong for what was to come.

"Also, on my walk just now I ran into a friend who is in town. It was quite a surprise," Morane said. "He said he will help you get out of the city. He's coming over in an hour."

"Can he be trusted?" I asked, uneasy that she had told someone about us and feeling like I'd never trust anyone again fully.

"Yes," Morane said with conviction. "He's in the Resistance. Like you."

At dinner, I had no appetite but forced myself to eat some of the delicious omelet Morane had prepared. I was preoccupied with raw grief and a sense of foreboding, contemplating our next move. We couldn't stay here much longer and risk the lives of Morane and her family. An attic armoire would be the first place the Germans would look for us if they searched the house. Somehow, we would have to leave Tréguier tonight.

Josette sat next to me and took tiny bites, no doubt sharing my worries. Morane's *mamm*, whose actual name was Enora, eyed us both suspiciously the entire dinner despite the polite smiles we gave her. Thank God for little five-year-old Bleuenn. For the whole meal, she entertained us with some new songs she had learned in school.

Josette and I cleaned up after the meal while Morane put Bleuenn to bed. Enora, a woman of very few words, nodded good night and, after frowning at us, gave a deep, dramatic sigh and made her way up to the second floor to her bedroom.

It was quiet, the fire in the fireplace crackling quietly. The home's first floor had walls constructed with thousands of pale-gray stones, and the ceiling was bright white stucco with dark exposed beams going across it. It was warm and whimsical, and yet I couldn't stop shivering.

I wanted to let myself tumble into the deep pit of grief that now filled my heart and made breathing difficult, to just go on reliving the horror, my screams, the cold clamminess from the shock, and to fall to pieces, mourning for my dream of a future that would now never come. But I knew if I did that, Josette and I might die. And the intelligence I still had in my purse would never save anyone. All the sacrifices would have been for nothing. Henri would have found that unacceptable. I would have to go on in his honor, to save the lives I could.

Morane came back out and reached for a bottle of red wine in the back of a cabinet, pouring us each a glass.

"How are you?" Josette asked, looking at me with worry in her eyes as Morane came over to the fire with our drinks and sat down.

"Shattered . . . much like you. I'm only twenty-five years old, and I've lost a husband and what may prove to be the love of my life. And they're not even the same person." I tried to smile, my eyes filling up with tears again as I bit my lip and tried to compose myself.

Josette looked at me and nodded.

"Morane," I started. It was hard to get the question out. "Do you . . . Henri's body . . ."

"The priests of Saint-Tugdual are taking care of him," she said, putting her hand on mine. "There will be a mass and a burial."

"That we won't be able to attend," Josette said with quiet anger.

"No," I said, heartbroken at the thought of Henri's funeral with only strangers, nobody who loved him there to say good-bye.

"My friend will be here soon, but, if you can, please tell me . . . Just give me a little understanding of what happened?"

Morane listened while Josette shared a high-level summary of the events of the past few days, being careful not to share anything that might be dangerous for her to know. I got up and started pacing the room.

"I am so grateful for your generosity, Morane, but we can't stay here tonight," I said, taking a sip of wine. "Keppler, the German officer looking for us, is not going to stop until he's searched every house in the city. I'm sure of it. We need to try to get out while it's still dark."

There was a knock at the door, and Josette and I both jumped. Morane put her drink down and her hand up.

"I think this is my friend," she said in soft voice. "But quickly and quietly make your way upstairs in case I'm wrong."

Josette and I tiptoed upstairs two flights to the attic, but as soon as we reached the top, Morane called to us that it was safe to come back down.

When we reached the bottom of the stairs, I gasped, shocked to see the swashbuckling SOE agent Bernard Fairfax standing next to our driver, Siméon, who was no longer wearing a hat and had a white bandage wrapped around his head.

"What the hell is this?" Josette said, her face turning red with anger. "Bernard . . . you're supposed to be with Tatiana and Pauline, and you . . ."

"You!" I hissed, pointing at Siméon. "You left us there in that truck, like lambs to the slaughter . . ."

Bernard held up one hand to me and the other across Siméon, as though afraid I was going to reach out and strike him.

"He did not leave you," Bernard said. "He was detained by the Gestapo. Notice the bandage? They gave him a good whack when he went around the corner to relieve himself."

"We were doomed from the start," Siméon said in a deep, scratchy voice. "Yesterday, the Gestapo arrested the agent we were supposed to meet. He told them we were coming. Somehow, they figured out you three would be here too. I have no idea how."

*Keppler.* Keppler had figured it out. The thought of him filled me with rage.

"But how did you get away?" Josette asked, frowning. "How are you here now?"

"I got lucky," Siméon said. "When I came to after being knocked out, there was only one Gestapo guarding me. When he thought I was still out cold, I surprised him with a couple punches in the face and ran."

I raised my eyebrows at this.

"I'm faster than I look." Siméon shrugged. "An old man, a veteran of the last war, saw me and knew why I was on the run. He let me hide out in his house. As it turns out, like me, he is a friend of Bernard's. He's helped hide many others."

"Bernard, but how are you here? And how do you know Morane?" I asked, my head spinning, trying to piece it all together without enough information.

"From our days together at the Sorbonne," Morane said. She motioned for us to sit down as she poured wine for Siméon and Bernard.

"I must tell you how devastated I am about the loss of Henri," Bernard said after we were seated by the fire. My eyes teared up, and my raw grief bubbled to the surface again as he leaned over and gave me a hug. "I am so sorry for both of you. And about Georges's capture, too. It's too horrible; there are no words."

Josette just nodded as he hugged her, too emotional to speak. And then she turned a little green and ran into the tiny bathroom on the first floor, where, even with the door shut, we could hear her vomiting.

"I'm also very sorry," Siméon said, holding his head as he sat on the small sofa. He gave Josette a sincere, sympathetic nod when she came out and sat down. I was softening toward him now. "I have helped smuggle dozens of Allied soldiers out of France through the underground network; that's how Bernard and I know each other. I've never lost a man before today. And they captured those two American boys too."

"Oh no," I said, holding my hand up to my mouth, thinking of the two earnest young men in the back of the truck, hoping they were still alive. "We didn't know they had been captured."

Bernard explained that Tatiana had arrived at the Terriers' safe house in Avaray in the middle of the night and told him everything that had happened, including about the secret weapons intelligence we still had. He sent word to London via wireless that we were coming, but the two of them stayed up for the rest of the night, hearing more news about the many Resistance members who had been rounded up in the Gestapo dragnet in Paris that night. He referred to this kind of Gestapo mass arrest as a *coup dur*—a hard kick.

"Tatiana had a bad feeling and begged me to come here, to make sure you got out. Her instincts were not wrong," Bernard said.

"I don't understand," Josette said, looking like she might get sick again. "How are they finding out about our plans? About where people are?"

"Keppler was here waiting for us, Bernard," I said. "How could he know?"

"I have thought a lot about this, and I suspect the Germans have found a way to listen in to some of our wireless transmissions."

"And they've cracked our codes?" I asked.

"How did they know about Georges's rendezvous at the Passy metro? Or Nora's exact location last night? And exactly how did Keppler know you two would be here? It's the only explanation," Bernard said.

"Bastards of boches," Josette said, spitting out the curse.

"So now what?" I asked. "What happens next? We still have to get to London."

"I know, and that's why we are here, to get you out," Bernard said. "First, can you please show me this intelligence Tatiana told me so much about?"

I nodded and picked up my purse, which I had stuffed underneath the wooden chair I was sitting in. I laid the papers out on the small coffee table in front of the fireplace.

Siméon stared at it, tilting his head, looking at it from different angles, swearing about the Nazis the whole time.

"Incredible," Bernard said. "She wasn't exaggerating at all."

"No," I said, "she wasn't."

"And that's why, right before I came to Tréguier, I messaged London and made alternative arrangements in case your plans fell through. There is a fisherman who lives here, who will take you by dinghy to a waiting Royal Navy motor gunboat; he's done it before, and he's an expert at navigating the mines. Siméon and I will take you to meet him. We have a car parked down the street."

"Good," I said, feeling relieved and less trapped. We had a way out. "When do we leave?"

"Tonight," Bernard said.

"Now?" Josette asked, looking as exhausted as I felt.

"Yes," Bernard said with a nod. "I saw a few more German trucks coming into the city on the ride over here. I assume they're here to help with the search for you two. Every minute you stay here increases your risk of getting caught."

"Okay, that's all I need to know," I said, standing up and pushing down the emotional stew of grief, anger, and fear stirring within me. If I wanted something meaningful and good to come out of the horrible past few days, we had to move fast. "If I don't get these papers to the SOE and OSS in London soon, I feel like I am going to lose my mind. Let's go."

"I'm feeling the same way," Josette said. She was the only one in the room who could understand.

"Good. Siméon and I will go get the car. We'll make sure you get off safely," Bernard said. "We'll both be carrying guns."

"Thank you," I said. "I pray you won't have to use them."

# *Chapter Forty-One*

Bernard and Siméon finished their glasses of wine and went to fetch the car. We hugged Morane good-bye and thanked her profusely as we stood just inside her doorway, waiting for them to pick us up. It was close to eleven o'clock, and we had nothing but our purses, mine containing the only thing that mattered, and the clothes on our backs. I put on my coat and felt for the peacock pin in my pocket, rubbing my finger across its stones. It had not turned out to be the talisman I had hoped it would be, but being a gift from General Donovan, it still had meaning.

Donovan. I wondered if he would be in London when I arrived. I felt the need for him to see the papers himself, still wanting to prove myself to him after all this time. And I hoped he understood that I would return to France to continue to help the Resistance after delivering the intelligence.

We heard Bernard's car approaching and stepped outside just as it pulled up. Siméon nodded to us with a grunt, and Bernard opened the trunk and motioned for us to climb inside. Josette and I got in and lay down next to each other like sardines.

"It's about a thirty-minute drive to the boat launch," Bernard whispered. "But any cars on the road are suspicious these days, so I don't want to take any chances."

"Just drive carefully. I don't want us knocking heads back here," I said, already feeling claustrophobic.

He closed the trunk, and Josette and I were in darkness as Bernard started the car. It smelled like petrol and dirty socks.

"This is terrible, like being in a coffin," Josette said.

"Josette, that is not something I need to hear right now."

"Well, honestly, isn't it?"

"I don't know. I've never been in a coffin, and I don't plan to be anytime soon."

"Me neither."

We were both quiet for a moment, and then she started to laugh.

"What's so funny?" I said, getting annoyed.

"This," Josette said, whacking the top of the trunk with her hand. "I'm sorry to laugh. I'm just so very tired, and I'm horribly sad, and I'm sick about everything, but being stuck in the trunk of a car? It's so odd."

"It is," I said in a quiet voice. "Back at Sciences Po, this is not exactly what I thought we'd be doing when we reunited."

"No. And I never thought Henri . . . I had hopes for you and him." Her voice broke on the word *him*.

"So did I," I said, squeezing her hand and wiping my face with the other.

We shed some more tears for Henri and didn't say much for a while.

"Are you scared?" Josette asked. "About this boat trip? About what's to come?"

I thought for a moment before I answered her. "Am I scared? Surprisingly . . . no. I feel like the worst has already happened to me. I've got nothing to lose now. And there are too many lives to save with what we have. I'll be damned if Henri's death is for nothing."

"And Georges's capture," Josette said.

"We'll get him out."

"I'm trying to convince myself that is true, Anna. Because the alternative is unimaginable to me."

"We will."

The car turned and slowed down, the sound of gravel and sand under the tires. Then it stopped.

Siméon opened the trunk with one hand, holding a long, ugly Sten gun with the other. It was suspended from a thick strap around his neck.

We were parked next to a tiny harbor, and down below I could see the silhouette of someone standing on a wooden dock, a dinghy next to it. The air was damp, and the fog made it hard to see the ocean much beyond the shore.

"That is Ewen," Bernard said in a whisper, pointing to the dock and also holding a Sten gun. "He'll take you out to the Royal Navy boat. It's a straight shot to Plymouth from this part of the coast; you should be there before dawn London time."

"Will the fog be a problem?" I said.

"No. Ewen is almost seventy and has lived here all his life. He knows this water, including where the German mines are," Bernard said, holding a finger to his lips. "It's low tide, so many of them are visible. No more talking; there are German pillboxes close by. We don't want them to take notice of us."

We walked down to the dock on soft feet, flanked by Bernard and Siméon. I was shivering, and I felt a wave of anxiety and a lump in my throat. I had to leave France for now, but I desperately didn't want to. Josette sensed how I was feeling because she put her arm around my elbow.

The air smelled of seaweed and saltwater, and when we arrived at the dock, Bernard silently introduced us to Ewen, a small, soft-spoken man with white hair and a matching beard, wearing a scarf and baggy sweater.

"We should go now," Ewen whispered. "More boches around today than ever."

Siméon motioned that he was going to go back up near the car to keep a lookout. He blew us a kiss, and we mouthed our thanks.

"Thank you for everything. Love to Tatiana," I said, kissing Bernard. "We will be back as soon as we can."

"Good luck," Bernard said. "I will let London know if I find out anything about Georges."

"I feel like I'm abandoning him," Josette said, her voice shaky. "Please, please try to find out where he is."

"And Nora," I said.

"Yes, Nora too," Bernard said.

Ewen cleared his throat, and we took that as our cue to climb into the small, darkly painted wooden boat.

As Ewen untied the mooring line, pulled up the anchor, got settled, and rowed away from the dock with the strength of someone half his age, Josette and I sat together, watching the shore with a feeling of paranoia that was now like an old friend. As the coast of France became smaller and we were enshrouded in fog, I started to cry again, thinking of the love I had found and lost here. The only thing I knew was that I'd be returning. And I wouldn't leave again until France and my friends were free.

$\approx$

In my limited experience, I had found that grief either makes you want to sleep constantly or robs you of sleep completely. Right after Connor died, all I did was sleep for the first few weeks, because it was easier to sleep and shut it all out than deal with all the things I felt about his death. Mary, dear Mary, had been the one who rescued me from the depths and got me back to the land of the living. But then for a few months after he died, I had barely been able to sleep at all. I would stay awake, sitting up with the cats, reliving my last conversations with him, wallowing in the guilt of what had been said. Wondering, if I had the chance to do everything again, would I have done things differently? Would I have broken off my engagement and stayed in Paris, giving us both the chance to live different lives? I knew now more than ever that the answer to that question was yes.

We were safer than we had been in months, in one of the officers' cabins on a Royal Navy boat, but I couldn't sleep despite how fatigued I felt. I listened to Josette's quiet breathing next to me, as I kept going over every detail of the last two days with Henri, standing in the street in front of the café, at the hospital, saying "I love you" to him for the first time and the last, aching to say it again, to kiss him once more.

The trauma of the moment Keppler shot him was so vivid and raw. It tormented me, replaying in my mind even though I tried to block it out. Was there anything that could have changed Henri's fate? If he hadn't come with us, he would still be alive. He had yelled and fought the guards to give us enough time to get away. He had to have known Keppler was going to try to shoot him. He had sacrificed himself so we would have a chance to escape.

I wiped the tears off my face and turned over. At some point, despite the constant thoughts running through my brain, I must have dozed off, because the next thing I knew I heard knocking.

"Ladies, we've almost arrived." One of the young officers of the Royal Navy gunboat peeked his head into the officers' cabin, which the crew had generously let us have to freshen up and get a little sleep. "You're almost on British soil. Come up to the bridge to have a look, won't you?"

Josette had spent her first hours on board in the officers' head vomiting. She had blamed it on being seasick, but the trip had been calm, and I suspected there might be another reason she was ill. It was no surprise when she didn't even stir at the sound of the officer's voice. I stretched and put my shoes on, tiptoeing out to let her sleep a little more.

I went up to the bridge and looked out at the coast of England, just as the sun was rising. As a result of being so close to the French coast, the city of Plymouth had suffered greatly, being bombed by the Germans during the Blitz that had started in 1940. It had resulted in hundreds of citizens killed or wounded, and most of the children had been evacuated shortly thereafter.

Somewhere in the early morning hours, the fog had lifted, and it was the dawn of a clear, crisp March day. The HMNB Devonport, the Royal Navy base, stretched out in front of us, much of the damage to its buildings from the bombings still visible.

I felt like I had lived a thousand years in the months since I had left England.

Josette came up behind me and just stared out at the landscape, her complexion still a little green, her lighter brown hair still a surprise.

"How are you feeling?" I asked her.

"Okay. Not as bad as a couple of hours ago. Do you know what happens when we get to shore?"

"Someone is meeting us at the dock, then taking us to London. I've no idea who. When was the last time you were in England?" I asked.

"Ten years ago, with my father. It's odd, to be back."

"For me too."

As we docked, we thanked the crew that had transported us through dangerous waters and walked off the boat. It felt strange to have no luggage, just my purse.

"We'll get more clothes in London," I said to Josette.

"We better. I'm about to burn these culottes."

"I don't even know what we're supposed to do now," I said, feeling disoriented and grief-stricken and so exhausted. I looked around at the bustling navy yard, boats being constructed and repaired, officers hurrying by us. "I thought . . ."

"Anna, over here." I looked over, and Edgar Huntington was there on the road, standing next to a sleek black Austin, waving to us. The sight of one of my favorite people at the OSS made me tear up again, just when I thought I had no more tears left to cry.

"Huntington," I said, giving him a hug. "It's so good to see you."

"And you, my girl," he said. "I'm so sorry for all you have been through, my dear. And so happy you made it back in one piece. I almost didn't recognize you with the new hair."

I started to introduce him to Josette, but he interrupted me.

"Oh, your reputation precedes you, Ms. Rousseau," he said. "It's truly an honor to finally meet the renowned spy Amniarix. Thank you for all of your brilliant work."

"Thank you, sir," Josette said, her complexion changing from green to pink.

The driver opened the door for us. Josette and I climbed into the back, while Huntington sat up front.

"I don't understand. Why are you here to pick us up?" I asked him. "Not that it isn't good to see you but . . ."

"I've been in town since last week," he said. "When I heard what had happened with you, and that you'd be arriving today, I volunteered. I feel partly responsible for getting you into this job, this world. And the general wanted me to do it, to vouch for the fact that you had arrived here safe and sound. He'll be here in a couple of days. He wants you back in London for a while. Your parents are getting very anxious, as you can imagine."

I bristled at this, and Josette gave me a look. I did miss my family, my sisters, and Mary, so much it made my heart ache—and I would write them more letters from London, maybe send some telegrams too. But I didn't want to be in England any longer than I had to be.

"Yes, I do miss my family," I said. "I'm anxious to get an update on how they are all doing."

"Also, to be very honest, I wanted to be the first to see this intelligence firsthand," Huntington said, nodding at the purse I was still holding tight. "If it's truly what the wireless messages have hinted at."

"You won't be disappointed, sir. I promise you," I said, sinking back in the seat, feeling depressed but safer than I had in months.

# Chapter Forty-Two

**March 28, 1943**

*3/3/43*

*Dear Irene (and Anna too, wherever in the world you may be),*

*I am writing you from somewhere in China (yes, China!), although you know I cannot reveal exactly where I am in this vast country. I was recently transferred here along with Paul Child, Betty McIntosh, who has become a dear friend, and a few others from Ceylon who were recruited for the new OSS office here. We flew here last month. It was a treacherous, stormy flight, and the plane shook violently. I read a book the whole time, while the rest of the group was nearly hysterical and sure we were all going to die. But we made it over the Eastern Himalayas, or "the hump" as the pilots call it, and when I stepped off the plane the first thing I said to Paul was, "It looks just like China!"*

*It is even more exotic and beautiful than I antici-pated it would be. I am billeted with nineteen other OSS women in a modernistic building with a tile roof and lovely balconies. It's protected by massive wooden walls. The building's name is Mei Yuan—or "beautiful garden"—and it has a courtyard landscaped with a reflecting pool, plum trees, and bamboo. We have fabulous parties on the top-floor balcony.*

*Paul says the American food here tastes like it was cooked by grease monkeys, and I have to agree. All of us try to eat out at the local restaurants whenever we can. You will be happy to know that Paul and I continue our courtship. He is older and shorter, but he's brilliant and has a wicked sense of humor—and he loves to eat just as much as I do. Girls, I think this might be love! We will see.*

*Though at times this life abroad has been hard, and I've had bouts of homesickness as I'm sure you've had too, it's all been such a wonderful, life-changing adventure. I needed to break free of where I came from to find out who I truly am. I hope, my dear friends, that your adventures have done the same for you, that you have had more laughs than tears, more joy than heartbreak. And more than anything I hope we reunite someday in the future so I can hear all about your time abroad.*

*With love,*

*Julia*

Irene finished reading the letter to Josette and me and put it down on the coffee table in front of her. Her blonde hair was a little bit longer than when I had last seen her, and that lightness about her was still there. She had come to visit us after work, to bring us some new clothes and toiletries.

It was early evening, and the three of us were sitting under blankets in the posh suite at Claridge's that the OSS had generously arranged for us. After living under occupation, it felt like staying in a palace.

It was our second day in London, and since our arrival, we had done little more than sleep a great deal and eat a little. Josette had not stopped vomiting off and on, and I was trying to convince her it was time to see a doctor, but so far she had refused. I think she was afraid to learn what I already suspected.

"Julia's in *love*," Irene said. "It's so fantastic."

"It is," I said. "I can hear her talking through her letter. That voice."

"Can't you?" Irene said with an amused smile.

"I miss her," I said. "Especially her laugh. I hope you get to meet her someday, Josette."

"She sounds lovely. I hope so too," Josette said, trying to sound enthusiastic. Despite a shower and the fresh clothes Irene had found for us, Josette looked terrible, with dark circles under her eyes and a ghostly pale complexion. "If you don't mind, I am going to the bedroom to lie down."

"Of course," I said. "Are you sure you don't want me to call for a doctor?"

"I know of one—he's excellent," Irene said.

"Not yet," Josette said, shaking her head. "But thank you. Irene, it was lovely to meet you. If you'll excuse me, I . . . ." She put her hand over her mouth and ran to the bedroom and slammed the door behind her. I heard the adjoining bathroom door slam as well.

"The poor thing," I said. "The vomiting has been terrible."

"Does she have a fever or chills?"

"No," I said.

"Do you think she could be . . . ?" Irene tilted her head and gave me a pointed look.

"Pregnant? Yes," I said, dropping my voice and nodding. "It's possible. It's been such a horrible couple of days we haven't discussed it yet, but she's got to go to a doctor while we're here."

"I'll leave you the name of mine so you can set something up. And now . . . what about you? How are you, my friend? Really?"

"Not well," I said. "I'm still in shock, still sickened by it all. I loved him, Irene. Watching what happened . . ."

I blinked fast, trying not to cry. I was so tired of crying, but I found I couldn't help it; the grief was so raw.

"I know you loved him," she said, reaching over to give me a long hug. "And I'm so sorry he's gone."

"Thank you," I said. I wiped my eyes. "It's so good to see you. I've missed you."

"Me too. What are you going to do? You said, 'while we're here'—are you saying you're not staying long?"

"I have to go back," I said. "I can't explain it. I have to try to help Georges and Nora get out of prison somehow if I can. And doing the type of work I was doing there . . . that's what will help me recover from losing him."

"I don't know if the general is going to go for that," Irene said, giving me a grimace.

"I'll just have to convince him."

"And that should be a piece of cake," Irene joked.

"Um, probably not," I said, giving her a small smile. "I haven't even asked yet—how have you been? How has life been here? You look wonderful, so I'm guessing it's been good."

"Very good," Irene said, smiling wide. She explained that her divorce was going through. She told me that her husband had finally realized there was nothing to salvage in their relationship, and while things between them weren't exactly amicable, they were civil. David was also in the process of divorcing his wife, but it was taking a little more time than expected.

"It's so great to see you like this," I said. "To see you truly happy."

"Thank you. Now . . . you haven't asked about Phillip Stanhope. But he was in town a couple of weeks ago."

"Was he?" I said. "I've been wanting to ask, but then, so much has happened, I don't even know what I'd say to him if I saw him."

"He did ask if I'd heard from you. And he was definitely disappointed when I said I had not."

"Where is he now?"

I thought of our last night in London, a warm glow around a memory, which felt like it had happened so many years ago instead of just months earlier. I didn't want to see him because I *had* cared for him, but I had loved and lost someone else since, and that had broken me. Phillip Stanhope deserved better than that, and I certainly wasn't ready . . . for anything.

"He left for the Continent," Irene said. "A new program. They're parachuting in teams of three men—one OSS, one SOE, one Free French or French Resistance—to help organize the Resistance, especially with so many more young men joining up, and . . ."

"And so many Resistance leaders being arrested or executed . . ."

"Yes, for that reason too," Irene said. "Anna . . . I don't know how you did it. How did you live with that constant danger?"

"My friend Tatiana described the life we live there as a drug," I said. "At first everything about it is terrifying, and the paranoia—you don't know if you'll be able to stand living that way. But then you adjust, the danger becomes a part of life . . . and living undercover, there is something thrilling about it, a feeling of being truly alive."

"You're a very brave woman."

"I don't know . . . I've come to think bravery is just an instinct. A will to survive. I think you'd be just as brave."

"Maybe," Irene said. "Though honestly London's air raids are enough danger for me. I love that they put you up in Claridge's, by the way. You and Josette deserve a little pampering after what you've gone through. Did you know that the exiled kings of Greece and Norway are staying here for the duration of the war?"

"Oh yes, the bellboy loved telling us that," I said.

There was a knock at the door of the suite. I looked at Irene and frowned, having no idea who it could be.

I gasped in surprise when I opened the door to see General William Donovan standing there, smiling at me. He was carrying a briefcase and wearing the same trench coat as the last time I had seen him, before I left London.

"Anna, my dear," he said, giving me a big bear hug, and once again I got choked up and felt weak for doing so. "I am so happy to see you alive and well—you have no idea. Now I can call your father and give him a report that I've laid eyes on you."

"Thank you, sir," I said. Irene came up behind me with her coat on and greeted the general too.

"I should go. I know you two have things to discuss," Irene said, giving me one last hug. "I will be seeing you again soon. Best to Josette, I hope she's feeling better."

"Josette is unwell?" the general asked, frowning. I was not going to share my suspicions about her being pregnant.

"Oh, just a little stomach virus," I said. "I think she'll be fine with some more rest and fluids."

He took off his trench coat, and I hung it in the closet next to the suite's door. I offered him a glass of wine, from the bottle that had been left for us in the suite. We sat down across from each other on the sofa and chair in the little sitting area, his briefcase on the coffee table between us. "My dear, I am very sorry for the loss of Henri Rousseau and for Georges LaRue's capture," he said once we were settled. "And for the SOE agent Nora Khan's capture as well, I understand she was a friend of yours."

"Thank you," I said, taking a breath, trying to stay composed in front of him. "I wish I could have done something to prevent all of those things."

"When you've experienced war as much as I have, you realize that some things—no matter how many times you relive them in your mind—you couldn't have prevented no matter what. You're only *one* person."

"I know but . . . ," I said. "But . . ."

"You did the best you could under the circumstances. Take it from an old man," he said. "There is nothing to be gained by beating yourself up. I'm proud of you."

"Thank you," I said quietly.

"I've reviewed the intelligence you and Josette worked so hard to deliver to us," he said.

"And?"

"I'm not going to insult your intelligence by asking if you know how remarkable it is. You must know what you have here, what you two have accomplished. We had almost zero knowledge about these weapons and where the test site was located on the island of Usedom. All of the details you were able to remember and include are absolutely extraordinary."

"Yes, but I've been living in fear that the intelligence isn't going to get into the right hands in time," I said. "That it's not going to matter."

"It's being reviewed by Dr. Reginald Jones, Churchill's advisor on scientific warfare, as we speak," the general said, and I felt my heart fill with hope. *Finally.* "I can't say more about what will happen next; nothing's been decided yet."

"But you'll tell me when you learn what the plans are? When they do decide?"

"I will," he said. "I suppose you've earned the right to be privy to that information."

I exhaled. This was the first glimmer of good news. It was in the right hands. It might make the difference I wanted it to make.

"Thank you. Yes, the not knowing if all our work, the sacrifice, has been for nothing? That feeling is the worst part," I said, clapping my hands together, feeling relieved, thinking of Henri and how happy he would be if he were still here. "We accomplished our mission. That means you'll let us go back?"

He leaned forward, rubbing his face with his hand. "I knew this question was coming," he said with a groan.

"We have to go back," I said. "There's still so much work to do. I know the rumors about an Allied invasion in the next year have to be true, yes?"

"Yes," he said, "but we're only in the initial planning stages now."

"I feel like I was barely getting started and everything went to hell. And frankly, I am just so furious, so angry because Henri is dead and my friends are in prison, and I want to do something about it. I have to. Josette feels the same. Please don't make us stay on the sidelines in England . . ."

"Josette hasn't even recovered from all you've been through. And you look well enough, but you're far too thin. I'll leave that detail out when I talk to your father."

"What have you been telling him, by the way? After Irene ran out of letters to send from me?"

"I told him you had been transferred from London to work with an experimental detachment of the US Army and that you had to reduce correspondence as a result. Of course, your dad is no fool; he immediately said, 'So my daughter is a spy.'"

"He did not." I laughed, thinking of my father on the phone, calling Donovan out on the lie.

"He *did*. And I didn't answer the question, or any others about your work . . . so assume he knows. I can tell he's very proud of you, Anna.

And he's telling your mother what he needs to tell her, so that she won't be a nervous wreck."

"Thank you," I said, feeling a wave of homesickness, more than I had felt in a long time. For my parents and Colleen and Bridget, and for Mary, of course, too. It was as if seeing Irene and Donovan had made me feel the strong ache of everyone I missed.

"I will write them as many letters as I can until . . . Well, are you going to let me go back? I'll bring the peacock pin for luck. I still have it—although to be honest, I wished it had given me just a little more luck the past couple of weeks."

"You're here in front of me, Agent Peacock," he said. "That took a little luck."

He looked at me, thinking, taking a cigar out of his shirt pocket. I pulled an ashtray out of the drawer in the coffee table and slid it over to him.

"The fact is, if you and Josette hadn't proven yourselves so valuable in the field, I would have an excuse not to let you go. But we need experienced agents over there, desperately. The main goal of the SOE and OSS agents in occupied France is to expand, unite, and arm the various resistance networks in anticipation of the upcoming invasion, whenever that takes place. And to help these networks engage in acts of sabotage—trains, bridges, anything to cripple the enemy—to coincide with planned bombing raids."

"Yes," I said. "This is exactly what needs to be done. So . . . it sounds like you're going to let us go back, right?"

He paused again, thinking.

"I will let you go back," Donovan said with a sigh, "but before I do, you must give yourself time to recover here for at least a couple of weeks."

I started to protest, but he held up his hand, making it clear this was nonnegotiable, so I let him continue. He was going to let us go back; that was all that mattered.

"While you're here, you'll be given new cover stories and new papers, new clothes—and keep the new hair color too. You will both work for Pauline and Bernard; they are moving their headquarters to a more secluded area in the Loire Valley. You'll work as a wireless operator primarily, Josette as a courier."

"Thank you, thank you so much," I said. "I need to do this . . ."

"I know you do," Donovan said. "You're like me that way. But there's one other thing . . ."

"Yes?"

"We've learned that your friends Georges and Nora are both being held in Fresnes Prison, just outside Paris, along with many other political prisoners. Hundreds were captured in the Gestapo roundup last week."

"But they're alive," I said, buoyed by another spark of hope. "Thank God. At least we know where they are and that they are alive. I cannot wait to tell Josette."

"They are alive—that's all we know. We don't know what shape they're in, but . . . well, the Gestapo are sadists in their brutality and torture, especially when they're trying to extract information from spies," Donovan said, giving me a pained look. I felt ill at the thought of them being tortured.

"Is there anything you can do to get them out?"

"I have people working on it. Georges LaRue has too much knowledge and expertise; he's very valuable to the Allies, and, believe it or not, your friend Nora did quite well as an operator for all three of her networks. We need them, but so many have been captured. It won't be easy, Anna."

"But you are trying?" I asked.

"Yes, we're trying," Donovan said. "In the meantime, you must promise me that, when you go back, under no circumstances will you go anywhere near Paris or the prison."

"Okay," I said. "I promise."

"Good." He tapped his cigar on the ashtray. "Your friend Keppler was enraged that they didn't capture you and Josette in Tréguier. You were lucky to get out when you did. They searched every house, every shop, and every church in that city. From what I've heard, they've now expanded their search into other parts of Brittany. All of his Gestapo friends will be on the lookout for you two. You embarrassed and shamed him, stealing that intelligence under his nose. You might say he's obsessed."

"He can rot in hell," I said. I clenched my jaw in anger at the mention of Keppler, my mind flashing back to his sick smile after he shot Henri. He embodied everything I hated about the Nazis.

"I have no doubt he will," Donovan said, taking a puff on his cigar. "Now one more time, promise me again: nowhere near Paris. It's not safe anywhere in France these days, but particularly for you in that city."

"Yes, sir, nowhere near Fresnes Prison or Paris," I said, nodding in agreement, if only to appease him. There was nothing I could do to get Henri back, but if I had a chance to help get my friends out of prison, it was a promise I wouldn't hesitate to break.

# Chapter Forty-Three

**April 20, 1943**

The moon was not full until the third week in April, so even if we had wanted to leave England earlier, it would have been difficult. Josette and I had needed the time to rest, to eat a little better than we had in France, and to at least begin to heal. We had gone to the pubs a few nights with Irene and David and their friends from the OSS and SOE, and I had actually been able to put my grief and worries aside for a couple of short pockets of time if nothing else.

It had felt good to be back at the OSS's Cover and Documentation offices. They had created new identities for us, complete with new wardrobes. We were to be sales representatives for a cosmetics firm, carrying suitcases of makeup samples with a hidden compartment for the messages we would really be delivering. I was given a newer model wireless; this one was only fourteen pounds and much easier to carry around.

On Tuesday evening in the third week of April, I looked out the windows of the Lysander as we began to make our descent into France, the makeshift landing strip lit up by the lights of the Resistance members awaiting our arrival. I thought of the first time I had taken this trip, excited and not knowing at all what to expect when we hit the ground. This time I knew exactly what I was getting into, and I could hardly wait to get back to that life, despite everything that had happened. I had craved it while in London, longing for the feeling of passion and purpose, camaraderie and solidarity. I felt like it was the only thing that would help me heal and move past my grief. I couldn't bring Henri back, but I could honor his memory by doing this work. And, if it was at all possible, by getting Georges and Nora free.

"Home," Josette said with an ache in her voice, her hands on the window as she looked down, and I remembered Tatiana doing the same thing on my first Lysander flight.

The landing strip was in the heart of the Loire Valley between Sancerre and Chambord.

"It's going to get a little bumpy on the landing, ladies. Apologies," the young RAF pilot said, just as the little plane started to rattle from turbulence.

Josette put her hand on her stomach instinctively, and I reached across to grab her other hand.

"Feeling okay?" I said.

"Yes and no," she said. "I may vomit before this plane lands, but I'm feeling better, now that I know for sure."

"It's nice to have some truly happy news for a change," I said.

Josette had gone to the doctor in London and learned what both of us had suspected—that she was pregnant and due in early November. She had made me swear not to tell a soul, because she knew they would never let her return to the field if they found out. But now that she knew, she seemed more herself again. The news of this baby, Georges's baby, had given us both joy when we so desperately needed it.

"You still promise not to tell anyone?"

"Of course I won't," I said. "Although at some point, you know you'll have to tell them yourself."

"I know," she said with a sigh. "And I will. But I've got some time. And in the meantime . . ."

"In the meantime, we've got to find a way to get this baby's father out of prison?"

"Yes," she said, "we do."

~

A half hour later, the driver and truck that had picked us up at the landing strip drove down a long, winding road past miles of fields and then deep into the woods. The air smelled like fresh dirt and burning wood, and it was cool but not freezing. Spring was finally coming to France after one of its darkest winters in history. We turned onto a gravel driveway flanked by trees on either side, and about a half mile later we pulled through the wrought-iron arched gates of Manoir Anoir, an impressive, abandoned fifteenth-century manor complete with turrets and a partial moat. It was the new headquarters of Pauline and Bernard's growing resistance network and where Josette and I would be staying, at least for now.

The manor's gigantic double doors led into an enormous room with high, dark-beamed ceilings and a stone fireplace that was tall enough to stand inside if there hadn't been a blazing fire in it. There were at least two dozen people there, mostly men, drinking and laughing and looking as if they were celebrating their solidarity and the fact they were alive. Despite the roundups and arrests, and all the grim news, there was a warm, welcoming atmosphere for the arrival of more agents and arms.

Tatiana came running across the room and nearly knocked Josette and me over, hugging us so tightly it was hard to breathe.

"You are back," she said. "Thank God, I was afraid they wouldn't let you come. And there are so few women around here, too many bad-smelling men. I've missed you so much, my friends."

"I was afraid they wouldn't either," I said.

"We've missed you too," Josette said.

Then Tatiana's eyes filled up with tears, and I bit my lip as mine began to fill too, just nodding.

She hugged me again, then Josette, not saying a word. She didn't have to.

"Have you heard anything more about Georges or Nora?" I asked.

"They are at Fresnes Prison, alive. They have not been moved anywhere else," Tatiana said. "I've arranged to have a friend in one of the Paris networks drop them care packages of food and toiletries when he can. Some guards are more amenable to that than others; my friend is building a relationship with a few of them, to see if they'd be open to bribes."

"Bribes—to help them escape?" I said.

"Exactly," Tatiana answered.

"Thank you so much for all you're doing," Josette said. "I wish I could deliver the packages myself."

"Hopefully they won't be in there long enough for anyone to have to deliver many more packages," Tatiana said. "Come, let me get you drinks."

"My new wireless operator and my new courier have finally arrived." Pauline came over and greeted us with kisses on both cheeks. "Oh, my friends, I am so profoundly sorry for your loss, for all you have been through. And you have no idea how happy I am to see you both back here. We are desperate for the help, as I'm sure you've heard."

While Tatiana went to get us drinks, we talked about what rooms we would be staying in and our schedules in the coming weeks. I had already told Josette that I would help her with the courier jobs. I didn't want her to be overdoing it, biking up to fifty miles a day.

"Bernard! Look who's here," Tatiana called out as she came back with our glasses of wine.

Bernard, looking as ever like a handsome pirate, was at the far end of the room with a small group, talking, but he hurried toward us, followed by two others, both of them dressed in military uniforms, which I was not used to seeing. The first man was short and stocky with dark hair and olive skin, and he was dressed in a US Army Air Forces uniform. It was the second officer who made my jaw drop open.

I had forgotten how tall he was, and his sandy hair was cut very short now, though he still looked boyish. He had not been looking in my direction, just following Bernard through the crowds, so he didn't catch my eye until he was a few feet away, and then he froze right where he was, tilting his head and giving me that mischievous, boyish smile. I had so many feelings when I looked into his eyes, memories of our brief times together before I left, wistfulness about what would have happened if my life had taken a different path. But overriding it all I felt a sense of loyalty and overwhelming grief for the love I had just lost.

"Dear friends," Bernard said, nearly picking me up off the ground with a hug.

Josette, never one to miss a thing, knew something was amiss as she looked at my scarlet face and then back at Phillip's expression.

"I don't think we've met," Josette said, holding out her hand to Phillip just as Bernard was about to make introductions. "I'm Josette."

"I know. I've heard a lot about you—all good things, naturally," Phillip said, giving her that disarming smile. "I'm Phillip Stanhope, with the SOE. And this is Anthony Ricci with the OSS—like you, Anna. Hello. It's, uh . . . it's good to see you again. Anna and I were, uh . . . friends . . . We worked in DC together, and well . . . It feels like it's been a very long time, doesn't it?"

"Hello, Phillip," I said, as he leaned down and gave me an awkward kiss on the cheek that made me want to cry. "It has been. A very long time."

"Phillip and Anthony and their French counterpart, Raphael, over there are part of a new elite group of paratroopers composed of OSS and SOE members, some Free French officers, and a few Canadians," Bernard explained.

"I heard that in London from Irene," I said, finding it difficult to look in Phillip's eyes for more than a second.

"Basically, we're here to help organize the Resistance so we can harass the Germans as much as possible before the invasions," Anthony said in a New York accent.

"Whenever those happen," Phillip said.

"Why are you wearing uniforms?" Josette asked.

"To decrease the likelihood of being shot as spies if we're captured," Anthony answered, and Bernard looked at him like he might punch him.

"Anna . . . ," Phillip said. "Might I have a word alone outside? I promise it will only be a minute."

"Oh, um . . . all right," I said.

He headed in the opposite direction of the front door, and I looked back to see Josette looking at me with concern.

We found a rear door through the kitchen and stood against a stone wall with a view of the expansive gardens in the back of the house. Neatly trimmed hedges and flowering trees were looking neglected and wild now, but I imagined they would still be beautiful when they bloomed in the coming months. I wrapped my arms around myself and looked up at the clear, starry night. Charlotte, the moon, looked back at me.

"Are you cold?" Phillip asked. "I could get you something . . ."

"No, I'm fine, really," I said.

"I almost didn't recognize you with your hair."

"Yeah, it was a necessity, unfortunately."

"I like it," he said. "You look, well . . . you're as beautiful as ever."

"Thank you," I said. "You look well too."

We stood there for a moment, not knowing what to say or where to begin.

"Anna, I . . . I heard about what happened in Tréguier recently, before I knew who it was . . . ," he said, carefully choosing his words. "I can't believe that was you, and . . . and I'm so bloody sorry about Henri

Rousseau. Truly. What a devastating thing to witness. What a horrific, unspeakable act."

"Thank you," I whispered. He put his hand on my shoulder, and I wanted to pull away and melt into him at the same time. I wanted comfort, but I didn't want to give him the wrong impression.

"I . . . ," I began, falteringly. "Obviously Henri and I . . . we knew each other before the war. I feel like I need to explain to you about . . . well . . ."

"No, you don't, darling," he said, holding up his hand, and I couldn't tell if he meant it or he just didn't want to hear about my relationship with Henri. "You don't have to explain anything. This is wartime and . . . things happen. Because, in some ways, we are all just living for the day, aren't we? And you and I didn't know if we'd ever see each other again. But I must admit I . . . I regret sending you that letter . . ."

"Please don't. I loved that letter. I wanted to keep it . . . I cherished the words in it. Phillip, I'm sorry that so much has changed. I'm grieving, and I feel so . . . in pieces." My voice cracked, and I gripped the stone wall with white knuckles, just trying to keep myself composed. "I have to focus on the work because that's the only thing that will get me through this . . . this loss."

"I understand," he said, taking his hand off my shoulder, his voice thick with emotion. We stood with our thoughts for a few quiet moments, looking out at the gardens and the stars. And then he spoke, his voice as soft as a prayer.

"You know I understand loss and how it can suffocate you and color everything. We are all going to have scars after this war, a whole generation of us. Most of them will be the kind you can't see. You have now had to deal with two profound losses at such a young age. Quite honestly, I don't know how you've done it. And yet, here you are. Again. I told you before you left London, you are a wonder. And if nothing else, I am fortunate just to know a girl . . . a woman . . . like you. And

. . . if I could . . . I'd like us to be friends, Anna Cavanaugh. I promise you, I want nothing more than that. Would that be okay?"

I looked up at him and just nodded. I knew if I said one word, I would start to cry. He lifted his arms to hug me, and part of me wanted him to so badly, but then he stopped himself, and I stepped back from him. There was an anguished look in his eyes.

"Good then," he said, clasping his hands together. "I'm going to be traveling all over France with my team. In fact, I should go find them. We're leaving tonight." He pointed his thumb at the door behind us. "But I'll be back in the area. Please stay safe, won't you? And I'll . . . I'll see you soon."

"Yes, you too," I said. "I'll see you."

He started walking backward toward the door, but then he took three long strides forward and gave me a quick kiss on the forehead.

"It breaks my heart to see you hurting this way," he whispered in my ear. And then he was gone.

Wiping the tears off my face, I stood there for a few minutes, arms wrapped around myself, taking deep breaths. I heard the back door open and turned around to see Josette.

"Oh, ma chère," she said, putting an arm around me as I shed a few more tears into her shoulder. "That was the one you told me about, isn't it? I knew it from the moment I saw him look at you."

"It is," I said, and I told her about our conversation.

"He sounds like a very good man."

"He is," I said. "But I am a mess, Josette. Maybe I shouldn't have come back. I don't know if I can do this."

"Oh, no. No, no, no. Don't be ridiculous and start doubting yourself now. We have no time for that, do we?"

I took a deep breath and blew it out.

"No, you're right. We don't," I said.

# Chapter Forty-Four

**June 11, 1943**

I reached into my navy cotton culottes and pulled out the Colt .32 pistol strapped to my thigh. For me it was small and manageable, and, unlike with the more powerful Sten guns, we had ample pistol ammunition to practice with. The gun no longer felt awkward in my hands as I took aim at the target twenty yards away and hit just outside the bull's-eye for the fifth time in a row. Some of the men had built a homemade shooting range in a far corner of the gardens at Manoir Anoir. There was also an area for guerrilla warfare training, and on some evenings before I left on my bicycle, I would go outside and practice shooting. In the guerrilla course, I would take aim from various distances, while on the run, and in the dark. Though it was just a .32 pistol, I was still always careful not to waste too much ammo on my practice sessions. But if I was going to live life as a spy, I had to learn how to use a gun. I never wanted to feel as utterly helpless as I had during my last days in Paris or on that horrible day in Tréguier.

It was almost summer in the Loire Valley. The late-day sunlight bathed everything in the gardens in a warm, soft glow. The flowers were a wild, untamed explosion of colors—lavender lilacs, pink peonies, and white and red roses.

Despite the odds still being against us, despite the continued arrests and the losses throughout Paris and beyond, the Resistance had proven to be resilient. Pauline and Bernard, with the support of the SOE and OSS, had brilliantly organized, recruited, and trained thousands of new Resistance members and had built up numerous networks that stretched across much of France. Their success, our success, could not be denied, particularly with the sabotage campaign we had waged against the Germans. Railway tunnels and factories, electric pylons and trains, were being blown to pieces all over France, thanks mostly to the meticulous planning and execution of our two leaders.

And the latest developments in the war had given us renewed optimism—the withdrawing of U-boats from the Atlantic and the surrender of German and Italian troops in North Africa, as well as the air bombings of Germany by Allied planes—these were all signs that gave us hope that maybe the tides were finally turning in the Allies' favor.

I was preparing for another fifty-mile nighttime bike ride through the Loire Valley. I delivered messages to various resistance groups in the region, as we never wrote or telephoned. I'd also learn of their supply needs, among other information they needed to share, reporting back to Pauline and Bernard, and communicating with London. Tomorrow night, I would go out again, locating additional landing sites and parachute drop zones for the supplies and agents coming from the UK every month. My new cover as a sales representative for a cosmetics manufacturer seemed absurd in a way, but it had worked so far. I had a straw basket on my bike with a hidden compartment for any messages or arms and explosives I needed to pass on.

The night before, I had been stopped at a checkpoint by a young German soldier, who had inspected my papers and searched through the case of sample beauty products in my basket. I had smiled and flirted and handed him a round of goat cheese from the *fromagerie* in the village, and he had sent me on my way. But I never forgot what the

Germans were capable of—that had been branded on my psyche forever after Henri's death.

I still missed Paris, but life in the Loire Valley had done Josette and me both a world of good. The bike rides could be exhausting, but I felt stronger and healthier from all the exercise and from a diet that was much better than the one we'd had in Paris, thanks to country life. There was goat cheese and milk, river trout, and a sizable vegetable garden on the property. My skin had bronzed from time spent outdoors, and my auburn hair, which I had kept up per Donovan's suggestion, had grown long enough to braid.

And I felt stronger inside as well. My grief over Henri was still raw, washing over me when I least expected it, particularly when I was alone at night, biking under the stars. The tears would fall, and I would have to stop riding to wipe them away and catch my breath. But all my hard work was a salve that was slowly helping me heal.

With London's permission, I had taught Josette how to use the wireless, so I could do the bulk of the courier work. Now, nearing the end of her fourth month, she had realized it was for the best, as she was vomiting less but feeling tired much of the time. It was no surprise she had picked it up quickly, sticking to the schedule, moving locations often, and always having someone look out for the German detector vans.

I took one last shot at the paper target, imagining it was Herbert Keppler, my heart rate rising with my anger as I pictured him. This time I missed the bull's-eye entirely and let out a groan of frustration.

"Well done," Pauline said as she came up behind me, wearing khaki trousers, army boots, and a white shirt. She never wore makeup and kept her hair in a neat bun or ponytail, as if she couldn't be bothered.

"Not that last one," I said. "But your lessons helped tremendously, thank you. I was hopeless before."

"You're shooting like a natural now," Pauline said, shielding her eyes from the late-day sun, examining the target.

"I'm trying," I said. "Is everything okay? I thought you weren't going to be back until later."

"Yes and no . . . ," she said, a frown on her face. "I know you are heading out soon, but I wanted a word alone. Let's sit over at the table on the patio."

I nodded, worried about what she might have to discuss.

We sat down at the wrought-iron table on the patio, right next to the trail of lavender wisteria climbing up the back of the house.

"I have to tell you, your work has been brilliant, Anna," Pauline said. "And you have been tireless in the field. I don't know what we'd do without you."

"Thank you," I said, pleased at her words, blushing a little. "That means a great deal coming from you."

"It's true," she said with a laugh. "Josette has also done an exemplary job, and she's picked up the wireless from you with no trouble. Wireless radio operation—coding and all of it—is not one of my strengths, so that's been a huge relief."

"Yes, I knew she'd be terrific at it," I said.

"But tell me, when is her baby due?"

"Ah," I said, grimacing. "How long have you known?"

"Tatiana and I have suspected for a while now. We're women living together; it doesn't take much guesswork. Also, she's very petite, and she's starting to show, despite her efforts to hide it."

It was true. She had been trying to conceal her growing belly under her windbreaker, but I had noticed it, too.

"She's due in November," I said. "The baby is Georges's, obviously. She didn't think London would send her back if anyone knew. And it . . . it wasn't my secret to tell."

"I understand your loyalty. And for the record, you're right. London never would have, for good reason, I might add," Pauline said.

"I know, I know," I said. "But she's . . . well, you know her enough now. She had to come back."

Pauline sat there for a moment, thinking.

"I wanted to talk to you alone, because I just found out Georges LaRue and Nora Khan were transferred out of Fresnes Prison a few days ago. One of the guards we've been working with at Fresnes just informed us yesterday."

Our network in Paris had established relationships with two of the Fresnes guards. They had been the main link to Georges and Nora, making sure they got additional food when possible and allowing notes to be delivered. All this for a price, of course. But the guards had proven to be trustworthy, and the Paris contacts were about to offer them an enormous bribe if they agreed to assist in our friends' escape. It was a devastating setback.

"Oh God, where? Please don't say Poland." I put my hands over my face, scared of the answer. I knew that if they had been sent to one of the prison camps in Poland, it would be impossible to get them out.

"They've been transferred to the prison on the top floor of 84 Avenue Foch." Pauline looked at me, her eyes serious and sad.

"But why? Why there? Why now?" I said, feeling sickened at the thought. I recalled Dr. Jackson describing the screams. "And good God, what are they going to do to them there? That's a Gestapo torture chamber. They're going to kill them, aren't they?"

"They have recently figured out just how valuable Georges LaRue is to the Resistance. And yes, I think they are going to torture and execute them," Pauline said. "To make them a very visible example to the Resistance members trying to rebuild the Paris networks."

"Pauline, is there anything we can do? We can't . . . Georges . . . I feel responsible for what happened to him and Nora. Can we get to them?"

"We can try. There is a guard at Avenue Foch who recently started working as a double agent for us. Bernard has already met with him and discussed a possible plan to get them out. It's going to require a large amount of money for bribes and a great deal of risk. But if we don't do it soon, I'm afraid they'll end up dead. And, frankly, we need Georges. He is a gifted leader and organizer, and with the Resistance growing larger in numbers every day, we need his expertise. But if we're going to get him out, we should of course get Nora too. And we're always short on wireless operators, as you well know."

"I'll go. If there is a plan, I want to be a part of it," I said. "It's the least I can do."

I thought of Donovan's words and the promise I had known all along I wouldn't be able to keep. He had much more to worry about than one agent's activities in France.

"Bernard and I were taking bets on whether I'd even have to ask," Pauline said, sitting back, crossing her arms and smiling. "Yes, we want you to be a part of it. You know Paris well and the neighborhood in particular. Dr. Jackson is willing to help, and Tatiana is going to go with you too. We'll talk late tonight after you return. After Josette is asleep."

"You don't want me to tell her, do you?" I asked. I hated the thought of keeping this from her.

"I don't. I know you two are very close, but she's already sick with worry about Georges. And you know she would want to go. I think you should keep this a secret from her for now, for her own good."

I stared up at the pink-and-gold sky, feeling conflicted. Josette was trying to be strong, but she couldn't go with us. Not now. I looked back at Pauline, still torn.

"Okay, I won't tell her."

# *Chapter Forty-Five*

I came back from my courier duties at ten thirty that night to a feast cooked by Bernard and Tatiana: fire-roasted chickens, fresh asparagus, potatoes, and leeks. After my time in occupied Paris, I would never take adequate food for granted again.

After dinner, several of the men staying at the house went to smoke cigarettes by the fireplace while I helped Tatiana clean up the dishes. Poor Josette was leaning on her elbow, almost falling asleep in her chair. I grabbed the dishes in front of her and whispered in her ear.

"You should go up," I said. "You need your sleep."

"I know, but you know nobody talks about anything serious until after dinner," she said with a yawn.

"I'll tell you in the morning," I said, feeling a pang of guilt.

Josette got up from the table and was about to bid everyone good night when there was a knock at the door. Even though we had guards with Sten guns at the gated entrance of the manor, all of us froze for a second—our paranoia never abated.

I heard Bernard greeting whoever was at the door. Josette raised her eyebrows at me when Phillip Stanhope and his American counterpart, Anthony, walked into the dining room. The fact that she didn't stay to find out why they were there spoke to how exhausted she was.

I hadn't seen Phillip since the night I had first arrived at the manor, and I was genuinely pleased to see him again. His was a familiar face, but more than that, he was someone I still cared about, at least as a friend.

"Hello, Anna," Phillip said. "Wow, you look brilliant."

"Um . . . thank you. Are you saying I looked bad the last time you saw me?" I said, giving him a mock dirty look.

"Ah, no," he said, looking nervous. "You looked well before, but . . . Are you . . . oh, are you teasing me?" He gave me a smirk that I remembered well.

"Thank you for coming, Phillip, Anthony," Bernard said, one arm around Tatiana. They were inseparable when they were both at the manor.

Pauline greeted the men and asked that the five of us join her outside for a glass of wine, at the table by the wisteria, where she and I had sat earlier in the day.

"Um . . . what are you two doing here exactly?" I said, frowning at the two men as Bernard refilled our wine glasses with Sancerre.

"Pauline said she needed help with a job," Anthony said, looking at me. And then, looking at Pauline, he added, "Our third team member, Raphael, sends his regards. He's up in Normandy for the next couple of weeks."

"What job, Pauline?" Tatiana said, eyeing Anthony with suspicion.

"You and Anna are going to need help getting Georges and Nora out of Avenue Foch," Pauline said and then, amused, added, "I recently learned there is a bounty on my head of one million francs, so it would be very unwise for me to be the one to go."

"And my sabotage teams have several missions planned that night," Bernard said. "I have to be here to make sure they execute properly."

"Wait . . . you two are going with *us* to Paris?" I said, pointing at both of them, not believing what I was hearing.

"We're going to march onto Avenue Foch with two men in *uniform*? That's ridiculous," Tatiana said, and I was relieved she agreed with me.

"We aren't going to be wearing uniforms," Anthony said, in a condescending tone. "Sweetheart, we're way better trained than you two for this type of thing."

"You really think so?" I said, getting defensive now. "Who has been working in France longer? Didn't you just get here?"

"Anna, do you have any idea how dangerous this is going to be?" Phillip said.

"I watched Henri get shot in the head so, yes, I think I'm well aware," I said, clenching my jaw in anger.

There was an awkward pause at the table.

"I'm sorry, that was foolish of me to say," Phillip said in a quiet voice.

"It's okay. I'm sorry I snapped," I told him, taking a deep breath. "We're talking about our friends in a prison known for torture. I just want to get it right."

"Everyone listen, please," Pauline said, holding her hand up, calm and measured as ever. "Phillip and Anthony are part of the program known as the Jedburghs—it's an elite unit, and they are extremely well trained for these types of scenarios. Also, the SOE and OSS have agreed to send a gargantuan sum of money to use as bribes to get Georges and Nora out . . . but . . . they insisted that these two be a part of it. And once you hear the details of this outlandishly risky plan, you'll understand why you will need them."

Phillip kept looking over at me, his eyes apologetic.

"What?" I said, looking at him, blushing and hating myself for it. I couldn't quite believe he was back in my life, and I still didn't know how to feel about it.

"Again, I apologize for my daft comment. It's a bad habit around you," Phillip said, leaning forward, anguish in his eyes. "We made a good team once, didn't we? And Anthony here is one of the best of the OSS—besides you, of course. I promise we won't let you down."

Tatiana gave me a sideways glance. She knew of my history with Phillip. I looked around the table, and then at Pauline and sighed.

"Okay, if this is how it has to be. When do we leave?" I asked.

"The night after next," Pauline said. "Phillip will drive the four of you in a Red Cross ambulance to the American Hospital, but you won't make any moves until just before curfew. Bernard, why don't you explain what our double agent has in store."

Bernard explained that the double agent had given the two prisoners each a screwdriver to loosen and remove the bars of the ventilation shafts in their cells. The night of their escape he would equip them with a flashlight and rope. At the end of the guard's shift, Nora and Georges would climb up to the roof through the shafts, make their way to the back of the building, and rappel down to the next building's terrace, where Tatiana and I would be waiting for them. Phillip and Anthony would be watching from the shadows with guns drawn in case the two escapees were spotted.

"But the guards around the perimeter of the building will be bribed to look the other way, and the double agent, of course, is expecting a very large bonus for the evening *if* we're successful," Pauline said.

Tatiana and I looked at each other with skepticism. Anthony's eyebrows were raised, and Phillip's expression was difficult to read.

"What happens if and when they make it to the terrace, to us?" I asked.

"You will wait to make sure there are no alarms sounded regarding the escape, give them a change of clothes, and exit the building. You'll cut through the little square in back and take the side streets—Rue Pergolese to Avenue de Malakoff to 11 Avenue Foch. We will map it out."

"Eleven Avenue Foch—Dr. Jackson's home?" I said. "Is that wise?"

"It's a fourteen-minute walk, and he's been hiding escaped POWs and downed pilots there for months," Bernard said. "His home office entrance can't be seen from the street."

"Wouldn't it be better if we left the city immediately?"

"You will," Pauline said. "Phillip and Anthony will pick the four of you up from Dr. Jackson's home."

"In the same ambulance?" Phillip said. "We'll need another car—preferably a black Citroën from that friend on the inside, one with some Nazi flags? The Gestapo in Paris is more paranoid than ever. We can't take any chances. Getting into the city in an ambulance is one thing, but driving out past curfew, with two escaped prisoners? That will never work. We would be stopped a dozen times."

"Phillip's right. That's suicide," Anthony said. "We need one of their cars."

Bernard and Pauline looked at each other.

"It's possible we can get that arranged," Bernard said, hands behind his head. "It's going to cost more, but you're right . . ."

"Well, you weren't wrong when you said this plan was outlandishly risky, were you?" Phillip said. "Will you two be armed?" He looked at Tatiana and me.

"We'd better be carrying guns, because this whole plot you've concocted? It's insane," Tatiana said, as Bernard lit her cigarette. "But I kind of like it."

"I'm a little worried about Nora climbing up through a ventilation shaft and rappelling down a rope. Remember her in training?" I looked at Tatiana, and she nodded. "And to answer your question, yes. We'll be armed. I'll bring the Colt .32."

"I'll bring the same," Tatiana said.

We went over a few more details and then got into discussing other topics, including the popular sport of trying to predict where and when the Allied invasion of Europe would happen. Then people started yawning and saying their good nights. Phillip was the last one at the table, and I nodded my good night to him as everyone else trickled inside.

"Stay outside and sit with me for a moment, won't you?" he called to me just as I opened the back door.

I walked back over. There was a cool summer breeze, and the air smelled like fresh grass and lilacs. Somewhere in the vast acreage around us, something was howling at the night sky.

"When I first saw you tonight, you just looked so much healthier than the last time I was here," Phillip said. "More back to yourself, are you?"

"Thank you. I'm . . . I'm not, but . . . I'm getting there," I said, sitting back down at the wrought-iron table next to him. "It's been incredibly hectic, but the work has meant everything. And living here with good food and fresh air, despite the war raging around us. That has definitely helped. Josette and I are both doing better."

"Yes, where was she tonight?" he said. "I was surprised she's not involved in this."

"Sleeping," I said. Then, with a deep breath, I added, "She's pregnant."

"Oh," he looked at me, eyebrows raised in surprise as he poured the last of the bottle of Sancerre into my wineglass.

"Please don't say anything to anyone," I said. "Georges is the father."

"Does she know anything about this plan?" he asked.

"No," I said, tracing the table with my finger. "We're meant to keep it a secret. I'm not sure I can do that."

"I understand," he said. He put his hand over mine on the table, and I started to pull it away but then changed my mind. Because I still felt something for him, despite Henri, despite everything.

"Phillip, I . . ."

"Anna, please, hear me out," he said, not taking his hand away. And he paused before speaking again. "I have no expectations of you. I know you are broken and hurting. But we are about to embark on yet *another* mission together—mercifully without ladders or ex-convicts involved."

I couldn't help but smile at this.

"I wish I could convince you to stay behind with Josette," he continued, "but I know you well enough by now to know that I would be a damn fool to try."

"That is true," I said, still smiling as we caught each other's eye.

"So, let me just say, if we must do this kind of dangerous work, since that seems to be our fate in this war . . . well, there is no one I'd rather have by my side."

I'd had Henri, someone I loved, by my side for a cold, dark winter only to lose him in the most brutal way. I'd had Connor before that. A man who, before he died, had preferred I stand in his shadow rather than beside him in the light. I swallowed, choked up, so moved by the words of this man, who still would not give up on me and still believed in me. I turned my hand over and held his tight.

"Thank you," I whispered. It was all I was ready to say.

# Chapter Forty-Six

*June 13, 1943*

The day of the mission to Paris, Josette and I bicycled into Varennes-sur-Loir, the closest village, to get some provisions. We were both thrilled to discover that the boulangerie actually did have the sugary pastries with strawberry jam that were rumored to exist. We sat on a bench under a chestnut tree and didn't talk as we tasted our first real dessert in what felt like a hundred years.

"I want to go back and kiss the owner. I had forgotten how fantastic sugar tastes," Josette said, closing her eyes and licking the white powder off her fingers after she finished. It was a warm June day, but she was wearing her windbreaker to try to hide her small pregnancy bump.

I had not slept the night before, thinking about our trip to Paris, agonizing over the fact that Josette knew nothing about it. And I had made a decision.

"Before we head back, there's something I need to tell you," I said, my stomach tight as I wiped my hands on my culottes. She turned deathly pale.

"Is this about Georges? Is he dead? What do you know? I knew I was being kept in the dark about something. Tell me." She jumped up from the bench, pacing and balling her fists as if preparing to fight.

"He's not dead, but please sit down," I said. "Josette, I can't lie to you even if it's to protect you. Because I know you wouldn't lie to me."

"Just *tell me*, Anna."

I told her everything, starting with the fact that our friends knew about the pregnancy and then revealing where Georges had been moved. She put her head in her hands and started to cry.

"Oh my God, he's as good as dead there," she said.

"No, there's more. We have a plan," I said, putting my arm around her shaking shoulders. I quietly told her what was happening that night, and she stopped shaking and sat up, wiping her face with her sleeve. After I finished talking, we sat there together, watching the pigeons eat the sugary crumbs at our feet.

"Before this," she said, pointing to her stomach, "I would have insisted on going with you, of course. But now, things are different. Going with you . . . it would be out of pride, thinking nobody could rescue him as well as I could. That feels selfish now."

"You are going to be such a terrific mother," I said, my eyes tearing up.

"Please get him back safe, Anna. Both of you have to come back safe," she said, holding my hand and resting her head on my shoulder. "I can't have this baby alone."

"We'll get him back safe," I said with conviction, praying it would be true.

~

We pulled into the American Hospital that evening in the Red Cross ambulance. Dr. Jackson was in the courtyard, and Tatiana and I had a warm reunion with him as he gave us each a hug and expressed his condolences about Henri.

I introduced him to Phillip and Anthony, and Dr. Jackson suggested we go to his office. It hurt to walk back inside the hospital, remembering the last time I had been there, with Henri. All the memories came flooding back, but I knew I had to push them down if I was going to make it through this night.

"How are you?" I said to Dr. Jackson as we all sat down. He looked gaunt and more tired than the last time I had seen him, and he was wearing the same cotton sweater filled with holes under his white coat.

"I'm just trying to keep all my patients fed and cared for, but the food situation is worse than ever. In some of the poorer neighborhoods, they're dying of starvation," he said. "People are growing angrier all the time; you can feel it simmering underneath the surface. Every night, I pray for the Allies to invade soon."

"We all do," said Tatiana.

We had gone over it dozens of times, but we reviewed our plan once more with Dr. Jackson, and he gave us a key to the side entrance of his house at 11 Avenue Foch. His home office was where he sometimes treated patients, although lately most of his "patients" had been men escaping through the underground network.

"My wife and son are at our cottage in the country, so the house is empty," Dr. Jackson said. He looked at us with worry in his eyes. "Please be careful. Make it out of the city tonight."

We thanked him and said our good-byes, realizing it would soon be time to go. We separated to get changed into appropriate French-made clothes for a "night out" in Paris.

"Everyone's got their papers and their guns? I've got the keys to the car. You gals have the keys to the empty apartment?" Anthony asked us.

"Got them," I said, holding them up and then stuffing them into the large purse I was carrying with a change of clothes for Nora.

"Tatiana, sweetheart, you're with me. We'll pretend we're couples on a double date," Anthony said.

"Fine," Tatiana said, scowling at Anthony. It was clear she had never met a New Yorker. "But if you call me 'sweetheart' again, I will punch you."

"All right, suit yourself, Frenchie." Anthony shrugged and continued, "Phillip and I will walk with you until we're one block down from the apartment building, and then we'll split up. The two of us will take our places at the back of 84 as planned."

Like Anthony, Phillip was wearing French-made clothes—black pants and a dark-gray button-down shirt—colors that blended into the night. I couldn't deny he looked especially handsome.

Tatiana and I were happy to ditch our culottes for floral dresses. Even now, Parisian women were still wearing pretty dresses and lipstick.

"Shall we?" Phillip said, holding his elbow out for me as I finished pinning my peacock brooch to my dress. We were about to embark on an insanely risky mission, so the nervous fluttering I felt in my stomach when I took Phillip's elbow was a welcome distraction as we walked down the street toward Avenue Foch, Tatiana and Anthony behind us.

"You look lovely," Phillip said, looking over at me as we walked. "As always."

"Thank you," I said.

"Are you nervous at all, Cavanaugh?"

"Am I? Not really. It's amazing what you get used to, isn't it?" I said, and he smiled because he understood. "I'm more just . . . ready to get on with it. To get it done. I was there the night they both were captured. I have a desperate need to make this right."

He nodded and was quiet for a moment as we kept walking. "Back in DC, I know I questioned whether you'd be good at this job."

"You weren't the only one . . ." I smirked.

"I was bloody wrong—we all were. You are brilliant at this work."

I glanced up at him, and he looked me in the eyes.

"Thank you," I said. "It means a great deal coming from you." He smiled and pulled me closer, putting his free hand over mine.

"This is where we split up; the apartment building is there," Anthony said, pointing. "If all goes well, we'll pull the Citroën up to the doc's house in a couple hours."

"And if it doesn't?" Tatiana said.

"We'll improvise," I said. "Like we've learned to do."

"Let's hope it won't come to that," Phillip said. "Good luck and God bless."

Tatiana and I were turning to walk away when Phillip grabbed my hand and kissed it.

"See you soon, Cavanaugh," he said in a whisper, and his eyes told me so much more than what he was saying.

"See you soon," I said.

≈

The apartment building on the small square behind 84 Avenue Foch was completely empty. Either the residents had fled with the first exodus of Parisians after the occupation, or the Nazis had evicted them when they commandeered most of the neighborhood.

Tatiana and I stood in the window of the darkened apartment on the top floor, our eyes on the small terrace outside it, the one that Nora and Georges would be lowering themselves onto within the hour. My heart felt like it was beating outside my chest, and I couldn't sit still. I wanted this plan to work and this night to be over. I reached down to feel the cool metal of the gun strapped to my thigh, to make sure it was there.

"That roofline is so steep, and I still don't understand where the hell they're going to secure the rope to climb down," Tatiana said, voicing my own concerns as we stared out the window. The roof of Avenue Foch was thirty feet above the apartment's terrace.

"Georges is resourceful; he'll figure it out," I said.

"He better," Tatiana said. She stepped back into the shadows of the apartment and lit a cigarette where she couldn't be seen from outside. "He loves you, you know."

"Georges?" I said, laughing.

"Phillip," Tatiana said. "He's completely in love with you."

"I don't know about that," I said. I was glad she couldn't see me blushing in the dark. "As you know, we have a little bit of history, that's all."

"Anna, he loves you, and you know it," Tatiana said. "And I can tell you care for him, too. Before you say anything, I know how heartbroken and devastated you are about . . . about losing Henri. I'm not saying you should do anything about how you feel. Yet. But don't wait too long. The longer this war goes on, the more I think we should not wait too long for anything that brings us happiness."

She wasn't wrong. But I wasn't ready. I was opening my mouth to explain it to her when I saw movement on the roof of 84 Avenue Foch.

"Tatiana," I whispered, pointing up.

Two silhouettes were clambering across the roof high above us, and I could barely breathe. One false move and they could fall to their deaths. 84 Avenue Foch towered over the building that we were in, and, the way the two buildings were situated, it was possible to rappel down from the roof of 84 and land directly onto this particular apartment's terrace. Our guard on the inside had told us this was Georges and Nora's best possible option for escape.

Somewhere in the darkness below, Phillip and Anthony were keeping lookout, but right now we were all powerless to do anything but watch and pray.

Tatiana and I stood side by side, frozen as they reached the spot overlooking our apartment and crouched down. A minute later, a thick, dark rope was dangling onto the apartment's terrace. We both looked at each other, slid open the door, and got ready, in case whoever climbed down first needed help. I saw the smaller silhouette position herself on the edge and wrap herself around the rope, shimmying down it. At one point a summer breeze blew through the square, and Nora paused, dangling halfway between the roof and the terrace. I heard Tatiana gasp as she pointed up at something glowing on Nora's wrist.

"Oh my God," I said, sick to my stomach. Nora was wearing a watch with an illuminated dial, as bright as a flashlight.

"Damn it, Nora!" Tatiana whispered, hands over her face as if she was too scared to look.

The breeze stopped blowing, and Nora resumed rappelling down, and it was my turn to gasp as we saw her badly scarred feet, then her emaciated body as she collapsed onto the terrace and let out a barely audible cry. Tatiana got to her first, arms around her as she half pulled, half carried her inside and shut the door.

"My friends, thank you," Nora said between quiet sobs. She had lost at least twenty pounds since I had last seen her, and the dress she was wearing was filthy. The soles of her feet were covered with burn scars, and several of her toenails were missing.

"Oh, Nora," I said, stroking her matted, greasy hair. "I'm so sorry."

Tatiana pointed to the terrace, and Georges was coming down the rope, looking even filthier than Nora. He was dressed in the clothes he had been wearing the night he was captured, but they were barely recognizable as they were ripped in several places and stained with dirt and blood. They hung on his frame—he looked like a ghost of his former self.

As soon as he hit the terrace, I scrambled to open the door and help him inside. When he realized it was me, he tackled me in a hug, and for the first time since I had met him at Sciences Po, he started to cry.

"Josette?" Georges said, upon seeing Tatiana. "Is she . . . where is she? Why isn't she here? Anna, tell me she's okay . . ."

"She's fine," I said, getting the clothes and shoes out of my bag for Nora while Tatiana did the same for Georges. "She is back at the safe house. I'll explain later. Right now, you both have to get cleaned up and dressed quickly. There's no time."

Georges started to speak. "But . . . I—"

"Please, we have to leave here in five minutes. Get changed," I said.

Tatiana shoved the clothes in Georges's hands, and he went into the bathroom.

Nora was still so emotional that Tatiana and I had to help her get undressed. I found a washcloth in the kitchen and wet it in the sink so she could at least clean up a little. As I helped her pull her dress off over her head, she winced and closed her eyes. Tatiana was behind her with her hands over her mouth, a horrified expression on her face. I stepped over to see what she was looking at on Nora's back and gasped. Nora's skin was covered in large, long welts, from a belt or perhaps a horse whip. Some were old and starting to scar, and some looked like they might have been inflicted that morning.

"Bastards," Tatiana said, and she let out a torrent of swears, kicking the sofa next to us.

"Oh, my poor friend," I said, looking in Nora's eyes, blinking back tears. "How you have suffered. Let's get you out of here and safe."

After she had carefully fastened a new bra and stepped into new underwear, cringing the whole time, I unbuttoned the cotton floral dress we had brought her and, with great care, pulled it over her head and down her body. Then I gently helped her into a cardigan sweater.

Georges came out of the bathroom a minute later, walking with a limp, grimacing in pain.

"It's a fourteen-minute walk to where we are meeting our ride out of the city. Can you both make it?"

"If I have to crawl, I'm making it," Georges said.

"I'll be fine," Nora said, wiping her face with the cloth.

The four of us descended the stairwell of the apartment building, light on our feet and not saying a word. We cut through the back alleys off the square and then took the route we had mapped out with Phillip and Anthony. I kept scanning the streets around us for signs of Gestapo, but there wasn't a person in sight. Five minutes from Dr. Jackson's home, I heard sirens and I knew they were for us. I was scared now but refused to panic. We were so close to the house, so close to getting them out of the city.

"We're almost there. I think we should run. Can you run?" I hissed.

Nora and Georges just nodded; they could do it.

More sirens, and louder now as we bolted down Rue Chalgrin, the last side street before we were at the intersection near 11 Avenue Foch. I wanted to cheer when we finally arrived at Dr. Jackson's office door on the side entrance of the home. I fumbled with the key in my dress pocket and quickly opened the door. We all slipped inside.

But as soon as I shut the door, I sensed something wasn't right. The lingering scent of an odd citrus cologne I recognized was hanging in the air, and the hairs on the back of my neck stood up. I unstrapped the gun from my thigh and held it in both hands, trying to stay calm. And then, I heard music from a record player on the floor above us.

"Dr. Jackson?" Tatiana whispered. I shook my head. Whoever was upstairs was not Dr. Jackson.

That was when I heard a distinct creak, the sound of a footstep at the top of the staircase. I held my finger to my mouth and looked at my three companions to stay quiet. Tatiana pulled out her gun, and I motioned for her to follow me to the door to the stairs.

I opened the door, and he was standing at the very top of the staircase. His cold, dead ice-blue eyes were rimmed with red, and he had spittle at the corners of his mouth like a rabid dog. He was a man who had lost his mind. He started coming down the stairs toward me, and I lifted the gun.

"You foolish, foolish girl. I knew you'd come back," Keppler said. "You think you can escape *me* twice?"

"Yes I do, you evil Nazi bastard," I said, spitting out the words. "May you rot in hell."

He reached for his gun, but mine was locked and loaded, and I fired two shots in a row straight at his chest. He stumbled backward and collapsed at the top of the stairs in a heap. I thought it was the recoil from the gun that knocked me to the floor like a hard shove, just as I saw our black Citroën pull up out front, but Nora let out a high-pitched cry.

"Is he alone?" I said, struggling to get up. "Are there more?"

Georges looked at me, eyes wide, grabbed the gun from Tatiana, and ran up the stairs to see if there were more Gestapo. I tried to call out to him because if there were more, Georges was as good as dead.

"Anna, stay down. You've been shot," Tatiana said.

"What?" I said. "No, it was the recoil . . ."

I followed her eyes to my right shoulder and touched the inkblot-sized stain of red blood on my white cardigan that was blooming larger. I felt a wave of heat and burning and then coldness wash over me, and my teeth started chattering.

Nora opened the door, and Phillip rushed in. His face blanched at the sight of me.

"Oh no—no, no, *no*," he said, scooping me up in his arms. "Let's go, darling. We have to get you to the hospital."

Phillip and Tatiana placed me across them in the long back seat of the car, my head against Phillip's chest as he put pressure on my shoulder to stop the bleeding. Nora squeezed in with us in the back, and Georges sat up front with Anthony but stayed low. Anthony hit the gas and navigated the streets of the city like a professional.

"There was nobody else upstairs," Georges said. "I can't believe he was by himself."

"Is he dead?" I asked through chattering teeth, my cheeks wet.

"He's gone, Anna," Georges said, peeking over the seat to look at my shoulder, unable to hide the worry in his eyes. "Well done."

"She's pregnant," I said, my voice hoarse and shaking.

"What did you say?" Georges said.

"Josette. Pregnant," I said, my teeth still chattering.

Georges LaRue was at a rare loss for words and buried his face in his hands at this revelation.

My feet were on Nora's lap, and she took off the cardigan we had just given her and covered me with it, revealing reed-thin arms covered with burn scars from cigarettes.

I started seeing spots in my vision and let out a moan, turning my face into Phillip's chest as the heat and pain of the wound grew worse, burning like a firecracker. He continued to apply pressure, and Tatiana reached over to assist.

"Stay with me, darling. Try to stay awake. Please, my love," Phillip whispered in my ear.

*My love.*

And then everything faded into blackness.

# Chapter Forty-Seven

**June 14, 1943**

From the very beginning of the war, the Nazis had grossly underestimated the strength and intelligence of women. Herbert Keppler had epitomized this attitude, and that was what saved my life, what saved all our lives, the night we fled Paris.

The double agent who had helped orchestrate Georges and Nora's escape had decided to play both sides, since he was also aware of the bounty Keppler had placed on my head as well as Josette's. Keppler had suspected at least one of us would be involved in Georges's escape, and the double agent received a hundred thousand francs for tipping Keppler off to our entire plan.

Keppler had come to Dr. Jackson's home armed but alone, wanting to personally extract his revenge after our betrayal of secrets and our escape in Tréguier. Due to his huge ego and low opinion of women, it had never occurred to him that I would ever have the courage and training to face him as a formidable foe. That was his fatal mistake.

The tale of Georges and Nora's escape from the wretched Gestapo headquarters gave the French Resistance and the Allies a story. And stories have power—they are something to unite around in hope, the kind of hope that makes people persist in their bravery and sacrifice, the kind of hope that has changed the course of wars. There had been far too many captures and killings in 1943. Georges and Nora's daring escape was a small but significant thing to celebrate. And because of that, the Germans were desperate to find and kill anyone who was involved. And that was how I ended up wounded but alive, hidden by some benevolent nuns at a hospital in Blois, a hillside city on the Loire River.

When I woke up the next day, I had no idea where I was or how I had gotten there. The clock in the hospital room said it was well after noon. The sun streamed through the windows like a promise. In the corner, next to the windows, was Phillip Stanhope, his chin on his chest, fast asleep in a lounge chair that could not accommodate his tall frame. He looked even more boyish when sleeping, except for the two days' worth of blond stubble on his face.

I cleared my throat a couple of times, and then, when he didn't stir, I said his name, my voice hoarse and scratchy. He opened his eyes and jumped out of the chair.

"Oh dear God, I have never been so happy to see someone open their eyes," he said, sitting on the bed and holding my hand. He put his other hand on my hair and stroked it. He looked haggard and pale. "How are you?"

"I've been better," I said, cringing as I tried to sit up a little more.

"Take your time," he said, passing me a cup of water from the table next to the bed. "You were in and out of consciousness. What do you remember?"

"Not much," I said. "Where are we?"

Phillip explained that Anthony had driven like the "lunatic American" he was and arrived at the hospital in Blois in just under two hours. They had pulled up to the front door of the hospital, and Phillip had carried me inside. The doctors had decided to give me a plasma transfusion as a precaution against shock, as well as IVs of fluids and morphine for the pain. But the bullet had not hit any major arteries as it tore through my shoulder and exited the other side. I did not share this with Phillip, but it was an eerie coincidence that the procedure involving the use of plasma that helped save me had been developed at Harvard Medical School, with the help of my deceased husband.

"You were very lucky," he said, kissing my hand.

"How is everyone else? Where are they?" I said.

"Nora and Georges are here, under different names, like you," he said. "They are being treated for dehydration, malnutrition, and some of the atrocities that were inflicted on them while they were captive. Tatiana and Anthony are back at the manor. Josette is desperate to see Georges, but we all have to take more precautions than ever. Although the nuns that run this place are happy to help protect us."

"When can I get out of here?"

"In the next couple of days," he said. "I will stay with you until you do."

I squeezed his hand and felt my eyes well up as I looked out the window, emotional for too many reasons to say.

"You don't have to stay with me," I said, frowning and looking into his eyes, feeling a tear slide down my cheek.

"I know, darling. Trust me, I know by now you're bloody well tough enough to do it all alone," Phillip said, clearing his throat. "The thing is, I want to stay with you. Because when you love someone, you want to take care of them, don't you?"

I nodded, smiling through tears as he leaned down and kissed me on the forehead.

~

A week later, we were back at Manoir Anoir, around a crowded dinner table with even more recent arrivals. Georges and Josette had been joyfully reunited, and Nora was enthralled with her hard-fought freedom, walking around the back gardens every morning with the wonder of a child.

Phillip had been true to his promise, staying by my side the whole time I was in the hospital, and again when I returned to the manor. I still mourned Henri, I was still healing emotionally, and the nightmares of watching him being shot in the square in Tréguier still woke me most nights. As did the dreams of a postwar life in Paris with him that would never come true.

After what we'd been through in the past few days, I couldn't deny that I cared deeply for Phillip. But with that caring came feelings of guilt and disloyalty to a love that was still in my heart, even though he was gone from this earth. I knew that only time could help me reconcile my conflicting emotions about the two men who had both, in their own way, taught me what it was to love someone completely. And how courage—being brave, taking risks, and opening your heart—came from unconditional love.

Phillip sat beside me at dinner, and with Georges and Nora now free, the gathering had a celebratory feel. But there was still a world war raging beyond the confines of our hidden manor in the country, and that lingered over the meal as well. Phillip was quiet, and I could tell something was on his mind. And after a couple of days' rest, I knew I would be getting back to the work that had given me purpose beyond anything I'd done before. I would remain in France until the war was over, that much I had decided.

"Come outside with me," Phillip said after dinner was over and we had finished cleaning up. He took my hand, and we walked out to the patio. It was warm, and the sky was clear and so full of stars I couldn't stop gazing at it.

"What do you have to tell me?" I asked, as he put his arms around me from behind. He didn't speak for a few moments, but then he said what I had guessed he would say.

"I have to go," he said. "They need Anthony, Raphael and me, and the other Jedburgh teams of OSS and SOE and French Resistance. We are needed up north, near the coast. To prepare for what's coming."

"The invasion," I said.

"Yes."

He turned me around, his arms encircling my waist now as he looked at me.

"We're star-crossed," I said, giving him a sad smile. "Again."

"We are," he said, taking my face in his hands. "But you need to understand something. I am coming back to you. Wherever I am in the world after this war ends, I will find you and come back to you. Someday our star-crossed story will be at an end."

My heart ached so much I put my hand on my chest. Another good-bye, and he talked about it as if there wasn't a risk he might not come back at all, but I knew better. I might be worrying and waiting for a very long time. But I couldn't even hesitate, because taking the risk to give your heart to someone else? That made life worth living. Now that I had been so close to death more than once, I understood that more than ever.

"I am still healing my scars, inside and out," I said, looking up at him. "But I can't lie. I love you, Phillip Stanhope. And I think we're worth waiting for."

"Me too," he whispered, leaning in for another long, slow good-bye kiss.

# Epilogue

**August 26, 1944**
**Paris**

*7/5/44*

*Dear Anna,*
*I received your letter requesting an extension on your con-*
*tract, and I am inclined to agree to the terms. Because*
*even if I didn't agree to the terms, you might go ahead and*
*stay in France anyway, like some maverick American spy.*
*After all, I told you to stay out of Paris, and instead you*
*went back and became a hero. As I told Huntington, I*
*would be angrier with you if you weren't so much like me.*

*So, you may stay in France. Lord knows we're going*
*to need people over there, at least for another year. My*
*only condition is that you come back and see your family*
*for a few days. I am sure you miss them too, and they are*
*desperate to see that you are alive and well. But when*
*you do come back, make sure that bullet wound is con-*
*cealed—that is not something I will be able to explain*
*to your father.*

*I have only given them the high-level version of your service in the field, but know that your family is very proud of you. Huntington brags about you as though you were one of his own children. However, I don't think anyone is prouder of you than I am. When you started at the OSS, you were so smart but full of self-doubt. I wasn't sure if you would be able to get beyond that. But you showed us all, didn't you?*

*Anna, my relationship with you has helped me remember and celebrate Patricia, not just mourn her. Please keep that peacock pin close. I think it's brought you more luck than you know.*

*I hope to see you very soon. My wife and the president both think I'm getting too old to be at the front lines of the war. But you won't be surprised to know that I cannot seem to help myself.*

*Warmest regards,*

*General Donovan*

*P.S. One other piece of information that I promised I would tell you once I knew for certain: Peenemünde, on the island of Usedom, was bombed as the result of the intelligence you and Josette provided, setting back their weapons capabilities for months. The Allies were also able to better prepare to meet the threat of the German missiles. What you did mattered and saved thousands of lives.*

I folded up the letter, which had been delivered through the Resistance's letter-box network, and put it back in my skirt pocket. It was one I would save for my grandchildren to read someday. After so long away I couldn't wait to visit home, to hug my parents and sisters, and to reunite with Mary and hold her new baby girl. But my life and my work were here now, in France, a country that, having endured horrible fighting and heartbreaking sacrifice, was finally liberated.

After four years, the church bells in Paris were ringing again. It stopped Parisians in their tracks, and old men cried in the streets. The war was not yet over, but Paris was free. Josette and I watched the parade from the balcony of Josette's family-owned apartment on the Champs-Élysées. She held her chubby, nine-month-old daughter, Chantal, in her arms, showing her how to wave to the crowds below. Chantal had Georges's wild blondish-red hair and Josette's big dark eyes.

Millions of people were in the streets, wearing the best clothes they could muster after four years, to watch Général Charles de Gaulle, the leader of the Free French Government, as well as his troops, the Allies, and members of the French Resistance march down the Champs-Élysées from the Arc de Triomphe to the Place de la Concorde. Girls wore red, white, and blue ribbons in their hair, and skirts with the American, French, and British flags sewn together. From the men who remembered the Great War, to the women who had grown too cynical and too thin, many in the streets could not help but weep openly out of relief and happiness. It was a magnificent and messy carnival atmosphere. Allied jeeps and tanks were covered with flowers, and soldiers were showered with food and wine, handshakes and kisses.

The cheers and applause were thunderous, and I found myself overcome with emotion just watching it all. I knew for the rest of my life I would never forget the city's delirious, collective joy.

"Look for Papa," Josette said to Chantal as we watched the procession. "And Tatiana and Bernard."

"And Nora," I added.

The invited members of the French Resistance were the last group in the grand procession. Josette and I could have joined them, but ultimately we'd decided to stay back and enjoy the parade on the balcony with Chantal, and to prepare for the celebratory dinner party we were having that night.

We had all spent the year working for Bernard and Pauline in the Loire Valley, where their army grew by several thousand more by the time the Allied invasion happened in June. It had been equal parts exhausting and exhilarating, terrifying and soul-crushing, particularly when members were killed or captured. But what I would remember most was the camaraderie we had with each other and our passion for the cause. I would remember that more than the fear or the bad times—more than anything.

Things would change now. De Gaulle was keen on bringing the French Resistance into his military's fold, and it was clear my role as an OSS agent would be changing too. I had not received news about Phillip for months, and I would often wake up in the middle of the night thinking about him, wondering if he was alive and safe, and tormented by the not knowing. He had been in the Normandy area in the months leading up to D-Day, so the invasion only heightened my anxiety, because so many Allied soldiers had been killed on those beaches. He had promised to come back to me, but the more time that passed, the more I was heartbroken by the possibility that, like Henri, he might be gone forever.

There was a knock at the door, and I heard a familiar voice holler, "Bonjour! Anna, are you up there? Are we in the right place? Paul, this is the right address, isn't it?"

"Is that your friend?" Josette said, smiling.

I rushed down the stairs like a kid at Christmas.

Julia McWilliams and I screamed at the sight of each other, collapsing into an embrace, laughing and hugging. She looked tan and beautiful and even taller than I remembered. Standing next to her was a bald man with glasses, shorter than her, who was delighted at our ridiculous behavior. He was holding a paper bag with bottles of champagne peeking out of the top.

"Oh, my old friend, you look *wonderful*," she said, in that distinctive voice I remembered so well. "I have missed you. And I cannot believe we are finally in the same country again. And Anna, this is my fiancé, Paul Child."

"It's such a pleasure to meet you," I said, giving him a kiss on both cheeks. "Congratulations to you both. To have you here working for the OSS? It's like a dream come true for me."

"For me as well," Julia said. I brought them upstairs to introduce them to Josette and baby Chantal. After the parade to celebrate the liberation, the rest of our friends would be joining us to welcome my American friends. I wished Irene and David had been able to join us too, but we would see them at their wedding in September.

Julia and Paul made themselves at home. Julia held Chantal, talking with her all the while, and Paul found an apron and started chopping vegetables with Josette in the kitchen. An hour later, I heard another knock at the door.

"Are they back from the parade this early?" Josette said, frowning at me, wiping her hands on a towel.

"I don't think so," I said. "I'll get it."

I went downstairs and opened the door, and my mouth dropped open in shock. Phillip Stanhope stood there in uniform, sunburned, his hair lighter than I'd ever seen it. He was holding a bouquet of red and white tulips in his left hand and a bottle of champagne under his right arm, which was leaning on a wooden cane. I looked down to see his leg bandaged from the knee down.

"Hello, Cavanaugh," he said in a quiet voice.

"I can't believe it," I said, shaking my head, holding my hands up to my mouth.

"Now why on earth are you crying?" he said, smiling. "This is supposed to be a happy surprise."

He put down the flowers and champagne, and I jumped into his arms, careful of his cane and bandaged leg.

"I was convinced you weren't coming back," I said in his ear. "Thank God you're alive. I wasn't sure . . . Your leg?"

"It's okay," he said. "It's going to be just fine in a few months' time. My darling, how I have missed you."

"Me too," I said. "More than you know."

We stood there kissing, forgetting the celebrations in the streets all around us.

"Anna?" Josette called from above after five minutes. "Who is down there? Are you all right?"

"Yes!" I called. "I am perfect. How long can you stay?" I whispered to Phillip.

"As long as you'll have me," he said, smiling.

I beamed back at him and nodded. "Come on," I said, as I picked up the tulips and champagne and grabbed his hand. "We have to get ready for the party. That is, if you're up for it?"

"Sounds brilliant," he said, kissing my hand.

We walked upstairs together and spent the night celebrating with our friends, toasting to life and love and freedom in our beloved Paris, City of Light, finally no longer darkened by war.

# *Author's Note*

Though this novel is a work of fiction, it is based on some of the incredible stories of the women in the OSS, SOE, and French Resistance in World War II. For those who are curious about what is fact and what is fiction, here are a few notes regarding the story.

At its height in late 1944, the Office of Strategic Services employed nearly 13,000 men and women, with approximately 7,500 employed overseas. Their identities remained classified until 2008, when the National Archives released all the OSS personnel records. While the impact of the OSS continues to be debated by historians, Dwight D. Eisenhower once said of it, "If [the OSS] had done nothing else, the intelligence gathered alone before D-Day justified its existence."

What is beyond doubt is that the founder of the OSS, General William J. Donovan, was a WWI hero with a larger-than-life personality who was beloved by the members of the organization he founded. He took risks and pushed America forward in the espionage game in ways that still reverberate today. Many of the details in this book about him and his life and work at the OSS are based on my research.

Julia McWilliams Child did serve as a member of the OSS, starting in its DC headquarters and then in both Ceylon (Sri Lanka) and China. I took some liberties with her dates of service and where and when she met Paul Child. Her letters here are based on some of her actual letters home during her service. Julia and Paul did move to Paris, though not until 1948, when Paul accepted a job as an exhibits officer for the State Department. Of course, from that point on, Julia's story is American culinary history.

The story of the embassy break-in by a team from the OSS is based on my research regarding the actual event. It was orchestrated by a spy code-named Cynthia (a.k.a. Betty Pack, a.k.a. Amy Elizabeth Thorpe) and her French lover, Charles Brousse. An ex-convict known only as the Georgia Cracker was also involved, and he was not the only ex-convict the OSS employed. There are differing accounts regarding the details of the embassy break-in, including the layout of the embassy and exactly where the safe containing the codebooks was located, so the version in the novel is fictionalized.

Anna and all the women characters in the OSS and SOE are based on the many amazing and heroic stories of these women from World War II. I drew particular inspiration from the stories of Virginia Hall (OSS and SOE), Betty Lussier (OSS), Andrée Borrel (SOE), and Pearl Witherington (SOE). The character Nora Khan is based on real SOE agent Noor Inayat Khan, a.k.a. Nora Baker. The real Noor Khan made a brave and daring attempt to escape 84 Avenue Foch, similar to the one described in the book, but her attempt failed. Despite repeated torture, she never revealed any information to her captors. Sadly, she was executed at the Dachau concentration camp in September 1944.

Josette Rousseau is based on the real French spy Jeannie Rousseau de Clarens, code name Amniarix, alias Madeleine Chauffour. She was an extraordinary and brilliant woman who graduated from École Libre des Sciences Politiques at the top of her class. She first spied on the Germans while living with her parents in Dinard. When accused, she was forced to leave the city and move back to Paris, where she ended up working for the Druids resistance network.

The experiences of Anna and Josette working with the Germans at the Hotel Majestic, and obtaining the extraordinary intelligence about the Germans' secret weapons, is all based on my research about de

Clarens and her astounding accomplishments during the war. However, in the true story of de Clarens, she did not have an OSS associate working with her, nor did any of the German officers volunteer information to help her in her efforts. Still, she was able to charm her German associates and extract some of the most important weapons intelligence of the war. In the summer of 1944, de Clarens was captured and sent to Ravensbrück concentration camp. Despite horrendous treatment and torture, she survived and married another concentration camp survivor, Henri de Clarens. Jeannie Rousseau de Clarens died in 2017 at the age of ninety-eight.

The building at 26 Rue Fabert, on the Left Bank near Les Invalides, was a safe house for the Druids network.

Christian Dior did work at the fashion house of Lucien Lelong, and Lelong has been credited with saving French couture from the Nazis. Dior's sister, Catherine "Caro" Dior, did not work at Lelong, but was a member of the Polish intelligence unit working with the French Resistance. She was captured and sent to the Ravensbrück concentration camp and was released in 1945. Christian Dior's perfume Miss Dior is named in honor of his brave sister.

Florence Gould was an American socialite who lived very well in Paris because she was both incredibly wealthy and a German sympathizer. She had weekly parties at the Hotel Bristol and at her apartment on Avenue de Malakoff, and her guests included undercover resisters, artists, authors, and German officers.

Dr. Sumner Jackson was a native of Maine and a surgeon at the American Hospital in Paris. During the war, he and his wife, Toquette, decided to remain in Paris and become involved with the Resistance. Their house on Avenue Foch became a safe house for undercover agents and for sharing intelligence. Jackson falsified documents of prisoners of war treated at the hospital in order to facilitate their escape. Sumner, his wife, and their teenage son, Phillip, were arrested by the Germans just before the war's end. Toquette and Phillip survived, but Sumner tragically did not.

Finally, the actor John Wayne did apply to the OSS, listing "acting and horse-back riding" as his pertinent qualifications. He was not offered a position with the organization.

# *Acknowledgments*

I have so many people to thank who have helped bring this novel into the world, and others who have continued to help me navigate this writing life.

To Alicia Clancy, my primary editor at Lake Union: I am so incredibly fortunate to be able to work with you on this, our second book together. Thank you so much for your always spot-on feedback and your excellent management of the publishing process from beginning to end.

To my developmental editor, Faith Black Ross: How lucky am I to have you in my corner since the beginning of my fiction-writing career? Thank you for your attention to detail and your brilliant instincts. You make me a better writer in every way.

To Danielle Marshall, the editorial director at Lake Union Publishing: Thank you for first bringing me into the Lake Union Publishing fold. I'm so happy you are at the helm.

To Nicole Burns-Ascue, Lindsey Alexander, and the fantastic copyediting and proofreading teams at Lake Union: I am so grateful for your hard work, expertise, and meticulous attention to detail. Your efforts always make my books better. Thank you.

Thank you also to Jeff Miller and Faceout Studio for a gorgeous cover design.

A million thanks to Gabrielle Dumpit and the entire Lake Union marketing team for all the many terrific things you do for me and all Lake Union authors.

To my agent, Mark Gottlieb, at Trident Media: thank you very much for your continued support and hard work on my behalf.

To historian Nigel Perrin: Thank you for the walking tour of Paris. Your knowledge of Paris during the occupied years and the details you provided helped shape the narrative of this story in ways large and small.

To Corinne Abitbol-Terrier: Thank you for offering feedback on Josette's letters, and thank you to you and your husband, Remy Terrier, for always being so wonderfully hospitable whenever we visit Paris. I am grateful for our friendship.

To French translators Christine Gemenne and Manon Chraszez: thank you for your thoughtful feedback from both a language and cultural perspective.

There are so many people in the writing community that continue to be an amazing source of support. Thank you to all the authors I've met over the past few years that I now consider friends.

Also thank you to local writer friends Susanna Baird, Julie Cremins, Jennifer Gentile, and Amanda Stauffer. I cherish our coffee talks about all things writing, and your thoughts and feedback are so valuable to me.

To the iconic Dick Haley of Haley Booksellers: Thank you so much for helping me connect with readers through your terrific events. I look forward to more road trips this year.

To book influencers Andrea Katz and Suzy Leopold: Thank you for being so supportive of me and my books from the very beginning. I am so grateful.

To the many book bloggers, bookstagrammers, and Facebook book influencers: Your enthusiasm, creativity, and support mean the world to me. Thank you for all that you do to support the literary community.

To the librarians and local bookstores of New England: thank you for everything that you do for my books and all books.

Thank you to all the book clubs I've met with all over the country. It's been such a gift getting to know so many of you.

To my parents, Tom and Beth Healey: you're the best, and that's why this book is dedicated to you.

To my daughters, Madeleine and Ellie, always my inspiration and my greatest accomplishments. Thank you for putting up with Mama when she's on deadline, and for being the amazing young women that you are.

And to my husband, Charlie: I never would have come this far in my writing career without you. This is our most collaborative book project yet, and I'm grateful for your help with the French language and Parisian culture. There are no words for how lucky I am to have you by my side. As I've said before, my favorite story will always be ours.

# About the Author

Photo © 2018 Sharona Jacobs

Jane Healey is the Amazon Charts and *Washington Post* bestselling author of *The Beantown Girls* and *The Saturday Evening Girls Club*. When her daughters were young, Jane Healey left a career in high tech to fulfill her dream of writing historical fiction about little-known women in history. It was a passion that has turned into something much more. Jane shares a home north of Boston with her husband, two daughters, and two cats. When she's not writing, she enjoys spending time with her family, traveling, running, cooking, and going to the beach. For more information on the author or upcoming events or to schedule a book club visit, please visit her website, https://janehealey.com.